D0319602

Restitution

ELIZA GRAHAM

Restitution

Macmillan New Writing

First published 2008 by Macmillan New Writing
an imprint of Pan Macmillan Ltd
Pan Macmillan, 20 New Wharf Road, London N1 9RR
Basingstoke and Oxford
Associated companies throughout the world
www.panmacmillan.com

ISBN 978-0-230-70913-3

Copyright © Eliza Graham 2008

The right of Eliza Graham to be identified as the
author of this work has been asserted by her in accordance
with the Copyright, Designs and Patents Act 1988.

1 3 5 7 9 8 6 4 2

A CIP catalogue record for this book is available
from the British Library.

Typeset by Intype Libra, London
Printed and bound in Great Britain by MPG Books Limited
Bodmin, Cornwall.

For Mungo and Eloise Graham

Part One

Part One

One

Alix
January 2002

Even now I don't like leaving the house on foggy days, though soldiers are unlikely to jump on me in Richmond. The scar on my hand aches in the cold.

But this morning I barely have time to note the weather. All my nervous energy is given to preparing for my visitor. I change my outfit twice, finally selecting a long cashmere tunic and silk scarf. I add a silver necklace strung with chips of Baltic amber. I plump cushions that don't need plumping and fiddle with the Christmas roses in the vase. All the time I'm listening out for footsteps on the front path. As a child I had sharp ears, always attuned to whatever grown-ups didn't want me to hear. I'm seventy-four now and my hearing is still good.

None of the displacement activity works. I can't distract myself from my fear. I'm almost as scared now as I was in that misty forest more than fifty years ago. But I'm excited too.

Someone's coming up to the door. The bell rings and my heart lurches. I force myself to take deep breaths before I go to open up. Before me stands a tall, broad-shouldered, middle-aged man in smart un-English clothes with a wide un-English smile that shines through the fog.

'Alexandra?' American accent – Midwestern?

'Yes.' I extend a hand and he grips it, his grasp warm and dry.

'I'm Michael.'

Of course he is.

Everything spins; I clutch the door handle.

He must have taken my arm and led me to my armchair in the drawing room because I find myself sitting down. I rally. 'There's coffee in the cafetière, just waiting for me to boil the kettle, I'll—'

'No. Let me. Where's the kitchen?'

I direct him, almost relieved to have a minute to catch my breath. He finds everything and returns with the tray. His fine, strong hands are nimble as he pours the coffee and places the cup in front of me. I gulp down caffeine, trying not to stare but unable to resist. Very dark blue eyes – those haven't changed. A good head of greying hair. Who does he look like? I realize he's studying me too.

'It's good of you to see me, Alexandra. Is it all right for me to call you that?'

'Alix, please.' Only my governess ever called me Alexandra.

'You must have been very surprised to hear from me, Alix.' For the first time I notice a chink in his ease.

'I was delighted.' Wretched, inadequate word. 'As I said on the phone, I lost contact with your adoptive parents when they returned to America.' And even if the Whites had stayed in Germany I doubt I'd have kept in touch. 'Adoptions were handled differently back then and wartime made things . . . complicated.'

'I do understand.' He looks around the room at the photographs and ornaments. 'I've been researching your mother and father. I had no idea my grandma was a famous movie star and my grandpa a Resistance hero.'

The carriage clock strikes the quarter-hour five minutes early. Michael frowns at his watch.

'Your grandfather may have been a hero but his clock repairs were less than heroic. That clock's always fast.'

'He repaired his own clocks? I'd have thought a baron would have servants to do all that kind of thing.'

'Papi was always disembowelling some unfortunate time-piece.'

'And that clock came from the old house, from Alexanderhof?' He stands to take a closer look at it.

'Yes, and I can't tell you how much money I've spent over the years trying to get it to tell the right time.' He looks at the photograph of Mami on the fireplace beside the clock – the only one I have, given to me by my cousin Ulla as a wedding present. Mami is dressed for her own wedding to my father in 1926. Her eyes are focused on something beyond the camera lens; her lips form a perfect bow, as though she's

5

about to smile. Her veil is pushed back over her hair and looks a little like a halo.

'She was stunning.' He picks up the picture. 'More beautiful than Dietrich or Garbo. Or even Bergman.'

'Schoolboys used to collect cigarette cards with her pictures on them.'

'You inherited her bone structure.'

'But sadly not her talent.'

'The best teachers often have something of the actor in them.'

He replaces the frame on the fireplace and comes back to his chair, a more guarded expression on his open face.

'Alix, there's something . . . I need to ask you . . .'

I close my eyes to give me strength. We've reached that moment.

'I've only just met you again and I don't want to bombard you with questions, but obviously there's one big thing about myself I need to know.' He swallows. 'I didn't want to ask you when we spoke on the phone.'

'You need to know about your real father. Of course.' I'm going to make this as easy as possible for my son. The least I can do for him.

His dark eyes fix themselves on my face.

I find myself speaking very carefully while my heart pounds. 'Germany had collapsed. I was only seventeen.' A young, sheltered, seventeen at that.

He looks up. 'Same age as my Mark.'

One of my grandsons. In our preliminary telephone conversations I've lapped up details about these children. My greed to know every detail of their lives to date is almost insatiable.

'I know you came from the east.' Michael frowns. 'The Soviets . . .'

Oh God. I know where this is leading. Even after all these years my body stiffens at the mention of those men in their filthy, stinking uniforms, their eyes wild and greedy. 'Yes.'

'The Red Army must have been very close.' He taps a finger on his lower lip.

I nod. *So close you could taste the vodka on their breaths.*

He takes a breath and now that American ease has gone and he looks very young and unsure of himself, just as his father did when he reappeared in my life so unexpectedly all those years ago. 'Alix, a month ago, just after I first called you, I watched a documentary about Bosnia, the Muslim women . . .'

'Ethnic rape,' I prompt him, some courage coming to my rescue. I was born a Prussian officer's daughter, after all.

'I saw young girls running from the Serbs through misty forests.' He stops, perspiration gleaming on his brow. 'I don't know why it didn't strike me at the time the Bosnian war was on. Mom and Dad – sorry.'

I nod to indicate that I have no problems with his using these titles for the Whites but my mind is on what's coming.

'They were still alive then and I could have asked them. But I didn't.' He's looking at my arm. 'That scar on your wrist . . .' I look down at the white crescent just visible below the tunic sleeve. 'I couldn't help noticing . . . I thought, I wondered whether . . . ?'

'Whether a Russian had stabbed me.' I nod.

A look of pain flashes across his eyes. 'Oh God . . .' He looks like the small boy he must have been once, the child I never saw grow up. I wish I could go over to him, run my fingers through his hair, fold him into my arms. But I don't know my son well enough.

'No!' It's intolerable, evil, that my child should imagine he was the result of an act of violence. My voice shakes. 'It's not what you're thinking, Michael.'

He leans across to take my hand. 'I've come here and met you for the first time and asked you terrible questions. Can you forgive me?'

I stroke his long fingers. Last time I held his hand it was small enough for me to encase completely in my own.

I still don't how to explain his father, how to explain Gregor. I've had a whole month since he first rang me to prepare myself but I still feel at sea. I lean forward and clasp his hand.

'You're right in one respect. Your father *was* the enemy. But he was also the great love of my life.'

My most feared, most adored enemy.

Part Two

Part Two

Two

Alix
Pomerania, eastern Germany, February 1945

They'd reached a small village when the planes swooped and fired. The world blasted itself into millions of fragments of snow, earth and stone. The horses were screaming and Alix couldn't hold them. 'Steady,' Lena called.

The wagon swayed. Debris blinding her, Alix pulled on the brake, tugging at the reins with her other hand: *stop, stop, stop*. The wagon careered past refugees, barely missing people dashing for cover. She called the horses' names, trying to convey calmness, trying to remind them of days spent pulling the trap round the estate or moving logs in the forest. At last they slowed to a trot, coming to a halt just outside the church. Alix let out a long breath. Her clothes felt clammy and her skin sticky, despite the freezing air. The planes seemed to have vanished. She removed a glove and wiped her eyes and forehead with her shirt sleeve.

Two hundred years earlier Alix's ancestors, the von

Matkes, had driven along this very road into the morning sun to take possession of their new country house in Pomerania. The four bays in the harness of the gleaming liveried carriage tossed their sleek manes, kicking up dust as they cantered along. The coachman in his velvet jacket and tricorn hat looked down his nose at anyone who dared gaze at the spectacle.

Now here she was: Alix, properly Alexandra, seventeen, last in the line of von Matkes. Sitting, heart pounding, on this ancient farm wagon creaking its way west along the road. They'd packed the wagon with cooking pots, flour, bedding and a cageful of hens, rather than trunks full of finery. Beside Alix sat Lena, last remaining servant of the von Matkes. Alix's ancestors had worn the finest silks from Paris. This morning Alix was encased in three layers of woollens, an old coat of her mother's, chosen for warmth rather than fashion or its crimson colour, and a beaver hat of her father's.

A chicken reached through the wicker bars and pecked at her scarf. She turned round to push the basket back and blinked hard. She wouldn't let herself down by snivelling and reminded herself not to slump on the wagon seat, even though a little voice inside her murmured that nobody would now reprimand a von Matke for poor posture. Alix was just a refugee, like the farmers, peasants and tradesmen fleeing the Soviets.

It's over. Of course it was; she'd known this in her head for months, years now. But that was different from feeling the end in her cramped, cold muscles and churned-up stomach. Beside her on the wagon seat Lena let out a long sigh but said nothing. There was nothing to say.

Flames curled round the roof of a distant barn. Almost pretty.

She pulled herself together and clicked at the horses. 'Walk on.'

Around them hundreds of others picked themselves up and walked, rode, shuffled and cycled their way on through the grey slush. No men, except the very old. Even the boys had gone now, dressed in uniforms so big their mothers had turned up their trousers and sleeves.

Some of the refugees looked bewildered. Others showed comprehension in the set of their mouths. Children sat blank-eyed in wagons or clutched the hands of their mothers and elder siblings. Dogs trotted behind their owners. Parrots and cats were crammed into cages stowed in handcarts. It was a cruel pastiche of long-ago picnic trips to the beach – Mami overloading each member of the party with parasols, towels, badminton rackets and hampers, even a gramophone, which they'd carried with happy grumbles through the pine trees.

Guns rumbled to the east. Closer now. Occasionally planes whined again behind them. Alix silently begged the German troops – supposed to be protecting the Reich – to fall back.

Thoughts like that could get you into trouble. *The Wehrmacht continues to demonstrate success in protecting the Reich*: that's what the wireless broadcasts had told them last night as they packed up their boxes and hid precious objects that couldn't travel with them.

The horses flicked back their ears and shivered. They were bred for steadiness but they'd never encountered anything like this before. Alix made encouraging clicks with her tongue. As long as they could just keep moving west . . .

Lena tightened the scarf round her neck. 'If we get separated don't wait for me.' Her voice was tight, her normally pink-cheeked face already grey with fatigue, though they'd only been travelling for an hour or so. Alix focused on the tips of the horses' golden ears to calm herself.

A moan above them told her the planes were overhead again. Through the dirt encrusting her eyes she saw them dive towards the earth. The wagon shook. Lena called out something she couldn't hear and slumped sideways out of the seat. Alix shouted at the horses but then she was falling herself, watching dark particles blow past her. Parts of her earlier life floated with her: falling off a pony at eleven; tumbling off the orchard wall as an eight-year-old; toppling downstairs as a toddler; falling, falling, always falling. She heard the horses scream before someone turned off the volume.

The earth rose to meet her. For a moment she couldn't tell which way up she was. Her eyes stung. Apart from that nothing seemed to hurt. High above, planes still buzzed. She stayed down, blowing snow and dirt from her mouth and nose. It was all taking such a long time, as though she were watching a film in slow motion.

Time shot forward again. The planes were still screaming but becoming more distant now and people whimpered around her. Alix rose, checking herself for injury and finding herself unscathed – all those layers of clothing – and the rucksack still fastened to her back. She turned to the wagon and saw it lying on its side, suitcases and boxes spilling out from the canvas covers. One of Papi's clocks had fallen on top of the fur rug Mami had told them to take. At least it would have cushioned its fall . . . But this was no time to bother about trifles. The chickens had broken out of their basket and were running into the forest edging the road. Alix glimpsed a cream-coloured tail splayed across the snow. One of the horses shrieked and twitched and then they were both motionless. She couldn't look at them. She'd cared for them when they were colts and helped Papi break them to harness. She began to run back along the road. 'Lena!'

Alix's heart lurched. There she was, face-down in the snow, recognizable only because of the blue scarf she wore, the one Alix had knitted as a Christmas present with wool unravelled from an old jumper. Finally Lena sat up, a hand to her brow. She looked suddenly old and confused, far from the sturdy middle-aged woman she normally was. Alix threw herself down beside her.

'What happened, Alexandra?'

'The planes shot us.'

'Are you hurt?' Lena's eyes swept Alix.

Alix shook her head.

'And the horses?'

She couldn't answer.

Lena clicked her tongue. 'Ach, that's too bad. Is there anything we can salvage from the wagon?'

'Probably. I didn't look closely. All our things have fallen out onto the road. The hens escaped into the forest.'

'We'll catch them.' Lena started to rise to her feet and fell back onto her knees. 'Just give me a moment.'

Slowly she pushed herself up. Alix knew better than to offer assistance. At the sound of aeroplanes, Lena looked up at the sky. 'Under the trees, quick!'

The air was acrid, painful to breathe, the sun hidden

behind smoke. Alix followed Lena through the beeches and silver birch, her racing pulse starting to slow now they were away from the road. She heard clucking and spotted the tail feathers of one of the hens. As she went to catch the bird Lena stopped and put out an arm in warning. 'There's a soldier over there.' She nodded to the right.

'A Russian?' Alix whispered. 'It can't be. They haven't broken through yet.'

'I tell you it's an Ivan.'

'But—'

Lena put a finger to her mouth and pulled Alix down behind a bush. 'When I say run, make for that track. I think there's an old bridge down by the stream. We can hide.'

Alix nodded, feeling her panic as a knot in her chest. Lena looked to the right.

'Now!' She pushed her towards the path. Alix ran, head down, fists pounding the air. Spotting the bridge, she scrambled down to the stream, branches scratching her cheeks, her breath harsh in her throat. She squatted below the single span, the icy scum at the water's edge soaking her boots, feeling her blood scorching her veins. She glanced up the bank.

'Lena?' she whispered.

A deer shot down the bank from the path, hurling itself into the water, ice splintering beneath its hoofs. A gun fired once. Alix hugged her knees to her chest and lowered her head. She thought she heard a shout. Then there was nothing. *Count to a thousand*, just like she'd done as a child when she'd played hide and seek with Gregor.

A thousand came and went and still Lena didn't reappear.

Alix pulled herself up the bank, peering along the path, listening out for the crunch of frozen leaves or the crack of a twig, trying to pick up the scent of unwashed Russians and their discharged guns above the reek of smoke. How many times had Papi taken her out hunting? 'You must use all your senses,' he had said.

No sounds of a human running through the trees, no low boughs swaying . . .

But then there was something – an engine rumbling further along the track. Alix stooped behind a tree and strained her ears. A car. It sounded like the Mercedes that Preizler used to drive when he came visiting Mami. The Russians wouldn't come to Pomerania by Mercedes. *Unless they'd stolen it. Be quiet*, she told herself. *Listen.*

The car was large and black, the swastika on its bonnet hung limply in the smoke-filled air. Alix stepped forward. The driver's window opened. He was young, probably only a year or so older than Alix, very pale, black shadows under his eyes.

'Nearly shot you.' He waved the revolver in his hand. 'Thought you were a Russian. They've already got hold of one woman.' Words were rushing from him. 'I couldn't do anything for her.'

'Where—?' The world spun.

He pointed back along the way he'd come.

'What did she look like?'

He shrugged. 'Hard to say now.' He frowned at her. 'Jump in, I'll take you as far as I can. It's not safe for you here.'

'No.' She stepped back. '*Danke.*' She was turning down

her best chance of escape. But she couldn't get into the black Mercedes. Cars like that scared her.

'Please yourself.' He wound up the window and let out the clutch.

Alix turned and ran back into the trees, crouching behind a bush until the car had pulled away.

Almost evening now. The birds were making roosting sounds and the faint sunlight was fading. How long had it been since the planes had attacked?

Oh, Lena . . . But she pushed away her longing for the older woman. No time for that now. Get back on the road. Find the abandoned wagon. Grab the fur rug, food and water. Continue the journey. Mami would meet her in the little village on the other side of the Oder, just as they'd planned.

Keep heading west. Alix found herself shivering. An owl hooted beside her and every shadow seemed to host a menacing figure. The Russians might already have reached the wagon. Suppose they were already squabbling over Papi's clock, the cooking pots and the woollen blankets? The soldiers might be waiting in the gloom for the owners of these goods to return so they could rob them in turn. She already knew the kind of treatment she could expect from the Ivans, if they caught her.

Alix took a single step along the track and came to a halt.

She could creep back home through the trees. She knew this forest. Within a kilometre or so it became part of the von Matke estate. She could find something to eat in the house. They'd left some food behind in case Papi had been released and found his way home. Some of Alix's clothes still hung in the wardrobe. She could change into something warm and clean. The stove in the kitchen would still be hot – Lena had riddled and stoked it for the last time this morning so they'd have warm water before they set off on their long journey. The stove also heated some of the bedrooms. The house would give out its own particular scent of wood smoke and beeswax, mixed with the cinnamon and nutmeg Lena used when she baked.

She could approach the house from the back garden, check for signs of occupation. If it was safe she'd lock herself inside for the night. At dawn she'd leave for the west again. At least she'd have one more night at home. In the warm. With Papi's few remaining clocks ticking round her.

Three

They'd waited so long that when the news came Alix could barely believe it.

Lena bustled into the salon where they were covering furniture with dustsheets in the hope that the announcement would come in the next week. 'You'll never guess!' Her face was the colour of the plum velvet cushions on the sofa. 'The Preizlers are packing up that house of theirs. Frau Preizler's moving to the south, the Tyrol or Bavaria, they say.' She looked at them both. 'So we can leave too, can't we? We can go west now?'

The pupils of Mami's eyes contracted into tiny dots. 'Anton said nothing of this when I saw him last week.'

'I heard it in the town this morning from a girl who works at the house.'

'What does it mean for Papi?' Alix asked. It had been six months since the black car pulled up outside his office in Berlin.

Mami shrugged. 'Who knows?' She reached for her cigarette box. 'We need to start sorting things out, packing up the wagon. And quickly.' The telephone rang and she got up. 'I'll take it.' She went out into the hall, closing the salon door behind her. Alix sat on a chair and fixed her gaze on one of the nymphs in the mural on the opposite wall.

The conversation was short. When Mami came back in she looked pale. 'Gestapo headquarters. They want to see me in Berlin. Tomorrow.' She caught sight of Alix's face. 'No, *Schatz*, not what you think, it's fine. Anton Preizler will be there, he's arranged this interview, he says it will help Papi.'

'The excuse he needed to run away from the Russians.' Alix couldn't help saying it.

Mami appeared not to have heard. 'I'll go up to town on the afternoon train, if it's still running.'

She might have been talking about a shopping trip.

'You'd better get our things packed up while I'm away,' she went on.

'We really are going?' Alix asked.

'If the Preizlers are moving out it means they can't stop us now. It also means the Russians are closer than we thought.' Mami drew on her cigarette. 'We'll leave these dustsheets now and concentrate on getting you and Lena ready for the journey.'

'When do we go?' Lena asked.

Mami rested the cigarette on the ashtray. She'd been rationing herself; this was the first one Alix had seen her smoke in days. 'The day after tomorrow. Before dawn. They'll stop watching the house while I'm in Berlin. Go and fetch Papi's map, Alix.'

Alix went into her father's study. Already it seemed to have lost some of its particular aroma, a mingling of Papi's bath oil and his leather boots. On his desk the photograph of Mami as Cressida in her last film, *Troilus*, sat in its usual place, next to the silver blotter. Alix found the map in his desk drawer and brought it back to her mother. Mami opened the red calfskin covers, flicking through the pages until she found the section of Germany west of the Oder and south of Berlin. 'Somewhere around here.' She ran a finger over the page, pointing at villages Alix had never heard of. 'Perhaps this junction. And from there we will make for the Elbe. Magdeburg, perhaps. Then south-west through either Kassel or Erfurt to Cousin Ulla's in the Rhineland.' She looked at Alix and her soft eyes were suddenly hard. 'Repeat that to me, Alix.'

'West to the Elbe at Magdeburg—'

'Avoiding Berlin,' Mami interrupted.

'Avoiding Berlin, then head for either Kassel or Erfurt.'

'Good.' Mami nodded.

'I don't think I've ever met Cousin Ulla.'

'I've only met her a couple of times myself, years ago, but she was close to your father when they were children. She's a kind woman, and one of . . .' Mami waved a hand in place of the missing words.

One of us, she'd meant: someone who approved of what Papi had done. Mami bent her head to the map again. 'This whole journey depends on the bridges. We must pray we can cross the Oder and then the Elbe. We'll stay with Ulla until the worst is over.'

Ulla must be brave to offer to take in the family of Peter von Matke.

Mami gazed out of the window and the small wrinkle on her brow became a furrow. She was probably thinking of the snow, of the weeks to be spent in a wagon, of the Russians closing in, of the bridges across the great rivers and what would happen if those bridges were blown. She'd be remembering the stories that had already reached Pomerania with the first waves of refugees from East Prussia. Of how the Reds had killed women and children, had burned, looted and destroyed. Mami didn't know that Alix had overheard her and Lena whispering about these horrors. She didn't know that Alix had gone to her bedroom and sat on the bed staring at the familiar photographs in their silver frames without moving until it was time for her to go out and milk the cows.

They'd talked of heading west for months, written lists, sent the cattle on ahead a few at a time so as not to raise suspicions. Serviced the farm wagon in preparation. Checked the horses' hoofs. But it had all seemed theoretical somehow. And Alix had never imagined travelling without Mami.

Alix went to see Jana in the cottage that housed her and the other Polish workers. 'You've heard?'

Jana raised her head from the pine table in the little kitchen. Alix saw she'd been packing her possessions: her flute and a few books Alix had given her. 'I heard.' Behind her glasses her eyes flickered with something Alix had never seen before. Not hope, exactly, but some spark that might represent the precursor to hope: an acknowledgement that things were changing, that she might yet go home, back to her parents and her music career. Assuming the academy still stood and the professors had survived. A shift was occurring in the girls' relationship: the slave worker would soon be free, and as for Alix – who knew?

'Are you heading west?' Jana asked.

'First light the day after tomorrow. We're to meet Mami south of Berlin.'

'Ah yes, her interview.' Jana paused. 'Lena told me. The baroness must be nervous, no?'

'It's routine. She seems more worried about the Red Army getting here before we've left.'

'One hears such things about the Soviets.' Jana's eyes were owl-like behind her glasses. Alix didn't ask her what she'd heard. 'One barely knows what to believe. I shall come and say goodbye before I leave.'

Already the relationship was growing more formal. Jana would go home and agree with her friends and family – those who'd survived – that Germans were monsters. No reason for her to think any different just because one family had treated her well. Alix made her excuses and crossed the stable yard to return to the house. She had to consult her list. Most of her clothes were already packed in a suitcase, ready for a quick departure. In a rucksack she would take a torch, water bottle, hairbrush, soap and toothbrush. A small towel. A clean shirt and underwear. An additional thick wool jumper.

Much would have to remain in the house. A few days ago Mami had loaded valuables into concrete pipes and one of the Polish men had dug trenches in the vegetable garden and helped her lay the pipes in them. Rows of cabbages, neatly replanted, now grew on top of the Sèvres dinner service, the Bohemian crystal and the silverware. There hadn't been time to bury all the treasures in Alexanderhof, though. Shame they couldn't bury the grandfather clock, the Steinway, the tractor and the threshing machine, Mami had said.

The Polish worker had left the following morning without a word, desperate, Jana said, to find his wife and children in the Tatras.

'If I'd known he was leaving I'd have given him food for the journey,' Mami said. 'He's taking a risk, there are still SS patrols out there.'

'He just wanted to go home,' Jana had replied.

As Alix returned from the workers' cottages to the main house, an explosion to the east rocked the white, three-storeyed building and the ground beneath her. A chimney pot crashed down to the snowy flowerbeds where Mami had once, a thousand years ago, grown night-scented stocks.

The last night in the house. Alix walked through every room, saying silent farewells to tables and chairs, the portraits of relatives long dead, the Meissen circus animals in the cabinet in the salon. The Gobelin tapestries in the dining room. A Chinese urn in which she'd been able to secrete herself as a child when she was playing hide and seek. The photographs of Mami in all those film parts and from earlier in her career when she worked on the stage in Vienna. And Papi's clocks. They were taking two of his favourites in the wagon. The others, including the grandfather clock and the porcelain lyre clock in the drawing room – admired, family history had it, by the Kaiser himself – would have to stay. The golden Haflingers with their blond manes and tails were sturdy creatures but too small to pull a heavy load so far. Alix wound the clocks for the last time. As she did every night she adjusted their times, moving some hands forward and some back. Papi's clocks never ran accurately after he'd repaired them. If only he'd been a little more methodical, perhaps he and his friends would have succeeded with their plans.

Mami had left this morning for Berlin. Alix had driven her the seven miles to the nearest station in the trap. The station had been crammed with people attempting the dash west. The police had stood in the entrance hall, grabbing would-be absconders and pulling them into the waiting room to interrogate them. 'You are perfectly safe,' Alix heard one of them tell an elderly couple with a canary in a cage and a single suitcase. 'Return to your home.'

Mami had no problems because of the papers summoning her to the interview. She looked the police in the eye, without a flicker of fear. Alix could see admiration in their faces. Mami wore a Chanel charcoal-grey winter suit and her smartest fur, a dashing little hat angled on her sleek head. She looked every inch the baroness, the famous actress, the woman whose face had graced the backs of prewar cigarette cards. Not a woman scared for her family. The doctor had been to visit her a few days ago to give a further prescription of the sleeping tablets she took every night. 'If I can sleep, I can fight,' she'd told Lena and Alix. Something unreadable had flickered across Lena's placid stare for just a second.

Mami'd given Lena directions for where they were to meet, a crossroads away from the main roads. If that meeting failed, they were to keep on going west, ultimately heading for the cousin's house hundreds of miles away in the Rhineland, taking the route Mami had described to Alix. 'Keep away from the cities,' Mami warned. 'But I'll be with you by then anyway.' And she'd smiled that famous smile of hers; the one that had melted hearts across Europe and might yet persuade the Gestapo to free Papi. Alix had felt like she had as a child when Mami had left her at boarding school in Switzerland.

'Can't I come with you?' she'd begged.

'It's madness for you to risk the bombs in Berlin when you don't have to.' Mami checked her handbag for powder compact and lipstick, her props. 'And how would Lena manage the wagon without you? You need to be strong, *Schatz*, a proper Prussian, steady and purposeful.'

Alix straightened her shoulders.

'Just get across the Oder as quickly as you can. And check the horses' hoofs again. Those icy roads . . .' The train hooted. Mami got into the carriage, negotiating the steep steps with the easy grace of one trained in stage movement. She might have been boarding a first-class carriage for a holiday trip. She waved one last time and the train pulled out. Alix walked back along the platform, reminding herself that Mami wasn't a prisoner.

In the ticket office the policeman was still watching everyone who passed. The posters warning against defeatism and assuring civilians of the protection of the Wehrmacht glared down from the walls. The man in the trilby stared at Alix. She made a point of putting her hands into her coat pockets and sauntering out of the entrance hall. On the steps outside the station a woman with two small children hovered.

'Was that the Berlin train?'

Alix nodded.

The woman sighed.

Alix glanced at the Gestapo man.

The woman's pupils contracted. 'It's my sister in Jüterbog,' she stammered. 'She's not well. She needs me to help her with the children. Just for a day or so. Then we'll come right back home.' She rubbed her nose.

Alix looked at the woman's stuffed suitcase.

'Perhaps I've over-packed for a short visit?' the woman whispered.

Alix nodded again.

That evening she walked upstairs to her bedroom for the last time, trying to make the ascent last for ever. She could have climbed these stairs blindfolded; she knew every creaking step, every worn patch of carpet, the uneven section on the banister where the oak felt rough under her fingers. She went into her parents' room and sat on the bed. Mami had decorated this room just before the war and it had lasted well. No rips or marks sullied the periwinkle Toile de Jouy wallpaper: the young men still pushed the girls in their swings, the roses still bloomed round them. The blue satin quilt was pulled tight across the bed, creaseless, impregnable. Mami had made her bed herself these last years. Mami said Lena had enough to do elsewhere. Sometimes Mami had to be firm with Lena or she'd wear herself to the bone.

Papi had shared this bedroom with Mami, but of his presence there was now very little evidence. Mami had given away some of his clothes to the Winter Appeal. She'd packed up his hunting clothes and country suits and hidden them in the attic, putting aside only a few essential garments for him to wear when he was released and they could finally head west. *When*, Mami had always said. Not *if*. The only things of Papi's left in the room were his old dressing gown on the back of the door and the silver hairbrushes he always kept at home. Alix picked them up and looked at the initials engraved on their leather backs. *P.H.E.v.M.* Peter Hubertus Ernst von Matke. All the von Matkes were called Peter, Hubertus and Ernst. In various combinations. Mami had insisted that her daughter would not be called Ernestina or Petronella. Or Huberta, assuming there were such a name. They'd consulted the family tree and chosen the name Alexandra, which had belonged to Alix's great-great-great-aunt and was a nod towards the name of this house: Alexanderhof. Alexanderhof was the town in Brandenburg where the von Matkes had lived before they'd moved here in the middle of the eighteenth century to enjoy their new estate and the house with its fashionable plasterwork and its terraces and gardens landscaped in the English fashion.

Alix examined her own reflection in the glass: Alexandra Elisabeth Henriette von Matke: last of the line. And about to forsake all the glories of the family seat like a frightened scullery maid.

Mami had packed a small case to take to Berlin; the rest of her luggage would go in the wagon. A pair of oyster-pink silk pyjamas still sat folded on the pillow. On the dressing table sat her bottles of scent. Alix walked to the table and picked up the Jean Patou, spraying a wrist. The perfume didn't smell like it did on Mami. But then Alix wasn't Maria Weissmüller, was she? Mami'd taken to using her famous maiden name when she took calls from the Gestapo, probably in the hope of jogging a sentimental memory of her

29

best-loved roles: Anna in *Anna Karenina*, Effi in *Effi Briest*. Tragic and beautiful women. Only yesterday Alix had watched Mami sitting at this dressing table, her face smiling out from the glass looking familiar but different because it was a reflection. Mami was supposed to have a very symmetrical face; film cameras liked symmetry. So in theory the features in the mirror should have looked exactly like their original. But as she watched her mother apply the rouge and eyebrow pencil Alix perceived a difference between the two faces. The reflection smiled like Mami but wasn't really her. *Go away and give me back my mother.*

On the dressing table stood a photograph of Mami as a little girl in Tyrolean dress. Alix picked it up and studied her mother's features. Impossible to work out from looking at her whether this child, this little Marie, had ever imagined she'd grow up to be a famous actress and live so far away from home. And to plead for her disgraced husband: her most important role ever.

Four

Marie
South Tyrol, April 1919

The Angelus bell was tolling and she ought to be heading straight home. Marie stopped and watched the old man and the younger woman unload their handcart. Together they pulled up the panel on the top of the cart and Marie saw it was actually a frame, hung with purple and white striped curtains. The old man untied a board from the side of the cart, pulled out a piece of chalk from his pocket and wrote on the board the words: *The Adventures of Kasperl.*

The bell ceased its toll. She was now late for lunch. Hannelore, the housekeeper, would scold. Marie broke into a run, disobeying the rules of the nuns, who maintained that young girls should always act with decorum on the streets of Meran, just as they would in the presence of Our Lady herself.

As they sat in the dusty dining room over the meal Marie tried to explain to her father what she'd seen, the little stage and the sign about Kasperl, whoever he was. He gazed at the watery soup with the few dumplings floating on the surface as she told him about the frame and the curtains and the sign. 'A little puppet theatre.' A thin smile briefly warmed his face.

'Puppets!'

'Kasperl is a rogue, I seem to remember. They used to come here most market days but I haven't seen them for years now, not since . . .'

Before the war.

She didn't need him to finish the sentence. The puppets belonged to a time long before that when young men had started to limp home on crutches and so many women had started wearing black dresses and hats.

'Can we go?'

'Go?' He looked puzzled.

'To the puppet show. I want to see Kasperl. *Bitte*, Papa!'

Marie's father ate his last dumpling and gazed at the empty bowl. 'I wonder if Hannelore has any cheese for us today? Eat some more bread, child.'

She helped herself to another slice and chewed obediently on its hardness, knowing better than to repeat her plea. He watched her. 'At least we'll have some lettuces growing in the garden soon. And the hens have started laying again.'

She swallowed hard on the bread.

'Why not go to the show?' He shrugged. 'It won't cost much. Come and find me this afternoon and I'll give you some money. Take young Preizler and Lena.'

Marie's two closest friends.

'Won't you come, Papa?'

'I've essays to mark. One of my pupils, young Johann, writes a fine Latin prose.' His expression darkened. 'Once I'd have been sending him to the seminary. Now I don't know. But perhaps a good education will still count.'

The three of them, Marie, Anton Preizler and Lena, sat at the front of the crowd in the church square. Behind them stood a line of women, mostly black-clad – mothers, wives and sisters, some of them young enough to be girls who'd only left the convent school a year or so ago. A few sullen-faced men, some on crutches, loitered on the periphery.

'I wonder where the puppet-master went during the war.' Lena was staring at the little stage. 'My sister said he was Italian, but he can't be because he wouldn't dare come back here now, would he?'

'Why not?' said Marie. 'If we're going to be part of Italy anyway?'

Anton scowled. 'He's Bohemian, everyone knows that.' He sounded so certain; he always did. 'The Italian puppets were marionettes, on strings. These are glove puppets.'

A thin drumbeat announced the start of the show. The curtains drew to reveal Kasperl, wearing a long velvet cap with a bell on the end. '*Tri-tra-trulla-la, Kasperl ist wieder da*!' he sang. 'Are you all here?'

The children looked at one another.

'Are you all here?'

'Yes,' called Anton.

'Are you all here?' Kasperl called yet again.

'*Yes*!' shouted Lena and Marie. And something was happening to Marie, she *was* . . . here, wherever *here* was. Already the sounds and smells of the church square were fading. This little man in his funny cap was pulling her away from the town and the women in their mourning, the men with their missing legs, the empty shops, the shadow that passed over people's faces when they talked about the province passing to the Italians.

Kasperl boasted about his bravery. He wasn't afraid of the monster, oh no, not he! And he wasn't just a piece of wood and cloth now, he was . . . himself, someone other, someone different, tugging her into his own world.

She was crossing the river with him, and it wasn't made of blue and black cloth, pulled backwards and forwards by the puppet-master's assistant, it was an African river, deep and deadly. She jumped when the crocodile appeared, even though the creature looked as though the moths must have eaten part of his tail, and clutched her knees, wide-eyed. The crocodile taunted Kasperl and Kasperl responded with more bragging, beating the crocodile with his stick to the cheers of the crowd. After he'd won his duel with the crocodile he met a pretty girl who kissed him, a robber who stole his money and chased the girl away and a policeman who helped him retrieve both money and girl. Marie sat on the hard ground in silence and watched the glove puppets in their faded costumes. Only a small part of her was still aware of the hard stones beneath her, of the stale smell of the black dresses. She had drifted away into the world on the little stage.

When they'd finished clapping and the old man and woman were putting away the puppets into the box Marie still sat silent. 'Come on.' Anton tugged at her sleeve. 'Your father said we had to go straight back home.'

She stood mechanically as though she were a puppet herself, her mind still in the forest, beside the river, in the prison cell. The familiar outline of the parish church came slowly into focus.

As they walked across the cobbles Lena cried out.

'What?' Anton and Marie turned to her. The girl put a hand to her back.

'Something hit me.'

Anton picked up a stone. 'This.'

Two boys sprinted past them. 'Dirty Italian,' one of them hissed.

Anton threw the stone at the boys but missed.

A tear ran down Lena's cheek. 'I can't help it.'

'What did they mean?' Marie put an arm around her. 'You're not an Italian.'

'They mean my mother.'

Marie and Anton nodded.

'The man she left with was an Italian. Now they say we're all dirty Italian-lovers and we should leave too.'

'But that's so unfair!' Marie tightened her embrace.

'It's illogical,' Anton said.

'I'm going to have a word with them.' Marie spoke with a resolution that amazed even her. She let go of Lena, brushed away Anton's restraining arm and marched across the square. The four boys were loitering beside a shop window. She approached them, anger driving out the fear she'd normally feel at confronting lads three years older than her – and from the rough side of town.

'Don't you dare say that about Lena!' She put her hands on her hips.

'Who the hell do you think you are?' The largest of them put his hands on his hips, mimicking her pose.

'She can't help what happened with her mother. You leave her alone.'

'Or else?'

She thought quickly. 'I'll tell the police I saw you breaking windows.' She'd never seen them doing such a thing but their quick exchange of looks told her that the guess had been a good one. 'My father's school has lots of broken windows and I'll tell him I saw you doing it. He'll call the police. So leave Lena alone.'

Another of the four tugged at the largest boy's shirt. 'Let's go,' he muttered.

Marie returned to her friends. Anton stared at her with wide eyes. 'I was just about to go over and help you.'

'You were like a lioness.' Lena blinked slowly. 'Nobody's ever done that for me before.'

'What do you mean?' Marie felt tired suddenly. While she'd been talking to the boys some internal energy had driven her; she'd felt no fear. Now she felt as though her legs might give way.

'Stood up for me.' Lena's eyes were bright with an emotion Marie couldn't interpret.

They turned up another cobbled street, the shops shuttered in the arcades on each side. The nights were lighter now spring had come and the cherry blossom would be out soon. 'They used to sell doughnuts and gingerbread when the puppet man came,' Anton said. 'But they don't any more. Because of the war, my father says.'

For a second Marie thought she could smell the sweetness of the sugar on the frying doughnuts and the spices in the gingerbread. A woman was talking to her in a low voice and wiping crumbs off her mouth with a white handkerchief. Then the scents and the woman's gentle touch were gone. Perhaps her mother had taken her to the puppet show when she was a little girl, long before the war.

Lena was watching her. 'What were you thinking about?'

'I'm going to be an actress when I grow up,' Marie told them.

'Of course you will be.' Lena sounded matter-of-fact. 'One day you'll stand on a stage and people will clap and cheer you. And I . . .'

'You'll what?'

'I will make your costumes. I will make sure you always look perfect.'

And something like a shiver ran down Marie's spine at the tone in Lena's voice.

Five

Alix
Pomerania, February 1945

Alix forced her legs to keep moving, pushing damp strands of hair off her face and refusing to look back. The house was further away than she'd imagined. Her legs shook underneath her and the backs of her eyes seemed to be filled with sand. She longed to stop and close them for a moment but she trudged on, finally emerging from the forest and seeing the house ahead of her, a grey silhouette in the gloom. It was the only time in its history that it had ever been abandoned. Even when the family had gone off to their apartment in Berlin or to take the waters at Baden Baden, there'd been family or retainers to keep fires and lights burning.

Snow was starting to fall, clinging to her crimson coat and scarf. She stopped and listened. Nothing except the whine of the wind in the pine trees. The house was barely visible from the road and Mami had taken down the sign at the end of the drive before leaving for Berlin. A vain hope, thinking they could fool the Red Army.

Alix trudged across the fields. The snow had now settled thickly enough to produce a scrunching sound at each step, something she would normally have found satisfactory, almost enjoyable. Now each scrunch was a reminder that the temperature was dropping further. The quickest route required her to scale the ha-ha and cross the lawns. She hauled herself up, willing the weary muscles in her arms not to fail her. The stable yard was in sight. Only this morning she'd harnessed the two Haflingers to the wagon. When they'd first made plans for the exodus Alix had assumed that Papi's old horse, Piper, would make the journey, too. But Mami had taken the bay out into the field a few evenings ago and one of the Poles had shot the animal. He'd done it very cleanly, he said. For the best, Mami had said. Piper's weary legs would hardly get him to the front gates, and even the Russians wouldn't want such an old horse – except for meat.

Kinder to shoot him.

Alix listened and heard nothing except the mice scrabbling in what remained of the straw. Lena's cat Mischi should be here, too. He'd bolted out of the house when they'd taken the boxes out of the attic to pack for the journey. 'Mischi?' Her whisper sounded too loud. She sprang round.

Nobody behind her. A few snowflakes fell onto her hand.

She mustn't be a coward. The von Matkes were always brave: in battle, in politics, in everything.

Alix crept to the back of the house. The key to the room they called the boot room was kept under a terracotta flowerpot which had once contained geraniums. She forced her numb hand to remove the key and insert it in the lock. The door was already open.

She slumped on the low bench running across the room to remove her boots; old habits died hard, even in wartime, even when the end had come. She could no more have entered the house in such sodden footwear than she could have sworn in front of her father or eaten with her mouth open.

Something rustled inside the house. Like a rabbit she froze. One boot was half undone, its laces dangling. The thing moved again. She ducked behind the coats smelling of Mami's Jean Patou. Mackintoshes, dog leads, whistles and riding crops dangled round her, symbols of that old life of hacks in the forest, shooting parties, picnics and croquet on the lawn. Alix hadn't hidden here for years, not since she and Gregor had played hide and seek as children. If Papi caught them he would tickle them until they squealed for mercy. If these people caught her there would be no mercy. Papi had impressed that thought on her and Mami: *Expect no quarter because we gave them none.* And what had happened to Lena proved how right he'd been.

The door leading into the house opened. Papi. Her heart missed a beat. Idiot, of course it wasn't.

'I'm armed.' Fluent German from a Bolshevik maniac? She shook underneath the coats, feeling simultaneously as though icy water were trickling down her neck and hot towels suffocating her.

'Come out slowly,' the voice continued, 'with your hands where I can see them.'

She bit her lip and parted the furs, stepping over the bench with one boot still on. Very slowly she lifted her eyes to stare

40

at the enemy soldier. What she saw made her wonder for a second if the exhaustion of the day had caused her to hallucinate.

Gregor Fischer, dressed in Red Army uniform, with what looked like Polish insignia on his tunic. She put a hand to her eyes and rubbed them. He still stood before her. Was she certain? It had been such a long time ago that they'd last seen one another. And in that time he'd become . . . *this*.

She tried to open her mouth but found herself rendered dumb. Her legs seemed to be beyond her control; they shook so much she was finding it hard to stay upright.

'Alexandra von Matke?' She heard hesitation in his voice. He sounded almost scared, too. He hadn't seen her since she was a little girl. Now here she was – seventeen, hair pulled back into a single plait with bits of it escaping and sticking to her face, which was probably still smeared with soot. She couldn't say a word, just stood gazing at him while her heart threatened to burst out of her chest. If only he'd put down that gun in his hand.

'It *is* you, Alix, isn't it?'

She forced her head to move in an approximation of a nod.

'Hang on.' He reached his spare hand into a pocket and pulled out a torch, which he shone onto her face. She tried not to flinch. 'You still have those extraordinary-coloured eyes. My God. I dared not hope . . .' He broke off. 'Let's get inside to the kitchen before we both freeze. I've only just got here myself, I came on ahead.'

He'd taken a risk. For all he knew, the house could have been booby-trapped by the SS. Or have concealed a couple of

Heimwehr soldiers threatened with hanging if they didn't defend every inch of German soil. Alix still couldn't utter a word. Her legs still wanted to take her out of this room and into the snow. He had a gun . . . This could be a bluff, couldn't it? The Russians were skilled at intelligence. Perhaps they'd sent someone here pretending to be Gregor to fool her into doing or saying something incriminatory. She eyed him again. That long narrow nose and the questioning eyes certainly looked like Gregor's. But that uniform, that feared, dreaded, abhorred uniform . . . It seemed impossible that someone like Gregor would ever wear a uniform like that. But then again, he'd been driven out of the country. Forced into exile. If this young man was Gregor he must surely hate all Germans. He must surely wish for revenge.

She was a von Matke. She would try to be brave. Perhaps this person-who-might-be-Gregor would shoot her quickly and have done with it. Alix squared her shoulders and kicked off her remaining boot. She nodded at the door, indicating the way to the kitchen. He walked behind her. She tried not to think about the gun.

Inside the kitchen she lit the lamps on the dresser and the candles on the table, then turned to the stove. That was always the first consideration in this house in winter – keeping the stove alight. It still burned. Noting how her own mind attempted to distract her from the soldier's presence, she riddled the stove and opened the valves for a few seconds to allow more oxygen to fuel the fire. 'This will need topping up shortly.' How squeaky her voice sounded, like a school-girl's or one of those silly creatures in the League of German Maidens.

42

He drew back, removing his coat and cap, perhaps trying to look less threatening. 'Why don't we sit.' He frowned. 'Is there anything to eat here?'

Naturally. It was all his now, all *theirs*. Their house, their food. The Russians were entitled to everything.

'You look so cold,' he said. 'Have you soup? Bread? Let's see if we can warm ourselves up.' She was watching him all the time. He limped slightly, but his movements were still those of the old Gregor: quick and neat. Like an otter's, her mother had once said, with approval, an otter hunting fish. But this grown-up Gregor couldn't be the same as the old Gregor she remembered, even if he had Gregor's eyes and Gregor's way of moving. War must have changed him. It changed everyone, some for better, some for worse.

'What about your . . . comrades?' Her voice came back to her at last but her words sounded squeaky.

He blushed. 'I don't think they'll be here this evening.'

In Lena's pantry she found brandy, a jug of milk, a basin of soup, sausage and bread. None of it touched. Gregor whistled. Now it was her turn to colour. Mami'd saved all this in case, by some miracle, Papi was released or escaped and came back here after they'd left. Papi would be starving, Mami'd said, he'd need to build himself up. She didn't know if Gregor would understand.

But he simply smiled. 'A feast!' He stroked the tins as though they were kittens and pulled out a couple for her to open.

She found saucepans and heated milk and soup. He'd already fallen on the bread, tearing off great chunks and stuffing them into his mouth. Alix stared at him, remembering how his mother had fretted over his table manners. 'You're a good socialist,' Papi had once taunted Eva over a lunch table covered in fine linen and porcelain. 'What do *you* care about such bourgeois niceties?'

'I care,' she had said, turning those intense dark eyes of hers to Papi. 'It's not just the Junker class who like to do things properly, Peter. Consideration and politeness are class-less traits.'

'I couldn't agree more.' Papi had refilled Eva's wineglass. Behind them, unnoticed by either, but audible to Alix, Lena had emitted a small sigh.

Alix pushed away the memories and excused herself to wash in the cloakroom. Her reflection in the glass told her the story of the day's events – that darkness under her eyes wasn't soot to wash away. Lena, the horses, the soldiers . . . She closed her eyes and clutched the basin. *Don't think about it.*

'I'm trying hard to save you your fair share but you'd better hurry,' he called as she walked back through the hall. Through the windows the snow now fell with more determination. She sat next to Gregor and ate too, with increasing appetite, slurping spoonfuls of soup, cramming bread into her mouth and wiping crumbs off her face with the back of her hand. Breakfast had been a long time ago.

She watched his long, slender fingers crumble bread. Musician's hands. Gregor's hands. Her fear seemed to have abated a little as she'd eaten. He was looking at her own hands with their blackened nails. 'Dirt's ideologically sound. Cleanliness is decadent.' He grinned and she found her own lips stretching into an answering smile.

He finished the soup, sat back and sighed. 'That's the best thing I've eaten for at least three years.'

'I made it.' At least she sounded less scared now.

'You?' His lips curled.

'Why are you grinning like that?' He'd never believed her capable of anything practical. She remembered how he'd smirked when she attempted to pump up a bicycle tyre or sew on a button, on one of the rare occasions when no servant was on hand to do these things.

'Just never had you down as the type who'd be in the *Küche*. You used to prefer being outdoors, riding around on those ponies of yours.'

'Lena had me in the kitchen learning how to make cheese and sausages.'

Amusement lit his face. 'Not what your mother had in mind for you: finishing school in Switzerland and history of art in Florence, wasn't it?'

'Something like that.' She eyed the insignia on his tunic, which looked as though it had been made for a broader man. The uniform of the barbarian. How did he really regard her? A beneficiary of the enemy system which had done all those terrible things Papi'd told her about? She blushed again. Gregor had half-closed his eyes, as though he were trying to blot out something. Last time they'd sat this close it had been a July night. They'd still been children then, but there'd been a moment when they'd felt something more than mere childish affection. At least, she had. It had only been a single kiss. Chances were he'd forgotten it.

The shutters rattled. The snow was blowing itself into a storm. Good. It would cover her footprints and slow down the Red Army. On the other hand, it might bring others here seeking shelter. She shouldn't be in this warm kitchen with its blue and white Dutch tiles above the stove, and the pots and pans hanging from the ceiling and reflecting the light of the gas lamp. She'd been a fool to come back, she should have obeyed Mami and kept on going west, no matter what. She'd promised and promises mattered. Papi had always told her that. Then, about a year ago, he'd shaken his head and said that therein lay the officer's dilemma. If you'd promised a monster you'd serve him it was still a promise.

Terrible things everywhere. Memories of what had happened during the day stormed inside her head. She put a hand to one temple, trying to push them away.

'What is it?' Gregor asked.

She got up. 'I'm going now. This isn't safe.'

'You can't.' He put out a hand and grabbed her wrist. 'You'd freeze out there.'

'Better to freeze than be shot. Or raped.'

He flinched, as though she'd slapped him round the face.

'I didn't mean you.' Not the boy who'd shared a bath with her when he stayed here in the holidays. Who'd crept out of bed to share midnight feasts. Though God alone knew what he'd done since she'd last seen him. Impossible to imagine how he'd survived, what life had forced him to become.

'Please sit down.' He pointed at her chair and their eyes locked. She sat. 'You'll be safe here tonight.'

She let herself slump back in the kitchen chair with its faded padded cushions made by Lena when she'd still had time to sew non-essentials.

'What happened today, Alix?'

She wanted to throw the question back at him and ask him what the hell had happened to *him* in the last six years, but found herself answering him instead. 'Lena and I were in the wagon heading west to a cousin's, meeting Mami on the way.'

'Where'd she been?'

'Berlin. Trying to find out about Papi. They'd arrested him, you see. Because of the July Plot.' She looked at him to gauge his reaction but his expression gave nothing away. 'They kept moving him round and we'd lost contact with him. The parcels we sent were returned to us.'

Gregor nodded.

'We'd packed up the wagon when we heard the Reds – the Russians – were so close. The police were watching us. We couldn't leave till the very last moment or they'd have arrested us for defeatism.'

'Especially with your father being involved with the Bomb Plot?'

She nodded.

'What exactly did he do, Alix?'

She shrugged. 'Mami said he'd made a few telephone calls on the day, trying to garner support. She doesn't know the details.'

'Your father probably thought he was protecting her by keeping her in the dark. It must have been dreadful for you both.'

'You can have no idea, Gregor.'

A strange expression twisted his face for a moment. She wished she hadn't said the last bit.

'Mami grew more and more desperate as the Russians

47

came nearer. She said we owed the local people as much protection as we could give them. Refugees came here from East
Prussia and they told us . . .' Alix paused, remembering those
last weeks, Mami looking at the big map of Pomerania and
East Prussia hanging in Papi's study and biting her lip. Lena
packing bag after bag, saying nothing and hushing Alix
whenever she mentioned the Russian advance. The women
and children from the east who sat silent in the kitchen each
night and wouldn't say what they'd seen on their trek.

Gregor wasn't hurrying the narrative. He sat waiting,
without saying a word. The old Gregor liked to jump in and
finish your sentences, your thoughts, for you.

'A plane attacked us on the road west, we lost the wagon.
Lena and I went into the forest to shelter. We hadn't realized
that the Russian advance had got so far today. They were
already in the forest. They got Lena. She . . .' Alix put a hand
over her mouth.

His eyes hadn't left her face. One of his hands found hers
across the oilskin tablecloth. 'It's all right, I know . . . They're
like mistreated children. No sense of morality.' He sounded
weary. 'Poor Lena. Tomorrow at first light we must get you
back to the road. You might be able to slip through the line.
You've probably got a better chance without the wagon and
horses.' He sounded like her childhood friend again, gentle,
thoughtful. Mami always said that Gregor was a sweet boy.
But those missing years . . .

'You sound as if . . .' She didn't seem able to finish a single
sentence. She forced herself to continue. 'You seem concerned
for me.'

He looked baffled. 'Of course I am.'

'You say that, but you're wearing that uniform and I don't really know who you are now.'

'Who I am?' he dropped her hand. 'What do you mean? The same person I always was.'

She said nothing but looked closely at his uniform again.

'No, you're right. Probably not. How could I be?' He made a rectangle with his thumbs and index fingers.

'I don't know anything about what happened to you. Or why you . . .' She eyed the cap on the table in front of them.

'I couldn't have survived if I hadn't joined the Soviets.' He looked at the shape he'd made with his fingers.

'Tell me.' At last she had found the courage to ask him.

'Where should I start?'

'You and your mother went to Warsaw. Papi said it was sudden, that they'd deported you with lots of Jews. I can't remember the exact year.' Alix remembered her puzzlement at the news. Why would anyone want Eva and Gregor to leave the country? There'd been telephone calls, Papi ringing friends in various ministries, cajoling, shouting, despairing; Mami sitting silent in the salon smoking cigarette after cigarette.

'They phoned us one night in our apartment in Berlin, a few months after we were here that summer of '38.'

That last summer.

'You remember where we lived in Berlin, don't you, Alix?'

She did. 'I remember a street of smart apartment blocks with cherry trees in blossom and a courtyard at the back where cats sunned themselves.' The Fischers' apartment had housed Eva's piano and gramophone. Books had spilled out of shelves and cupboards; they even piled up on the wooden

49

floor. Matthias had loved books. 'What do you think of this?' he'd say as he pushed books of poetry, short stories or political essays onto the von Matkes. 'Read it and tell me what you make of it. He's a new Bulgarian author, very daring.'

Alix thought of something else. 'But there was a garage on the corner. I remember the smell of the rubber and petrol.'

'Spoilt the street's tone, some said. But Papi thought it gave us a touch of proletarian authenticity. With comments like that you can see why they . . .' He shook his head. 'They rang one night that October and told my mother she had to be out by the following morning. Anyone with Jewish blood who wasn't born in Germany had to leave the Reich.'

'Jewish?' Alix sat up. 'I had no idea.' Alexandra von Matke had probably been the most naïve girl in Europe.

'She'd kept it quiet. Until the summer of 1938 when suddenly the Gestapo knew all about my grandfather. He was a rabbi's son. They lived in eastern Poland before the first war.'

'But your mother . . . ?' Alix frowned. 'Mami never mentioned she was Jewish.'

'Collective amnesia. In Vienna, when they first got to know her, my mother lived a secular life. She'd left Poland as a small child, spoke German like a native and looked like a Gentile – her own mother wasn't Jewish, so she wasn't even properly Jewish herself, either.' He shifted his weight in the chair. 'Nobody ever suspected. Until 1938.' His eyebrows locked into a frown.

'Surely when she married your father she could have got German citizenship?'

Gregor shrugged. 'She had a German passport all right. But they confiscated it when they arrested my father. Back then they didn't *want* us to leave the country. Then suddenly we couldn't leave quickly enough for them. They stuffed us into sealed freight cars and transported us east. Then we were unloaded into a field on the Polish border. There was nothing, no shelter, no water, nowhere to . . . no sanitation. The Poles said Mama's birth certificate, showing she'd been born in Poland, meant nothing. They didn't want to take in stateless Jews. And I had a German passport, so I should go back to Berlin.'

'Without your mother?'

'Naturally I couldn't do that. Even though your father begged me.'

'Papi?' She sat up, remembering something. 'Your mother rang here, didn't she?' A telephone call late at night, Papi and Mami talking in hushed tones, Papi running out to the car with blankets and a thermos.

'My mother told me he came to the frontier with food and warm clothes. And money. He must have paid someone to pass it to us. I remember Mami opening the parcel and crying because she was so relieved to have those things. They'd stolen our suitcase at the station and we had nothing. We bribed a guard to let us sleep in a stinking barn with the cows. It was freezing: small children and old people were just lying in the open.' Gregor paused. 'At least we had what your father'd given us. The next morning Mami paid the farmer to post a letter to friends in Warsaw. They must have pulled some strings because two days later a policeman came to the barn and stamped our papers, said we could travel on to Warsaw and told us we were lucky not to have our Jewish arses whipped.'

He shook his head. 'Mama and I knew Poland wasn't safe. It was only supposed to be temporary, until we could get south to Hungary or Romania, and then to Palestine or South Africa. Hard to imagine, but the Poles hated Yids even more than the Germans. But my mother got sick when we arrived in Warsaw, probably because of those nights in the barn. We missed our chance of getting out.'

'Tell me about Warsaw.' She leaned towards him.

'Not much to tell. We stayed with some second cousins of my mother's, the Gronowskis. They had sons a little older than me and a couple of little girls. They . . .' He let out a breath.

'Tell me?'

He turned his eyes to hers and the intensity of his gaze was like a blow. 'It was only six years ago, that's what I keep telling myself. It feels like another century.'

Something rumbled outside and the house shook. 'Tell me.' She clutched at his hand.

Six

Gregor
Warsaw, September 1939

'Tanks.' Mr Gronowski closed the windows to block out the rumbling. 'They'll be here within the half-hour.' His face was shadowed and he and his wife looked a decade older, no longer the cheerful middle-aged couple who'd found room for Eva and Gregor in their spacious apartment in fashionable Marianska Street. 'Just three weeks for them to reach Warsaw.'

'We'll just throw the bastards right back where they came from.' Reuben the eldest boy seemed to simmer with furious energy. His mother put a hand on his sleeve.

'Keep out of trouble.'

He shook her off. Through the window came the sound of feet pounding over cobbles. Polish soldiers in their square-topped caps trying to regroup, to think of something else they could try, knowing it was too late.

*

A few weeks later, when the news of the partition of Poland with the Russians reached the Gronowskis, Reuben and his younger brother Jacob sat with Mr Gronowski's road atlas spread out in front of them on the carpet, muttering about joining the Polish Home Army and resisting the invaders. Gregor and his mother and the Gronowski parents sat in pairs on the two elegant sofas arranged facing each other. The two girls were playing a board game in a corner, oblivious, apparently, to the tension in the room. Gregor wished he could join the boys on the floor but hadn't the nerve. They thought he was a kid. From where he sat he could see Reuben's pencil mark, a north–south line dividing the country into the German and Russian sectors.

'We need to fight them. I've got friends who can put us in touch with other patriots.' Reuben kept his eyes on the map as he spoke, obviously knowing the reaction his words would arouse.

'For God's sake, do you want to face a firing squad? Get yourselves sent off for forced labour?' Mr Gronowski got up and reclaimed his touring map, previously used only to plan the family's annual holidays in the Tatras. He stabbed the sheet. 'We should all head south for the mountains.'

'People are saying—'

'What people?' said his mother. 'You mean those types you meet in Nalewki Street?'

'Jews, Mama. Just like us.'

'*Not* "like us".' Mrs Gronowska glanced round the drawing room with its Persian rugs and the Monet hanging over the fireplace. 'We are assimilated, Polish-speaking professionals.'

'I'm sure Himmler'll take your word for it.'

'Don't speak like that to your mother, Reuben.' Mr Gronowski sounded more sad than angry.

'I should have taken Gregor straight to Hungary.' Eva's eyes were still puffy from lack of sleep. 'I failed my own son.'

'You were ill,' Gregor said for the fortieth time.

'They probably wouldn't have let you in.' Mrs Gronowska spoke so quietly Gregor could hardly pick up the words. 'It's not your fault, Eva.'

'It is. Perhaps I should have left him with the von Matkes in Pomerania. Nobody in Germany bears him any ill-feeling. He's still got his German passport.'

In the weeks preceding the invasion the Polish officials had fortunately failed to remember this fact. On the carpet, Reuben and Jacob exchanged a glance.

'I'm not leaving you,' Gregor tried to make the words authoritative.

His mother reached across the sofa and pulled him to her. He could hear her heart beating under her angora jumper. Eva had always loved fine clothes. He could feel her ribs; she'd never regained the weight she'd lost from her influenza. She even showed a few grey hairs now, and there were fine lines round her eyes. But she still drew glances when they took their Sunday afternoon strolls down Nowy Swiat to admire the art deco buildings and buy a cheap nosegay at a street kiosk, or picnicked on something cheap but perfectly presented in the Lazienki Park.

'How did they know, Gregor?' Her voice was controlled, her stage training never left her. 'Who told them about my father?' It was a question she could never answer to her satisfaction.

A few days later Gregor found her sorting through their clothes in the little room she shared with one of the young Gronowska girls. 'You've got a German passport, a German name and you're only one-quarter Jewish.' She let out a breath. 'You understand what I'm saying, don't you, Gregor?'

'You can't *still* believe I'd be safer in Germany?' He flopped down onto the bed. 'We've been through this again and again.'

'Don't crease those shirts.' She lifted them from the bed. 'They may have released your father from that camp by now.' Matthias had been arrested for publishing left-wing books before Eva and Gregor had fled Germany. 'If war's coming they'll need every man they can get to fight.' Her hands tightened around a wool cardigan. Gregor tried to picture his father in the Wehrmacht and failed. If they gave him a weapon Matthias Fischer would probably manage to shoot off his own foot. He'd always been useless with any kind of tool or machine except a typewriter; when he'd visited the printers they'd refused to let him within a metre of their precious presses because of his reputation for jinxing equipment. And, almost uniquely for someone of his generation, he had problems with taking orders. Gregor looked at his mother and felt a deep pity. Perhaps her longing for Matthias cut her like it did him. She must pine for one of Matthias's rib-crushing hugs or deep guffaws.

'The German authorities here will probably send you back to Berlin, they'll regard you as one more ethnic German who needs to return to the Reich,' she went on. 'But while you're with me, you're at risk.'

'Perhaps you're right.' There was no point in rerunning the conversation. But God knows what they'd do with him in Germany – place him in some dreadful youth camp, probably. Or foster him out to the kind of family who thought Picasso and Chagall were alternative names for Beelzebub. His mother didn't need to hear these thoughts. He tried to rally himself. 'I'll probably be back with Papa in our apartment before long,' he assured her, his fingers tracing the Paisley pattern on a silk shirt he remembered his father giving her one Christmas. After they'd arrived in Warsaw Eva had written to Marie asking her to send on some of their clothes. Marie had gone to the Berlin apartment and packed up a big trunk. Gregor and his mother were well turned out. They didn't look like refugees even if they could only pay rare visits to the cafés and cinemas Eva loved so much. 'But where will you go, Mama?'

'East across the Bug. To my father's old village. I still have cousins there, remote ones, but they'll take me in. Perhaps I can find some kind of work.'

'God, Mama!' He could use *language* with her now; she seemed to treat him almost as a grown-up. 'What kind of work would a trained actress find in a rural Jewish village? And the Soviets—'

'Have no quarrel with me. Remember the books by that Russian engineer your father published? About Soviet construction triumphs – the dams and canals? They went down very well in Moscow.'

He didn't like to tell her that he didn't remember. And his father had probably destroyed all the remaining copies of those books years ago; they'd have been death warrants after 1933.

'This will only be a temporary measure.' Eva sounded almost jaunty. But she was an actress, practised at feigning emotion. 'The French and British will soon be making a nuisance of themselves, I expect. And that'll be the end of Hitler.' Her defiant expression made her look like she had in the photograph of her as Joan of Arc in a Vienna production.

She stared at the shirts. 'Clothes will be in short supply now. Take care of your things. I'll write to you once a week.'

'How will you get out of Warsaw?'

Eva bent her head down to study a button on a velvet dress. 'A friend has transport.'

'Which friend?' She'd never mentioned anyone like this before. Sometimes she slipped out of the house for an hour in the early evening. For fresh air, she said.

'His name is Viktor. He has contacts in a construction company working for the Germans. Their trucks leave the city all the time.'

'Viktor who?'

'Viktor Vargá,' she said slowly. 'I know him from Vienna days. I didn't realize until recently that he was in Warsaw too.'

'Vargá. Is that Hungarian?'

She nodded. 'But I don't think he's lived there for a long time. He spent some time in Russia before the war.'

'And it's this Vargá's idea that you should go to the Soviet sector?'

'What is this, an interrogation?' She was almost annoyed with him now, he could tell.

'Mama, it sounds dangerous. Do you trust him?'

'Viktor will get me out of the city safely. He's an old friend.'

'He could be a spy for the Germans.'

'His sympathies were for the other side, as I remember.' She gave a wry smile before her expression became more sombre. 'I really believe this is the best for both of us, Gregor, *Liebling*.' She sounded as though she were repeating a line she'd told herself again and again.

He wanted to ask her more about this Vargá fellow but she smiled that famous dazzling smile of hers and he knew she was trying to deflect further questions. 'I want to come with you. It's not right that you should go by yourself. Papa wouldn't have wanted me to let you do this.'

Eva bent down towards a silk dress and twisted one of its buttons between her fingers so the thread grew tighter and tighter.

One morning a few days after this conversation he woke to find his mother gone, the white quilt pulled neatly up over the pillow on her bed. Mrs Gronowska put a hand on his shoulder. 'It happened very suddenly in the early hours. Vargá got hold of a timber wagon leaving the city with all the right papers and someone knocked on the door for her. Chances like that don't come up often.'

Words seemed to fill his throat, twisting together, choking him. 'She didn't . . .'

'Say goodbye. No.' Mrs Gronowska's touch became a clasp. 'She was worried you'd want to go with her. It's only temporary, Gregor, just for the next month or so.' She gave a forced laugh. 'Eva had to wear an old pair of overalls with a turban round her hair. She wouldn't have got many cabaret parts dressed like that.'

She was trying hard to console him. Gregor forced himself to stretch his facial muscles into an amused expression. 'She left this.' She took an envelope from her dress pocket and he ripped it open.

Darling Gregor,

Forgive me for leaving without saying Auf Wiedersehen. I actually said it to you while you slept. I couldn't bring myself to wake you. I knew you'd want to come with me and I wouldn't have been able to resist letting you. And you're safer away from me.

It's only for a short time, Gregor. The Russians and the Germans will reach a stalemate, some people believe, and life will ease for us. Or the Allies will do something.

I found the address of the German office you can approach about repatriation as an ethnic German and the Gronowskis have the details. I didn't make the application for you myself because we need them to forget all about me. You can honestly say that you don't know where I am at the moment. But I'll send you an address in due course.

Try and keep up your piano practice. Sometimes your left hand is unsteady at speed. By the time I see you again perhaps you'll have mastered that mazurka! I look forward to hearing it.

All my love, Liebling.
Mama

When Mrs Gronowska went to supervise breakfast Gregor sat on the stairs, letter in hand, staring at the front door through which his mother had crept so silently hours earlier.

'What the hell are you doing staring into space like an idiot?' someone said below him.

He hadn't heard Jacob coming out of the dining room.

'Your breakfast is waiting. Hurry up or one of the girls will eat it.' His hand was gentle on Gregor's back. 'You wouldn't believe what greedy little devils they are. And don't worry – Vargá would have done everything necessary to make sure your mother's safe.'

'Have you ever met this Vargá?'

'None of us have, except your mother. They met at one of those cafés in Nalewki Street. That's what Reuben said. He's got friends who know Vargá.'

So that's where Mama had gone on those evenings when she'd pleaded headaches and said she was going to walk in the evening air. Gregor felt a kind of impotent exasperation. The Gronowski boys seemed to know so much more about what'd been going on than he did.

'How did Vargá know she was in the city?'

Jacob rolled his eyes. 'You'll never make a Varsovian, Gregor. Word travels in this city. Particularly among us Jews.'

'But you're not really . . .' He stopped.

'Observant? No. The Gronowskis have lived a pretty secular life for the last half-century or so. But we still have friends and family in the Jewish community.' He slapped Gregor's back. 'Come on, little German boy.'

One afternoon he came into the drawing room and found Reuben smoothing down the Persian rug. Reuben looked up. 'Damn thing's never sat properly.'

Gregor sat on the floor beside him, the question almost hanging out of his mouth. Reuben raised an eyebrow. 'What?'

'Why are you nice to me?'

'What do you mean?'

'I'm German. I'm supposed to be getting myself repatriated to the glorious Reich. You should hate me.'

Reuben shrugged. 'Vargá obviously trusts your mother.'

Once again, this man's name. But other things were on his mind at the moment. 'I'm caught in the crack.'

'What crack? What are you talking about?'

'I don't belong here and if I go home I won't belong there. They'll stick me in some institution, try and make a Nazi out of me.' The words fell from his mouth.

Reuben studied him. 'What do you want to do?'

Gregor shrugged. He didn't even know how to fire a pistol. He was probably a useless fighter like his father.

Reuben stroked the rug, saying nothing for a while. 'I'll speak to a friend of mine who's close to Vargá,' he said at last. 'Perhaps he'll have some suggestions.'

'This Vargá . . .'

'What about him?'

'Everything seems to come back to him. And yet everyone's always so vague about who he is exactly.'

Reuben nodded. 'No bad thing in wartime, a bit of vagueness.' Gregor sensed no more information was to be obtained on the subject of Vargá and stood.

'Thank you,' he said. 'I mean it. Thank you for accepting me.' God, he'd probably sounded like an idiot.

Reuben was still staring at him. 'You're almost one of us really.'

'How d'you mean?'

Reuben ran a finger round one of the flowers on the rug. 'A *Mischling*. A mixture. That's enough.' And there was a note in Reuben's tone that told Gregor he'd been accepted in a way he hadn't been before.

A single postcard of girls in embroidered headdress came from Eva, with an address in Brest on the river Bug. Eva had written a brief message saying she hoped to travel on to the countryside east of the city within the next week. She didn't sign the card.

Rumours came of arrests and executions both sides of the new border. Mr Gronowski got out his map again. Mrs Gronowska packed cases. 'We're going to a farm near Zako-pane where we used to spend summers,' she told Gregor. 'Come with us. I promised your mother I'd look after you.'

Gregor watched her fingers flying through piles of wool-lens and shirts, sorting them into piles to be taken or left, just as his own mother had a month earlier. Mrs Gronowska's once perfectly manicured fingernails were bitten to the quick. She came from a rich family who'd made their money in the jewellery business. This large Marianska Street apartment, so tastefully decorated with paintings and porcelain and formerly the venue for so many literary and artistic soirées, had been her childhood home. Now she was stuffing blankets and woollens into cases and abandoning most of the family treasures.

'Mama wanted me to try and get myself repatriated to Germany.'

'She gave me the name of the official you need to see. I have it in the desk in my room.'

Reuben had come into the room and stood listening. 'The more I think about it the more I think it's a bad plan, Gregor,' he said. 'You can't just waltz in and hand yourself over. It's too risky.'

'Precisely. Besides, I don't want to go back to Germany. I hate them. I want to go to my mother.' He handed Mrs Gronowska a shirt.

'Join Eva in the east? Is that wise, Gregor? You've heard about the Russians,' she said.

Word had already reached them of the deportations from eastern Poland.

'Perhaps we can still get to Hungary. From there – who knows?'

Mrs Gronowska stared at the pile of jumpers and socks. 'Reuben and Jacob are heading off to a forest somewhere between here and the border,' she said at last. 'I'm not supposed to know but I saw them looking at that map again. They'll help you get to the Soviet sector.'

Gregor helped Mr and Mrs Gronowski and the two girls carry their bags to Warsaw Central. The station was crowded with passengers clutching bags and attaché cases and trying not to make eye-contact with the Gestapo men at the ticket office.

Gregor lifted Lydia, the smallest Gronowska girl, into her mother's arms, handed Mrs Gronowska her jewellery case and wished the family a safe journey. 'Zakopane's always fun.' Mr Gronowski was trying hard to inject enthusiasm into his tone. 'We could do far worse. At least we'll get some fresh air.'

'It's too early for skiing.' Lydia wrinkled her nose. 'It'll be so boring. Lucky you, staying here, Gregor.'

'Little town mouse.' Her father ruffled her curls.

When the train had left, Gregor made his way back to the house. On the streets people walked with eyes fixed somewhere in the middle distance, ignoring the soldiers. There were still plenty of well-dressed middle-class women. Women who looked as though they hadn't noticed that they lived in a defeated city; who held themselves as though they were inhabitants of Paris or Rome or New York. But perhaps it was more important now than ever to step out with lipstick perfectly applied and clothes pressed.

When he reached the house he found Reuben and Jacob pulling up the drawing-room floorboards. They removed a lumpy object wrapped in canvas. Reuben glanced at Gregor before cutting the string with a pocketknife.

Gregor blinked at the sight of the guns.

'We can find a third one if you want to join us.' Reuben pulled a handkerchief out of his pocket and polished the barrel of one of the guns. 'We can't hang around here any longer. Haven't got the fucking work cards. Even Vargá can't get them for us. The Nazis will send us to Germany as slave labour.'

'What are you going to do, Reuben?'

'Help the Union of Armed Combat – that's the Home Army's proper name.' Reuben sounded proud.

'You're going to fight?' Reuben wasn't yet sixteen, Jacob barely fifteen, hardly older than Gregor.

65

Reuben scratched his nose. 'They won't actually let us fight yet, some nonsense about being too young.' He scowled. 'But we can make ourselves useful carrying messages and supplies.'

'I need to find my mother.'

'Your mother left you here because she thought you were better off without her. Now you're doing just what she didn't want you to do – following her.'

'I have to find her. She can say what she wants, but it's not right for her to be alone in times like these.'

'Frankly, you'd be a spineless little bastard if you didn't think like that.' Reuben tucked the handkerchief back in his sleeve.

'Pack your rucksack, Fischer. Travel light. No need to take the entire contents of the Brothers Jablkowski department store.'

Gregor managed a smile as pale as the autumn sunshine, remembering the trips they'd made to admire the stock when they'd first come to Warsaw.

'And find that old touring map of Papa's and learn the geography of Poland. Rivers, roads, forests, railway lines.' Reuben stood, his face serious. 'Your life may well depend on knowing the country better than you know your own arse.'

The three of them left Warsaw together. À la Fourchette, Gregor's favourite café, was still serving its famous open sandwiches and Reuben agreed to one last visit on the way to the station.

'Who knows?' Jacob crammed bread filled with cold beef

and cucumber into his mouth. 'We may all be back here soon.'

'Shame to let the German pigs eat everything.' Reuben licked mayonnaise off his fingers. 'Whoops, sorry Herr Fischer. Keep forgetting you're one of the Master Race.'

'Easily done when he's dribbling sour cream down his chin like that,' said Jacob.

Reuben's grin turned to a frown. 'You're such a kid, Fischer. How on earth are you going to manage?'

Gregor shrugged, scared to speak in case the cowardly thoughts in his head burst out and he begged them to take him with them.

They travelled with him as far east as they could, almost into Brest itself, sitting in a railway carriage populated by people with grey faces who clutched suitcases and children to themselves, hardly talking and visibly stiffening when the Polish police boarded to check papers. The forged documents Vargá had supplied to Reuben and Jacob were examined without comment. Gregor's German passport caused raised eyebrows and muttered consultations. Finally they handed it back. Gregor tried to concentrate on the landscape through the window, strips of field then forests, fields again, then forests stretching on and on. He fell into a near-reverie for the hours that passed, staring at the trees and hardly hearing the whispered conversations or the wail of babies. He thought of Warsaw, now gone from his life like Berlin before it: the markets with the women in their brocade shawls and bodices, the streetside shrines where tapers flickered before saints. And now he was travelling even further away from the city he still thought of as home, and even further away from his father. And from Alexandra. He wondered what had brought her memory back to him. He'd hardly thought of Alix since the war had started. She was German, after all. Perhaps she thought the invasion justified. He felt ashamed. She wouldn't approve of the invasion; not with parents like hers.

It had all started back there. Someone back in that old Pomeranian house with its scent of spices and its gardens full of roses had said something, done something, which had drawn attention to Eva. Not Peter, not Marie. There'd been another man at Alexanderhof that evening, a man he had despised and feared. Gregor shuddered, remembering him. There'd been a dinner party and a storm and—

Reuben was nudging his arm and nodding towards the corridor. Jacob was already waiting outside for them.

'The train will slow in a minute,' Reuben muttered when he'd closed the door. 'Grab your rucksack. As soon as we've crossed the river be ready to jump. Jacob and I don't want to end up in the town.' The smooth chunter of the wheels turned to a hollow clatter as the train reached the bridge. Gregor did what he was told.

Gregor watched Reuben. The older boy seemed to be listening out for something. The engine was braking. Suddenly Reuben nodded and sprang up, opening the door and jumping out of the carriage. Gregor hesitated a second before forcing himself to step out after him, feeling the rush of air on his face and the nothingness beneath him. He landed on his feet at the top of the escarpment like a parachutist before losing his balance and rolling down the slope, coming to a halt at the bottom, winded but unhurt. A grunt behind him announced the arrival of Jacob.

'Quick.' Reuben pulled them to their feet and led them across a field, not letting them draw breath until they'd reached a clump of trees where they doubled over, gulping in air. 'Brest's close.' He pointed over the field towards its church spires and fortress. 'Find your mother before they close the frontier. Bring her west to this village.' He stuffed a piece of paper into Gregor's hand. 'Leave a message for us if we're not there. You can trust the baker.'

Gregor peered at the name on the scrap, thanking God for the hours he'd spent with Reuben before they'd left Warsaw, memorizing the touring map and the new boundaries.

'It's a long walk but just keep heading west. You'll know you're going the right way if you keep the railway on your right, but stay out of sight of the carriages.'

Gregor folded the scrap and was about to stuff it into his pocket.

'No.' Reuben stopped him. 'Memorize it. Nothing written down.'

Gregor tore the paper into tiny fragments, which the wind blew away. In turn Reuben and Jacob shook his hand. 'If the Russians get you, remember to swear like we taught you,' Jacob told him. 'Act rough, not like a good little boy who practises piano and knows his French irregular verbs.'

'Sod off, *psia krew.*' He only knew the one Polish curse: dog's blood. Lydia had taught it to him. She said she'd picked it up from the men who delivered the coal. Gregor'd kept it up his sleeve for a suitable occasion.

Jacob turned and grinned. 'Dog's blood yourself.'

And they were gone. For a few minutes Gregor stood watching their retreating backs and swallowing hard. It took all his willpower not to run after them. At last he managed to turn himself round and direct his feet towards the town.

Nobody stopped him or questioned him when he reached Brest after a short walk through fields and smallholdings. A solitary policeman on a street corner stared straight through him. The town seemed empty. Most of the shops were boarded up. Stray dogs sniffed around garbage bins, eyeing Gregor with interest and approaching him on crouched legs, half pleading, half calculating. Gregor tried not to think about how hungry these animals might be.

He found an old man sitting on steps outside an apartment block and showed him Eva's address. The man sucked on toothless gums and muttered directions in an accent so thick Gregor could barely understand a word. He thanked him and walked on, taking wrong turn after wrong turn, feeling the strangeness of this place. No street kiosks selling newspapers and tobacco. No markets with their cackling geese. No Jewish urchins with their black pillbox hats and corkscrew curls.

Finally he found the street and walked along it, noting the shuttered windows and broken glass. He knocked on the peeling black-painted door that was his mother's. No answer. Again he rapped. This time he heard footsteps and the door opened a centimetre. Gregor's nose crinkled at the tangy odour of a scared human being. She peered out at him.

'There's nobody here. All gone east.'

'My mother, Eva Fischer . . .' Gregor fumbled in his rucksack and found a photograph – Eva at a picnic at the von Matkes', sitting on a plaid rug, head tossed back so her long neck was exposed, dark hair falling like a curtain over her shoulders.

The woman took the picture between grubby fingers and stared at it, a grin forming on her face. 'I remember her. She go east too.' She handed back the photo.

'Who took her?'

'Who you think? Fairies?' She cackled and the door slammed in his face.

Gregor walked very slowly back the way he'd come, feeling nothing, neither pain, nor grief nor fear. No time for that now. *Make plans*. His rucksack held bread, sausage and apples and a bottle of water, along with a change of clothes. How long would these provisions last? He'd been banking on his mother having additional supplies they could take with them on the journey to meet the Gronowski boys.

Two mongrels jumped out of a side-street, ears back, teeth bared. He kicked out at them and they moved away, growling. He walked on, ears straining for the sound of the dogs' feet padding up behind him.

He found he was standing beside an abandoned school. The dogs had vanished. He walked round to the back and broke a ground-floor window, managed to squeeze himself through like a cat burglar and found himself in what had been the cloakroom, still smelling of damp clothes. A sign in Polish – which he could read well now – told him not to wear outdoor shoes in the gymnasium.

Gregor brushed the shards of glass to one side and made

himself a makeshift bed with his rucksack as a pillow and his overcoat wrapped round him. He daren't try the light switch. If only he weren't so damn scared of the dark. But the dogs couldn't get him in here; there was nothing to be frightened of.

As he lay there he caught sight of something red and metallic on the tiled floor beneath the benches. He reached out and picked it up. It felt cold as stone in his hand. A mouth organ. Some schoolboy had dropped it here. Gregor was about to place it on the bench when he stopped himself. What chance was there its owner would ever come back? He slipped it into his coat pocket. Why should the Russians have it?

As he lay there, too tired for sleep to take him immediately, his mother's image floated into his mind. *What happened to you, Mama? Can your friend Vargá still save you?* He blew a single plaintive note on the mouth organ, very softly, for company, and stared out of the broken window-pane.

Seven

Marie
Vienna, May 1924

The window shattered and glass cascaded to the ground a foot away from the table where Marie and Anton sat eating their lunch. A man rolled through the window.

'God!' Anton sprang up, napkin in hand. 'Are you hurt, Marie?'

'Perfectly fine.' She put a hand to her new hat to check it hadn't been sprayed.

'My apologies. I believe I aimed myself so as to avoid any danger to you both.' The man got to his feet and removed a handkerchief from his top pocket, wrapping it round a bleeding knuckle.

'Viktor?' Marie couldn't resist a smile. 'What *are* you up to?'

'Marie?' His sleepy gaze swept her face and the length of her body, making her blush. 'I didn't recognize you in that very elegant but somewhat *concealing* hat. No doubt essential for keeping your admirers at bay.'

Shouts erupted on the street. 'There he is!' someone yelled.

He gave a little bow. 'Excuse me.' She looked away, wanting to laugh but conscious of the cold draught of Anton's disapproval. 'I don't think those hoodlums will bother you if I'm gone.' With a few strides of his long legs he'd already reached the kitchen doors, pushing a banknote into the waiter's hand as he passed him.

'Well.' Anton blinked. Marie took a sip of her wine. The waiter bustled over and insisted on moving them to another table. Seeing a group of angry uniformed men staring in through the hole in the window, he waved a silver tray at them and shouted something about his cousin's husband who was something or other in the town hall and they shuffled away.

'Political.' Marie spread butter on a piece of bread. Rehearsals had started early and she'd only grabbed a quick breakfast before leaving for the Academy where she was studying drama.

'That was Viktor Vargá, wasn't it?' Anton poured her another glass of wine. 'Have some more of this red. Eva's friend? He's the one with the missing fingertip, isn't he?'

'A dog bit the tip off when he was a child.' Marie sipped her soup, which had hardly cooled during the upheaval.

'Isn't he a Communist or something?'

'Viktor?' She laughed at the thought. 'Not really. He just doesn't like the Heimwehr, says they're a bunch of over-patriotic thugs.'

'Which makes him a Communist.'

'Not necessarily.' If Anton was going to dwell on the various militia groups and their ideologies she'd forgo pastries and coffee and make her excuses.

'He's probably Jewish,' Anton went on. She looked up at the use of the word. 'What is it?'

'Nothing.' She helped herself to another bread roll. 'I just don't remember people talking about who was Jewish and who wasn't when we were growing up.'

'Well there weren't so many of them, were there? It was only after the war that they swarmed in from Russia and Poland. And they've done very well for themselves.'

Marie blinked. 'I suppose so. But there are lots of poor Jews. Some of the students at the Academy are Jewish and their families have lived here for generations. They don't have money to throw around.'

He made a sweeping gesture with his hand. 'You're probably right. I'm no Jew-basher. Remember that old baker back home? He used to give us the misshapen gingerbread at the end of the day. Besides, this political stuff is no conversation for a day like this.' He gave that quick smile of his, the one that had disarmed the nuns, and probably disarmed God himself, Lena always said. Lena had followed her friend to Vienna, finding odd sewing jobs to keep herself afloat (she had a talent for running up imitations of the latest fashions) and using her spare time to help Marie learn lines or alter costumes.

Anton was watching her now. 'So how does it feel?'

'Terrifying.' The coldness in Marie's stomach returned and she sipped the wine to try and warm it away, wishing he hadn't reminded her. Poor Anton, he meant so well. She was Sonja in *The Lieutenant's Girl,* a new play about a young woman engaged to an Austrian officer but in love, against her better judgement, with a Croatian nobleman. Sonja reminded her of herself, a little naïve, perhaps, but capable of great emotion, which jostled uneasily with her dutiful desire to please her family and friends by marrying the worthy young adjutant.

'You'll be wonderful as Sonja. Brilliant.' He remembered something. 'Shame your father won't see it.'

She felt her face drop. 'He just couldn't afford the train fare.'

'It's a scandal, a man like your father left high and dry like that.'

There were problems with Papi's pension. The town was in a kind of limbo, still not yet properly Italian but no longer really Austrian. It took even longer than normal for complications to be ironed out. Papi was relying on savings, only they weren't worth what they should have been, because of the war. And he'd started a new venture.

'Did I tell you about the little brown cows?' Perhaps this would will him into a better humour.

'The what?'

'Swiss cows. Farmers in the Po Valley love them but they can't breed them down there. So instead of buying them from Switzerland they're importing them from the South Tyrol. Papi's put some money into a small farm with a man who used to teach at his school.'

Anton put down his soup spoon. 'Your father's raising cows? A professional man reduced to that?'

'I find it rather sweet.' He'd sent her a photograph of himself with a couple of newborn calves. She kept it on her dressing table and it always made her smile when she looked at it. Her father was one of the few Austrians of his generation who'd adapted to postwar life with some degree of grace. But she couldn't say this to Anton.

'My father's fruit rotted in the orchards last year.' Anton's gaze switched to the bowl of fruit on the pastry counter. 'We couldn't sell it in Austria and we can't compete with the Italians. Look at those cherries. Before the war they'd have come from our valley.'

He was going to start on the subject of the Treaty of St Germain and its appalling treatment of the South Tyrol. Marie looked round the restaurant for a distraction and couldn't find anything suitable. She racked her brains for a change of subject. 'What are your plans for the summer, Anton?'

He gave her a sharp look, probably knowing what she was up to.

'Will you do any hiking?'

He scowled. 'The Italians don't know how to look after the mountain huts. It makes me sick how they've let them fall into disrepair.' Disgust deepened his voice. 'This summer I'll stay this side of the Brenner for my hikes.'

The waiter had finished sweeping up the shards of glass. How unruffled Viktor had appeared as he'd sprung through the window, as though he were diving into a pool for a dip. He'd probably run down the back alleys behind the kitchen and jumped on the first tram he'd spotted. He would lose himself in one of the big apartment blocks outside the Ring, the wide boulevard encircling the city. This evening he'd appear for the performance at the theatre because he'd promised them both he would. Viktor was all the things Anton accused him of being but he kept his word.

But why was she letting Viktor preoccupy her like this? Anton was asking about Eva. 'She's nervous, too,' she told him.

'Her part's not nearly as big as yours. What is she, the Croatian's crazy sister or something?'

'His cousin.' Marie shook her head, unable to deny it but almost wishing he'd hide this unnecessary pride in her career. Eva was good, very good in fact, as the jealous and suspicious girl, giving the role an element of just-controlled hysteria which drew all eyes to her whenever she was on stage.

'Is her affair with Vargá serious?' he asked.

'I'm not sure it even is an affair yet.' Why was she so reluctant to discuss it? Loyalty to Eva? 'Viktor comes round some afternoons if we haven't got rehearsals.' She realized with a shock that the reason she didn't want to talk about the relationship was that she didn't like thinking about Eva and Viktor as a couple. Silly really, there'd never been any possibility of Viktor looking at *her*. He'd made it clear at that first meeting in the *Heuriger* in the forest that he preferred Eva. He'd stared at her with those sleepy eyes of his while he sipped his wine. Men generally considered Eva more attractive than Marie, more unusual, more exotic. It wasn't surprising Viktor would prefer her. And yet that didn't stop Marie taking tea with the pair of them, enjoying his teasing and his accounts of his travels. Viktor had seen the world and could talk to them about Paris, Rome and London.

He liked their apartment, which belonged to a distant cousin of Eva's. 'Such porcelain,' he'd say, holding the cup so that his tipless finger stuck up incongruously. 'And everything so fashionable and neat.' He spoke in that slightly clipped German of his which made people say he was Hungarian. Or perhaps Slovakian. Or was it Ruthenian? People were like rivers, Viktor always said when pressed about his nationality; they assumed, temporarily perhaps, the territory through which they flowed. Calling them German or Austrian was reductive.

Eva had thrown one of the butter-yellow cushions at him. 'How dare you imply my apartment is bourgeois!' He caught the cushion with one hand, easy and graceful. Did Viktor ever appear off-balance?

The concierge's cat had wandered in again – Eva always forgot to close the door – and strolled into the room with a proprietorial air. Marie and Eva each put down a hand and made encouraging noises with their tongues. The cat ignored them both and leaped onto Viktor's lap, rubbing her black head against his jacket. Eva watched the animal, perhaps wondering what it would be like to be so close to him.

He stroked it in a single long movement from its ears to the tip of its tail, his face losing its easy expression for a second and showing pleasure. Eva had told Marie that Viktor liked visiting the Zoo. And he'd once kept a monkey in his apartment. The cat on his lap curled up and purred. 'When I was a lad I used to help my father with the cats and dogs he looked after,' he said.

It was unusual for Viktor to volunteer information about his childhood.

'Was your father a veterinary surgeon?' Marie asked.

He nodded and continued to murmur nonsense at the cat.

'What rubbish are you muttering to that animal?' Eva asked.

'Not rubbish at all. It's a bit of English poetry, exclaiming at feline beauty.'

Eva looked confused. Her English wasn't good. Marie's lips twitched. Viktor looked at her with approval. Perhaps there was still a chance that he and Eva weren't . . . ? That he might yet prefer *her*?

Anton was saying something to her across the table.

'I'm sorry.' She blinked.

'Be careful, Maria.'

She forced herself back to the present, her napkin crumpled on the table, her half-full wineglass.

'Vargá moves among disreputable people. Your career is just beginning, you can't afford to be associated with the wrong sort.'

'I'll be careful.' But mention of the 'wrong sort' of people had made her recall Viktor's impersonation of a Communist concierge forced to hold open a door for a countess and her poodle. 'But don't worry about Vargá,' she added. 'He's harmless.' She shivered suddenly, recalling how Viktor had gazed at Eva when she'd come into the sitting room wearing a backless gown on her way out to a restaurant. His casual air had disappeared and he'd looked like a wolf, longing to consume Eva. She'd seen him often enough waiting for women by the Goethe statue in the Burggarten. Always a different girl, some of them fellow students from the Academy. But come to think of it, she hadn't spotted him there in the last weeks. Which probably meant he really *had* fallen in love with Eva.

Anton must have been struggling with his mood because he suddenly produced one of those dazzling smiles. If only she could find it in herself to desire this handsome and athletic young man like all the shopgirls and flowersellers did. She'd seen how his presence caused them to fiddle with their hair and look up at him through lowered eyelashes. 'I'll settle up with the waiter so you can be back in the theatre in good time.'

Her stomach turned a somersault at the thought of what was to come. 'Oh Anton, suppose I forget my lines? Or where I'm supposed to stand? Sometimes I go wrong in lighting rehearsals. My mind just goes blank. Or what if—?'

'I promise, you won't forget your lines.' His dark blue eyes burned. 'Or where to stand. And you won't trip over, either. Your Sonja will be wonderful, Maria, just wonderful. You're doing it for us, for the old place, for our little town, for your family and friends.'

And she'd felt just as she had when they were kindergarten children and he'd cajoled her down a steep slope on his toboggan, assuring her she'd be fine.

He looked at her glass. 'You've hardly touched your wine!'

She drank a mouthful. 'Delicious.'

'From the Burgenland.' He'd probably ordered a bottle more expensive than he could afford. Dear Anton.

They smiled at each other over the glasses.

Eight

Alix

Pomerania, February 1945

Gregor finished telling Alix about the abandoned town on the river Bug from where Eva had vanished. For the last half an hour he'd pulled her out of this kitchen with its familiar blue tiles and range and its sense of imminent danger. She'd travelled to that Warsaw family with him and Eva, felt his bewilderment when his mother had vanished. Alexandra von Matke no longer feared Gregor Fischer, uniform or no uniform.

He stood and helped himself to glasses from the kitchen dresser, pouring shots of the vodka he'd removed from his jacket pocket. 'Here.'

Alix took a glass from him. 'So your mother trusted this Vargá to get her to safety.'

'She trusted him all right.' Gregor downed his vodka. 'She'd known him for years, since Vienna.'

That mysterious, excitement-filled time in Vienna that Mami hardly mentioned any more.

'You never heard another word from her after you left Brest?'

He shook his head.

Alix closed her eyes. All around them rolled this dark mist, all-consuming, all-concealing, inescapable.

Gregor was holding her hand again.

'You haven't finished your story.' Her voice sounded harsh.

'No.' He made no attempt to continue. She didn't press him. Perhaps she was being selfish, shielding herself from knowing any more. She looked at him, at his restless eyes and full, set mouth. This was *Gregor*. She'd known him since they were both infants. He shouldn't be making her feel like . . . this. Whatever *this* was. He was an enemy. If she forgot that she'd be lost. But then she remembered that kiss in the cellar and felt her cheeks flush.

He stroked her fingers. 'If Vavilov hadn't come this way, you and I might never have seen each other again.'

'Vavilov?' Her voice sounded high-pitched. She wished he'd stop touching her. No she didn't. 'Who's he? What do you do for him?'

He made a sweeping movement with his free hand, reminding her of the old Gregor, who'd dismiss anything or anyone he found uninteresting with a single wave. It had annoyed her once; now it made her feel relieved. Gregor was still Gregor. He brought her hand to his lips and kissed it. 'Do you mind?' His voice sounded thick.

'No.' Warmth was spreading through her body, from the base of her spine to her heart. She laughed, disconcerted.

He raised an eyebrow at her.

'It's nothing. Just strange how things turned out. Tell me more about this Vavilov.' She needed to distract herself away from this madness.

'He's a major in the Polish unit. At least, officially. He's actually intelligence rather than combat. I suspect he sometimes works with SMERSH or the NKVD as well.'

She'd heard of both Soviet intelligence units and repressed a shudder. 'He sounds dangerous.'

Gregor didn't deny it.

'Why do *you* work for him?'

'I was in Kolyma.' He looked at her as he said the name, which meant nothing to her. 'That's a camp in eastern Siberia where the Russians eventually sent me. He got me out.' A part of his story he hadn't yet described. 'The deal was I'd help him.'

'What sort of "work"?' A note of coldness in her voice now, she observed.

'It's our brief to visit the big houses in captured territory and make notes on their status. I came on ahead today.' He spoke as though reading from a sheet.

'Why?' Some of the doubts she'd brushed aside were returning. She'd perhaps been foolish to dismiss her earlier fears. Whatever had happened between them in the past, Gregor and she were on opposite sides.

'Vavilov was overstretched – there are quite a few big houses in these parts. A combat unit was supposed to come with me but they found alcohol in an abandoned van in the town.'

'What exactly do you mean by the "status"?'

He put his free hand to the lobe of an ear and rubbed it. 'What we know about the owners, who they are, what they did.'

'What do you do with the information?' she asked.

'Keep as much of it as possible to myself.'

'Really?'

The itch he'd felt on his ear seemed to have spread to his cheek.

'What *do* you know about us?'

'That they arrested your father after the July Plot. And that high-ranking Gestapo officers came here regularly.'

'One of them did, all right.'

Nine

August 1944

Alix squinted through the sun at the gleaming black Mercedes as it cruised up the drive, throwing up clouds of dust. Anyone who still had petrol was almost certainly someone she didn't want to meet. But her feet seemed incapable of moving her off the terrace and out of sight. By the time she'd identified the car's passenger as Preizler it was too late to run away. He waved at her like a jolly old uncle visiting a favourite niece. Alix concentrated on setting her features into a neutral pose.

'My dear Alexandra.' He sprang out of the car, his figure as slim as ever. Apparently he'd taken up rock-climbing again, when he could spare the time to head south to the Alps. Surely such jaunts were frowned on, with the Allies now in mainland Europe? Perhaps it was different for the likes of Preizler.

'What are you doing nowadays?' he asked.

'Working on the farm.' As if she could be doing anything

else, dressed in breeches and old shirt and carrying a pitch-fork. He probably didn't approve, no doubt believing that she should be working in some signals job or manning an ambulance. But farming was essential work, thank goodness.

'And how the fresh air suits you. You'd make a perfect photograph for *Die Woche*.'

She grimaced at the thought. 'You're here to see Mami?' Papi *obviously* being in no position to offer hospitality, incarcerated as he was by this man's colleagues.

He put a hand on her shoulder as they walked up the steps. One of his shoes creaked as he moved. 'A Patek Philippe, I see?' He was looking at the watch Papi'd given her for her birthday.

'Yes, I'm very lucky.' She tried not to let her shoulder stiffen where he touched it. She wouldn't let him see her uneasiness; keeping her poise was a matter of pride to her.

'Indeed.' A pause. 'My own childhood wasn't notable for expensive presents.'

'I'm sorry.'

'My father lost his job as a janitor soon after we South Tyroleans were handed over to the Italians. Kicked in the teeth when he'd already lost a son.'

Mami had mentioned Preizler's brother, blown up fighting the Italians in one of the battles of 1917.

'I'm sorry,' she said again. She took him into the salon. They'd covered the furniture in the drawing room with dustsheets now but still used this room on the rare occasions visitors arrived. He looked at the Tompion table clock and checked it against his watch.

'You're three minutes fast.'

Alix excused herself and went to find Mami, who was helping Lena remove the stalks from blackcurrants in the kitchen. Mami looked up as Alix walked in. 'I heard the Mercedes.' She stood and rinsed her hands under the tap. 'Just let me do my hair.' She put her hands to the chignon on the nape of her neck and checked for stray hairs. Each movement was sure and graceful. All those years of being trained in movement, Mami would never lose that. She reached for her handbag and pulled out lipstick to touch up her lips. 'Makes me feel more confident,' she explained. She barely needed cosmetics; Mami was thirty-nine now and still retained the smooth, plumped-up skin of a woman a decade younger.

Alix thought of her own face, still that of a girl, tanned by being out of doors all year round. She hadn't experimented much with cosmetics. There was something shameful in being seventeen and not knowing how to put on lipstick, tidy your eyebrows or do anything more with a mane of thick hair than simply plait it.

When they entered the salon Alix and Mami found the visitor adjusting the minute hand on the Tompion. 'That's better.'

Mami's cerise lips formed a smile. Preizler gave her an approving nod. 'You look well, Maria.' His wife Clara favoured the scrubbed look, Mami said, rosy cheeks from working in her garden and kitchen. That's how the Party liked their homegrown women. When they were away from home in Warsaw or Prague or Paris it was a different matter. They enjoyed *mademoiselles* with painted fingernails, red lips and waved hairdos.

Alix watched Preizler's fingers close the clock's glass and

imagined them flicking through the pages of police files, pausing now and then so he could linger over details and make notes. She shivered in the warm air. He pulled a handkerchief out of a pocket and wiped the glass before taking Mami's hand and kissing it. 'Maria, I need to ask you something.'

Mami sat on the chaise longue, her face suddenly pale beneath its rouge.

'I'm sorry, I've startled you. So indelicately phrased.'

'Yes,' Alix said.

Mami frowned up at her.

'Clara begged me to ask for the recipe for those delicious preserved plums you served us once.'

'A little early in the season for plums, isn't it? Mami raised an eyebrow. 'Ours are a month away from ripening.'

'She likes to be well prepared.'

'Alix, pop into the kitchen and ask Lena to write it out.'

Alix shot her mother a look heavy with gratitude.

'No, please.' Preizler raised a hand. 'The poor girl's been working out in the heat. Clara can wait until next time.' It didn't sound as though he particularly minded the inconvenience to his wife.

'It's no trouble.' Alix decided she'd get the wretched recipe anyway, even if he preferred her to stay in the salon. If he wanted to play little games with them, so be it. He'd have to *order* her to stay here.

'You might want to hear this.' He turned to her mother. 'I've news of Peter.'

Peter. Alix had only ever heard her mother and close friends call her father by his Christian name. Before the arrest, Preizler had always used Papi's title: baron.

'They've moved him.' He reached over and took one of Mami's hands. 'Now it's not necessarily bad news, Maria. I'm sure it's simply because of the bombs.'

She was so white now her lips looked like a clown's against her skin. 'Where?'

'I'm not sure. Probably somewhere to the south.'

She closed her eyes for a second or two. 'Is there nothing we can do, Anton?' On her lap her hands wove in and out of each other.

'I rang a . . . someone I know in Prinz-Albrecht-Strasse and asked them to go through the file one more time. There may be something they've missed, something that shows Peter had nothing to do with the . . . treachery.'

Alix looked away. Preizler surely knew her father was up to his neck in it. Someone must have talked, or written Papi's name down on a list. He was playing a game with Mami, pretending he could find evidence to the contrary.

'You're so kind,' Mami said in a tight voice. 'I'm grateful.'

What for? As though reading Alix's thoughts, Mami shot her a look. Alix recomposed her features. 'Thank you,' she said.

He dropped Mami's hand.

'I'll find Lena and get you that recipe now.' Mami stood. 'Oh yes, the plums.'

'I'll go, Mami.' Alix made for the door. On the way her eyes met those of Aunt Friederika in the portrait on the wall. Friederika's thin, disdainful lips seemed to curl. Alix wondered what she made of this play-acting. If she were alive today she'd probably tell Mami and Alix to throw Preizler out and to the devil with the consequences. But they couldn't. Not while there was still a chance he could help Papi.

Lena stared at Alix when she asked for the recipe. She reached for an old envelope and wrote it out on the back in the precise handwriting taught her by the Tyrolean nuns. 'Here you are.'

Mami was sitting again when Alix returned to the salon, her eyes on Papi's carriage clock, one manicured hand pressed against her mouth. Preizler was standing in front of her. 'I tell you this only so you have all the facts, Maria.'

'I wish I didn't know.'

'We might be wrong—' he broke off, seeing Alix.

Had Papi been tortured? Perhaps he was dead after all.

'Thank you, Alexandra.' Preizler took the recipe.

'We don't have much paper,' she said, explaining why it was written on the envelope.

Mami started to get up. 'I'll show you out.'

'No need, Maria.' He took her hand and kissed it before leaving the room, his shoe still creaking. Surely the Gestapo must have people who could sort out footwear problems. Mami's face was now composed, almost cheerful. She could have been one of those witty women in the Noël Coward comedies she admired so much.

'He won't come back, will he?' Alix said, when the Mercedes finally pulled away. But her mother looked at her and sighed.

'I don't know.' She picked up the box of cigarettes. 'There was once a time when Anton Preizler was the one person I could turn to for anything. But now . . .' She flicked the lighter. 'Now I'm not sure.' Her pupils dilated as she drew on the tobacco.

'How can you be friends with someone like that?' Alix caught sight of her mother's face. 'I'm sorry, I didn't mean . . .'

'No, you're right.' Mami let out a puff of smoke. 'As a boy he was so strong and reliable. We all grow up, that's the tragedy. We all grow up and have to deal with the mess we make.' She drew on the cigarette. 'And Anton may be the only person who can still get anything done these days.'

'What did he tell you, Mami? When I was out of the room?'

Her mother examined the cigarette box as though the answer might be engraved on it along with her initials. 'It was nothing.'

Alix waited.

'Nothing for you to worry about darling. Just some minor detail. Be an angel and ask Lena to boil more water. I might make a *tisane* with some of those chamomile flowers we picked last week.'

'A bad headache?'

Her mother looked at her. 'Like a hammer pounding my temples. I think I need more sleeping tablets, I'll ring the doctor when I've drunk my *tisane*.'

Ten

Alix's account of Preizler's visit seemed to have brought them to a silence they couldn't seem to cross. Gregor sat staring at the tiles above the stove. 'And you don't know what, if anything, Preizler did to help your father?'

Alix shook her head. 'I only wish Mami hadn't felt she had to involve him.'

'He came here before the war, didn't he?'

So Gregor had remembered that dinner party, years and years ago. He narrowed his eyes and seemed to want to say something further. But instead he bent down to his pack and pulled out a packet. It couldn't be. Alix sat up to take a closer look. 'Real coffee?' It certainly smelled like it. The scent brought back pictures of prewar breakfasts: Mami pouring Papi's coffee, Papi reading the newspapers and grumbling, she begging her parents to come out and watch her put her pony over the jumps.

'This packet was gratefully liberated from an SS mess in

93

East Prussia and has joyfully allied itself with the cause of anti-Fascism.' Gregor's grin gave her a glimpse of the boy who'd loved pranks. She fetched the coffee pot, much lamented by Lena but not regarded as essential enough to take west. But Lena would never again make coffee. First Papi, now Lena. How many more of them would she lose?

'We asked about Papi everywhere we could.' The words tumbled out of her mouth as she found the cups. 'His name wasn't on the list of those executed after the bomb plot, but that doesn't mean he isn't dead.'

'It must have been terrible for your mother.'

'She became very practical, taking charge of things here.' She was amused at the surprise on his face. 'I know. It's strange how war changes people.'

'I remember her so well. She was vibrant, that's the best word to describe her.' And there was a look in his eyes that seemed to reflect images of Mami singing in the mornings as she arranged flowers in the salon or teasing Papi about a malfunctioning clock. The flash of memory flickered and went out of Gregor's eyes, and in its place Alix saw thousands of miles of empty steppe and burned-out cities.

He blinked and she had the impression that he was dragging himself into the present. 'Is the Steinway still in the salon?'

She nodded. He got up, holding out a hand. 'Come and show me. I haven't played for months. We found a piano in a house in East Prussia that hadn't been wrecked. Before that I had to make do with a mouth organ.'

'A mouth organ?' It seemed a very plebeian kind of instrument for someone like Gregor.

'Don't mock. I'm actually not bad. Played all kinds of Russian folk tunes for the guards.' He came to another abrupt halt. Again she had the impression of leagues of emptiness between them.

She took the lamp and led him through to the salon, pulled the dustsheet off the piano and opened the lid.

'I hardly know where to start.'

She put the lamp on the Steinway and lit the candles above the fireplace.

'Just play a scale or something.' She sat on a sheet-covered sofa. Gregor played a C major scale with his right hand, then added the left. Stopped. Shook out his hands. Started again, working up through all the scales, majors first then minors, then arpeggios, broken chords, his long fingers gliding over the keys. His shoulders relaxed as the notes became smoother and more even.

'Vavilov is missing the tip of one of his fingers. But he can still play almost as well as I can.'

'Almost?' The old Gregor Fischer had never believed in false modesty.

He grinned. 'Even if he had all his fingers Vavilov'd still lack a certain seriousness of purpose in his music-making.'

She didn't want to think about the intelligence officer now and turned her concentration to Gregor, noticing how his hair was growing long at the back of his neck. Red Army barbers must be scarce. The curls looked soft, as though they belonged to a sleek young animal rather than a political enemy who'd survived imprisonment and war. She found herself wondering what the curls would feel like to stroke.

'It's all still here.' He tapped his head. She rose and pulled out a Prelude from the pile of Chopin sheet music kept in a mahogany box beside the Steinway. He played, stumbling at first before regaining control. Against the chords, distant tanks rumbled a malevolent percussion – the war rolling on, unstoppable, unyielding. She and Gregor could sit inside and listen to music but they were chaff, nothing more.

Gregor glanced at her and then to the shuttered windows.

'No more. It's too cold. And it reminds me of my father. He used to like hearing me play. He taught me, you know.'

He hadn't mentioned Matthias before.

'Gregor?' He might not know what had happened. Alix remembered Mami telling her the news about his father, her face white. She'd sat next to Alix on the stone steps leading down from the terrace and told her, her hands shaking so much she couldn't hold her cigarette lighter. That had been the year before Papi was arrested. 'Have you found out what happened to your father?'

'He was executed. Dachau.' Gregor's eyes took on a cold fire. 'Vavilov told me. For a time I took great pleasure in seeing our men shoot German soldiers.'

Alix shivered and he must have noticed. 'Wait by the stove,' he ordered, getting to his feet. 'I'll bring in more logs.'

She opened her mouth to tell him not to, but what point was there hoarding wood now?

'In the front porch,' she told him.

As he made for the door something caught his eye. 'Your mother's gramophone. I remember this.' His face lost its steeliness and looked like a child's as he opened the mahogany lid.

'She used to take it on picnics. Needle looks fine.' His face fell. 'No records, though?'

'Mami put them away after . . .' After Papi's arrest. She blinked.

'So I can't ask you to dance?'

'Dance?' She tried to remember when she'd last danced. At one of those wretched parties for young officers due back at the eastern front.

He put his arms around her waist. 'I'll hum.'

'We'll need to roll back the rugs.' She could hardly meet Gregor's eyes: she might have been a girl at her very first dance. He held out his arms to her and started to hum 'Roses from the South'.

He had been taught well. Strange that the aggressively modernist Eva had taught her son something so old-fashioned. After a while Gregor stopped humming, but the waltz continued in her ears. The cold, dusty north German room became a ballroom, chandelier-lit and scented with hothouse flowers. Around her ankles rustled the taffeta of a magnificent ballgown, while medals twinkled on Gregor's mess jacket. Onlookers sipped champagne, girls flirted and giggled, the orchestra wore roses in their lapels. The occasional sprinkles of light against the windows weren't rockets or mortars; they were fireworks. The rumble of tanks was carriages clattering over an elegant cobbled street.

Dancing without music . . .

Gregor stopped. The sparkling ballroom dissolved and they were just two castaways, clutching one another. From the wall a series of black and white photos of Mami in her various film roles stared down at them, her mouth in that

97

photogenic half-smile, her eyes deep pools of indescribable emotion. Gregor released Alix. 'Go. Wait in the kitchen.'

She did what he said and blew the candles out and took the lamp back to the stove, hearing him walk to the inner porch, where Lena always stored a day or two's worth of logs in case they were snowed in. The resinous scent of pine reached her before his tall figure came through the kitchen door. When had skinny Gregor Fischer become a man like this, a male creature with broad shoulders who could carry armfuls of heavy logs without seeming to notice? He was still thin but there was a sinewy grace to his movements, despite the limp, visible even in that ill-fitting uniform. She rose to open the stove door for him and he added the logs one by one. Flames curled round the wood, hissing and popping, their shapes reminding Alix of human figures running, writhing, dancing.

He closed the stove door. 'That should keep us going.' He paused and caught her eye. 'Alix, there's something I must tell you—'

He stiffened suddenly and turned, eyes narrowed.

She'd heard it too.

'The door.' While they'd been fooling around in the salon the war had sent this reminder of their vulnerability.

Gregor's hand went to his holster.

'Perhaps it was just logs falling off the pile,' she said. Please God.

'No.'

There were other noises now. She knew the squeak the front door made. Now someone was treading across the marble tiles in the hall, past the antlers mounted on the walls. Whoever it was wore heavy boots.

'Stay in here.' Gregor walked to the kitchen door, gun in hand. 'Stand still,' he ordered the intruder. 'Hands on your head.'

Lamp in hand, Alix moved from the stove to stand behind Gregor. A man in a greatcoat glared at Gregor and raised his hands. 'You,' she said. No way of telling from Gregor's expression whether he recognized him too.

'Alexandra?' He sounded baffled. 'I thought you'd left for the west.'

'Shall I shoot him?' Gregor asked. 'I can take him outside.' He sounded as though he was worried about making a mess on the marble floor.

'I wouldn't if I were you,' said the captive. 'There are still a few SS units in the woods – with nothing to lose if they think you've killed someone of my position.' The slight accent still betrayed Preizler's Tyrolean origins. Snow from his boots fell to the floor.

'Drop it.' Gregor nodded at Preizler's gun, which clattered onto the marble, its Walther brand mark visible on the barrel.

'Has he mistreated you, Alexandra?' Preizler asked.

She shook her head without meeting his stare.

'That was a very sudden push we made this morning,' said Gregor. 'Must have caught a lot of people out. Shame your Führer doesn't listen to his intelligence.'

Preizler looked surprised. Probably not expecting fluent, unaccented German from a Red.

'You still don't recognize me, do you?' Gregor's scorn

seemed to fill the entrance hall. Preizler's eyes betrayed confusion, followed by a flash of something else – recognition? Dismay? Whatever it was he immediately reset his features to a stony indifference. 'I expect it'll all come back to you. Where's the cellar key, Alix?'

Preizler blinked at the familiar use of her name.

'I'll fetch it.' But first she lit the small lamp on the table in the hall, not liking to leave Gregor in the dark with this man. She went back to the stove, where Lena kept the key hanging on a nail.

'Before you incarcerate me you may wish to know why I'm here,' Preizler said when she came back.

Alix said nothing.

'I've been working to free your father, Alix.'

'That's what Mami said.' She tried to keep her voice neutral but her tone conveyed everything she felt about Preizler. 'Doesn't explain why you're here now, though.'

'We – I – wanted to check he hadn't come back here.'

'Kind of you.' She heard her voice shake.

'This has all been quite a business. Treachery's something they take very seriously.'

They. He must think she was stupid. 'I thought you were in Berlin. In some high-level meeting with my mother.'

'Enough of this.' Gregor waved the gun towards the steps leading down to the cellar door. 'Go and unlock it, Alix. He can stay down there until Vavilov gets here. We'll question him then.'

Alix had reached the steps when she heard the front door squeak again. 'Now you'll see something you weren't expecting,' Preizler said, behind her.

'Anton? *Liebling*?' a voice hissed. Alix stiffened. It couldn't be . . . Tiredness had confused her senses. She turned very slowly and looked at the figure standing in the hallway.

A woman, clothed in furs, a silk scarf wrapped around her face to keep out the worst of the snow. It couldn't be her . . . That *Liebling* . . . In north Germany an endearment only for men in your close family. Or men you loved: lovers, in fact. Even if you moved in theatrical circles . . . She looked back at Gregor. He'd tell her she'd got this wrong. She saw the confusion on his face. Perhaps he didn't recognize this woman with her famous face – it had been seven years.

While Alix's mind was throwing up all these jumbled thoughts she'd taken an involuntary step towards the woman. There was the click of a released safety catch on a gun.

In the confusion, Preizler had reached inside a pocket and pulled out a small pearl-handled gun. He pointed the delicate object at Gregor's head. 'Your turn to drop your gun.'

Gregor's revolver thumped down to the floor beside Preizler's Walther.

'Clara's pistol,' Preizler said. 'I gave it to her so she could shoot the children and herself if the Reds caught them. But she's safe across the Oder now.' He sounded highly satisfied. 'Is there anyone else in the house?'

Alix shook her head, seeing no advantage in pretending that there were Soviets upstairs. Any words she might have spoken were trapped inside her. The blood raced so violently through her veins it must surely be audible. She clenched her hands.

'Alix?' the woman said. Alix closed her eyes and opened

them again, willing them to tell her something else. She must be hallucinating. The slender figure in the furs she must have retrieved from their Berlin apartment, that woman who'd lavished that endearment on Preizler, couldn't be Mami.

Eleven

'You have all the information you require,' her governess used to tell Alix. 'How is it you can't complete the equation, Alexandra?'

Well, Alix had all the solution right in front of her now, didn't she? Mami plus Preizler. Of course the two of them had been lovers all along, playing this game of trying to free Papi as an excuse for their assignations. How much of Mami's grief for Papi had been guilt? And what a performance it had been! Worthy of anything she'd done at Babelsberg studios with all those famous directors.

'Alix?' Mami was coming towards her, arms outstretched, anxiety furrowing the smooth skin 'What on earth are you doing here? You were supposed to be on the road by now. Where's Lena? What happened?' Her eyes swept Alix's face. Alix stood back. 'What is it?' Then she saw Gregor and put a hand to her mouth. 'My God!'

'Baroness.' Something seemed to be caught in Gregor's throat.

'It *is* you, Gregor Fischer! After all these years. But tell me, your mother—'

'I suggest we sit in the warm.' Preizler nodded towards the kitchen. 'I'll interrogate this one first.'

'Interrogate him! Anton, this is—'

'Go and lock the front door, Alix.' She crossed the marbled floor, wondering if she could run for it. But who would help her? And she was still in her stockinged feet. She pulled the thick iron bolts across the door and returned. '*Gut*. Now put down the lamp and pick up those two guns,' Preizler told her. 'Lay them in front of me on the table when I've sat down and then bring in the lamp.'

She obeyed him, wishing she had the courage to use one of them to shoot off the back of his head. She'd shot rabbits and hares for the pot without giving it a thought. And once even a deer while hunting with Papi. If only she could shoot this man. She cursed her cowardice and let the guns clatter onto the table, before sitting down herself.

Mami came into the kitchen and fixed those famous eyes on Alix, questioning, pleading. Alix looked away. Who was her mother this evening? Still Anna Karenina, perhaps. Or Cressida, a part Marie had always detested? Yes, let her be Cressida, soiled and despoiled. Pity and contempt jostled in Alix's heart. She couldn't meet her mother's eyes. But surely she had this wrong? Mami and *Preizler*?

'Marie, *Schatz*, take off your furs and those wet stockings,' Preizler said without taking his eyes off Gregor, and exchanging the pistol for his own Walther. 'You need to warm yourself.'

Again that familiarity, that assumption that the Baroness

von Matke would do as he said. Gregor stood beside the stove, watching the guns.

'Alix?' said Mami again, slipping off her coat. 'We saw those poor people on the road. Is that why you came back?'

'I could ask you the same thing,' Alix said.

'Now, Maria.' Preizler shook his head at her. 'First things first. Alexandra, heat some food for your mother. There are tins of soup in the basket we left in the porch.' He replaced his wife's gun in his pocket with one hand, retaining his own pistol in the other. Gregor's gun still sat in front of him on the table, too far away from Gregor to be of any use to him. Alix got up to bring in Preizler's basket. Even under the cover of the porch, so much snow had fallen she could hardly make out its outline. Soup. Tinned asparagus. Oranges! What looked like fresh bread. A ham. Mami's adventure was certainly well provisioned. Alix stared out at the white and black blurred outlines of the forest. She should run away. Even if there was nobody out there to help her, she'd survive somehow. No, she couldn't leave Gregor. Or Mami, damn her.

She brought the basket into the kitchen and began opening one of the cans. 'Will mushroom soup be acceptable?' Her voice sounded mocking. She couldn't forget that *Liebling*.

'Perfect.' Mami sounded composed now. 'Thank you, *Liebling*.'

Alix's hand shook.

'Anton,' she went on. 'Alix and I know this young man, he's not—'

'What in hell's he doing here?' Preizler glared at Gregor and put out a hand to prevent Alix ladling out soup for him. 'Where's the rest of his unit? Waiting outside for him to signal to them? Sit down here, Comrade.' He pointed the gun at the chair opposite him.

Gregor shrugged and sat, still keeping his eyes on the weapon. 'I'm alone. Just wanted to see if the family was still here. I thought I might be able to help them.'

'Help them?' Preizler seemed to bare his teeth at him. 'Or line them up in the cellar and shoot them?'

Gregor glared at him.

'Shall we all have coffee?' Mami might have been concluding one of her prewar dinner parties. Any moment now she'd be asking Alix if she wanted to come upstairs and powder her nose. Alix picked up the coffee packet Gregor had produced earlier. Preizler held out a hand for it.

'Looted, I see.' He gave it back to her and turned to Gregor. 'Is that what you intended to do here, help yourself to the von Matkes' property? Or was there something else?'

Gregor said nothing.

'Thought so.' Preizler glanced at Mami. 'Come to spy on his former friends, just as I suspected.'

'What are you talking about?' Alix looked from one to the other.

'Alix—' Mami began.

Alix swung round to glare at her. 'I've worked it out, you know, I've got nothing to say to you.'

'What do you mean, worked it out?' Her mother sounded distressed, but then she'd know exactly how to convey that emotion. 'Let me explain at least . . .'

Alix shook her head.

'Where's Lena?' Mami asked, sounding desperate now.

'The Russians got her.' Alix stared down at her coffee cup. 'She's dead.'

Her mother flinched as though receiving a physical blow. 'No! Poor, poor Lena,' she whispered.

'You see?' Preizler glared at Gregor. 'So much for the noble Red Army.' His hand tightened on the Walther. Alix imagined those same fingers stroking her mother's skin and wanted to be sick.

'Remember what your people did in the east?' Gregor almost spat out the words. 'I've seen it. You tell me one story of Soviet cruelty and I'll tell you ten of German depravity.'

'Tell me what happened, *meine Liebe*?' Mami said to Alix, as though the men weren't there. Alix closed her eyes to try and block out the force of her mother's anguished face.

Preizler thumped the table. 'But you were a German citizen, Fischer! And not really Jewish at all. You had no reason to turn traitor – nobody would have touched you. There's no reason for me not to put a bullet through your traitorous head.'

'Anton!' Mami shouted. 'Listen to me when I tell you you're wrong about him!'

He dismissed her with a shake of his head.

Gregor's eyes looked like cold stones. 'What did you think I'd do when you locked up my father and hounded my mother out of Germany?'

'I didn't have anything to do with your parents. My responsibilities were directed at a specific group of people that included neither left-wing intellectuals nor Jews.'

'You were assigned to watch landowners, weren't you?' Alix said. 'People with connections. Like Papi?'

'It appears others may have similar interests.' Preizler nodded at Gregor. 'Ask him what he's snooping around for.'

Alix folded her arms. He was the enemy, not Gregor.

'Where's the wagon?' Mami whispered to Alix.

'We left it on the road,' Alix replied. 'The horses were blown to bits, too.' She almost enjoyed watching Mami's face blanch. Then she felt a prick of shame. Mami'd always cherished the little Haflingers, fellow Tyroleans.

'So tell us how you made friends with the Soviets, Fischer,' Preizler said.

'I was in good company.' Gregor snorted. 'Remember the Molotov–Ribbentrop pact?'

'Are you hurt?' Mami asked Alix. 'Did they . . . ?'

The loyal mother bleeding for her children: that was in some play or other. 'I'm fine,' Alix snapped. 'Where's Papi? Did you ever even go to that meeting in Berlin to talk to them?'

'Of course I did.' Mami leaned forward. 'He wasn't there, Alix. They told me they'd sent him to another camp.'

'So much for *his* help, then!' Alix glowered at Preizler.

'You still wear their uniform, Fischer.' Preizler was pointing the gun at Gregor's tunic. 'Even when you've seen what they're really like.'

'And I've seen what your side is like, too,' Gregor said.

'I have nothing to be ashamed of.' Preizler sounded stiff.

Mami reached a hand across the table to Alix. 'Is there anyone else here?'

'No.' Perhaps she was worried that Gregor had comrades posted upstairs who'd come down to liberate him. Alix moved her own hands into her lap and heard her mother's sigh.

'So, Comrade. What have you been up to here? I think we've established you're not combat.' Preizler removed a handkerchief from his left pocket and dabbed at an invisible speck of dust on the gun's chamber, all without moving his eyes from Gregor.

'Anton,' said Mami. 'I wish you'd put that gun down. Gregor's going nowhere. There is nowhere for him to go tonight. It must be possible for us to be civilized about this.'

Alix noted the familiar '*du*' she used to address Preizler.

Mami refilled their coffee cups. Preizler nodded his thanks but ignored her request to put down the gun. 'There was a man not five miles from here who had his arms and legs chopped off this morning before the Reds fed him to his own pigs,' he said. 'Another refugee told me he'd seen two little girls crucified, nailed to their kitchen table. You've been very busy, Fischer.'

Alix clutched the edge of the table and watched the kitchen turn black around her.

'There are atrocities,' Gregor said in a flat voice. 'I save who I can. It might surprise you to know I still think of the people here as my countrymen.'

'Then surely you'd want to throw off that somewhat ill-fitting uniform and put on ours?'

Gregor said nothing.

Preizler sipped from his cup and raised an approving eye-brow. 'So long since I've had real coffee.' Out in the forest the tanks started rumbling again. The teaspoon on Mami's saucer picked up the vibration and rattled against the cup like a warning drumroll. Mami put it on the table.

'I cannot wear a German uniform.' Gregor sounded weary.

'What better way to defend German schoolgirls and nuns?'

Gregor flung out an arm and knocked his cup and saucer to the floor. The porcelain broke into neat shards and the coffee spread over the tiles in a fast-moving dark stain. Mami was sitting on the edge of her seat, staring at Gregor.

'Sorry, Baroness.' He shook his head.

'*Macht nichts*,' Mami whispered.

Preizler studied the mess. 'Strange. I remember your mother as an eloquent woman.' He nodded, as though recalling past examples of their eloquence. 'You seem somewhat inarticulate, Fischer, throwing china around. Probably the influence of your lumpen comrades.'

Alix rose. 'I'll fetch a cloth.' She couldn't bear to see the dark liquid seeping across the floor through the fragments of white porcelain.

'Not now.' Preizler pointed his free hand at her chair.

'The Red Army won't mind a few stains,' said Gregor. 'It won't be the worst thing the floor will see.'

'Oh Gregor.' Mami sounded tired. 'Anton, why don't you just let him go? He hasn't got a gun and perhaps he can keep the others away and—'

Someone pulled the bell at the front door. The eyes of the other three widened. Gregor leaned back and folded his arms. 'That will be one of ours.'

Mami bit her lip. '*Ach, du lieber Gott*.'

Preizler got up, his pistol still trained on Gregor.

'What'll you do now?' Gregor sounded amused. Mami sat back in her chair, examining one of her nails, all signs of fear gone. She must still be scared but her acting training was reasserting itself.

'Answer it. Tell them to leave,' Preizler hissed.

Gregor smirked. Preizler aimed his Walther at Alix's temple. She could almost feel it burn through her skin. She swallowed hard, forcing back the cry that wanted to burst from her mouth. Mami made a sound like a whimper.

'All right.' Gregor scraped back his chair and stood up, making for the door.

'Anton?' Mami pleaded with him. 'Don't do this. Not to Alix!' Alix felt wave after wave of coldness wash over her. The room was spinning.

He kept his gaze averted. 'Such a wonderfully Germanic little head. Perfect proportions,' he said. 'I never really believed all that racial purity stuff, but sometimes when I see someone like your daughter I can almost understand what Himmler and Goebbels meant.'

'How can you?' Mami whispered. 'She is my only child.'

'She's a young woman. All across Europe young women are part of the front-line now.'

Alix heard the front door screech open. Gregor said something in Russian and slammed the door.

'Well?' Preizler asked as he came back in.

'They asked if we had any pretty ones in here and I said no. They'll be back in the morning, though. To talk to Vavilov.'

'Who's Vavilov?' asked Mami.

Gregor slipped back into his seat, ignoring the question. 'You can put that down,' he told the older man. Preizler lowered the gun, but kept his fingers tight round the handle. He looked at Alix.

'I trust you understand that was all show, Alexandra. You and I have never been fond of one another but I would never harm you.'

She tried to give a nonchalant shrug and prayed she wouldn't be sick in front of them all. Now the immediate danger was over it occurred to her that Preizler had taken a huge gamble. For all he knew Gregor might have been unmoved by the prospect of a bullet piercing her skull; his loyalties to his comrades might have overridden old affections. Maybe Preizler had seen something between them that had given away their feelings. Gregor and she had been parted for all these years but there was still something between them, some pull from the past which placed them on the same side, despite the intervening years. All the time she'd been watching him and Mami, he'd been watching her and Gregor. Four people staring at one another over a kitchen table trying to make sense of one another's relationships as though they were in some comedy of manners. While outside a snowstorm raged, an empire fell and chaos rushed in to fill the vacuum.

For whole minutes nobody spoke. Alix could almost feel the electrical charges flying between them. The rumbling of tanks hushed. Even the Red Army had given up tonight. A crashing sound a mile or so away rattled the plates on the dresser. Then there was only the moan of the wind against the shutters.

'Another bridge or railway line being blown to pieces,'

Gregor said. 'Germany's nearly finished.' Alix couldn't read his tone.

'Old Prussia, you mean.' Preizler sounded satisfied. Even now he couldn't seem to refrain from expressing the old Austrian prejudice against the Junkers. As though Hitler had grown up in a Pomeranian village! 'Churchill hates Prussia. He'll let Stalin consume it.' Preizler shrugged. 'We'll make for the mountains, my love.'

'You won't get far. It's prison camp for you, for years,' said Gregor. 'Worse, if my comrades get you.'

'The Russians will hang you,' Alix added.

He might be armed but it seemed they had him at bay, she and Gregor. Alix thought she'd go mad if they had to stay like this much longer. Let him shoot them all if he wanted, it would break the spell that kept the four of them sitting here throwing these conversational barbs around while the world crumbled. Laughter threatened to burst from her lips. Or perhaps a scream.

Something scratched at the door. They all swung round to look, eyes frightened, even Preizler's. Lena's tabby strolled in, eyed the group and appeared to sum up each of them before she jumped onto Gregor's lap. He stroked the animal from the top of its head right down to the tip of its tail. Alix noticed her mother give a little frown as she watched Gregor.

'Tell me about Vavilov,' Preizler said. 'Bearing in mind that you have no choice but to talk.'

Gregor's nostrils flared as though he'd smelled something bad.

'Gregor,' Alix said. 'Tell him.'

Preizler raised his gun again. 'Come on, Comrade. I've

already heard a little about Vavilov the Polish Communist,'
he said.

'Then I won't bore you further.' Gregor still sounded flip-
pant, even when that monster was threatening him with a
bullet.

'Continue or I'll shoot you.'

'You wouldn't kill me in front of the women.'

'Correct. I'd take you down to that cellar.' Preizler placed
a slight stress on the last word. 'You were telling us about
Vavilov. Where does he come from?'

Again Gregor shrugged.

'What language do you use to talk to him?'

'Polish.'

'But you don't think he's a Pole, do you?'

Gregor said nothing.

'Does he speak German?'

Gregor nodded.

'With an accent?'

Gregor looked down at the floor.

'You know I can extract this information from you, don't
you? It doesn't have to be a bullet. There are other ways.'

'No!' Marie put out a hand. 'I won't have this!' She
looked at Gregor. 'It can't hurt anyone to tell us that, can it
Gregor?'

Whole seconds passed until he spoke. 'It might be a Hungarian or Slovene accent.'

'How old is he?' Mami asked. Alix glanced at her, startled
by this interest in a Communist intelligence officer.

'Forties.' Gregor shrugged. 'Could be younger. Most people

coming from the east are younger than their faces. We never discuss these matters.'

'Of course you don't, Fischer. You'd be very careful not to talk about personal matters because Vavilov doesn't know you're a German, does he?' Preizler spoke softly but with an air of triumph. 'I see your predicament. God help you if your comrades find out you're really one of us.'

'People are like rivers, they have no nationality but take on the nature of the terrain they pass through. No human spirit can be confined to a single state.' Gregor folded his arms.

Mami leaned forward. 'What was that?'

He repeated the words.

'That's what he says, this Vavilov?' Preizler snorted.

Mami's face could have rivalled the shattered porcelain for whiteness.

'What is it, Marie?' Again Alix winced at the familiar use of her mother's name.

'Perhaps the baroness finds your interrogation rather tedious,' Gregor said, stressing Mami's title. Alix couldn't resist a small smile. Preizler stiffened in his chair but didn't rise to the bait.

'Someone else used to say that,' Mami muttered. 'Those exact words. Who was it? Is it a quotation?' Her puzzled eyes sought Alix's as though begging her daughter to help her out. Alix shrugged.

Gregor was silent.

Preizler shook his head at Mami indulgently and gestured at Gregor to continue.

'His finger,' Mami said. 'He was missing a fingertip.'

Gregor blinked. 'I don't have to say any more. You are only entitled to name, rank, number.'

Mami was staring at her cigarette box. 'The little finger on his left hand.'

Gregor must have made some sudden slight movement. The cat jumped down to the floor, making Preizler start. In the second that his attention was diverted Gregor and Mami had exchanged glances. Something about that missing finger-tip. Alix noted how Mami's hand holding the cigarette now glistened with perspiration. 'I need something from my bag,' she murmured. 'Pass it to me, Alix.' Alix picked up the leather vanity case and handed it to her mother. Mami pulled out a pillbox. 'Terrible headache,' she said.

'Pour your mother some water,' Preizler ordered. Alix stood and reached for a glass and the pottery jug of water from the pump which Lena kept on the dresser. Mami crumbled a tablet in her hand and kept watching Preizler.

'How did you come to work for Vavilov, Fischer?' demanded Preizler.

'He came to Kolyma and asked if I could fight in the Polish unit.'

'Kolyma?' Preizler shifted in his chair and there was something else in his expression now when he looked at Gregor. Almost a respect. 'You were there?'

Gregor nodded.

'How did he know you?'

'I don't have to answer any more.'

Preizler half-pulled the trigger. Alix heard someone cry out. Herself. Gregor glanced at her. 'It was opportunistic, he simply needed someone with medical experience. I'd been working in the camp hospital.'

'But you haven't been acting as a medic since he took you out of the camp?' Preizler asked.

Gregor said nothing.

Mami and Preizler exchanged one of their speechless looks. Now it was as though the two of them were transmitters tuned to the same frequency, picking up signals nobody else could receive. Preizler drained the last of his coffee. 'Let me refill your cup.' Mami reached for it.

'Fetch me some rope, Alexandra,' he said, ignoring the ministrations.

Alix sat there, mouth open, blood running to ice, unable to protest.

'Do it, Alix,' whispered Mami. 'Anton won't hurt Gregor.' Her hands were shaking as she poured the coffee.

'I just want to tie him up so I can put this gun down.' Preizler twinkled like a kindly old uncle. 'Then I can relax a little.'

Relax. As though they were all on holiday.

'All right.' She rose and took one of the candles. 'I'll go to the boot room to get it.' She tried to meet Gregor's eye but all his attention was given over to an invisible mark on the oilskin tablecloth. His mouth was set, as though he were clamping it shut.

In the boot room Alix eyed the door to the garden. But if she failed to return, Preizler would certainly use his gun on Gregor. No way of knowing whether Mami would try and stop him. And Preizler's affection mightn't be strong enough to stop him from shooting her, too, if she did.

Alix picked up a coil of rope from the peg by the door and

brought it back into the kitchen, setting it down on the table in front of him as though bringing tribute to an emperor.

'Fischer, give your knife to her. Cut four lengths about this size, Alix,' he ordered, holding out his hands to show her.

Gregor removed the knife from his belt and handed it to her. For a second their fingers made contact and she felt something like an electric shock. She thought of trying to stab Preizler but Mami was watching her and furtively shook her head.

'Let's go down to the cellar,' he told Alix when she'd finished. 'Take the lamp with you, Alexandra.'

She swallowed hard. The man's memory was impressive. All those years ago yet he remembered about Gregor and the cellar. She picked up the lamp and led the way. The steps were steep. Behind her the two men clattered down. Had Mami followed them or had she stayed in the kitchen? Alix undid the bolted door. They'd filled the cellar with boxes packed with the china and glass that hadn't been buried in the garden, hoping without any conviction at all that the Bolsheviks wouldn't find them. Beside the boxes stood an old wooden chair, placed down here so it could be chopped up for firewood. 'Sit,' Preizler told Gregor. 'Tie his hands and feet to the chair,' he ordered Alix. 'And remember, I'll shoot him if you try anything.'

She put the lamp on the floor. If she turned it off, Gregor'd have a chance to make a run for freedom, if he could move fast enough in the dark.

'Get on with the knots.' Preizler must have read her thoughts. She did as he asked. 'Tighter,' he said.

Gregor blinked back at her.

'Now upstairs we go,' Preizler said, leading the way. 'Bring the lamp.'

Alix couldn't bear it. She remembered the last time he'd been left down here. Preizler had been in the house on that occasion too. Something had started that night but she hadn't understood what it was, what it meant. 'We could leave the lamp—'

'No.'

She took a last look at Gregor, apologizing with her eyes, aware that she was saying sorry for more than just this imprisonment in the cellar. She was telling him how much she regretted all that had happened here seven years ago, all those things she had failed to comprehend.

Twelve

July 1938

The day would probably end with a thunderstorm, Lena told Alix as she pushed the window sash up and opened the shutters. 'You slept through a beauty last night.'

Shame. Alix liked storms: the drama, the noise. 'I didn't hear it.'

'Didn't you hear me come in to check the shutters?'

Alix got out of bed. 'It feels lovely now. Fresh.'

'Won't last. You know these July days, moody as a chestnut mare.' Lena walked to the wardrobe, taking care not to disturb the row of toys on the carpet. She was smiling. 'You've forgotten, haven't you?'

'What?'

'Your birthday.'

Alix let out a squeal. 'I had!' she sat up. 'Fancy forgetting your own eleventh birthday.'

'*Alles Gute zum Geburtstag*!' Lena pulled a small

wrapped parcel out of her apron pocket. Alix sprang out of bed and hugged her.

'*Danke*, darling Lena! What is it?' She took the parcel. It was something long and thin.

'Open it.'

Alix's fingers tore at the paper. Pencils from Switzerland in their own tin, with a picture of the Eiger on the front. Beautiful. 'You always know what I like!'

'Of course I do.' Lena disentangled herself from a second hug. 'I'll press your frock for tonight.'

'I hate that dress.' It was white silk with a blue taffeta sash. Mami had brought it back from Berlin last week. Alix had groaned as she'd undone the tissue paper. 'She always chooses things I don't like.' Mami seemed to want Alix to be a girl in a Winterhalter painting, all white-dressed and glossy-haired, instead of the scruffy gamine Papi said she was.

'Be grateful for your kind mother.' Lena's tone was tart. 'She does all kinds of things for you nobody else would.'

'You would.' Alix threw her arms around Lena. 'You're always good to me. You wouldn't make me wear a dress designed for a silly doll.'

'Nobody could ever be as good to you as your own mother.' But now Lena's hands were stroking her hair. Alix remembered the story of how Lena's mother had disappeared one Sunday morning while she and her sisters were at mass in Meran, the Tyrolean town she and Mami came from. 'She left without a word,' Lena had said. 'While we were on our knees in church. When we came home the stove had gone out and there was no lunch waiting. My father pulled out a bottle of Schnapps and didn't put it down until he died ten years later.'

'I know it was dreadful for you,' Alix said now. 'I know Mami loves me.'

'Never forget how lucky you are to have a woman like her as your mother: beautiful, accomplished, kind. She could have been a Hollywood star, too. She made those few films at Babelsberg studios before she had you and she dazzled them all.' There was a catch in Lena's voice that morning, as though she were starting a sore throat. 'When people saw her on the screen as Anna Karenina they couldn't believe a woman could be so beautiful.' She gave Alix's hair a last stroke. 'Don't forget to tidy up these toys on the floor.' And she went downstairs.

Alix washed and dressed. When she reached the dining room the others had already finished breakfast. Mami wouldn't be pleased she'd slept late, even if it was her birthday. *When we have guests we are first out of bed . . .* Tinkling sounds from the salon told Alix that Gregor was already practising at the Steinway, working on a Chopin Prelude even though it was the holidays. When she'd finished her rolls and chocolate she went to find him. The maids had been working hard: vases of flowers covered every surface in readiness for tonight's dinner party. Gregor looked up when she came in but didn't break his playing. 'Happy Birthday, Alix. Just wait a minute and I'll find your present.' She listened for a while.

'You used to play those rude songs saying funny things about Hitler and Himmler. You never play them now.'

'Are you mad! Course I don't.'

'Stop being so scared all the time.' Surely he knew he was safe here?

Gregor snorted. 'Just let me get on with my practice.'

Alix stood so one of the maids could plump up the cushions on the sofa. They'd dusted the portraits of the ancestors and polished the picture-glass so they looked less gloomy. But the ancestors still pursed their lips, nostrils slightly flared as though they could smell something unpleasant. Alix had grown up thinking her forebears disapproved of her. Then she realized they wore the same expression regardless of who was in the room. Papi had told her his great-aunt Friederika had once sent the future Kaiser out of the room for impertinence. Family lore had it he'd teased her pug.

Gregor played a last chord and stood. 'Come on. Let's find your present.' They went upstairs. Gregor went into his room and returned with a small parcel, wrapped in plain paper. 'I'm afraid it's not new.'

Emil and the Detectives. 'I've been longing to read this!' She threw her arms around him. Usually he hated physical expressions of affection. This morning he let her embrace him.

'What did your parents give you?'

'I haven't had it yet but I'm pretty sure it's a new saddle for Florian.' She wrinkled her nose. 'And a new dress.'

They'd found their way into Alix's bedroom. Gregor stared at the rows of soft toys and dolls on the floor and the single large stuffed dog facing them, flanked by a small blackboard. 'What are you doing with these kids' things?'

She felt her cheeks burn. 'Nothing.' She'd forgotten to tidy them up. At eleven she was too old to be doing this.

'It looks like you were playing some kind of game?' He gave a slow grin. 'You were playing schools, weren't you?'

Her cheeks burned on.

'Go on, own up.'

'It's all right for you,' she burst out. 'You get to go to a real school.'

Something flashed over his expression, but in her indignation she didn't stop.

'I've never even been in a classroom.' Her parents wouldn't send her to school in Germany. She'd had governesses, the latest one had just gone home to England because of the Unsettled International Climate, whatever that meant. 'I like to pretend.'

'So you do this?' He touched one of the bears with his foot.

She nodded, humiliated.

'It looks just like a real classroom,' Gregor stooped and straightened a slumped toy rabbit in the front row. 'You did a good job.'

She blinked. It might just be imagination, but Gregor seemed kinder this year. Quieter and more sympathetic to others.

'Let's go and find your father. Perhaps he'll let you have the new saddle.' Gregor'd always had a fascination with Papi, but this year it seemed almost to have become an obsession. Perhaps it was because his own father was away being re-educated in that camp near Munich. Gregor and his mother were here to recover from the shock, Mami had said. A camp didn't sound too shocking to Alix. She'd imagined wood fires and tents, but Papi said it wasn't that kind of camp and changed the subject.

They wandered into the garden. Mami and Eva were two cool figures in white linen dresses, examining the rosebeds and chatting in low voices. Mami pulled secateurs from a trug and considered a fat red rose. She seemed to change her mind at the last moment, moving away from the bush towards one of the yellow rose trees and cutting one of its blooms instead. Alix studied her and decided her mother's frock was too short, only just covering her elegant knees. And nobody could ever say Eva would fit into one of those frothy Winterhalter portraits; those intense dark eyes of hers were too unsettling.

And there was Papi, ambling across the terrace with his cigarette. He hadn't seen Gregor and Alix and stopped at the top of the steps beside one of the wooden boxes filled with dwarf lilies, watching the two women cutting flowers, a strange expression on his face, one which Alix couldn't remember seeing before. Alix heard footsteps behind them. Lena. She stopped too and watched Mami and Eva at work, turning to stare at Papi, some emotion puckering her calm pink face like a pulled thread on a piece of linen. Cream souring in the heat? A shortage of napkins? Lena walked on, still wearing the same expression. Papi finished his cigarette and turned the opposite way, probably making for the stables and the new horse he wanted to try over some hurdles.

How funny, Alix thought. All of them watching one another and not saying a word. Something about the scene confused her. As she and Gregor moved away she turned to take one more look at the women. Eva was looking at Papi's retreating back and there was an expression on her face that made Alix think of a little girl looking into a toyshop window.

Suddenly she wanted to run away from all of them and spend the morning alone in the forest, even if it was her birthday.

Alix was lying on her bed reading *Emil and the Detectives* when the guests arrived, the new saddle sitting on the end of her bed. It had been too hot to ride this afternoon but she couldn't bear to part from the saddle; it smelled so delicious. Mami had agreed that Alix and Gregor could come down to the kitchen in their finery and sample the left-over chocolate mousse and fruit tarts. Until then, they were to rest and recover from the heat of the day.

Her bedroom door was open and she heard Mami's light feet on the stairs. 'Eva?' There was a strained note in her voice. Alix heard her knock on Eva's door. 'I need to tell you something.'

The door opened and closed and Alix could hear no more. She put down her book and tiptoed to the landing. 'Just a bit of a surprise, that's all,' Papi was telling someone she couldn't see.

'I'm still just Marie's old friend from home,' another male voice said.

Along the passage Eva's bedroom door handle rattled. Alix fled back to her room.

'I could just have a migraine,' Eva said as she came out. 'You haven't actually *told* him I'm here, have you?'

'No. But if he finds out you're in the house and he hasn't

seen you, it would look very suspicious, Peter says.' Mami's voice.

'And this is *Anton*, after all.' Downstairs the bell rang and a servant walked across the marble floor to open it. 'Listen, there are the other guests arriving. Thank goodness, the more the merrier, this evening.'

The women walked past Alix's door to the stairs, their footsteps uneven and hesitant. Alix thought she heard an intake of breath, as though someone was bracing themselves for a dive into a cold pool.

Lena came upstairs at half-past nine and took them downstairs. Alix paused outside the dining-room door. 'Shouldn't we go in and say *Gute Nacht*?'

Lena glanced at Gregor and then away. 'Not tonight.'

'Oh.' Papi was usually so keen for her to greet guests. Admittedly it was now very late. All that money wasted on the new frock. Perhaps Mami would send Lena back to Berlin to exchange it for something more wearable.

In the kitchen they piled high their bowls, running their tongues over their spoons so not a molecule escaped. Lena brought in tray after tray of dirty glasses and crockery, then stood at the kitchen door watching all the guests troop into the salon for coffee.

Magda the cook came to stand beside her. 'Frau Fischer wears that dress of hers like a second skin.'

'A dress like that is dangerous,' said Lena.

'What do you mean, Lena?' asked Alix, from the table. 'How can a dress be dangerous?'

'Don't talk with your mouth full, child,' she replied. 'Five minutes and it's up to bed with you both.'

'Tsk, look at that outfit.' Magda was watching another guest. 'What is that, some kind of Bavarian costume? Is she trying to make a point?'

Lena shook her head. 'It looks like *Tracht*, you're right. See that hair plaited round her head like a big snake?'

'She's the perfect wife for someone like him, though.'

'Someone like who?' Alix asked.

'Never mind, birthday girl.'

'She's certainly not as elegant as the baroness,' Magda said. 'Or as striking as Frau Fischer with her big dark eyes.'

Lena made a small sound with her tongue but said nothing.

Alix waited until both women were distracted with washing-up. 'I want to see that lady they were talking about, the one in the costume. There was a bit of a commotion when she arrived with her husband.'

'Commotion?'

'Your mother and my mother were whispering together.'

Gregor ate a last raspberry and looked pensive.

'Finished now?' Lena turned back towards them.

'It's my birthday,' Alix said. 'I should be allowed to stay up later.'

'You already have. Up you go.'

'*Gute Nacht*, Lena,' said Gregor.

'*Schlaf gut*.' Lena kissed her and ruffled Gregor's hair. 'Don't forget your teeth. And I'll be out to check you're not sitting up on the stairs when you should be in bed.'

As they walked out of the door Alix grabbed Gregor's

sleeve and drew him down the passageway connecting the kitchen with the back of the house.

'We can wait in the cellar until Magda and Lena are finished in the kitchen. Lena'll check the stairs for us in a minute, but if she doesn't see us there she'll think we've gone to bed. Then we can go and sit up there and listen.'

Gregor sighed. 'Do we have to? I'm tired.'

'I want to and it's my birthday.'

'Have you got a torch?'

'No need. There's electric light down there now.' She descended the steps and flicked the switch beside the door, before opening the cellar. Gregor followed her. The light revealed an old sofa, part of its stuffing discharging itself from an arm. 'Let's sit down.'

But Gregor walked over to an old trestle table, laden with clocks missing their innards. 'Your father's as crazy as ever about his clocks.'

'Mami says he's a man obsessed.' She heard something above them, ran to the door and switched off the light, hearing Gregor's gasp as the room darkened. 'Don't worry,' she hissed as she came back inside. 'It's just for a minute. Then we'll creep upstairs.'

'It's a lot of unnecessary effort for a bit of eavesdropping.'

'Not very adventurous, are you Gregor?'

'I just don't see why your adventures have to be so uncomfortable.' He was probably thinking of what had happened when she'd made him camp out in the forest with her a few nights ago and the tent had collapsed in the rain.

'Lucky for you they wouldn't have you in the Hitler Youth.' She bit her tongue.

'Shut up, Alix. What the hell do you know about it?'

She blinked and peered at him.

'You've no concept, have you, of what it's been like since . . .'

'I'm sorry.' Her cheeks burned with shame. 'I didn't mean it. You haven't said much about Berlin, Gregor.' But then she hadn't asked him, had she? Everything felt different this summer. Even Gregor. Especially Gregor. Perhaps it was her. It had once been so easy – he and his family came to Alexanderhof each summer and Alix and Gregor slotted back into the long days of playing out of doors and keeping one another company. He'd changed. Or perhaps she had.

She heard him flop onto the old sofa. 'There's not much to say about Berlin because nothing much happens these days. It's boring. We don't go out. I used to play football with some boys from school, but their parents won't let them now because of Papi being so dangerous.'

Alix tried to imagine Matthias with his rumpled jackets and big grin as dangerous.

'At least they don't know . . .' He glanced at Alix and then down at his shoes.

'Know what?'

'What I think of them.'

She didn't think that was what he *had* meant but decided not to press the point. 'So what do you do with yourself?'

'Play the piano. The teacher won't come any more but he left me some pieces to play. Sometimes I take my tennis racket to the courts and practise my serves very early in the morning, before anyone's around. But it's boring when there's nobody to return them.'

'It must be.'

'Sometimes I see Dieter.' Gregor sounded brighter.

'Dieter?'

'Dieter Braun. Remember that garage on the corner? The one my mother finds so ugly? His father runs it.' He gave a fleeting grin. Alix had visited the Fischers several times in Berlin and knew the garage. It was supposed to be an eyesore but she liked looking at the cars in the showroom. Once she'd even crept round the back to peer at the mechanics changing tyres in the yard. It had smelled of rubber and leather and oil, an almost exotic mixture. 'Shouldn't think Dieter's the kind you'd have come across, Alix.'

'No,' she said with regret.

'He hates them too: Hitler, all of them. Once Dieter let down a party official's tyres. He got his *Arsch* whipped then. Sorry, Alix. But that's the way Dieter talks.'

'He sounds fun.'

'He is. And so are his parents. His father had to beat him because of the tyres. But he didn't really mean it. He gave Dieter money for chocolate afterwards.'

'Does he have brothers and sisters?' Alix felt deep jealousy of anyone with siblings. One of the reasons she liked Gregor was that he wasn't so blessed.

'Two of each. Werner's the eldest, then there's Dieter, Erik, Sabine and Ute. His mother got one of those breeding medals. Dieter says it's a shame Adolf didn't buy them a bigger apartment too. Dieter's parents don't mind that Mama's . . . That we're not socially acceptable these days.'

'Because of your father?'

He hesitated a second before giving a half-nod. 'The

woman in the apartment opposite used to invite my mother in for coffee. Not any more.' Gregor yawned. 'I'm tired. Can't we just go to bed?'

'All right.' Hearing about Gregor's life in the city had made her feel foolish. How brave he was, putting up with this treatment day after day. How spoiled he must think her. And how immature, planning silly tricks, hiding from adults. Perhaps Mami was right when she said the time had come for Alexandra von Matke to go away to school in Switzerland for a year and see more of the world.

She led Gregor back up the cellar steps. They'd nearly reached the hallway when the salon door clicked open. Alix waved Gregor down to his knees on the steps. Voices reached them. Mami was talking about Lake Garda, *pensione* and good restaurants. Papi explained to someone that the clock on the fireplace was English and lost three minutes a day. The door swung wider open and light fell on Alix. She heard Gregor slip softly back down the cellar steps. Mami gasped. At least she hadn't spotted Gregor.

'Alexandra?' Mami came out frowning. 'Surely Lena sent you to bed hours ago?' Unlike her to be so angry, especially with someone who was celebrating a birthday. Perhaps it was the sultry weather. Or—

'A young absconder?' A tall man appeared beside Mami and Alix gasped. The man was strongly built, but slim. He looked like the kind who'd be happier on an athletics field or climbing mountains. 'I see it's the birthday girl herself.'

'What were you doing in the cellar?' Mami asked.

Alix thought of saying she'd seen the light on and had

gone down to turn it off, but the man's eyes seemed to see inside her mind. He smiled at her and she felt her face heat.

'Looking at the sofa.' It was true; not a lie. The one unforgivable transgression in this house was lying. 'Sometimes there are baby mice in it.'

'What about Gregor?' Mami sounded sharp. 'I hope he's gone to bed?'

'He's very tired.' Not exactly a lie but not exactly an honest answer either.

'Good.' Mami slipped an arm through the man's. 'Come and smell these night-scented stocks.' Something caught her attention. She stopped and frowned. 'You left the cellar door open, Alix.' She dropped his arm. 'Excuse me, Anton.' She tripped down the stone steps in those dainty little evening shoes of hers. Alix felt her muscles stiffen. The man in uniform watched her.

'Everything all right, *Fräulein*?'

'Fine.' She managed a tight smile. 'Thank you.'

Mami would see Gregor. The half-truth would be discovered. But Gregor had obviously managed to hide from Mami's view. She bolted the cellar door and came back up. 'There.' She smiled at the man. 'Let's go out onto the terrace. Off to bed with you, Alix.' She didn't sound cross now but her companion was scrutinizing Alix, his eyes expressionless. He wore a NSDAP membership pin on his lapel.

'*Gute Nacht*,' Alix mumbled and ran upstairs to the first floor, waiting for them to walk onto the terrace. If they caught her downstairs a second time . . . Mami and the man were murmuring by the front door; the other guests must still be chatting in the salon. On the landing the grandfather clock ticked out the seconds. Gregor was still sitting in the dark cellar, probably thinking that Alix had gone off to bed and left him there. Mami and the man came back inside and stood in the hallway beneath Alix, half in shadow.

'I had no idea you were interested in an organization like the Gestapo,' she hissed.

'You're making it sound as though it's something to be ashamed of.' Anger in his voice.

'I'm sure you had your reasons.' Mami sounded soothing now. 'It was just a bit of a surprise.'

'The world's changing, Maria. For all of us. Even you. This place won't be the quiet little backwater it's been for so long.'

She laughed. 'Hardly a backwater. Peter says just about every army in the history of the world has marched along that road at the end of the drive: French, Poles, Russians, Swedes.'

'The people you mix with—'

'You mean Eva. You've known her as long as I have, Anton.'

'We were never close.' He took her hand.

'She's one of my dearest friends.' Mami's voice shook.

'But it's a risk, Maria. If they find out . . .'

She made a dismissive gesture with her free hand. 'It's all nonsense. She's Austrian, like me.'

'She came from Poland originally.'

'*Galicia*, Anton! Part of Austria back then, remember?'

'But her father came from further east, from Russian Poland. Funny how it all comes back to me now.' He shook his head.

'You always did have an over-retentive memory.'

'I knew your lines better than you did.'

'Remember how bad I was at learning them?' She led him towards the salon. 'If I hadn't had you to practise with I'd have been lost when I came to play Sonja.' She stopped at the door. 'What happened to you, Anton? I thought your timber business was doing well. Why the career change?'

He didn't have a chance to answer because Papi came to the door. 'There you both are! We were wondering whether the wolves had got you.'

'Wolves?' Eva said from inside the salon. 'There are wolves in the forest?' She sounded strained.

'Not many these days. But I saw one here, years ago. And I've heard him at night.'

Alix felt a pang. She'd never seen or heard the wolf.

One of the guests inside let out a howl and everyone laughed.

Alix pulled off her slippers and tiptoed downstairs, using her knowledge of the location of every creaking floorboard to descend without a sound. She took a deep breath and plunged across the door, praying nobody would be looking in her direction, that the Gestapo man's hand wouldn't fall on her shoulder. Still barefoot, she reached the cellar, unbolting the door with gritted teeth. 'Gregor?' Too dangerous to switch on the light again. She groped her way towards the old sofa.

Something scuffled at her feet. Alix jumped back in case it was a mouse. It was his foot. He'd been sitting on the sofa in the unlit room, waiting for her.

'Are you all right?'

'Fine.' He sounded exhausted. 'You took your time.'

'They were talking at the front door. I had to wait.' She took his arm. 'Come on, I'll guide you out. Mind you don't make a sound. That Gestapo man's suspicious, I swear.'

'Gestapo man?' A note in his voice Alix had never heard before.

'Yes. I don't know what he's doing here. Papi hates all that stuff.' She pulled him towards the door.

'My God, Alix. We can't stay here now. Why didn't your father tell me? Why didn't my mother tell me?'

'You're only a boy, Gregor, a child. They don't tell children anything.'

'You're right.' He sounded so despondent she wanted to hug him, but he'd only push her off. She found herself taking his arm, anyway.

'I didn't mean that. You're thirteen, that's quite old, actually.'

'I feel old.'

He sounded it. They needed to hurry up and return to their rooms before the guests started leaving, but she couldn't bear to see his sadness and say nothing more in comfort. 'You know we're your friends, don't you, Gregor?'

'You're mad if you want to be friends with us. It's dangerous.' His voice gave a slight quiver.

'We don't care. I . . .' she took a breath. 'I don't care. I'd like you even if you were an escaped murderer.'

He snorted.

'Maybe not that, then. A robber.'

'If you just like me for myself, that's enough.'

She leaned over and kissed him on the cheek as though he were Papi. But then something strange happened. He turned to her and grabbed her by the shoulders and kissed her lips. And for a moment it didn't feel like a friend's kiss but something more dangerous, more enticing. A shiver ran from her scalp to the base of her spine as she kissed him back. She could make out a reflection of herself in each of his eyes, a thin figure with an untidy blond plait over one shoulder. Just a child.

He pulled away. 'I'm sorry, that was stupid of me. You just made me feel like the real me, not this scared person I've become.'

She didn't know what to say. 'We should go upstairs now.' She pushed him up the cellar steps ahead of her, noticing how dusty his pyjama trousers were. He must have crouched down behind the sofa when Mami came in to switch off the light. His mother wouldn't be pleased. Eva hated any kind of dishevelment.

They crossed the hall. Alix paused for a second by the half-opened salon door before pulling Gregor on towards the staircase, heart pounding.

'Another fugitive?'

The Gestapo man – Anton, Mami had called him – had come out of the salon again so silently she hadn't heard him, perhaps because he wanted to smoke a cigar. Or perhaps because he was a policeman and had ears attuned to people who were in forbidden places. Alix stopped, a foot on the first stair.

'This must be Eva's son.'

The correct form of greeting was a salute that Gregor would never make. Alix bet her father hadn't made it, either.

'How do you do, sir.' He clicked his heels but his hands

stayed at his side. Alix could almost smell the emotion coming off him, fear and something else, anger. Good. She couldn't bear Gregor to be scared.

'Gregor Fischer, eh?'

Gregor nodded.

'You got locked in the cellar, no?' The man's eyes glinted. 'Tell me, Gregor Fischer, how did it feel to be shut in the dark?'

Gregor shrugged.

'Were you scared?' The voice was gentle. Gregor's mouth opened a little but still he was silent. 'I think you probably were.'

Alix couldn't stand it. 'We need to go to bed.' She gave a little curtsy that would have made Lena proud, and tugged at Gregor's arm.

The man nodded. Alix heard him walk across the marble floor as he made for the cloakroom on the far side of the entrance hall. He had a slightly uneven gait. Then she picked up another noise, a gentle patter. She turned. Nothing. She squinted into the darkness and saw a single yellow petal lying on the marble floor. It must have fallen from the rose Mami had cut in the garden this morning and placed in a vase on the hall table.

'God.' Gregor gave a short laugh when they reached his bedroom door. 'What a night this has turned into. Your parents have some surprising friends.'

Alix let out a breath. 'I don't think they knew that he was Gestapo.'

His hand was on the door handle. 'Sorry.'

'What for?'

'Being such an idiot. It's ridiculous being so scared of the dark at my age.'

She reached for his hand. 'Lots of people are scared of the dark.'

'You're not and you're only a . . .'

'What?'

'It doesn't matter. The fact is, you're braver than I am.'

'Oh, I'm scared of lots of things.' She tried to think of some. 'I hate mice.' Gregor put a finger to his lips. Eva was talking to Mami. 'You know it's not like that . . .'; 'No place for us . . .'; 'Nothing to be scared of . . .'; 'Better to go now . . .'

Gregor's face seemed to grow even whiter.

When Alix went down to breakfast the next morning neither Gregor nor his mother had yet appeared. 'These townies,' Mami said, pouring the chocolate.

'What happened last night, Mami? Eva is scared, isn't she?' Alix sank into her chair.

'I take it you were listening in.' Mami sighed. 'You know you shouldn't – it's rude, *Schatz*.' Mami handed her a plate with bread rolls on it. 'I think this is just the beginning.' She didn't say what exactly was beginning. 'We're going to have to be very careful from now on.' She pursed her lips. 'After breakfast I'm going to make some telephone calls and find out about schools in Switzerland. We need to get you away from Germany.'

'I don't want to leave home, Mami.'

'You need to go somewhere where young people can talk freely.'

'I want to stay here.' Alix folded her arms. Last night had left her feeling unsettled, clingy. She knew this was the type of behaviour least likely to endear her to her mother. 'This is the best place in the world. I'm never leaving.'

'Oh darling, everyone has to leave home at some point.' An expression Alix couldn't read flitted over her mother's face.

'Not me.'

'If there weren't going to be a war I'd send you to one of those English schools.'

Gott sei dank for the war, then. 'If you make me go I'll just come back.'

'You love this house, don't you?' Mami's voice was soft. 'But things change. Sometimes we have no control over events . . . We can't always stay at home.' And she sat back in her chair, a distant look on her face.

Thirteen

Marie
Vienna, October 1925

'Tell me about your home,' said the young German, Peter von someone-or-other. Marie could tell he was a Prussian by the way he held himself, such a straight back. He'd probably find this Viennese party made up of theatrical types too silly for him. North Germans were supposed to be so serious, weren't they? Not the kind who enjoyed gossiping in the upstairs room of a restaurant following a student production of *As You Like It*.

'I come from Meran – Merano – in the South Tyrol.' She told him about the old castle and its rampart walkways, the flowering cherry trees, the skiing in winter, the housekeeper Hannelore's chickens and bees. 'My father still lives in the town.'

'It sounds idyllic.' His eyes were dark for a German's. She liked the way they crinkled up when he was amused, which seemed to be frequently.

'I do miss it,' she admitted. She still felt homesick for the town and the sweep of the mountains above it. But not tonight. Tonight was about celebrating her success. For it was *her* success; that's what everyone was saying. They kept telling her how wonderfully she'd played Rosalind. Even Fredi Brandt, the director, said that Marie had carried the play. So much praise – it was almost too much. And there was poor Eva, so convincing as Celia in her first scene but stumbling over a line in the second act and never quite recovering her poise. Marie had to admit that it was almost a relief that Eva *had* stumbled. 'What's in your parcel?' she asked the German, to change the subject. She flushed. He'd think her over-familiar or nosy. But he grinned – that was the only way she could describe the way his face broke into creases.

'It's a clock. There's a very good shop near here.'

'You collect them?'

He twinkled at her. 'Broken ones. I take them to bits and try to repair them. The clocks probably wish I wouldn't.' He patted the parcel. 'You should see my workroom.' He looked more serious. 'I enjoyed your performance, *Fräulein* Maria.'

She felt herself blush. If only she could learn to accept praise with grace. 'Thank you.'

Somehow they'd managed to squeeze themselves behind a table of empty glasses. 'Do you mind if we sit down?' Her legs felt tired.

He pulled out a chair for her. 'You said your father still lives in the Tyrol. Is his life much changed by the new regime?'

'He already spoke Italian, which was a help. But his

pension . . .' She stopped. Talking about money was supposed to be vulgar.

His gaze was thoughtful. 'These last years have been bad for many.'

'I suppose it's the same in Germany.' This was supposed to be a party, not a time for talking about sad events. 'And it's probably not as tough for him as for other people. Meran is still beautiful. It has a mild climate, you know, despite being so near the Alps. We have palms and oleanders.'

'And what about Vienna? How do you like the city?'

'It's exciting.' She chatted about Fredi Brandt and Xander Zeiler, the producer, and how much she liked the work of Michael Lander, who'd written last year's *The Lieutenant's Girl* and had said he'd nearly finished another play with a perfect part for her in it. Then there were the artists and the musicians. Last week she'd been to an exhibition of Expressionist art which had left her physically overcome. 'Everyone else has known about Kokoschka and Schiele for years but I'd never seen their work before.' She still felt embarrassed about having reached the age of twenty knowing so little about contemporary culture.

'Don't know them well myself, I must admit. Your life sounds fascinating.'

'It is! Every morning I wake up and hardly know what'll happen.'

'And you see yourself settled in Vienna permanently once you've finished at the Academy?'

She paused just a second too long. 'Probably. Sometimes I wonder if . . .'

He raised an eyebrow.

'As though it might come to a head, I suppose.' She rolled her eyes. 'Not that I know much about politics at all.' She hadn't really been referring to the political situation but had checked herself in time.

'These are restless times.'

Anton had found them. He approached, frowning. 'There you are, Maria.'

'I just needed to sit down for a moment.'

'People are asking for you.'

'I'll be along soon.'

Strange how she wanted to sit here with this eccentric German when she could be lapping up praise from her friends.

Peter von Matke stood. 'I should let you go back to your admirers, *Fräulein* Maria.'

'Marie,' she gave him her hand. 'Everyone calls me Marie.'

He held her hand for a moment. 'Next time I'm in Vienna I hope to see you again, Marie.'

Anton nodded a goodnight to the Prussian. 'Well, well,' he said when Peter had gone. 'That's a conquest. Young von Matke's had half the girls in Vienna chasing him.' His voice sounded tight, as though he had a sore throat.

'Nonsense.' Marie suddenly felt as though a headache was coming on. 'He was just being polite. Where's the champagne, Anton? And are there any more of those little cheese pastries? I'm ravenous.'

He gave a slight start at her tone but hurried off to fetch her refreshments. While she waited she saw a familiar figure lope through the door. Viktor – with a bunch of sunflowers.

'Sunflowers aren't bourgeois, it's official.' He handed them over with one of his rare smiles. Strange how, for all his amusing ways, one so seldom saw Viktor smile or laugh himself. Perhaps it was the Hungarian in him; they were supposed to be a melancholic race.

'They're magnificent. Where did you find them?' She took the flowers and admired their vivid gold before placing them on the table beside the carved wooden bowl Anton had given her.

'This very morning they were growing in a friend's garden near Szent Marton. Summer goes on a long time there.'

'You've come from Hungary?'

He nodded. Viktor never said very much about his supposed home in the west of the country and showed polite reluctance to provide information about his family. She'd assumed some kind of tragedy during or after the war. But now it struck her that he'd never actually said he was Hungarian at all. They'd simply assumed it, she and Eva. Perhaps he really came from somewhere else on the fringes of what had once been Austria-Hungary. Perhaps he had Jewish blood. Sometimes she thought Viktor symbolized all the rootlessness of their generation, young men and women who could barely remember the days of the old empire and swam in the turbulent, if exhilarating, waters of the new republic. Rootless he might be, but somehow he managed to acquire money. Last month had been her birthday and he'd given her a silver cigarette case.

She stroked one of the sunflowers. 'They'll look wonderful in our blue sitting room. Look, Eva.' For Eva had come in after Viktor.

'Lovely.' Eva's tone was flat. 'Where were you last night, Viktor?'

'I had business.' Nobody ever understood exactly what kind of business Viktor conducted. Perhaps it wasn't business at all but more of his politics.

'Oh.' Eva said, and turned her back on them to talk to a Matthias someone-or-other who was a friend of Fredi's. Marie knew she was angry. Why did Viktor have to make it all such a secret – where he went, even what nationality he was? Marie had once asked him why he was so dismissive of people who claimed pride in being German or Austrian or Hungarian or whatever. 'I've seen what nationalism does,' he'd said, a rare flash of emotion in his eyes.

She felt suddenly weary. Viktor was taking up too much of her attention. And she almost felt that she herself was taking up too much of everyone's attention with this party. No wonder Eva felt out of sorts. Her time would come, everyone said so. Marie had simply been lucky: she *looked* right as Rosalind. Soon it would be Eva's turn for parties and flowers. Already there was talk of her as a Joan of Arc. She had the presence for it, and the face – almost androgynous and stern in its beauty. And as for Maria Weissmüller, well, she would simply have to see whether her good fortune continued. She shivered.

'Cold?' Anton asked.

'How could I be on such a lovely night?' She touched his arm. 'It's a wonderful party, thank you again for the lovely bowl, Anton.' He beamed at her, reminding her again of the little boy who'd charmed extra apple slices from kindergarten assistants.

'Do you really like it?'

'You've got a talent for wood-turning.'

Anton was so practical, so gifted with his hands. Any woman who married him would never lack for fitted cupboards and shelves. He was Tyrolean through and through in his love of wood.

It was easy to be mesmerized by the Viktor Vargás of the world with their nonchalant charm, but people like Viktor could provide no defence against life's reversals. Take her own situation. Maria Weissmüller was essentially stateless. Rumour had it all the German-speaking South Tyroleans, loyal former Austrians, would be encouraged to migrate to Germany. Or stay in their homes – as Italians.

'Feeling safe and settled matters most,' Lena always said. Marie glanced at Viktor and doubted either of those feelings mattered at all to him. But, really, dear Lena, how old-fashioned she was. She'd refused to come tonight, saying the dressing room needed a good tidying before tomorrow's performance. Marie hated this mistress-and-servant role-playing. Lena was her equal, a fellow professional. Her tailoring skills were much in demand among women who liked the latest fashions but couldn't afford expensive designers.

'What amuses you?' Viktor said now.

Marie gave a start. 'I was thinking about someone.'

'Not that fine Prussian specimen I hear you were talking to?'

She flushed, annoyed. 'No, Lena.'

'A woman who never ceases to amaze me.'

'Really?' Marie frowned. She wouldn't have imagined Lena fascinating a man like Viktor.

He helped himself to a cheese pastry. 'These are good. Yes, Lena's one of those who'll sit by patiently for years judging a situation or a person. Then she'll jump. It'll seem sudden but it won't be at all.'

'You've only known her a few months.'

'I'm good at assessing people.' His eyes were shrewd.

'How do you assess me?' She could have kicked herself. Foolish, foolish question.

He glanced down at his plate.

'Save some of those for me.' Eva came up, cheeks pink from the champagne. Viktor handed her the salver of pastries and muttered something about finding the waiter so he could top up their glasses, but not before Marie had seen him glance at Eva, his face, for once, devoid of its neutral expression.

'Your dress really is lovely.' Marie noted how the silk clung to Eva's chest. Nonchalant as he liked to appear, Viktor couldn't resist Eva. He appeared at the apartment with boxes of cakes from Gerstner's which Eva wouldn't eat because they were so fattening. He bought her roses from the flower market and found her funny old books from the secondhand dealers.

Anton came back again with a platter of smoked fish on rye bread, looking awkward in his evening dress. He was the kind of male who looked best in shorts and walking boots, striding along an Alpine track. Indoors he appeared a captive animal. 'Very becoming,' he told Eva. How cold he sounded. Surely it couldn't still be this silly Jewish business? Half Vienna was Jewish. Even more, in their circle of actors, artists and writers. He'd never make friends with interesting people if he kept up this attitude. She'd stopped inviting him out with them on Sunday afternoons to *Heuriger* in the Vienna woods. He found it so hard to relax and enjoy the conversation and wine. Anton had no interest in discussions about the subconscious or music or the position of women in the arts.

And yet . . . Marie looked at his broad shoulders and remembered him rowing her out on the lake at home or picking her up off the snow when she'd fallen while skiing. Or that time he'd skated with her and they'd gone so fast she'd screamed at him to slow down but he wouldn't. A warm sensation ran through her abdomen and towards the top of her legs, just remembering it. 'Heard anything from the timber company?' She was careful to keep her voice neutral. He'd applied for so many jobs without success.

Anton examined his fingers. 'The job interview was last week. Forty applicants, they said.'

'None with your knowledge.' How fierce she sounded. He seemed to glow at her words.

Viktor came back with the bottle of champagne. 'The waiter seems to have grown invisible. Let me top you up, Maria.' Like Anton he called her by her full name, saying Marie was a name for a French maid. He still used *Sie* when addressing her, as well. These socialists could be awfully proper.

Eva moved closer to Viktor, slipping a hand through his arm and resting her head on his shoulder for a moment. Daring, like caressing one of the lions at the zoo. Viktor placed his free hand over Eva's and stroked her fingers. Marie blushed. Too hot in here. Too much champagne. Too much of everything. She turned away from the others and pretended to admire her sunflowers.

'Only me.' Peter von Matke stood beside her again with an apologetic grin. 'Forgot my clock. Here she is.' He picked his parcel up from the chair. 'Couldn't bear to lose her.'

'Are clocks female?' She felt refreshed at the sight of the young German.

'Mine are.'

She supposed they were flirting but it didn't feel like it. He was too straightforward.

'Have dinner with me.'

Such an informal way for a Prussian to phrase it! She couldn't help smiling. 'Now?'

'You've probably got better things to do,' he said. He'd take her out of this stuffy room with its empty champagne bottles, away from Viktor and Eva's enigmatic silences and from Anton with his stubborn pride.

'Let me find my wrap and say a few goodbyes.' It was probably rude to leave her own party while guests still remained. She glanced round the restaurant. Eva had moved away and was now chatting to the young Berliner called Matthias. She was smoking a cigarette in one of those long holders she favoured, looking cool and self-possessed. Anton was talking seriously with a group of men in faded smoking jackets. She knew it was politics because of the way the side of his hand intermittently struck the table to punctuate his words. Viktor was nowhere to be seen.

Fourteen

Alix
Pomerania, February 1945

We can't always stay at home, Mami had told Alix on the morning after the terrible dinner party. How heavy Alix's heart had felt at the words. Yet now she would have done anything to escape from this house, even if it meant a night in the snowy forest. Nowhere else on earth could fill her with the same sense of imminent violence as this kitchen.

Preizler was watching her over the kitchen table. 'You may as well rest, Alix, while it's quiet.'

She picked up her rucksack and coat and left the kitchen without a backwards look, ignoring her mother's imploring *Gute Nacht*. In her bedroom she locked the door and sat on the bed.

A light step on the landing told her Mami was coming to bed, too. She paused outside Alix's door and knocked. Alix said nothing. Perhaps Mami would think she was already asleep. '*Gute Nacht, Liebling*,' Mami said, her voice shaking. 'We'll talk in the morning when we've had some rest.'

Alix clutched the edge of the quilt and forced herself not to answer.

Twenty minutes passed. Preizler stumbled upstairs and across the landing. His footsteps sounded uneven, drunken, as though he were attempting some complicated dance routine. Maybe he'd found Papi's cognac. If so there was still a chance of escape.

He knocked on Mami's door. Alix took a deep breath. *Don't let him in.* She ran to her own door and put her ear to it.

'Marie?' he hissed.

A click as the door opened.

'I feel strange,' Preizler said, the words loud and slurred. 'Dizzy. Can I lie down?'

The sound of the door closing. Silence. Alix tried to block her imagination from picturing the scene in Mami's room with its Toile de Jouy wallpaper and thick wool carpet.

She took her torch out of her rucksack and went to the door of her bedroom, listening for Preizler. Nothing. Alix turned the door handle, willing the door to open without a creak. As she crept across the landing she felt herself spinning back through time to the night six years ago when she'd slipped downstairs to release Gregor from the cellar. Preizler had caught them that time: caught them and let them go. Not this time.

Pausing frequently to listen for signs of movement she edged her way through the dark house to the cellar, unbolting it slowly and carefully and waiting until she was inside before switching on her torch. Its beam flashed on Gregor's eyes.

'Hello.' He seemed to be attempting a grin.

'Are you all right? You must be frozen.' She wanted to throw her arms around him and warm him but caution told her to hurry as she released him. 'We should both leave this house now.' She sounded curt. 'I'll take this.' She'd spotted an old hunting knife of Papi's sitting on the table beside the old clocks. 'It's better than nothing.'

'The storm's even fiercer now,' Gregor said. 'Listen.' They heard the wind pounding the shuttered windows. 'We wouldn't get far out there.'

'But Preizler . . .'

'I saw your mother give him sleeping tablets when he wasn't looking. She dropped them into his coffee.'

More of those sleeping tablets. Mami must have been hoarding them for years.

'Suppose he wakes up?'

'He won't – not with that many pills in him.' He looked at the cut lengths of rope on the cellar floor. 'These may be useful, too.' Just as they had as children, they crept upstairs, stopping frequently to listen out for the sound of a creaking boot, but there was nothing. They sat on her bed, hands almost touching on the white quilt. Alix's skin tingled. 'Preizler must still be out cold,' Gregor whispered. 'We need to immobilize him.'

The thought of being in the same room as Preizler again made Alix shake. Gregor put an arm around her. 'Don't worry. I'll make sure he doesn't harm you. Stay here.'

He got up. 'Give me the rope and knife.'

'No.' She clutched his arm. Better to face that man – and Mami – than to sit here alone waiting, wondering what was happening.

Seconds passed before he answered. 'Very well.' He held out his hand for the knife.

Mami's room lay across the landing. The thick Persian rug muffled their footsteps. Gregor tapped softly on the door. 'Baroness?'

The door opened almost immediately. 'I was waiting for you. He's sound asleep.' Her eyes met Alix's and Alix looked away. 'You won't . . .'

'I won't kill him. But I will have to hand him over to my superior officer. You understand that?'

Mami nodded. 'Come in.'

How strange to be back in this room with its thick carpet, scent bottles and hairbrushes. Mami must have been sitting in a chair at the bottom of the bed. Preizler lay on top of the quilt, his mouth slightly open, breathing quietly. He'd removed his coat and slept in a civilian suit. Mami looked at the pieces of cut rope. 'Those aren't long enough.' She rose and went to a drawer and took out a pile of neatly folded silk scarves, which Gregor took from her. Preizler grunted as he approached the bed but didn't move. Gregor tied his hands and then his feet together and used a scarf to tie the bound hands and feet together so that his enemy was trussed. 'I need another one, to gag him.'

Mami shook her head. 'Please don't do that. There's no need. These walls are thick and who's going to hear him outside in a snowstorm?'

'You're so concerned about him, even now.' Alix hadn't meant to say the words aloud.

'Darling, it's not like that, it's just—'

Alix threw up a hand to silence her. 'I'll wait in my room.' She walked back to her room and curled up on the bed. Gregor returned minutes later.

'Can we trust her not to release him?' she asked.

He gave her a long look. 'At her own request I locked your mother into another bedroom. I gave her Clara Preizler's pistol. Just in case.' He stuffed Preizler's Walther and a smaller object into his pack.

'What's that?'

'Cyanide capsules. Found them in Preizler's pocket.' She dropped her head and examined the quilt.

'Don't think about that now, we've won a reprieve, Alix.' He squeezed her shoulder. 'A few hours before Vavilov gets here. We need to rest and then move you out of here before dawn.' Gregor flopped onto the bed. 'You know what I'd love more than anything else just now?'

She shook her head.

'A wash in hot water.' He was looking at the door to her en suite bathroom. 'I've had occasional field showers, but that's about it.'

'Go ahead. You could even run the bath if you're sure we're safe for a while.'

'We are. I told you.'

'There are towels in there.'

'Wonderful, thank you.' He sounded like a polite visitor.

She heard Gregor's sigh of pleasure as he got into the bath. Alix pulled an English novel out of the bookshelf to distract herself and found herself reading the same paragraph again and again and falling back against the bed's pillows but unable to sleep.

But then she heard him pulling the plug. He'd have to put on that tattered uniform again. She heard the taps of the basin running. Did Red Army soldiers carry toothbrushes? It sounded as though that was what he was doing, cleaning his teeth. The door opened.

He was wearing towels, one on top, one round his waist. 'I'm sorry, I rinsed out some of my clothes. Couldn't resist the opportunity. I hope you don't mind.'

'Hang them out on the towel rack.' The rack, like the bedroom, was heated by the stove in the kitchen.

He did as she suggested and reappeared in the bedroom. 'You should get some sleep, Alix. I'll stay on guard and wake you up in an hour or so. We'll leave together. I won't wait for Vavilov.'

Her heart leaped at the way he made it sound like it would be a shared escape. Perhaps he would come all the way to Cousin Ulla's with her. They could burn his uniform in the stove downstairs and borrow some of Papi's old clothes. Gregor could pretend to be an invalid from the eastern front.

'I'll make myself comfortable on the chair,' he said.

'I'll find you some blankets.' She handed him a couple from the mahogany wardrobe and got into bed, shivering in the cold. She heard him remove his revolver and load it. A metal object rattled on top of the table. Ammunition? No, the mouth organ. 'Tell me more about Poland.' Anything to take her mind off that creature trussed up in her mother's bedroom.

Years ago they'd shared midnight feasts, and Gregor had told her stories he'd read in books.

'You should sleep.'

'I will. But first I want to know what happened to you when you left Brest. Did you find your friends again? What were their names? Jacob and . . .?'

'Reuben. It's a long story.' Now he sounded weary.

Fifteen

Gregor
Poland and Russia, 1940–42

God alone knew exactly where he was. Gregor had lost the precious map that he'd bartered his watch for and was now relying on the sun to guide him west; difficult when he preferred to travel at night to avoid patrols. He'd tried to keep the railway to his right as Reuben had instructed, but the Germans had been moving freight along the line and there were too many armed guards on the wagons.

Impossible to calculate how far he'd walked now. Maybe eighty or a hundred miles east of the Bug. He must be somewhere near that wretched village where he was supposed to meet the Gronowskis. *Borki*, he still remembered its name but the other details of the meeting place had gone. He asked a peasant digging up potatoes in a field and the man stared at him in speechless amazement, either because of his unusual accent or because of his rough appearance after so many days in the open. He pointed along the track.

Gregor stumbled off. He still had no idea how far the village was. His empty stomach was trying to eat away at his brain. Soon he'd forget who he was, who his friends were.

At times he thought of handing himself in to the first patrol he could find and showing them that German passport. But they might take one look at him, filthy, scrawny, and decide he'd stolen it. He hardly looked like that sleek boy in the jacket and tie in the photograph. A suspicious patrol might just shoot him or throw him into one of those trucks they used to round up people for forced labour.

He was mad, trying to find the Gronowskis. Perhaps he should try for German-annexed western Poland, and from there head for Pomerania and the protection of Peter von Matke. The memory of the von Matkes made him forget the growling void inside him. The baron, baroness and Alexandra. Alix. What had they done the last holiday he spent at Alexanderhof? Forget that dinner party, remember something else, something that was like a small candle flame burning in the night. The kiss. He'd kissed Alix down in that dark cellar. And she'd kissed him back and even though she was just a kid it had felt like . . .

His tired imagination couldn't find the word.

He hadn't found the village by dusk but came across a farmer driving a cart who said Borki wasn't more than four or five kilometres away. Gregor could shelter in his stables. He even promised bread and cheese. But then the farmer's son came into the kitchen, heard Gregor's thanks and scowled. 'That's a German accent.' He grabbed Gregor's rucksack and pulled out his papers. 'You *are* German.'

'Yes, but—'

Bellowing like an ox the son grabbed him and dragged him into the farmyard. The father picked up a pitchfork. Gregor waited for the prongs to rip through his chest.

'You sons of dogs, can't a man get a moment's sleep?'

Gregor opened his eyes at the roar. Reuben Gronowski, whom Gregor had last seen just outside Brest, strode across the farmyard, bearded, looking years older, like some Old Testament prophet. The man and his son scuttled away. 'Who the hell—?' Reuben scowled at Gregor, blinked, looked again. 'I don't believe it. Gregor Fischer! What the devil are you doing here? How did you know we'd moved up here from the village?'

'I didn't know,' Gregor muttered, his legs shaking with delayed shock. 'I lost the map.'

'Just as well.' Reuben threw an arm round him. 'Turned out the Germans had their eye on the place. We were warned not to go there so we've been staying here and in other farms around the area.' He led him to the barn. 'Jacob's here too.'

Jacob sat up on a pallet, yawning. '*Psia krew*! It can't be you?' A grin stretched across his face. He hugged him so hard that Gregor feared for his ribs. 'Didn't you like Comrade Stalin?'

'Not much.'

'Bastard,' Reuben growled.

Jacob handed Gregor a piece of sausage. 'Sit down here. You were lucky to find us. Tomorrow we're heading to Section North. That's what the Home Army call the part of Poland east of Warsaw, you know.'

Reuben gave a slight frown at his brother.

'I've just come from there.' Gregor shuddered at the thought of walking all those miles back, dodging patrols, farm dogs, suspicious locals. 'Besides, I thought you wanted to fight Germans?'

'You've missed the news, haven't you?' Jacob laughed at Gregor's face. 'Jews have to wear stars now. If they catch you without one, it's a bullet.'

'I see.' Gregor ate the sausage.

Reuben frowned. 'You didn't say it.'

'Say what?'

'You didn't point out that you're only a quarter Jewish. And you've got a German passport. You could tidy yourself up and hand yourself in to them.'

'I want to stay with you.' Gregor thought of the lonely months he'd spent tramping cross-country.

Reuben drew in a breath. 'I wish you could, Gregor. But you're the enemy.' He couldn't meet Gregor's eyes.

'I'm not, you know I'm not.'

'You know what I mean. This occupation is getting even uglier. People hate the Germans more and more.'

Gregor dropped his head and studied the straw on the barn floor. 'All right. You don't have to say any more. I'll keep heading west, make for Pomerania.'

'To those friends in the big house?' Reuben walked to a corner of the barn, back to the others and stood silent for a moment. Then he turned back to them. 'No. We promised them, your mother and mine, that we'd try and look after you.'

'I don't want you to look after me!' Indignation choked Gregor's throat. 'I'm not some damn child.'

Reuben touched his shoulder. 'No, of course you're not. You're Gregor Fischer, known as *psia krew*. And who knows how useful those German papers of yours might prove?' His eyes were warm. 'Let's sleep now.'

Gregor pulled off his boots. 'Why are we going to the east?'

Reuben looked down at his own feet. 'Messages for the Home Army there.' There was still a note of caution in his voice.

They hadn't asked him about his mother and Gregor could have blessed them for this.

They kept away from roads and villages, trying to walk at night where possible. For whole days they managed to keep away from other human beings. At times the war seemed to belong to another world. As they made camp on the first night in a shepherd's hut Gregor thought of the Gronowski parents and girls. 'Have you heard from your mother?'

Jacob looked away. 'One letter. Lydia'd been ill. Pneumonia.' He shrugged. Gregor didn't ask again.

As they headed east fields turned to forest. The only sound was the snapping of twigs, animals rustling in the undergrowth, boots scrunching on snow. The Gronowskis had traded in Gregor's summer shoes for thick leather boots that kept his feet warm and dry for the first time in weeks. As they tramped Reuben told Gregor they were going to retrieve some children at risk of deportation. 'We're being squeezed in both directions now but there are still some parts of the country where you can hide out. These kids – we don't know how many there are – deserve a chance.'

The way he talked about kids made it seem as though Reuben were much older. Hard to remember he was still in his teens too.

They trudged on, the silence broken only by the rustle of bushes as rabbits and deer crept around; a jay's occasional flash of colour the only brightness.

They'd almost reached the Bug, heading north of Brest this time because Reuben was nervous about the major crossings. He stopped and pulled out a map. 'The border's close. Let's go through the plan one more time. Fischer, what do you do?'

'Head for the baker's in the village, opposite the church. He gives me papers belonging to his son, who's in bed with scarlet fever. Tomorrow morning I cross the footbridge and wait for you in the cemetery. If you don't appear I cross back the next day and wait at the baker's for a message.'

'Good. Try and keep your gob shut. That German accent's deadly.'

Jacob rolled his eyes. 'He treats us like kids.'

'Talking of kids, we'll be collecting the first one tonight. A boy.' Reuben sounded gruff. Gregor hadn't liked to ask for too many details of the Gronowskis' work. Jacob had talked of a meeting with Home Army leaders in which responsibilities had been handed out. Reuben had taken their orders and had refused to tell his brother much.

'He thinks I'd squeal if the Germans caught me.' Jacob sniffed. 'As if I would. It's just because I'm younger than him, he likes to rub it in.'

They trudged on through the snow.

The baker put Gregor up for the night and fed him on black bread and cheese.

'Sorry there's nothing more.'

'This is wonderful.' Gregor hadn't eaten as much in days. The baker's wife showed him up to the loft and he slept long and deep. 'Why are you helping someone like me?' he asked in the morning.

The baker snorted. 'The Germans are Christians, not like those atheistic monsters.'

The wife handed Gregor a parcel of food. 'We've hardly stopped fighting the Russians or the Ukrainians or the Lithuanians these last twenty years.' She sounded resigned. 'Poles have many enemies.'

At the footbridge the next morning the Russian guard barely glanced at Gregor's papers and waved him through with the peasants bringing jars of preserved berries to sell in the market. He found the cemetery and curled up behind a large gravestone to wait. War or not, chrysanthemums still sat in flowerpots, their petals frosted and crisp. Hard to tell how long they'd been here. The donors were probably hundreds or thousands of miles east by now. Like his mother. He pushed thoughts of her away. It only weakened you to dwell on missing loved ones, Reuben said. Keep your thoughts on the present, on surviving the next patrol, the next night shivering in the open, the next hungry day—

'Bang bang!' Jacob had slunk up to him without a sound, holding up his fingers in the shape of a gun. 'You'd be dead if I was a Russian.' He pushed a thin lad of about ten wearing a black cap and a coat several sizes too big for him

towards Gregor. 'This is Cyrek. Cyrek, this is . . . a friend.'
Cyrek extended his mittened hand and Gregor shook it. The
fingers felt light and fragile.

'If you lift that loose white stone,' Reuben pointed at the
cemetery wall, 'you'll find a space where you can stuff the
baker's papers. He'll pick them up when he comes to put
flowers on his aunt's grave.'

Gregor found the stone and as he replaced it his ears
caught the clink of metal. He listened again, heard a cough.
He crawled back to the others. 'Someone's coming.'

Reuben's eyes swept the cemetery. 'Take Cyrek out the
back gate and wait for us in the lane. There's a burnt-out
charabanc in the ditch you can hide behind. Jacob and I will
head them off. We'll come back for you later. Go!'

No time for discussion. Gregor grabbed Cyrek by the
arm. They zigzagged from gravestone to gravestone. Gunfire
burst out from the main gate. Gregor spotted the bus, a rem-
nant from the fighting in thirty-nine. They scurried up the
lane and crouched behind it and waited.

Jacob and Reuben never appeared. Eventually the gunfire
stopped. Each time Gregor thought of creeping back to the
cemetery he caught sight of Cyrek's scared face and dismissed
the temptation. They climbed inside the bus and shared the
bread and cheese the baker had given Gregor. Night fell.
Cyrek moved closer towards Gregor. Gregor told him about
his life in Berlin before the war and about Alix's big country
house with the ponies and lake. He described Alix's school
for toys and Cyrek laughed softly, catching his breath as
though the story were so amusing it hurt. They dozed,

huddled up together, Cyrek's fingers clasping the sleeve of Gregor's coat.

A light shining on Gregor's face woke him. Cyrek cried out.

'You boys think we not find you?' The Russian grinned through black teeth. 'Out you come.'

Gregor tried to stretch out his legs on the filth-encrusted wagon floor but the man next to him snarled an objection. Next to him the boy Cyrek groaned and whispered something about his school. Probably thought he was back in the classroom again. Yesterday he'd been convinced they were all sitting a Latin test.

'Dehydrated.' The old woman in the corner sighed. 'That wound's gone septic and he's burning up.' Her rosary beads rattled. Gregor wished he could believe in whatever she believed.

Cyrek hadn't even cried out when the bullet had grazed his skinny thigh in the cemetery, and Gregor hadn't noticed the injury, so desperate had he been to keep them warm and quiet while they waited in vain for the Gronowskis. If he'd seen the graze he could have cleaned it up a bit. It had only been on the third day of the journey that he'd noticed the swelling under the boy's threadbare trousers and pulled up the leg to reveal the infected wound.

He tipped the last of his water into Cyrek's mouth. Like trying to put out a fire. Cyrek had stopped calling out now, and lay still, his brown eyes dull and staring at nothing. Occasionally he'd clench one of his hands, as though he were trying to grab hold of something. Before the infection had taken hold Cyrek had talked about his old life in Warsaw. His mother was a friend of Mrs Gronowska's.

'I almost envy him.' The old woman put away her rosary and laid a hand on the boy's brow. 'He'll be out of it soon.'

Sixteen

Alix
Pomerania, February 1945

Alix waited for him to continue. 'What happened next?' she asked when he didn't.

'Tomorrow.' Gregor yawned. 'You need to sleep now while you can, while we're safe for a few hours.'

Alix switched off the lamp and tried to let herself drift off. Preizler in the next bedroom, Gregor in the chair at the foot of her bed, his story still unfinished—

Something howled outside, only metres from the window.

Alix sat up. 'I've never heard him before.' Please God don't let the wolf wake Preizler, bound though he was.

'I saw them in Russia, sometimes in Poland,' Gregor said. 'But mainly they kept away from us.'

'Why's he here tonight?'

'The fighting must have driven him from his territory.'

She got out of bed. Gregor had already crossed the carpeted floor, a blanket around him like a toga. Soundlessly Alix opened the windows and shutters.

The wolf sat on the snowy terrace, so close they could make out the black rings round his eyes. 'He's magnificent.' Alix wished her father could see him. 'He can see us watching him.'

The wolf studied them, his breath forming a mist in the night air, the snow falling round him.

'Wonderful,' Gregor said, his shoulder against hers. 'I wonder what he must think of the human race.'

'All those legends about bloodthirsty wolves, but we're the ones who torture and kill our own.' But staring at the wolf Alix felt some of the anger and fear drain out of her. The world had shrunk to this room: Gregor standing so close to her; the wolf gazing up at them both.

'Aren't you cold?' Gregor whispered.

She couldn't imagine ever being cold again.

She couldn't be sure which of them turned first to the other. She could feel his breath on her face, smell something that must be Red Army issue toothpaste, harsh and medicinal, and Papi's bath oil and something else warm and musky that must be Gregor himself. 'We shouldn't do this,' Gregor said.

She wasn't hearing his words; his physical presence was filling her senses. Her fear of Preizler, her longing to leave the house, all these things were fading.

'Alix if you stand this close to me, I . . .'

She put an arm round his neck. 'Don't push me away.'

'I won't.' His voice caught. 'But you don't know what you're doing. I'm – I'm a soldier. Where I've been men don't treat women with kid gloves.'

'You could never treat me badly.' She moved so they stood chest to chest. No mistaking his response now: she hadn't been sure at first. She and Jana, the slave worker from Warsaw, had spent hours discussing the mechanics of sex.

Gregor let out a long deep breath that seemed to express his sadness for all the years they'd lost. 'Do you remember that night in the cellar when I kissed you?' he said.

'Of course.'

He nodded. 'I thought you did.'

'Come to bed with me.' It seemed a natural conclusion to the music-less waltz, to the wolf's mysterious arrival. 'You want to, don't you Gregor?'

He made a sound that was halfway between a laugh and a gasp. 'I don't think you need to ask me that.' He held her chin in his hand. 'But there are things you don't know about me, things I should tell you—'

She put a finger to the hairs curling on the back of his neck. They felt as silky as she'd imagined when she'd watched him playing on the Steinway. 'Don't tell me. I can't cope with anything more. It's only one night.' She closed her eyes and leaned against him. 'It could be all that's left.' She closed the shutters and window, catching one last glimpse of the wolf still watching the window.

Outside on the landing Papi's wall clock struck the quarter-hour. 'This isn't really happening.' He put his lips to the hollow underneath her collarbone and kissed it and an electric thrill went through her and it was like that time she'd first galloped on Papi's horse, too fast, impossible to pull back.

Seventeen

Alix
Next day

She woke from deep, dreamless sleep. Beside her Gregor slept on, his breath warm on her neck. She had to force recollection of last night's events on herself: the horses blown to pieces, running with Lena through the forest, Gregor's smashed coffee cup. Preizler. Mami.

Gregor sat up, reaching across her for her Patek Philippe. She felt his muscles tense against her. 'We overslept.'

She buried her head in his chest and took in the scent of him, warm and sweet. Please let all the rest be just a bad dream. He reached for the blanket she'd pulled off him last night and wrapped it round him. 'I wish we could stay here for ever, but you're in danger, Alix. Let's get moving.' He handed her the watch.

Her body tingled. There were still whole inches of her body he hadn't had time to explore. The injustice struck her: *this* was what was important, the two of them together in this bed. Yet they'd be torn apart, forced to continue on divergent paths until powers they couldn't influence decided that the killing could stop and people could go back to bed with their lovers. Already last night's terror was catching up with her again.

Alix got up, too, shivering – no Lena to light her fire this morning. Her mind reluctantly switched to the immediate dangers. 'I don't know what to do about Mami.'

Gregor padded over to her and took her hands. 'We need to hurry.' His voice was urgent. 'Vavilov will be here any moment.'

She saw the strain in his face and felt scared again too. She stuffed on her shirt and pulled on her layers of woollens, one on top of the other. They still smelled of cordite and burned metal and Mami's cigarettes. 'Will Preizler have woken? How long do those sleeping tablets last?'

'If he wakes he can't do anything. He's trussed up like a chicken.'

Even so Alix couldn't help glancing at the door. She found her socks and watched Gregor dress. He held up his left foot awkwardly to put on his boot and then stiffened.

Alix heard the purr of an engine. Gregor cursed under his breath. 'We can get out through the boot room,' she said. 'They're at the top of the drive, they won't be able to use their vehicle, they'll have to walk through the snow.'

'Quick.' He grabbed her rucksack along with his own pack and pushed her out of the door. Her fingers clutched at the mouth organ he'd left on the table.

'What about Mami?' Adulteress she might be, but they couldn't just leave her here for the Reds.

'I'll come back for her.'

They'd reached the ground floor now, heading for the passage that led from the kitchen past the cellar steps to the back of the house.

Last night's snow had jammed the boot-room door. Gregor cursed again and shoved it with his shoulder. This time it moved; the porch had shielded it from the worst of the blizzard.

'Run for the forest, I'm going back upstairs for your mother!' he told her.

How close to the house were Vavilov's men now? Gregor should be leaving with her. But Mami . . .

'Alix, run!'

'I can't just leave you and Mami, I can't.'

'We'll catch you up in the forest. But don't wait, keep running. You swear?'

His eyes reminded her of the wolf's last night. She nodded and forced herself to turn away from him.

She waded across the snow-covered flowerbed, home, in summer, to her mother's night-scented stocks. 'Run,' he hissed again at her retreating back.

She cut through the whiteness, skirting the chestnuts under which aconites and celandines would bloom in a few months. The snow seemed to want to detain the last of the von Matkes at Alexanderhof, grabbing at her calves and threatening to trip her. At last she reached the stables. She brushed the snow from the top of her boots and kept on going, her breath coming in spurts, her muscles still tired from yesterday's run from the soldiers. The beeches and firs were in front of her now. If she didn't draw breath she'd die.

She thought she could still feel Gregor's gaze on the back of her neck like one of those searchlights she'd once seen in Stettin during an air raid.

She kept running, a von Matke, running like a scared doe. She wouldn't stop until he said they could.

Eighteen

Gregor
February 1945

Gregor ran back through the passageway and into the entrance hall. How far down the drive was Vavilov now? He flew upstairs to the door of the bedroom into which he'd locked the baroness and pulled out the key.

'Gregor!'

Marie stood in front of him. Even now, with perspiration drenching his neck and his legs shaking, he blinked at the sight of her. The tentative dawn light from the window behind her illuminated her face, showing faint lines that couldn't mar the purity of her skin, as luminous as the pearls strung round her slender neck. Her mink coat hung from her shoulders and she wore a fur hat. Anna Karenina. Leather boots on her feet, ready for the snow. 'Baroness, you need to get out of the house now!' Could they reach the boot room before Vavilov reached the house? 'Come on!' Any second now they'd be pounding on the bolted front door. He grabbed her hand and pulled her towards the staircase.

'I can't just leave him like that for the Russians.' She spoke very softly and it took a moment for him to work out what she'd said.

'Are you mad?' He seized her arm and dragged her out of the room. 'Get away now while you can. Your daughter is out there in the forest, go and join her!'

'I drugged him and we tied him up like an animal. He's defenceless. I only helped you last night so that you and Alix could escape.' They'd reached the sweeping staircase now and he was still pulling her.

'He's a criminal,' he hissed. 'Remember that gun pointed at Alix?' He tugged her down the stairs but she was surprisingly strong.

'I have to untie him, Gregor. You know what they'll do to him.'

'He deserves it!' At last they were on the ground floor. Gregor thought he heard voices coming from the front. He'd go and let them in, create a diversion so she could escape through the back. He halted beside the door to the salon. From his pack he removed Clara Preizler's pearl-handled pistol. 'Go out of the boot room and across the park. The trees will shield you and you can hide in the stables. If it's clear you can run for the forest, that's where Alix is.'

'But what about you, Gregor? Aren't you coming?'

He shook his head and pushed her towards the back of the house. It was too late for him to catch up with Alix now. The only thing he could do for her was to delay Vavilov and the intelligence unit and buy her precious minutes.

'I'm going to open the front door now.' He gave Alix's mother a last look. Her face was absolutely serene. She nodded and placed her hand on his.

'You've grown up into such a fine man. Your parents would be proud of you. Look after yourself, Gregor Fischer.' She ran towards the back of the house, her footsteps light, even in the boots.

And now Gregor could hear feet crunching through the snow at the front of the house. He walked to the front door and pulled open the bolts, which ran smoothly under his fingers. Vavilov stood under the porch, snow clinging to his boots, flakes floating around his outline. Below him in the drive the others blew on their fingers and stamped their feet. 'Fischer.' Vavilov's eyes were like chips of amber. 'You spent the night here?'

Gregor stood aside to let him in. 'Yes Comrade.' He'd planned it all out in his head. 'There's something upstairs you might like to see.' Vavilov's companions were still outside, pointing across the gardens at the farm workers' cottages. Please let them spend time searching those cottages . . .

Vavilov's gaze traced the antlers mounted on the walls, the marble floor, the portraits.

'One of the most successful examples of eighteenth-century architecture in this part of Pomerania.' Vavilov pointed at a cornice. 'The family brought an Italian out from Florence to do all this plasterwork. I believe he also did the salon as well.'

The older man appeared very relaxed this morning. 'Would you like to see that room before we go upstairs?'

Gregor nodded at the door. Enough in there to distract him for another twenty minutes or so. The more time they spent in the front of the house, the better for Marie and Alix; the parkland leading to the forest couldn't be seen from these windows. Vavilov strode into the room. 'You made yourself at home, then?' He was looking at the open lid of the piano, the music on the stand. The dustsheet rolled up on one of the sofas. The open gramophone player.

'Interesting to see how such people live.' Gregor closed the door quietly behind him.

'Indeed, Comrade, indeed.' Vavilov examined the plaster cornice. 'Such detail.' He stood admiring the work for some minutes. Then the photographs of Marie caught his attention. 'And the baroness, Maria Weissmüller, as she used to be.' He studied her with concentration.

Vavilov turned to Gregor. 'Now, what did you have to show me upstairs?'

'A Gestapo officer. He appeared last night, taking shelter from the storm.' Gregor opened the door and led him out.

'And you overpowered him single-handed?' Vavilov's tone expressed surprise. 'Most impressive, Comrade.'

'His pistol is in my pack.' They'd reached the top of the staircase, Gregor led the older man down the corridor to the bedroom in which Preizler lay bound.

The key was still in the lock but the door stood open. A pair of nail scissors and some cut silk scarves lay on the floor. A dent on the quilted bed showed where the man's body had rested overnight.

Nineteen

Alix

Two days later, west of the river Oder, February 1945

Trains were still running, someone told Alix when she woke, head spinning, throat parched, trying to remember where she was – in a station waiting room, crushed between the wall and a family with three children. Her legs had grown numb during the night and as she stretched her muscles screeched a complaint.

Loudspeakers blasted out military marches and Hitler's speeches. On the walls posters still advertised 'Strength through Joy' cruises, promising invigoration and fresh air for patriotic workers. The door swung open and the stationmaster waded through the refugees and eyed the loudspeakers, shaking his head. 'They make me play this stuff night and day, damned idiots.'

He was taking a chance, speaking out like this in a roomful of strangers. Alix had been dreaming of dancing with

Gregor. She had kissed him and he turned into a wolf, baring white teeth and lifting his head to howl.

When she'd dragged herself out of the forest, bleeding, dizzy, she'd promised herself she'd never cry again, that from that day onwards Alexandra von Matke would give all her energy to protecting herself, putting herself first always.

The music stopped and everyone sat up. The stationmaster held up ripped wires. 'If they give me trouble I'm going to say it was bomb damage.'

Except bombs didn't sheer through wires, leaving rooms untouched.

'Where are you going?' the stationmaster asked her.

'Berlin.' She'd decided Papi might be there, if Preizler's colleagues hadn't had him killed. Berlin was against Mami's instructions, but everything'd changed now.

'Don't.' He dropped his voice even though the family next to Alix were preoccupied with sharing out a loaf of bread. 'The Russians are well over the river now. Go south, make for Dresden and then head west. Try and get to the Americans.'

'What will you do?'

He fished something out of his pocket, a tattered card with a photograph on it. 'Communist party membership. Kept it safe for sixteen years.'

Alix stood and shook out her legs one by one to get her circulation going. An engine whistled and people began rolling up blankets and calling children to order. The train pulled in and the crowd surged towards it. Grabbing her coat and rucksack, Alix half-closed her eyes and let the throng propel her out of the waiting room towards the platform. Someone pulled her up into an open wagon. 'Where are we going?' she asked the man in the sheepskin coat next to her.

'God alone knows,' came the answer.

She clutched her knees to her chest, examining the soot falling onto her hand. She'd been on the train for three days now and hadn't eaten for two. They'd had water this morning, brackish-tasting, but welcome. Now it was night again and the train had stopped. Something had woken her. She concentrated and worked out what it was: the carriage was vibrating to the sound of planes, hundreds and hundreds of planes. She could see them above her in the night sky. Around her people whimpered and prayed, some of them on their knees on the soiled straw-covered floor. They'd stopped *meckering* – complaining – long ago. Papi had once told Alix that it would be a bad time for Germany when its people stopped moaning. She'd noticed how they'd quietened over the last year or so. Fear. Despair. Lack of energy. Terrible memories.

Don't think about it. Something in her breeches pocket was digging into her leg. Gregor's mouth organ. Alix almost welcomed the discomfort. She hadn't imagined that night together in bed, fingers placed to one another's lips in case they woke the others. She hadn't dreamed his whispering of her name, over and over again like a spell. She pulled out the mouth organ. It was blood-stained, like her clothes. *Don't let yourself remember what happened in the forest.* She'd hardly dared examine herself. The worst of the pain had subsided.

Alix put away the instrument. She needed to concentrate on more immediate needs. More soot fell on her. She followed the gazes of her fellow passengers and saw how the horizon blazed yellow and red. 'Where's that?' she asked the woman next to her.

'Where *was* that, you mean. Dresden.'

'Dresden?' They'd come further south. Porcelain shepherdesses and paintings. Mami'd taken her there just before the war had started and they'd visited museums and palaces.

Two men in the wagon returned from a foraging trip with cans of water, which they passed round the wagon. Two children had died in the night. Frozen, probably. When they tried to take them from their mothers, the women screamed. Nobody had the heart to insist. But now it was getting warmer. 'A thaw,' an old woman said. 'Sudden too.'

'Their tanks will get stuck in the mud,' said a girl with two long brown plaits.

Alix knew that nothing could stop them, nothing, nothing, nothing. Anything in their way would be ripped apart, tossed aside. She wanted to tell the people in the wagon what she knew about the Russians but there was no point. They'd find out.

They were supposed to be heading north-west to Leipzig now. Or so rumour had it. It was impossible to tell by observing the direction the train took. Sometimes they stopped for hours. Sometimes the train took them in circles, causing mutters of alarm when the morning sun blazed into the passengers' eyes and warned them they were heading east again. Nobody seemed to know if they were any closer to the Elbe now. They needed to cross the river to reach the Americans, but the bridges might all have been blown. The train seemed uncertain where to go, shunting from one place to another like a disoriented caterpillar, its passengers becoming more apathetic as each day passed. Perhaps they'd sit in the stinking straw until the end of the war.

A man climbed into the wagon as the train slowed to pass over a bridge and jumped down, landing on two middle-aged women who pushed him away with curses. He wore clothes like pyjamas and his eyes burned yellow in his thin face. He said nothing for hours. When Alix stood up to stretch her legs he stared at the bloodstains on the insides of her breeches. She caught his eye.

'A Russian?' His voice was educated, with a faint middle European accent – Czech, perhaps. She looked away. 'A Russian, wasn't it?' He cackled. 'A Russian got you, little Aryan girl, didn't he?' And tears of laughter fell from his eyes. She backed into the corner of the wagon, causing people to shout at her as she trampled on blankets and coats. When she looked back at where the man had been he'd gone. Perhaps she'd imagined him. Perhaps he'd jumped off the train again. Perhaps they'd pushed him out of the wagon.

Sometimes they could get out and stretch aching limbs, relieve themselves, fetch water from fast-melting streams and ponds. One day the engine gave a final shudder and a blast of its whistle and came to rest for good. Outside, a guard walked along the wagons, ordering them out.

'No more coal, the driver's abandoned the engine. He's walking up the tracks to the town.'

'Which town?'

'Don't know.'

'Where are we?'

'Don't know.' The guard looked dazed. 'All the signs have gone from the stations.'

'I'm not moving.' The man next to Alix pulled his hat over his eyes and folded his arms. Two or three hours passed. The passengers rearranged bedding and possessions and tried to sleep. Alix woke to the sound of engines and made out the faint lights of trucks on the track beside the line. As they came closer she saw the red crosses on their sides. Nurses approached the train, calling out for volunteers to unload wounded soldiers from one of the wagons. Alix stood, winced as the blood ran into her legs and pain shot through her pelvis. She waited until the worst of it passed before clambering out of her own wagon. 'You there!' called a nurse to Alix, as she moved back to allow a young private with a head wound to pass. 'Come and hold up this drip.'

'Where are they going?' She followed the nurse to one of the trucks.

'We're taking them west to the Americans. We have special passes.'

Another hundred-odd miles nearer to the Rhineland, to Cousin Ulla's house where she, Mami and Lena had been supposed to take refuge.

'Better than just sitting here till it's all over.' The nurse gave Alix the ghost of a smile.

Progress was slow. On several occasions they had to stop to move burnt-out vehicles and bodies off the road. Abandoned suitcases spewed photographs, clothes and food. A dachshund sat obediently beside a hat-box. Alix learned not to

look at these lost possessions unless there was a hope of sal-
vaging food or blankets. Sometimes they saw worse things:
scores of wagons and tanks and carts crushed together, bodies
hanging out of them. A shard of metal, the size of Alix's arm,
impaling a horse's neck; the horse, improbably, still whinny-
ing and pawing the earth with a hoof until a young Wehrmacht
officer pulled out a revolver and shot it.

She screwed up her eyes against the dying sun and tipped
water into a soldier's mouth. 'Where are we?' His hand
clutched hers.

'I'll ask.'

'They won't know.' His hand relaxed its grip. She reck-
oned he'd be gone before dawn. They'd carry his body into
a village graveyard and mutter a brief prayer. The Russians
were already in the village a few miles behind them and their
gunfire cracked in the dark. Frontline troops. The nurses muttered. Alix pulled the white apron they'd given her when
she'd joined them tightly around her body and said nothing.
When they stopped again to repair a flat tyre she found herself staring at a hoarding on the side of the road. 'It is thanks
to our Führer!'

When the Russians overtook the ambulances they threw
the nurses bread and sausage. 'Well, there you are,' said one
of the women. 'All that talk about Soviet atrocities, it was all
exaggeration.'

Alix tightened a bandage round a conscript's temples. Her
fingers shook and she dropped the pin she needed to fasten
it.

*

As quickly as they'd appeared the frontline troops vanished and in their place came regulars, accompanied by shaggy little ponies pulling supply carts called panje-wagons. Some of the soldiers had Mongolian features and dark skins and brought with them the miasma of thousands of miles on foot without adequate water and sanitation. Alix tried not to make eye contact. They gave food to any children they encountered but at night their kindness seemed to evaporate. The nurses learned to disguise themselves in men's clothes or hide under their vehicles. Sometimes Alix put her fingers into her ears to block out the sobs of women who hadn't concealed themselves well enough. An occasional stabbing pain from her pelvis would cause her to bite her lip, but most of the time she could ignore her body and concentrate on fetching water for men with fevers or scavenging clean rags to tie round wounds. Thank God she'd come away with the nurses – there was no time to think while she helped them. She kept her eyes on her patients no matter what they passed on the side of the road: a small dead child or, once, a nun, lying face-down and crumpled, like a shot and bloodied white stork, her stained habit and veil rising and falling in the breeze.

The convoy reached the Elbe and they unloaded the soldiers onto stretchers to ferry them across the river. Beside the banks stood hundreds of women, old people and children, clutching bundles and staring at the barges with intent. As they neared, the refugees surged towards the water and the Americans fired shots above their heads. 'No civilians,' called a sergeant. 'Uncle Joe's orders, wounded soldiers only.'

But still the civilians ran towards the barges, dragging

their children with them. The GIs jumped out and formed a cordon.

Alix stood back as the last soldier was loaded on. '*Schnell*,' urged a doctor. 'Last chance to get across. We only have until this evening.'

She glanced back at the crowd on the bank.

'The place in this boat is for you, Red Cross, *schnell!*'

'I'm not Red Cross, I only helped so I could get away from the Russians.'

'You've changed dressings and emptied bedpans for days now. You've written letters for dying men and helped bury them.' He grabbed her hand and pulled her towards the boat. 'I order you to stay with your patients, *Fräulein*. You're too good to leave to the Ivans.'

On the other side of the river they unloaded the soldiers into trucks which would transport them to a military hospital under American control in Magdeburg. Once this had been done Alix showered and washed her clothes. The Americans fed her, but when her clothes had dried they sent her on. 'No food for civilians, missy, but count yourself lucky to be in the US zone.'

It was hard to see how this luck would materialize. She wandered outside into the spring sunshine feeling scrubbed and almost naked without the layers of grime she'd acquired in the last weeks. For the rest of the day she stayed in the ruined town, walking from one shattered street to another as though she were searching for something or someone. It was the first time she'd seen the results of heavy bombing close to hand. She'd passed through Stettin after she'd escaped from the forest but had no memory of seeing anything except the sought-after carriages of the train, one of the last, which had carried her south. Now she noted houses like collapsed cardboard boxes, buckled strips of metal, the stink of decay. They'd been so cut off in Pomerania; she'd had no idea.

At dusk Alix found herself back at the military hospital, like a stray with nowhere else to go. A GI with a black face and kind, dark eyes gave her a bar of chocolate and something called a Spam sandwich. A white sergeant came out of a building and stopped in his tracks when he heard Alix thanking the GI in English. 'Hey soldier! Any more fraternizing and I'll haul your sorry ass into solitary.'

Alix stood and started walking again. She walked until she'd left the town behind and spent the night in a barn.

Weeks passed. She took off her coat during the mild days and tied it round her waist. Some days she felt too weak with hunger to creep further west and lay in the sunshine for most of the day, hoping the rays would energize her. She ate beechnuts, or dug at dead horses whose carcasses might yield meat that wasn't quite rotten. And still she didn't let herself remember. Perhaps, if she kept on walking, the motion would excise all memories from her. She'd start again as Alix Matke, aged seventeen, without possessions, family ties, home or lover. Born in the ashes of downfall, baptized in the showers of the military hospital, fed by kindly GIs and sent out as a newborn into the unknown.

Twenty

May 1945

When spring had become so intense a presence that it almost seemed to be mocking the world with its insistent birdsong and fierce bursts of blossom, a middle-aged woman at a water pump told Alix that Hitler was dead and the war was over.

'Dead?' The bottle in Alix's hands shook and water ran onto her boots. She instinctively looked over her shoulder in case someone was listening.

'Don't look so scared. He's gone, they all have.'

And Papi: this might mean that someone, somewhere, was unlocking a cell and letting him out. She couldn't think about her father, didn't have the energy for hope. Better to continue as this new Alix, untied to the past, unencumbered by optimism. She'd learned how to let her consciousness float above her when necessary, just as she had when the conscript had grabbed her in the forest that morning four months ago. *Here is Alix*, she'd tell herself. *With hands blistered from digging graves for dead soldiers. And here she is again, this time with*

her stomach filled with acid because she hasn't eaten and her
hands shaking so much she can't do up her shirt buttons. I
note all these things about Alix and I pity her.

She filled her bottle and carried on walking. Ahead of her
American soldiers danced in the road to the jazz music they
loved. 'Cheer up, *Fräulein*!' a GI called to her. 'No more fighting now.'

The countryside grew steeper. Alix turned slightly to the
south, into the hills and forests lying to the east of the
Rhineland where the unknown Cousin Ulla lived.

Still a long walk to go – two hundred or more kilometres.
But she kept going, surprised at how far she could walk in a
day if she allowed herself to retreat into semi-consciousness.
Apart from Gregor there was nothing worth thinking about,
anyway. Sometimes Papi accompanied her for a kilometre or
two, telling her that she ought to be grateful to him for insist-
ing she keep her boots in good condition, before springing
onto a glossy-coated Piper, waving a casual farewell. Or Lena
would walk beside her, muttering at Alix to keep her shoulders back and remember she was a girl from a good family.
*We can't all be like your mother but we can work on our car-
riage.*

Alix had reached the Thuringian Forest south of Erfurt when
she noticed the signs warning people not to travel. She spent
a night in a burned-out shepherd's hut, hoping the soldiers on
the road would move on, but by morning they still strolled
around barricades, inspecting papers and interrogating civilians.

'I'm going to my cousin's,' she volunteered in English.

'Not now you're not, *Fräulein*. Orders are all of you are spending time in a camp. Diseases.' The soldier shoved her papers back at her. 'Gotta stop 'em spreading.' Alix looked for an escape route but armed guards stood round the barricade. She allowed herself to be pushed into an open-topped truck.

The displaced persons camp wasn't a bad place: meals were regular, if sparse, and there were showers. But some of the women who'd trudged here from the east were slipping out of the huts at night to tie ropes around their necks. Some of them even evaded the guards and walked to the millpond in the neighbouring village, where they waded into the water until it dragged them down and relieved them of their worries. Most mornings there were two or three floating there. Others who couldn't bring themselves to give up on life were swelling like she was.

Alix forced herself to work out dates. Four months. But she couldn't be entirely certain. Starvation could make your abdomen swell, you only had to look at the children in this camp. Perhaps her symptoms were just those of exhaustion and trauma. She tried to drift back into her detached state, to watch herself dispassionately again, but something was pulling at her, forcing her back into her body, determined that she should feel life again: the growling of an underfed stomach, the itching of skin that bugs had bitten, the sour smell of clothes that could never be washed often enough. She tried to resist the pull – it was easier to stay in her twilight state, less painful, less demanding – but it was no use. Her body, that hungry, tired, grubby body of hers, demanded she pay it attention.

One morning in the queue for water a woman touched her arm. 'You came from the east, didn't you?'

Alix made a slight movement of her head.

'It's all right. I can see you're in the same condition as me.' Alix saw how the woman's abdomen pushed against her dress. She hunched her shoulders to try and hide her own swelling. 'You're not married are you? Me neither. Those Russian dogs.'

Alix nodded. No more explanations needed.

'Pity we didn't get here earlier.' The woman leaned towards her. 'A doctor gave some of the others something to take.' She dropped her voice. 'You know the Russians are coming here, too, don't you?'

Alix's heart thumped against her ribs. 'But this is American territory, they—'

'It was all agreed with Churchill and Stalin.'

'How do you know all this?'

The woman lowered her voice. Old habits. 'My brother had a job which meant he could travel to Sweden. He read foreign newspapers. The Russians are to occupy this part of the country. The Americans will move out.'

'When?'

'July.' The woman was speaking so softly Alix could barely hear her. 'Get out of here before then. Go farther west.' Again her eyes dropped to Alix's abdomen. 'You and I have had enough of them.'

Alix shuffled off. Next morning she swapped her breeches and shirt for a navy and white polka-dot tea-dress that covered her stomach. It looked a bit like the kind of thing Mami might have worn to entertain guests before the war. If you didn't look at the boots she wore with it and the coat she still draped round her shoulders when the sun went in and the air chilled.

The camp guards were distracted by a disturbance in the shower block and Alix slipped under the barriers. Late June now. The first berries would be ripening in the gardens at home. She walked with more purpose than she had before. But she wasn't heading to her cousin's house. She was following some instinct that sent her where she wouldn't be known, where she had no connections; away from the Russians. *Coburg.* Names from Papi's map floated through her memory. That wasn't far enough west. The Russians might still reach her. She needed to walk farther, to hide herself away. Perhaps she could find a job somewhere until the child was born. And then . . .? Her mind refused to imagine what would happen. Perhaps she'd lose the baby. If she worked very hard at some physical task, to the point of exhaustion, she might miscarry. But it was probably too late for that now. She set her gaze on the road ahead, letting her mind fall into a trance.

It was only when the car came up so close behind her on the bend that she could smell its hot metal, rubber and petrol aroma that she leapt into the ditch at the side of the road. Behind her brakes screeched. Someone shouted. Alix rose to her feet, brushing dust from her dress. Her rucksack lay in the road, squashed. She stared at it.

A man and woman, both in a uniform she didn't recognize, came towards her. She froze.

'*Sprechen Sie Englisch?* You hurt?'

'No, I'm fine,' she replied in English, forcing herself to meet the American man's stare. If he was going to punish her for carelessness, so be it, but Alexandra von Matke wasn't going to cower. Then she reminded herself that she was just Alix Matke, defeated civilian. 'I am sorry for causing an accident,' she said.

'We drove over your bag,' the woman said. 'Sorry. Couldn't help it.'

'Could have been *her* we drove over.' The man folded his arms. 'What were you thinking of, walking down the middle of the road on a blind corner in a daydream?'

Alix couldn't think of an answer.

'Joseph,' said the woman. 'Don't harass the poor girl.'

'Post-defeat trauma, that's what I call this.' His voice was thoughtful. 'Classic symptoms. Interesting how many civilians are involved in motor accidents. They just can't concentrate properly.' He approached her. 'Are you sure you're OK? In your condition . . .'

Alix put a hand to her abdomen. Funny, a week or two ago this would have seemed like the perfect solution. She felt the baby move. 'I think it will be all right.'

'Can we give you a ride anywhere?'

'Civilians aren't allowed to use private transport,' Alix answered, still in English, unable to resist a small, self-mocking smirk at her Germanic adherence to rules, no matter how inconvenient.

'We know the patrols on this stretch, they're OK. Where

you headed?' The woman pushed open the passenger door. Alix struggled to understand her rapid, accented English.

'Frankfurt.' She named the first place that came into her head.

'That's a long way,' said the man.

'And you're heading a strange way to get there,' the woman added.

'Anyway, Frankfurt's a mess,' said the man, handing her the squashed rucksack. 'We're on our way to Hammersdorf, a little village ten miles from the city.'

'We're child welfare officers, working at one of the DP camps.' The woman scrutinized Alix, perhaps interested to see how she'd respond. Alix met the gaze and nodded.

'You got family in Frankfurt?' asked the man.

'No.'

'Friends?'

'No.'

'There you go, pestering her again, Joseph!'

'It's all right, really,' Alix said. They could ask her whatever they wanted, couldn't they? They were occupiers. But they didn't seem like unkind people.

He frowned at her. 'No offence, *Fräulein*, but you're alone, you're expecting a baby and you haven't got a ring. And you speak English like your nanny used to push you round Kensington Gardens in your perambulator.'

The woman slapped his arm.

Alix waited.

'We'll need help in the house.' She saw his eyes were gentle. 'Someone to do light housework and cooking.'

'I ran my father's farm before the Russians came.'

'The Russians.' He frowned. 'Thought so. We can't pay much but money's worthless anyway and you'll have board and lodgings.'

'But—' She put a hand to her belly.

'We'll be able to help, we work for UNRRA – the United Nations Relief and Rehabilitation Administration. You heard of us?'

Alix shook her head and climbed into the car, which appeared to be an Opel. Alix hadn't seen one of these on the roads for years. 'You don't know who I am. Why do you want to help me?'

He shrugged. 'We've interviewed a few girls. Mostly they just look sullen. Mention what their country's been up to over the last seven years or so and they go all defensive or claim ignorance.'

'Then they're fools.' Her voice sounded harsh. She re-membered what Papi had said, what he'd left unsaid, before he was arrested.

He nodded at his wife. 'See? She's honest. An honest German.' He sounded amazed.

'Thank you.' There didn't seem any more to say. She slumped back in the Opel wondering if she was the first person in the family to take a maid's job and what Aunt Friederika would have said. Under her fingers she could make out the shape of Gregor's mouth organ in her dress pocket.

The work was light compared with what she'd done at home on the farm. Each morning, after she'd cooked their break-fast, the Whites would drive to the displaced persons camp where they worked with orphans, writing reports on their condition and arranging for those who had homes to return to them. Joseph White had been a psychologist in New York, he told Alix. His area of expertise was assessing children. Now he was trying to help the more traumatized before they left the camp. Emily had been a children's nurse in Philadelphia.

While they were at work Alix would clear the table, wash dishes and make beds. Then she had time to do her own laundry – they'd given her a couple of maternity smocks – read and rest. 'If you want to write letters, I'll help you get them delivered,' Joseph told her. 'I know it's hard making contact with family right now.'

She'd nodded and said nothing.

Later in the morning she'd pick currants or raspberries and collect eggs from the hens, trying not to remember how she'd done these things at home with Mami, Jana and Lena. The laundry van delivered clean sheets, smelling of unfamiliar American detergent and hot metal. Alix remembered how Lena used to hang their washed sheets on a line by the rosemary and lavender bushes in the kitchen garden so they'd bring the scent of summer into the bedrooms.

A young man the Whites called Frank, who spoke English with an accent Alix could barely understand, drove meat supplies to the house two or three times a week: tins of pork, veal cutlets, once or twice even a fresh chicken. Alix stared at the food, which apparently she would be allowed to share. 'Second trimester; calories are important now.' Joseph nodded at her stomach as she laid the table for lunch. 'Red meat, vegetables and fruit—' She must have made a sound expressing her amazement. 'What's so funny?'

'Most Germans don't know what red meat looks like any more.'

'Most Germans don't *deserve* to know.' He peered at her. 'Heard any more about your father?' She'd told him about Papi and he'd helped her send enquiries to the Red Cross.

'Nothing.'

'That's too bad. What your father did was remarkable.'

'They didn't accomplish very much.' She tried to keep the tremor out of her voice. 'All they had to do was detonate a bomb in a briefcase and kill one evil monster. It might have ended the war. Then some of them were *stupid* enough to write down the names of those involved.' She put a hand to her mouth.

'But they nearly managed, you know. Even without killing him. There nearly was a coup.'

'Nearly wasn't good enough.' She, a von Matke, was going to lose control, here, among strangers. She struggled with the flood of anger and grief which threatened her.

He pulled out a chair for himself and motioned to her to sit at the table as well.

'You resent your father for not succeeding?' His eyes were soft but Alix observed a cool flicker of professional interest in them.

'My father wasn't a practical man. He could start things but never finish them.' She told Joseph about the clocks, how Papi used to open them up to mend them and find he couldn't always replace all the parts. 'Some of the other conspirators seem to have had the same problem – they couldn't complete what they'd started.' Mami hadn't told her much about the reasons for the failure of the plot. Perhaps she hadn't known much herself. They'd pieced some of the story together by listening to the radio broadcasts and reading between the lines. 'The signals people didn't even know what was going on. They could have succeeded if they'd organized it better.'

Joseph leaned forward and touched her hand. 'He was brave, Alix. Remember that.'

'I'm trying to.'

'What was his role?'

'Mami thought he'd made telephone calls to senior officers on the day of the attempt, persuading them not to oppose the coup.'

'Just being on a list somewhere would have been enough to condemn him,' Joseph said. 'And the rest of your family? Your mother? What happened to her?'

She shrugged. She wasn't going to tell him about that last evening and morning in Alexanderhof. Besides, she tried not to think about Mami. Every time someone came to the door her heart thumped, half in terror it would be her, half in longing. At least by the time Mami found her, if she ever did, the baby would probably have been born and sent off to a good family in America. Alix had no intention of talking about Mami to Joseph White. He'd use his professional tricks to expose all those memories Alix was trying so hard to bury. She'd avoid Joseph from now on. He was dangerous.

And so was his wife. Emily White watched Alix clear the lunch table. 'You're blooming. I bet it's a boy. They say boys make pregnant women look even more beautiful.' A look Alix couldn't interpret passed over Emily's plump cheeks.

Alix couldn't work out how old Emily was – early thirties? Joseph looked older, perhaps the same age as Mami.

Alix stacked the cutlery on top of the plates. 'Boy or girl, it's all the same to me. I'll give it up.'

'And yet you didn't . . . You weren't tempted to do something to stop the pregnancy?'

Alix stared at her. 'No, it never crossed my mind.'

Americans were very free with their questions. Strange to talk about things so openly after years of being told to watch your tongue.

'You never talk about what happened. With the soldier.' Emily's voice was gentle. 'It might help. That's what Joseph does with some of those children, you know. He tries to get them to talk.'

Alix placed the pile of plates on the tray.

'You know you can trust me, don't you, honey?'

She nodded and picked up the tray.

'You must have been so frightened.'

The tray shook and a salt cellar toppled off. 'I'm sorry.' Alix put the tray back on the table.

Emily steered her to a chair. 'Tell me.'

'I don't remember.' She'd locked the memory up so securely sometimes she thought she'd never remember any of it. Except for handing over her watch, the Patek Philippe her father had given her for her birthday and which she'd worn every day until it had been taken from her in the forest by a man who thought that she and everything she owned were his.

Twenty-one

Pomerania, February 1945

Where are you, Gregor? She ran on through the forest, past
the spot where she'd hidden from the Russians yesterday
when the wagon had been hit. Every now and then she slowed
to listen out for Gregor. He was taking so long. The
snowflakes fell less thickly now and the light was turning
grey; Pomeranian fog sweeping in from the Baltic.

A tree rustled. A pair of eyes was watching her, Asiatic
eyes, slanted, amused. He stood on the other side of the track
wearing a blue scarf with his filthy uniform. Alix stared back.
For a second neither made a sound. Then another figure and
another joined the first man. They looked at each other and
laughed. Even at this distance Alix could smell stale urine and
unwashed clothes. For whole seconds she stared at them.

'*Uhri*.' The first soldier pointed at his wrist.

Then she was running like she'd never run in her life but
finding it hard to build up any speed in the knee-deep snow.
Each breath tore her lungs. She ran until her heart seemed

about to burst and she had to stop. She crouched by a beech tree. Behind it the ground dipped into a snow-filled hollow. Her best hope. She threw herself into the dip, shovelling snow onto her legs and torso and covering her face with leaves. The fog would help hide her but if they came close they'd see her. She lay motionless, heart racing, too scared even to pray.

Voices came towards her. It sounded like Russian but might have been some other Soviet language. Whatever it was she knew they were describing what they wanted to do to her: the hunger in their words was obvious. Closer now. A twig cracked and she held her breath. A pheasant coughed. Alix counted. When she reached two hundred she lifted her head, letting the leaves tumble off, so she could peer round the beech. She saw them shuffle away, arms round one another's shoulders. Alix stayed where she was and counted again.

A bottle smashed against a tree trunk; then another.

She let out a long breath. The mist cooled the perspiration on her brow but her tongue was swollen with thirst. In the rucksack there was a glass bottle of water. Still she waited, rubbing her leg muscles. Papi used to tell her stories about ancient people living deep in the forests, worshipping tree spirits and repelling even the Roman army. Swedes, Poles, Prussians, French, Russians, the trees had seen them all come and go, sheltering generations of women.

Alix took off her rucksack and pulled out the bottle, almost weeping as liquid ran down her dry throat. She stood and brushed snow from her coat. The fog hung round the trees like a grey veil.

As she stepped onto the path, a reddened, calloused palm

clasped her mouth from behind without a sound. Coarse wool scratched her cheek. She gagged at the reek of him.

'*Uhri!*' He jabbed at the Patek Philippe. She tugged it off with her right hand and passed it over her shoulder to him. He spun her round to face him and held the watch in front of her, grinning. She turned, hoping that she could sprint for the trees, but as though reading her mind he grabbed her arm with his free hand. A wave of his gun showed her what would happen if she tried to run away again. He tried to fasten her watch on his wrist but the strap wasn't long enough. He scowled at the watch, before stuffing it into a pocket. Perhaps he'd swap it with a comrade. He let go of her arm and offered her a vodka bottle.

'No.' She stepped back but he shoved the bottle at her. 'You, drink.' And she took it, tipping it up and letting the vodka brush her lips.

'Please.' If only she'd studied Russian instead of French and English, hopeless, useless languages.

He grabbed back his bottle and emptied it in a single gulp. Alix twisted round. Again she wasn't quick enough. He grabbed her by the hair. 'You *stay*.' He pointed at the ground. 'There.'

'No, *bitte*.' Her heart would surely burst out of her mouth.

He pushed her down onto the snow. She felt the coldness penetrate the back of her breeches. He was tugging at his own trousers with one hand, in an instant the other was round her throat, threatening to throttle her if she moved. Alix looked up and saw the silver-frosted bough of a birch tree above her, back-lit through the mist by the sun's ruby early morning rays. He was tugging at the belt of her breeches now. She knew what she had to do. Come what may, she had to keep looking up at that silver branch. It had to fill her mind, her world. From now on her body was just a husk; the real Alix would float above it to the sanctity of the tree, untouched by what was happening on the cold earth. All of this flashed through her mind, as though other women were calling up through the generations to help her. This scene had been enacted in these forests so many times in the past: soldiers speaking many languages but always the women pinned to the ground, bile in their mouths, lying in their own urine as they shivered and pleaded. She was just one in a pattern going back centuries.

He was cursing to himself, apparently incapable of completing the act. His sour smell filled her senses. He released the hand round her neck and picked up his vodka bottle, gazing at it as the idea took shape in his mind. 'You still now.' The bottle moved down her body.

The silver bough waved at her gently, as though promising it would not abandon her.

Twenty-two

Near Frankfurt, October 1945

Emily waited outside the room while the doctor, a young man from Milwaukee, examined Alix with a grave face, asking her questions in a low voice. Had Joseph White filled him in on Papi's role in the Bomb Plot? He stood up. 'You sustained some tissue damage when you were, er . . .'

'He stuck a bottle . . . into me . . . because he'd drunk a lot of vodka and didn't seem able to manage anything else. Then he smashed the bottle and cut me.' She showed him the mark on her upper wrist.

'Thank God he didn't use the broken bottle on you.'

'After that, fortunately, he passed out before he could do me any more harm.' She'd had eight months to rehearse a way of explaining what had happened and was surprised how matter-of-fact she sounded.

The doctor swallowed. 'So the baby . . .?' He looked down at his notes. 'I see.' He'd have noted that she wore no ring on her finger. 'You were lucky there seems to be no infection, just inflammation.' He washed his hands in the little sink. 'I suppose I could give you penicillin, just in case, but it'll be safer to wait until after you've delivered.'

Delivered. As though the baby were an eagerly awaited parcel.

Alix spent hours in the Whites' library, reading the books the German owners had left behind when the Americans requisitioned the house. In the long afternoons there was little else to do after all the washing, ironing and mending was finished and it was too early to start supper.

She found herself wandering through the empty rooms, staring at family photographs, wondering where all those people were now. Sometimes she'd sit for hours clasping Gregor's mouth organ, touching its worn metal surface. She became greedy for contact with the outside world. She chatted to Frank the driver, asking him if he'd heard news from the east. When would the Russians leave? What was this about a wonder weapon? Frank had regarded her with suspicion at first, but as weeks passed and her English became more fluent he started to talk back. 'You speak real good American,' he told her once as he brought in bags of flour and sugar.

'Thanks, I'd like to teach it some day.' She stopped, surprised. The idea seemed to have come from nowhere.

The labour pains caught her as she poured water at the lunch table. The jug crashed to the floor, water cascading over the parquet floor and reminding her – even then – of a white porcelain coffee cup smashing on another floor in another world.

'I'll fetch the doctor.' Joseph White jumped up, pulling his jacket off the back of the chair. She shook her head.

'It might take ages yet.'

There was a quarter-of-an-hour lull, during which she sat in the kitchen, sipping a glass of water and then pacing up and down, counting the floor tiles between the range and the kitchen table. So far from home. So far away from anyone who knew what had happened to her. 'Gregor,' she whispered. 'Where are you? We need you.'

We. This unwanted fellow traveller had somehow assumed a place in her life.

When the pains came in ten-minute intervals she allowed Emily to take her upstairs. 'You're young,' Emily told her. 'You'll do fine. Concentrate on your breathing.' Emily's sister was a midwife; her mother, too. Emily knew about these things, knew to keep Alix's lips moist and to let her walk around between contractions while she still could. Knew when to reassure, when to cajole, when to order. 'You can scream,' she told Alix. 'If it helps, just bellow, honey.'

But Alix knew the von Matkes didn't scream. They were brave in battle, when tortured in some Gestapo cell, when pinned to the snowy ground by a Russian conscript. Alexandra von Matke was a Prussian officer's daughter and she would act like one.

Twenty-three

They laid the child in her arms with some reluctance. His eyes were almost violet, not the usual baby blue. The baby's hair was dark, though Emily said it might fall out and be replaced with fairer down. Alix looked at him and knew he'd been himself from the moment of his conception, in her bedroom at home, while a wolf prowled outside. Her hands tightened on her sheet.

Emily sat down on the edge of the bed. 'Who's Gregor?'

'How did you . . .?'

'You were calling for him.'

'A family friend.'

Emily looked from the child to Alix. 'The Russian soldier. I thought . . .'

So the doctor at the base hadn't passed on to the Whites what Alix had told him. He'd been as kind as he looked. Or perhaps too embarrassed by the whole situation to wish to involve himself in matters of paternity.

'The Russian isn't his father.' She looked down at her son. 'He was too drunk.'

'How can you be sure?'

Alix stared at the infant. 'I just know.'

Emily stood up. 'I see. That changes things.' Alix saw something in her face she couldn't understand. Not unkindness, not exactly, but a new coolness, as though Alix had let her down. Well, she had let them all down, hadn't she? Mother of a bastard child. Her head throbbed. She longed to be alone with the baby; he was the only one who mattered. Emily stood.

'Try and feed him.' She muttered something to Joseph, who was standing in the doorway.

Alix dropped her head to the baby. He eyed her with those vivid eyes of his and seemed to sigh, his head heavy in the crook of her arm.

The doctor returned and examined her again. 'I'm pleased to say that you seem to have managed very well.' He swallowed. 'You should be able to undergo another pregnancy despite the damage. If you ever marry, that is.' His voice contained a note of doubt.

'It doesn't seem likely.' She turned her face to the wall.

'You never know. Some men don't mind as much as others about previous . . . encounters and, well, the consequences. Especially in wartime.'

Alix nodded.

Emily saw the doctor downstairs and returned alone. 'Does this change how you feel about the baby?' Her face was pale.

'What do you mean?'

'The doctor says you can still have other children.' The

old Alix would have felt indignant that they had discussed her health so freely behind her back, but what was she but a defeated enemy? 'So you might be more likely to . . .'

'To what?'

'To let him go to a good family.' Emily twisted her hands as she peeped at the baby. 'But this isn't the time for talking about this.'

'It doesn't change a thing.' Alix closed her eyes to blot out her view of the cot. When she'd fed him last night he'd stared at her with his violet eyes. She'd tried to look away but found she couldn't.

'Alix . . . we were wondering . . .' Emily was gabbling. 'Joseph and I can't have children.'

'You told me. I'm very sorry.' Alix knew how the Whites regretted their childlessness.

'Your baby – it seems so hard to send him to strangers.'

'You do it every day.' She hadn't meant to sound so curt.

Emily looked away briefly. 'Some of the DP children have absolutely no family or friends left.' The older woman put a hand on her arm. 'Would you consider letting us adopt him? He'd grow up in the States. We can give him a wonderful home and we'd care for him so well, believe me, Alix. We already love him.'

Alix had seen them: Emily cradling the baby, Joseph sitting beside her prattling to him. Tens of thousands of German mothers in her position would have jumped at the chance.

'It would be better for him.' Emily's grasp on Alix's arm tightened.

The grandfather clock on the landing struck the half-hour. Alix shivered.

Twenty-four

Gregor
Pomerania, February 1945

Vavilov and Gregor opened the bedroom door. Empty. They stared at the scarves and scissors on the carpet.

Marie. She must have crept back up here while they were examining the objects in the salon. Time enough for her to turn the key in the lock and release Preizler.

In an instant Vavilov had removed his revolver from its holster. Gregor darted to the window. Across the snow he made out two figures, a man and a woman. 'They're making for the forest.'

Vavilov's hand clasped his arm. 'Not so fast, Comrade.'

'They'll get away—'

'The regulars are on the way. He won't get far. You said "they". Who else is out there?'

Gregor made himself meet the amber eyes. 'I believe it's the baroness. She must have returned to the house.'

'Nobody else?'

'No.'

Vavilov let him go and walked towards the dressing table. He picked up one of the photos showing Marie with an infant Alix. 'I wonder how she got in here without you seeing her. You locked the doors last night, did you not?'

Gregor nodded. Vavilov sounded calm. But the key left in the lock, the two escapees. Such carelessness could merit a death sentence.

'Perhaps she was already inside last night? In a cellar or attic, perhaps?' Vavilov sounded as though he were trying to solve some parlour-game riddle. Gregor had heard him employ the same relaxed tones with captured landowners he was about to interrogate. He longed to put his hand into his pack and touch the cyanide capsules in their tattered enve-lope, just to be sure they were still there.

Shouts from the front of the house broke the tension. 'Here are our comrades. Shall we let them in?' A note of irony in Vavilov's voice now. 'You can brief them about the dan-gerous political prisoners and they will track them down for us.'

The conscripts had already pushed their way up the steps to the front door by the time Gregor and Vavilov came down-stairs. 'All right.' Vavilov looked at the watch he'd had since Gregor had known him. 'One hour to take what you can.' Something had flattened his tone, disapproval, perhaps? But of whom? The soldiers? Gregor? The Junkers who'd owned Alexanderhof and its contents? 'But you five,' he pointed at a group. 'Are to go into the forest immediately and catch a middle-aged woman and her companion, a senior Fascist police officer in plain clothes. There'll be extra soup if you bring them back here alive.'

The five selected did as they were told. Gregor heard their boots crunching through the snow as they ran for the trees.

The others came inside, eyes glinting. Down in the cellars they'd find the best vintages from Bordeaux, Burgundy and the Moselle, collected over a hundred years and recorded in a black leather book by Peter, his father and grandfather. Peter had also laid down a case of vintage port when Alix was born, in the English fashion. She'd been supposed to receive the bottles on her wedding day. Gregor watched as the conscripts ran below the antlers in the entrance hall, boots dripping snow over the marble floor, some of them pausing to blink at the chandelier and the grandfather clock. One of them turned towards Gregor and Vavilov. 'If they had so much themselves, why did they come to drive us out of our homes?'

'Well expressed, Comrade,' Vavilov answered. 'Now get on with it.' He glanced at Gregor. 'Talking of things taken, you'd better give me that gun you took from your prisoner.'

The men's excitement grew even greater with the discovery of Marie's lingerie drawer: confections of silk and lace the like of which they'd never seen and that seemed to fuel their conviction that German women were whores, and probably glad of the attentions of the Red Army. Their pillaging of the salon only took off when they'd slashed Great Aunt Friederika's portrait, claiming she was a witch and would put spells on them. Even as the knife tore the canvas round her face Friederika seemed to glare down at Gregor, as though asking him who on earth had allowed these Russians into her house. When she lay in tatters on the Persian rug a cheer went up and they enjoyed a celebratory smash of the Meissen ornaments Marie had left in the glass cabinet. Gregor left them to see what was happening upstairs.

They hadn't reached the maids' rooms in the attic where Gregor suspected Marie would have stored the particularly valuable china and jewels, along with the missing gramophone records. They'd wasted too much time trying to detach the clock from the landing wall. Their failure had engendered so much rage Gregor thought they'd smash the glass, but then someone shouted out that they'd found a room full of kids' stuff. *Alix's room.* They emptied the chest of drawers and took armfuls of her clothes downstairs. Her silver photo frames were valuable but the photographs themselves good only for throwing out of the window, where they fluttered down to the flowerbeds with the snowflakes. Her books made satisfying thumps as they fell the same way.

And to make it quite clear what they thought about people like this, two of them used her bed as a latrine.

Gregor felt a heaviness in his stomach. Several times his mouth opened to shriek at them to stop. But he couldn't. He knew what had happened to their own villages in Russia, houses burned with or without their occupants in them, women driven out into the snow with their children. People starved, shot, tormented.

When they'd finished in Alix's room he cleared up the worst of it and stood for a moment studying the emptied bookshelves, smashed ornaments and disembowelled soft toys. Then he went to find Vavilov. He might as well face him.

The cyanide was now in his tunic pocket, easily accessible. Best to know the worst. The five men who'd gone out into the forest still hadn't returned with Preizler and the baroness. Perhaps they'd shot them despite Vavilov's orders.

He found his superior in Peter's study, examining papers he'd taken from the filing cabinet. 'Not much here.' Vavilov snapped shut a roll-lever file. Propped up against the side of the desk was a photograph album. Vavilov must have found it in the salon.

Gregor peered at the documents spread over the desktop – farm invoices and receipts.

'I saw a threshing machine and tractor in one of the sheds,' Vavilov said. 'Nice equipment.'

Vavilov never missed anything.

'Have you had any more thoughts as to how long the baroness had been in the house?' he went on.

'Hard to be sure exactly, Comrade Vavilov.'

The older man's slow stare seemed to penetrate Gregor's mind. 'Tell me something, Comrade.'

Gregor willed the muscles of his face into inscrutability.

'There are four used coffee cups in the kitchen. You didn't have company last night, did you? Apart from the Gestapo officer, I mean.'

'The family must have drunk it before they left.' Gregor couldn't find the steel to tell Vavilov another direct lie. But dodging the question could be just as bad for him.

'Perhaps they had connections with the SS base we over-ran a few days ago.' Vavilov squared a pile of papers on the desk. 'We found the packet of coffee in the kitchen with the stamped label.'

He dropped his head to study the sheet on top of the pile, a list of grain yields. 'Amazing how efficiently the Germans farm their land. Even with all our plans we don't seem to match these percentages.'

Gregor repressed a shiver. Dangerous statements to make.

'When we get to Berlin we can see who's still around.' Vavilov scooped up the sheets. He didn't look disappointed that his search had yielded no results. He pushed them to one side and picked up the photograph album, flicking through the yellowing leaves. Gregor tried to retain a blank expression as pictures of himself and Alix, Marie and Peter, and his parents passed beneath Vavilov's fingers. Vavilov lingered over a photograph of Marie and Eva dressed for tennis.

A shriek outside in the kitchen garden pierced the silence. Vavilov frowned. 'Have they found someone?'

Not Alix, please God, not her. Or her mother. Let it be some other unfortunate female.

Gregor ran to the garden and shouted for order. When the throng dispersed he found it wasn't a woman they were fighting over but the tabby cat. 'We've got no food for cats, it'll just die,' he told them. 'You know Comrade Vavilov's fondness for animals, he will wish you to leave it here.' The soldier with the Asiatic eyes clutched the tabby even closer.

'And it might have been infected with a disease.' The conscripts had been fed so much propaganda about what they could expect from the Germans that they'd believe anything, even that the Nazis had injected domestic pets with germs. The soldier dropped the tabby, which shot into the stable, miaowing in protest. Gregor couldn't begin to explain to himself why he'd wanted to save the wretched animal: what was one cat? When he was back in that hulk on the way to Magadan, it would merit him nothing that he'd saved a single cat instead of the girl he loved. *Loved*. The word seemed to burn through his body. Alix, so long unseen, so suddenly rediscovered, his love, his link to the old world of meals served on linen-covered tables, arguments about books and houses filled with cut flowers.

The conscripts returned to the important work of loading up their plundered goods. Vavilov met Gregor at the bootroom door. 'You seem very at ease in this house, Smolinsky.'

'We've seen many similar properties since we entered German territory. I've got to know how they're laid out.'

'A shame you didn't use your knowledge to secure your prisoner.' Vavilov reached up and stroked one of the antlers on the wall. 'You're right though, these places are all fairly similar: the big entrance hall with the principal rooms opening off it, the grand staircase. Shame there won't be many of them left by the time our troops have finished.'

They'd already burned many of the old houses and blown up others. Gregor didn't rate the chances of this one surviving. 'Let's take a walk outside,' Vavilov went on. He'd already put on his coat and gloves and gave the air of one planning a stroll in a fashionable Alpine resort.

Gregor looked up at the white walls. You couldn't call it a beautiful building but its clean lines gave the house symmetry and a pleasing grace. As though reading his mind, one of the soldiers pulled a stone off the terrace wall and sent it flying through the salon window. The glass shattered but the shutter held fast. Built to last. Gregor remembered playing with Alix on the terrace in childhood summers. The grown-ups would drink their post-lunch coffees and talk theatre, politics and books. He and Alix would muck about in the fountain. Alix liked throwing in coins.

Vavilov was saying something. 'Sometimes one might almost imagine you were German yourself, Smolinsky, there's something about you. I can't pinpoint it but it's there.'

Gregor looked around. Nobody else in earshot. Not that it mattered. Suspicions like that could get him sent back east more quickly than you could spit, especially when connected to the escape of a dangerous political prisoner. Suspicions all the time, anyway, no matter what you did, or who you were. They'd deported a lieutenant last week because someone'd seen him reading an old French newspaper he'd found in an abandoned house.

'I am German.' The words seemed to fall out of Gregor's mouth. He was so damn tired, tired of it all, the deception, the shame, the despair and the even more dangerous moments of hope.

Vavilov stood back to examine the urn. His expression was as impenetrable as ever, but just for a second Gregor thought he'd seen a glimmer of surprise, almost of hurt.

'You were right when you asked me those questions in Kolyma. I lied to you. My name's Gregor Fischer. I was born in Berlin in 1927.' He was speaking rapidly now. 'My father is, or was, Matthias Fischer the publisher. My mother is, or was, Eva Mauer, the Viennese actress. They drove us out in 1938.' He felt like he imagined a Catholic would leaving the confessional box.

Vavilov said nothing for what must have been a full

minute. Then he turned very slowly and shouted at his driver to bring round the truck. 'We've finished here.'

He signalled to Gregor to sit behind him. As they skidded down the drive towards the main road Gregor would have liked to take a last look at the house but dared not. As they drove on through the last of the straggling line of German refugees, past the panje-wagons carrying food and water and the soldiers, always the trudging soldiers, Vavilov turned to stare at Gregor. Probably deciding what to do with him. Send him east? Shoot him? Keep him for some future unspecified purpose? Gregor felt for the cyanide capsules in his pocket.

If only he knew where Alix was now. He examined each group of women they passed, looking for a tall, thin girl with a blond plait.

'Very well, Fischer,' Vavilov said finally. 'Apart from this morning's carelessness your work has been good – German or whatever you are. You'll stay with me. For the moment you'll continue to call yourself Smolinsky.'

Gregor let out a breath. 'Thank you.'

The women they passed turned their heads to avoid eye-contact with Russians. Gregor felt the now-familiar coldness in his stomach. And he was no better. For all his professions of love, he'd taken advantage of a vulnerable girl, a friend, someone in his protection. He imagined the look on Peter's face if he discovered Gregor had seduced his only daughter. Shame heated his cheeks. *Alix, Alix, Alix*. Her name throbbed through his body.

On one of those nights when they'd sat together in a

requisitioned house in front of a fire, Vavilov had warned him not to expect any kind of private happiness for years. And Gregor had believed him. But then, only weeks after the fireside warning, Alix had emerged from the fur coats in the boot room and the feeble beam of his torch had illuminated that face, smudged, weary, defiant, but possessing something that had made him miss a breath. Her mother had been a beauty, acknowledged and treated as such. But Alix . . . her face that wasn't classically beautiful like her mother's but was even more heartbreaking because of its slight imperfections: a nose a little too long; a mouth a little too wide. Why? Why this woman? Because he'd known her as a child and associated her with comfort and warmth. But it was more than that; she'd mesmerized him.

No man could have resisted her after all those years in Kolyma, not even a saint.

He'd loosened her plait and pulled her hair round her body like a curtain. Then he'd swept it back like a conjuror to reveal her breasts and her long neck. The sight of her had been almost unbearable. Plunder. Not taken with force or threats, offered willingly, but plunder all the same. He was no different from the rest of the conscripts.

He remembered one of the first occasions he'd found himself under mortar attack, back in eastern Poland months ago. When the immediate danger had passed and he'd flopped, heart pounding, behind a shattered wall to rest, he'd found himself in a state of arousal. A civilian woman had passed him, huddling against what was left of the masonry, face black with ash and dirt, and his blood had raced at the sight of her begrimed female body. He'd felt simultaneously ashamed and elated. One of the medics had told him this was a normal physiological response to danger. Perhaps the male body sought to reproduce itself while it could, before the threat returned. Perhaps none of them could exercise free will or hope to act with any decency, let alone nobility; men were all just machines, driven by fear and hunger, just as Stalin believed.

The evening sun bathed the snowy countryside in crimson. On the road ahead of them a group of women staggered out of a hut, weeping, clutching bundles. Behind them strolled a couple of conscripts, grinning, adjusting their belts.

Gregor turned his head from the sight.

Twenty-five

Alix
Western Germany, March 1946

Alix wore the new shoes the Whites had given her for Christmas and the coat she'd brought with her from Pomerania, its rips darned and its buttons replaced. She almost looked like someone Mami would have recognized.

Emily White stood at the front gate, holding the baby – Michael, as they'd decided to call him. 'You've got our address back home?'

'Yes.'

'Write to us, tell us where you're living. I'll send photos.'

'Yes.'

She knew she wouldn't write.

'Make sure you don't lose those permits Joseph gave you and take care with the French, Alix. Some of them are . . . unforgiving.'

The Rhineland was under French occupation now.

'I will. Thank you.'

'No, we're the ones who should thank you. You've no idea what Michael means to us.'

Alix nodded. '*Auf Wiedersehen.*'

She got into the truck and didn't look round again as Frank took off the brake and they set off. Normally she enjoyed chatting to him; today she couldn't manage more than the occasional yes. 'Sure is hard for you to leave that baby,' he said at last. 'But the Whites are good folk. I've seen them with the DP kids; they've got hearts.'

'Why didn't they just adopt one of *those* children?' The words burst from Alix.

Frank blinked. 'They know you, they know about your dad – he was a hero, wasn't he? Perhaps that makes your kid special for them.'

'Perhaps.'

'Guess it's personal for me,' Frank went on. 'I was adopted. Worked out fine for me.' He broke off to negotiate a steep bend in the road. 'You done the right thing, honey.'

Alix looked out at the people they passed, old folk, boys and girls. Women in ragged clothes carrying babies, faces worn and grey, marching to some oppressive beat that kept them moving onward and onward.

What exactly *had* she done? She thought back again to that dance without music in the shuttered salon and trembled.

Part Three

Twenty-six

Marie
Vienna, 1925

Marie couldn't stop shivering at rehearsals for *Romeo and Juliet*. Her throat stung. Finally Georg, the director, sent her home, recommending honey and lemon gargles and an afternoon in bed. From the wings, dressed in the stiff robes of Lady Capulet, Eva watched her, inscrutable.

By the time Marie reached the apartment her temples throbbed and perspiration soaked her dress. She could barely pull the key out of her bag to unlock the door. She reached her bedroom and threw herself fully clothed onto her bed, too exhausted even to rifle for aspirin in the bathroom cabinet, and fell into a deep sleep.

When she woke, the shadows on the bedroom floor told her she'd slept until late evening. Last night's glass of water still sat on the bedside table. Marie drained it in a single draught and knew she had to have more. They kept a jug in the cool kitchen pantry. She had to pour herself another glass, she'd burn to ashes if she didn't. She rose, very slowly, pushed her feet into slippers and stumbled into the corridor. 'Eva?' No answer. As Marie passed the sitting-room door, the sound of movements reached her and she stopped outside, her feverish brain trying to grasp the image that confronted her. At first it seemed like one of the paintings she'd seen in a modernist exhibition: a jumble of unrelated shapes spelling out a message she couldn't interpret. The back of Viktor's head. His back. Eva's long legs and arms twined round him . . .

Eva was sitting in Viktor's lap, her face buried in his neck. A lock of her hair dangled loose over the chair's straight back. Eva made a sound like a cat's purr and Viktor answered it with a kind of exclamation and his back stiffened in response. They'd placed the straight-backed chair in front of a gilded mirror that usually hung above the chaise longue but was now propped up against the wall. In it Marie saw the reflection of Viktor's face. He gazed at her with blind eyes, his mouth curled in an expression of almost religious fervour as he stroked Eva's long cello-shaped back and buttocks, muttering something into her mahogany-brown head.

Then he gave a shudder.

Marie put a hand to her head and rubbed it to see if the image would dissolve. When it didn't she turned back towards the bathroom without a sound.

So that was that. Eva and Viktor – a couple in the fullest sense. And she was on the outside, looking in.

A technically efficient Juliet but one who shows little real emotion. Fräulein Maria Weissmüller shows great promise and will no doubt gain the necessary intensity as she

228

matures. At the moment one senses that her Juliet has never really woken out of innocent girlhood, never felt the mixture of rapture and despair that is her passion for Romeo.

'Great promise.' Lena nodded. 'He's right there. And he says your technique's good.'

Marie looked at the article again. 'He thinks I'm just a silly little girl up from the provinces.'

'Where does he say that?'

'It's what he *doesn't* say.' Marie shrugged. 'Anyway, what does it matter?'

Lena opened her lips as though to respond but then closed them again.

'Come on.' Marie folded the newspaper and left it on the café table. 'Let's get it over with.'

End of term at the Academy. Time to collect her things and take them back home for the summer break. They walked the short distance to the Academy, passing a number of Marie's fellow students who greeted her with smiles but said nothing about her review. Probably felt sorry for her. Georg, the director, hadn't said anything to her after the performance apart from a quick congratulations.

Lena watched her as she searched for hairgrips and character shoes in the dressing room, moving quietly among the chattering girls who leaned against lockers and exchanged home addresses and promises to meet up. 'You didn't have to come with me today, Lena. There's not much to take home.'

Very little, in fact. This was all she had to show for the years she'd spent at the Academy: a brush, a jar of cold cream, a scarf for tying back her hair during movement classes, and a pair of rather battered black character shoes: worn at the toes.

'Something scared you.' Lena stood by the tall mirror in the dressing room and stared at Marie with those sharp eyes of hers. 'You've been jumpy for weeks now. What was it, Maria?'

'I don't know what you mean.' Marie spotted a pile of hairgrips on the dressing table and picked them up. 'I'm missing one. Never mind.' She closed her locker door and turned the key.

Lena pointed at something on the tiled floor.

Marie picked the hairgrip up and dropped it again.

'You haven't been yourself since before the play opened.' Lena stooped and retrieved the grip. 'Something put you off. What happened?'

'*Es macht nichts*. Let's go home, Lena.'

But something had happened, Lena was right and all those theatre critics who'd dismissed her as a silly girl who'd never felt anything for a man, they were all wrong. She'd felt too much, for the wrong person, and only realized when she'd seen the irrefutable evidence that her feelings weren't reciprocated. She'd seen Viktor and Eva entwined on that chair and the discovery had shaken her. So this, the groaning and the awkwardly arranged limbs, the glazed eyes, this was sexual passion. This was what the poems and the plays celebrated: this animal performance. That's why Marie's Juliet hadn't convinced: she didn't understand sex.

The image of those two together haunted her. She pulled

it out of her memory to examine all the details and what she saw made her cheeks burn.

Marie kept to her room, pleading a headache. If Eva hadn't also been nursing some vague malaise it would have been awkward. As it was, only Lena seemed to notice Marie's depression when she visited each evening to tidy the bedroom and coax her outside for a walk in the Burggarten.

Anton, staying with one of his brothers in Vienna and still seeking work, called once or twice for Marie and she sent Lena out with messages saying she was indisposed. She couldn't face him. And yet, if she was honest, she could almost imagine her body and Anton's performing those *movements* Viktor and Eva carried out. The thought made her nerves almost fizz with electricity. Anton was a tall man with conventional Germanic good looks. In summer his eyes were intensely blue in his tanned face. His limbs were muscled from all those years skiing, hiking and climbing. She'd seen him throw a ball or vault a gate and admired his easy movements. She still found him desirable and this recognition was even more shocking than the recollection of Eva and Viktor together; it was like lusting after a brother. If only she could go to bed with Anton, just once, and learn how to do *it*. He'd always been kind and gentle with her. If only he would show her without demands for love, or, God forbid, proposals of marriage. But such a proposition would be anathema to him. Her lips curled imagining how he'd respond to the suggestion. He'd think she was mad. Or that she'd become what he feared: a debauched actress, a near-prostitute.

She must be suffering from some disorder even to consider such a thing. Although that doctor everyone talked about in

Vienna, the one who looked deep into your psyche and told you what he saw, said that *everything* in life came down to sex. Perhaps someone like him could decipher her conflicting thoughts. But imagine confessing such farmyard yearnings.

Viktor came to the apartment late one night when Marie was almost asleep. She heard him mutter to Eva in the hallway, '. . . a month or two . . . can't take you with me, Eva . . . keep in touch.'

There was a deeper edge to his voice than usual. 'I promise I'll come for you when I can. I promise.' His voice shook slightly. Eva was sobbing now.

The front door clicked shut.

In the morning Eva didn't appear for breakfast. Marie found her sitting in her room that evening, staring at nothing. 'Viktor's gone away.'

'Where?' Marie sat beside her on the bed.

'Hungary, he said. But he's planning on going to Romania afterwards. God knows what he's doing, he was so vague, Marie. Even to me.' She twisted her hands in her lap.

All that summer rumours reached them of Viktor. Someone said he'd been spotted in a yacht owned by an Englishman in Nice. Someone else swore they'd seen him sitting outside a café in Bucharest. But that was unlikely when Fredi Brandt knew for a fact that Viktor Varga had been spotted at the opera in Warsaw. And all the time Eva grew quieter and quieter. Marie thought of the ecstasy on Viktor's face the afternoon she'd come across them entwined. It seemed impossible he could feel that for Eva and leave her. She could still close her eyes and hear his muttered endearments. Viktor loved Eva. Not her; Eva. If only she could stop being in love with him.

Eva started to go out in the afternoons, saying she was growing claustrophobic. Often the young German, Matthias Fischer, would escort her round the shops or coffeehouses. Once or twice Alix heard the front door open in the early hours as someone left the apartment. Eva would sleep late and say nothing when the two girls ate their lunch.

Life grew dull. Even Anton was unable to offer Marie companionship. He'd gone to Innsbruck for another job interview. Marie stood at the window looking down at the street below with its respectable middle-class women out exercising their dogs and men buying newspapers from the stand. Vienna had once enchanted her. Now it felt oppressive. She thought of going home to Meran for a few weeks, but the heaviness that seemed to have claimed her prevented her from walking to the railway station to book the tickets.

Towards the end of the summer Eva arrived back in the apartment one afternoon, smartly dressed and flushed.

'It's done,' she said, looking relieved. 'Bit of a rush to get it all sorted out but here I am, Frau Fischer.'

'*Wie bitte*?' Marie stared at her.

'I've just married Matthias Fischer. Remember him?'

'You've done what!' Marie stood.

'You must have noticed how much time we've been spending together.'

'Yes, but—'

'Ridiculous making myself ill over a man who left me like

that.' She flopped in a chair. 'For God's sake, sit down, Marie. You remind me of my mother, standing there looking disapproving.'

'Eva, I don't think Viktor had any choice, I think—'

'He left me! I haven't had a word.'

Marie sat.

'It's been over two months now. Why should I have waited any longer?' Eva played with the ring on her finger. 'Shame Matthias couldn't come back for tea. He had to rush back to Berlin – some union problem at the printing press. Rather amusing for a socialist to have bolshy workers, isn't it!'

'I don't understand, Eva.' Marie examined her. Eva's eyes were cleverly made up but the lids drooped slightly and the skin was puffy. 'It feels so rushed.'

'Matthias Fischer is very amusing and he's got friends in interesting places. I'd like to try something a little more modern for the next stage of my career. Berlin's the place for that.' The words sounded as though they'd been composed earlier, rehearsed, perhaps.

Marie closed her eyes and saw Viktor's face while Eva writhed on top of him, blind and rapturous. 'Don't do this, Eva. Viktor adored you.' If Eva and Viktor had had *that* together, it was obscene that Eva could bear to marry someone else.

'Too late.' Eva put out a hand to show her the diamond ring. 'God my head hurts. I hope this stage doesn't last long . . .'

'What stage?' Marie asked. 'What are you talking about?'

'Nothing. Be a sweetheart and make us both a *tisane*.' She

grinned. 'I'm the bride, remember? It's my day for ordering everyone around.'

And Marie had the sense that all this was happening in some underwater dream, in which reaction or protest was impossible.

Twenty-seven

Alix
Rhineland, Western Germany, April 1946

Alix's trug was full. As she turned for the house she noticed how each movement she made felt as though it were happening leagues beneath the ocean. Must be the weight of the potatoes and carrots. Everyone was tired these days, Cousin Ulla said. The Whites had fed Alix well, but she'd been away from their well-stocked larder for some months. Ulla was generous with the few vegetables still growing in the garden and sometimes they managed to exchange potatoes for flour, but hunger seemed a constant presence.

She reached the top of the terrace and sat for a moment to take a breath.

'*Bonjour*.' Two Moroccan soldiers leered at her. The French occupying force in this valley had recruited far and wide. She wished she'd worn her coat and not this tight-fitting jumper of Ulla's.

They said something about the vegetables in her trug.

The first scaled the wall. '*Tu donnes.*' He held out his hand.

She pulled the trug towards her.

His companion hissed a word she couldn't understand and spat.

'It's all we've got.' Alix heard the pleading note in her voice and hated herself.

'*Tu donnes.*' They stood in front of her. Alix stood up to run, found herself sinking down again, head spinning, the world dark around her.

'What the hell's going on here?' The soldiers spun round, as surprised as she at the British accent.

Their hands shot to their heads in salute. '*Monsieur*. We check.'

'Then go and check something else or I'll report you for harassing civilians.' The British officer rested his bicycle against the wall and scowled at the soldiers until they'd retreated up the road. 'Did they hurt you, *Fräulein*?' His German was slow and accented. 'Those French officers need to teach their soldiers some discipline.'

'No, I'm fine, thank you.'

'Your English is better than my German.'

'I once had an English governess.' A lady from Norwich who'd insisted on a bowl of prunes each breakfast and quoted cricket results from a book specially imported from England. Alix laughed.

'What is it?'

'I'm sorry, it's just been so long since I spoke to anyone from England.' She stood.

'We don't often get down to the French sector. I'm only

237

here because I'm using my leave to do some cycling. I came here before the war and loved it then, the river and the castles, it's so beautiful . . .'

Alix had sunk down again. When the darkness passed, her rescuer was sitting beside her, holding her hand. 'From the look of your nails and the pallor of your skin, I'd say you desperately needed iron.' He let go of her hand. 'I'm a doctor. Before I came out here I was working in a London hospital.'

Dr Robin Macdonald visited every day of his week-long leave, bringing concentrated orange juice and iron tablets he'd wangled from God knew where. By the time he returned to Hanover Alix could walk without feeling faint, though he warned her it would take at least a month for her to feel fully recovered. 'Keep taking these.' He pushed another bottle of iron tablets into her hand. They were sitting in Cousin Ulla's tapestry-lined drawing room.

'I feel guilty about this.'

'Don't be. Your cousin told me about your father. You're a hero's daughter.' His face grew grave. 'I made inquiries about him, Alix. I hope you don't think it was presumptuous?'

She shook her head. 'I'd give anything for information.'

'I'm afraid it's not looking good.' He swallowed. 'It seems likely he lost his life at Flossenbürg camp.'

'Executed,' she said. He nodded and she stared hard at the peony pattern on the drawing-room curtains while Cousin Ulla held her hand and muttered words of comfort. 'I didn't really expect anything else by now.'

'And my mother?'

'No word.'

'They say millions died on the retreat to Berlin,' said Cousin Ulla, covering her eyes with a hand. '*Ach*, poor Maria. How could she deserve such a thing? I went to your parents' wedding, you know, Alix. She looked so beautiful.' Ulla nodded at a photograph of Mami in her wedding gown on the console table against the wall.

Mami. Papi. Lena. Michael. All gone. Only Gregor was left to her. And he couldn't reach her. They were as far apart as they had been when he was in Russia.

Cousin Ulla had told her she could stay in the *Schloss* for as long as she wanted, but Ulla's husband was due home. His leg wound had qualified him for early repatriation from a POW camp in Scotland. Ulla was planning the future: revitalizing the vineyard, marketing her wine to the American soldiers . . . Kind as she was, she wouldn't want Alix hanging around indefinitely.

'She seems very fond of you,' Robin said when she told him this. 'I'm sure she wouldn't mind you staying on.'

'Even so, I need to make my own plans once we're allowed to travel again.'

Cousin Ulla came into the drawing room where they sat. 'Robin! How nice.' You'd hardly think that he was a member of the occupying forces. Perhaps it was fortunate that Robin was only holidaying in this sector. Fraternizing – even with those related to Resistance heroes – was not looked on with approval.

'I brought you this.' Robin produced a package for Ulla. 'To help with supplies.'

'*Ach!*' She took it with delight and bustled off into the kitchen.

'Alix?' He sat down beside her. 'I really want to help you all I can, you know. No matter how great the difficulties.'

'You're not supposed to be friends with us.'

'Some of those restrictions will lift in due course.' He took her hand. 'I have to go back to Hanover soon but I'd like to write to you, if I may?'

Ulla came in with a teapot and cups on a tray. 'Real English tea, look, Alix!'

They sat sipping the tea. Robin said it was brewed exactly right even though they had to drink it black, without either milk or lemon. 'I haven't drunk Typhoo since before the war,' Ulla said.

'A friend of mine was part of a liaison party that went up to Berlin to see the Russians,' Robin told her. 'He had tea with a Soviet officer. It was Typhoo tea looted from a senior Nazi's home.'

'Those people drank English tea?' Ulla sounded astounded.

Robin sighed. 'Strange to imagine, isn't it?' His face grew more sombre. 'This Soviet chap told my friend grim stories about the battle for Berlin.'

'Someone told me they'd still be finding bodies in the forests next century.'

Ulla bit her lip.

The cup rattled in Alix's hand.

Robin was taking her other hand. 'How insensitive of us.'

She knew she could never tell him what she'd seen on her journey west.

Releasing her hands, she stood and picked up Cousin Ulla's teapot. 'I'll just freshen up the tea.' She felt their gazes, warm and sorrowful, on her back as she walked out of the room.

Gregor's long silence now made sense. He was dead. The fantasy she'd built up of him coming to find her, of the two of them crossing the Atlantic to reclaim Michael, perhaps settling in America themselves, crumpled.

A hiss brought her back to the present and the water bubbling over the edge of the saucepan onto the stove. 'Alix?'

Robin stood at the kitchen door. 'My dear.' He held open his arms. 'They've all gone,' she muttered, falling against him. 'All of them. I let him go. I let them take him.'

'You mean your father?' His arms were firm around her. 'How could you have protected him from those evil men?'

She opened her mouth to correct him but closed it again.

'You should feel proud of yourself, of your family.' He stroked her hair. '*I'm* proud of you.'

Robin wrote from Hanover a few weeks later, asking her to marry him.

> . . . *I know there will be some difficulties about this and we may have to wait some time before restrictions lift and we receive permission. I could wait a decade for you, Alix.*
> *Your loving*
> *Robin*

She thought for two days before finding a rare sheet of virgin writing paper.

Dear Robin

I was so very touched and flattered by your kind offer. I have grown fond of you too and I was very tempted to say yes. Perhaps if we had met in another time and place, where there had been no war, I would have said yes. But I cannot – not just because of the rules but because . . .

The pen stopped. How to explain that she already considered herself married? Married and widowed and not ready to marry again. She'd have to think of some other reason. She couldn't bear to hurt poor dear Robin.

I would like to go to university and study, if they ever let Germans have higher education again. I am only eighteen and I need to grow up. I lived a very protected life, even while so much death and suffering was all around. I wish I had known what was going on. Now is my chance to do something for my wretched country. I would like to become a teacher, perhaps of English. I would like to try and stop children believing in lies by teaching them to read other languages and talk to people from different countries.

Dear Robin, it would be so easy for me to say yes. It's such a temptation to be your wife . . .

Love. Security. A home – in England eventually, perhaps, where people watched cricket and the police weren't allowed to drag you off to prison in the middle of the night. And Robin was a nice-looking, clever, kind man. But . . .

. . . but I must pursue this ambition. How could I be both your wife and a student?

Your loving friend

Alexandra

Twenty-eight

Gregor
Berlin, early May 1945

They drove to a suburb in the south-west of Berlin to hunt
for a senior civil servant Vavilov was keen to interrogate. The
streets up here had escaped the worst. Gardens threw out the
scent of spring flowers and birds sang – almost like peace-
time.

'Smell that lilac,' said Vavilov. 'Was there ever such abun-
dance?'

Everyone said it was the most perfect spring they could
remember. Gregor shuddered: blossom-decked streets with
corpses in the gutters, tulips waving in the breeze beside children so hungry they couldn't stand. They turned a corner and
Gregor heard Vavilov's intake of breath. Outside a building
which appeared to be a hospital or clinic, a woman crawled
along the pavement dragging a bundle and trailing blood.
The men ran towards her. 'What happened?' Gregor shouted.

'What do you think? They even fucked us while we were

in labour. And the nuns, too.' She clutched her baby, wrapped in what looked like a ripped curtain. She frowned. 'What's a German doing in that uniform? Traitor!' Her spittle caught Gregor on the chest.

He reached into his pocket, dug out some chocolate. 'Take this. I'll find one of our medics—' She pushed his hand away and resumed her slow progress over the pavement. Gregor looked round for Vavilov. He'd reached the door of the hospital and had pinned a conscript to the wall. He was hitting him round the face with one of his leather gloves. Gregor had rarely seen his face lose its customary neutral sleepiness.

Nobody was watching him. Gregor walked off.

He walked all morning and part of the afternoon, without direction at first, circling the suburban streets. At lunchtime he started to head north-east to the rubble that had once been the *Mitte*, the city centre. By dusk he made out the dark outline of the Reichstag, from where gunshots had cracked only days earlier. He stopped, gazing at the rubble and dazed citizens and wondering what kind of victory this was. Seven years had passed since he'd left this city – it might have been seven centuries. From time to time he heard rustles and squeaks in the piles of bricks. Rats. Probably feasting. Gregor wanted to retch.

Knowing he wasn't far from his parents' old apartment, he headed east, cutting into Unter den Linden, the long avenue leading east from the Brandenburg Gate to the museums and the palace – if they still existed. The avenue, littered with burned-out tanks and collapsed masonry, bore no resemblance to the street he'd strolled along as a child on Sunday after-noon outings.

He'd be shot for desertion before he got very far, or else a German would lob a grenade at him; but he was going to try and find his parents' apartment. A group of Russians emerged from a side street. He walked on, expecting the shout, the hand on his shoulder. No one stopped him. Perhaps the Polish uniform confused them. He turned off, striding through anonymous roads, grateful for the few remaining road signs because there were no landmarks. Occasionally a rare surviving flowering cherry threw its colour over the muted canvas, or a tiny patch of unscorched soil bloomed yellow and green with narcissi, or a red Soviet flag would dance in the breeze, fragments of brightness which turned Gregor's stomach as he thought of the woman sprawling on the pavement by the maternity hospital. Better that the world throw itself into complete mourning; this gaiety was sacrilege.

On a whim he turned into a street that a wooden sign assured him was Friedrichstrasse, where his mother had shopped before the war, negotiating the piles of rubble and twisted metal that rose like the waves of a petrified ocean, to reach the corner where one of her favourite stores had been. The sign banning Jews had sprung up overnight one summer, must have been '33 or '34, preventing Eva from buying a new hat for Matthias's annual office boat trip along the Spree to Charlottenburg. Gregor kicked a burnt piece of wood.

An old woman hobbling past turned to flash a toothless grin at him. 'You tell them, handsome.'

At least she hadn't feared he'd rape her.

Gregor headed back to the Linden and continued east. During his time in Kolyma he'd sometimes dreamed of coming back here, confronting random Berliners and asking them if they knew what had happened to him and his parents. But now he was back he couldn't imagine confronting the wan-faced people. He'd thought he'd hate them but he felt nothing, only weariness. He could have curled up in the broken masonry and slept. But he forced himself on, grateful for the few surviving façades that acted as guides. Somewhere on this street had once stood a restaurant where Russian Cossacks flamed kebabs on their daggers, to the accompaniment of ooohs from the diners; his father had taken him for dinner on his tenth birthday. Now the Cossacks would be making a dash for the Elbe before their Communist brothers could catch up with them.

He walked on, disorientated. Somewhere here had stood the Catholic cathedral of St Hedwig. He couldn't locate its copper dome. Gone. He turned south, letting his feet drag past fragments of buildings until they stopped. He was standing on the corner of what had once been his own street. He doubted he'd recognize the apartment block. But there in front of him was Dieter's father's garage. It had lost some of its roof. The showroom windows behind which those shiny Mercedes cars had once stood must have shattered; singed timbers and sheets of corrugated metal now replaced the glass. The forecourt appeared to be acting as a store for piles of broken bricks.

A wooden board informed Gregor that the garage was now trading bicycle spare parts and providing repairs. Gregor had already felt a secret pleasure watching Russian soldiers falling off the stolen bikes they didn't know how to ride. Anyone who could provide spare tyres and chains would be doing well by Berlin standards. The shop next door that had sold newspapers and chocolate had vanished, as had most of the apartments on the other side of the street. But not his block, which stood only metres beyond the garage. As far as he could see in the gloom, its Biedermeier exterior was intact. No saying what the apartments would look like inside, though.

Among the rubble at the end of the street a small lake had formed and on it a swan was gliding. Amazing nobody had yet grabbed it for the pot.

He walked up to the garage door and knocked. No way in hell could his friend Dieter's family still live here. The door opened an inch or so and he smelled the familiar oil and rubber scent. The wary face of Dieter's mother appeared, flinching as she saw his uniform. 'It's me, Frau Braun, Gregor Fischer,' he told her.

She stared at him, wiping oily hands on overalls, her mouth making a perfect O. Then the door flung open and she enfolded him in her broad arms. The aroma of oil and old, tired clothes was the best he'd smelled since he'd left Alix's bed. 'Gregor Fischer! I knew you'd come back! I kept telling Dieter, Gregor's a clever one, he'll look after himself. And when the bombing started I said you were better off out of it.'

He could have clung to her for eternity and had to force himself to let her go. She touched his cheek. 'Did you think we'd all be gone, Gregor? Well you might. Dieter's father died in an air raid in February. Werner was killed in Normandy last year. Erik's fighting the Americans somewhere near the Elbe.' She shook her head, managing to express unspoken scorn for this endeavour. 'The girls are still here. Except for Marta – you probably never saw her. She was born in 1939. Died in 1943. Whooping cough.'

Werner, Deiter, Erik, Ute and Sabine. And Marta. Werner had been older than Dieter and Gregor and spent most of the time he could spare from Hitler Youth helping out in the garage. The other three Gregor remembered as small kids playing with old tyres in the repair yard. They were only allowed to join in with Dieter and Gregor's games if they agreed to play supporting roles.

'And Dieter?'

'Prisoner of war. Some camp near Moscow. Perhaps they'll let them come home soon.' The words were casual but the expression in her eyes was not.

Gregor tried to nod, remembering what he'd heard of the fate of the captured German soldiers he'd seen heading east, stinking, blank-eyed. She dragged him inside and bolted the door behind them. A couple of candles and a gas lamp illuminated the office. The family had lived in an apartment above the premises but Gregor noticed that they'd brought bedding and cooking pots downstairs, along with a portable stove. Frau Braun pointed to a photograph on the wall: Dieter wearing his Wehrmacht uniform. Even the official photographer hadn't succeeded in dampening the glint in Dieter's eyes. *Scheissköpfe*. Gregor could almost hear him say it.

'So it's just the girls and me now.' Her voice was matter-of-fact. No time for emotion when there was food to scrounge or daughters to hide from the Russians. 'But you'll be wanting the key.'

'The key?'

'To the apartment.'

After all these years he'd remembered that Frau Braun had the key. Or perhaps he'd simply retained some memory of her kindness. 'Before you left Berlin in thirty-eight your mother gave me a key so I could keep an eye on the place. Rushed down here, she did, said there was no time to explain. Where in God's name did I put it?' She rummaged in a drawer of nuts and bolts and handed him the key. 'Here we are. Those bastards turned over the place but they left most of your stuff and the Russians haven't come sniffing round here yet. I let a few folk sleep up there if they were desperate.' She looked worried. 'I hope you don't mind, it's about the only block still standing on this street. Apart from this garage.'

'How could I mind?'

'I'm going to find you some of Dieter's clothes, you don't want to be shot as a deserter.' She didn't seem surprised that he'd escaped from the Red Army. She vanished upstairs to the family's apartment, returning a few minutes later with underwear, shirt, trousers and jacket. 'Still a lot of wear in them. Dieter'd only had them for a few months when they called him up.' Her eyes had misted over. She pushed the clothes into his arms.

She still hadn't asked him where he'd been, what had happened. He could have hugged her for not probing. Perhaps people didn't ask questions any more. Perhaps exhaustion had deprived her of all curiosity. She put an arm round him and took him through a back entrance, leading to a rear door of the apartment block. 'Quieter, this way.' She gave him a meaningful look. 'Keep your head down. Let me know if you need food.'

She was gone before he could thank her.

The staircase had lost its carpet and stair-rods. Patches of brickwork showed through cracked plasterwork. Gregor climbed to the second floor. His mother had been so thrilled when they moved here in 'thirty-two, loving the closeness to shops and galleries and the view from their balcony, which she crammed with pots of flowers. She'd loved looking out of the rear windows too, at the *Hinterhof*, the inner courtyard where neighbours gossiped and cats stretched out in the sun. Not even the existence of the garage on the corner had dampened the family's enthusiasm for their new home. Anyway, back then the garage had featured a shiny plate-glassed showroom full of gleaming automobiles. Nobody had known about Eva's father then and the police hadn't really shown much of an interest in Matthias. But his name must already have been on some police file.

As Gregor reached the landing something moved and his hand went to the revolver in his belt. A woman – wild-eyed, dishevelled. Frau Schiffer, the woman who hadn't liked having a half-Jewish neighbour. He smelled the civilian odour of sour, empty stomach and decaying teeth which he hadn't noticed on Dieter's mother. He heard a dripping and saw she'd wet herself. 'I'm German.' He blinked. This was the second time he'd said the words. She didn't seem to hear him.

He unlocked the apartment door. It smelled of old newspaper, metallic – like an iron that had been left on too long. Nothing a good blast of fresh air wouldn't disperse. He could almost smell his mother's Mitsouko scent, hear her chatting to his father in the sitting room. The first door on the right was his father's study. Matthias Fischer, gone so long ago. Gregor opened the door. The desk was empty. When Matthias had lived here it had been covered in towers of paper. Gregor went into the sitting room. Someone had covered his piano with a dust cloth. He pulled it off and opened the lid. Not as grand as Alix's Steinway, but he'd missed it. At least the mouth organ had given him some limited musical outlet. Or had done until he'd lost it. It was probably sitting in some soldier's rancid pocket.

In a kitchen cupboard he found cans of potatoes and carrots, and asparagus spears of all things. With all those mouths to feed, Dieter's mother must have found these hard to resist. He wished she'd taken them. It would make him feel less . . . Less what? Guilty?

He opened the potatoes and found a plate and fork. Silly to stand on formality but he was damned if he was going to eat his first meal back in his home from a can. He ate at the kitchen table, remembering all those meals his mother had served him here. No running water, washing up could wait. It was getting dark and he knew the electric lights wouldn't work. He found a candle stub in a drawer and went into his old bedroom to change into Dieter's clothes. Tomorrow he'd burn the Polish uniform. Or cut off the insignia and buttons, at least. Perhaps he could swap it for a civilian coat. He'd have to do something about his gun, too; risky to keep it.

On his bedroom wall John Wayne and Gene Autry still aimed pistols and glowered, eyes clear and uncompromising under their Stetsons. *Hi*, Gregor greeted the yellowing posters silently. *What would you have done?* He looked away. His bed was made up, and despite their film of dust the sheets smelled reasonable. He hadn't slept in it since October 1938 but he recognized the quilt and the linen sheets with their blue edgings, now so thin they were almost transparent. Someone had left a small fluffy dog on the pillow. Gregor didn't think it was one of his. He was going to throw it onto the floor but something made him place it on the window sill above the bed before he went back into the sitting room.

Vavilov could chase him here if he wanted. He wasn't going to run any more. At least he'd have a day or two at home. Perhaps more if he was lucky. He'd keep the cyanide with him at all times. A patrol might not notice the tablets. The cattle wagon wouldn't take him very far east.

Something else was bothering him, something was missing from the room. Gregor peered at the furniture and photographs under their veil of dust and couldn't work out what it was.

A tap on the door roused him from his contemplation. He checked for the gun and then remembered that was the most dangerous thing he could produce.

'It's just me, Co—, Sabine.' Dieter's younger sister. He opened the door and blinked. Sabine wore large sunglasses, even though it was almost dark, slouchy trousers and a tight, short-sleeved blouse with low neckline. Her hair was long and slightly waved. Her lips were cyclamen red. Her neck bones protruded, but like her mother she didn't smell of chronic hunger. In her arms she held a gramophone player. 'It's very heavy, can I come in?'

He opened the door.

'I was only borrowing it.' She flicked the sunglasses back onto her head in a gesture that was pure Hollywood.

Of course, the missing object in the sitting room. 'Let me.' He held out his hands, trying not to think of that other gramophone player back in Pomerania.

'I put on a new needle last week.' She handed it over.

God knows where she'd found *that*. The mahogany case smelled of beeswax. 'You've certainly looked after it.'

'We loved it. We used to come up here and play jazz. One night when the bombers didn't come we sat down in the *Hinterhof* and danced. Frau Schiffer didn't like it. But she lost most of her hearing in one of the raids so she didn't bother us much.' Sabine permitted herself a small grin. 'But when the Ivans came, Mutti thought it would be safer to bring the gramophone to where we used to keep the coal.'

Clearly she didn't regard him as one of the enemy. Feeling touched, Gregor put the gramophone player down on the oak cupboard where it belonged. 'Jazz, you said?'

The girl's lipsticked mouth opened up into a grin. 'Swing. Benny Goodman, mainly.' She peered at him as though to see if he'd recognize the name.

'I've heard of him but I haven't heard a note of swing since about 1939.'

'Didn't mean anything to most people here. If they caught you listening the police could cart you off to a camp. They said it was antisocial, that we were all promiscuous or homosexuals.' Sabine grinned. 'Or both.' Then her expression grew more serious. 'We used to pretend we lived in New York or Chicago and all of *that*,' she nodded at the window, 'didn't exist.'

254

Gregor pointed at the sofa. 'Tell me about it.' He'd imagined Berlin had shown him everything, but this was new. He'd been too young to appreciate jazz when they'd been in Warsaw. Reuben had sometimes frequented a cellar bar before the Germans arrived to listen to American music. Gregor thought he remembered him whistling the melodies he'd heard there, tapping his hand on the dining-room table to the strange rhythms that made you want to sway.

'Most of the Swing Kids – that's what we called ourselves – were the kind that did well in the *Gymnasium* and gave their parents no trouble.' She gave an amused look round the apartment.

'Sounds like me.'

She snorted. 'But *not* like me. I only got into jazz when the raids got bad. Used to go to an unofficial cellar at the clothing factory with the slave workers who weren't allowed in the proper shelters.'

Gregor could only feel admiration.

'Some of the kids brought records there in the raids. Some had their own instruments. At one stage we had a saxophone and a trumpet. I did vocals.'

'You played jazz down there while the Americans and British bombed you?' Gregor found himself smiling at the image at the same time as it almost made him want to weep.

'It took our minds off it. That's where I met Agneta and Tomaz.'

'Agneta and Tomaz?'

'She was a Lithuanian slave worker in the factory. Tomaz was her son.'

'Was?'

'The cellar took a direct hit one night. I was on fire duty so I wasn't there.' She sighed. 'You'd think that would be more dangerous, out in the open. But not on that night.'

'Wait a moment.' Gregor went into his bedroom and found the toy dog.

Sabine took it and swallowed. 'We bought it for him for Christmas. It wasn't new, but nearly. He must have left it here before his mother took him to the shelter.'

She sat the dog beside her on the sofa and stared down at her knees.

Gregor gave her a moment. 'Do you have the records?' he said at last.

She blinked.

'Benny Goodman, you said?'

She stared at him for a few seconds, then her face broke out into a broad grin. 'Hang on.' At the front door she halted. 'By the way, it's Coca.'

'What is?'

'My name. The Swing Kids called me Coca.'

'Coca. I like it.' He really was sitting here having a normal conversation with this kid. But then he reminded himself that he wasn't that much older than her.

She looked pleased. 'We also had a Winston and a Teddy. Be back in a second.' She shut the door and he heard her feet tripping down the stairs in her wedge-heeled sandals. She returned in less than five minutes, clutching a pile of records. 'I'll start with some Goodman.' She took off her sunglasses and put the records on the sofa. As she leaned over them Gregor caught a view of the top of her breasts. He looked away. God, this was Dieter's little sister. He and Dieter had once taken her to the park to feed the ducks. They'd removed her from her pram and plonked her on the grass so they could use the pram as a racing car. Sabine – Coca – had crawled towards the lake and a policeman had rescued her, giving the boys a roasting. A long time ago – before policemen stopped being benign and protective figures.

'Gregor?' She was frowning at him. 'Am I boring you?'

'No, no, sorry.' He shook himself. 'I was just reminiscing.'

'You're as bad as my mother, she's always going on about this summer or that Christmas when we had such a large goose it wouldn't fit in the stove.' But the voice was warm. 'God, I hope I don't go on about the good old days when I'm her age.'

'Probably not something we need to worry about.'

A pounding on the front door made them both jump. 'Gregor? Coca, whatever you call yourself, open up!'

Dieter's mother. Coca ran to the door to let her in.

'There's a couple of drunk Ivans coming down the street.' Her face was pale and the lines of exhaustion were even more marked. 'Soon as they see the garage they'll be trying to loot something. But they're like dogs the way they smell out women and—'

Deserters, Gregor finished for her.

Sabine was bundling records together. 'Take the gramophone player,' she hissed at Gregor.

'*Um Gottes Willen!*' her mother called from outside. 'I can hear them on the forecourt, girl!'

Gregor strode to the cupboard and picked up the wooden box. He followed them out, locking the front door. The Russians could probably smash it down if they wanted to. He thought they'd go down into the basement, but when they reached the ground floor, Frau Braun put a finger to her lips and opened one of the doors off the entrance hall. It must have been the concierge's office but was now empty apart from a pile of broken chairs. Frau Braun pulled open a rear-facing window and raised a leg over the sill. With surprising ease she climbed out, holding her arms out for the gramophone player while Coca scrambled over. They were standing in the *Hinterhof*, now used for storing wood. 'You can get down to our cellar from here,' she whispered, pointing to the apartment opposite. 'Without going onto the street and through the garage.' From the front of the building came the sounds of male laughter.

Frau Braun led them across the courtyard and opened a window, repeating her agile manoeuvre over the sill and waving them on. She pointed at a rear door. 'It's open.' She pushed them through. They were in an alleyway, beside the garage's back office. He'd never come through this way with Dieter. Memories of that other cellar in Pomerania flashed through his mind. *Oh Alix.* They hurried down the steps and Frau Braun shoved aside the hessian sacks in a corner. 'Under you go, never mind your clothes now.'

Gregor tucked the gramophone player in beside Sabine. 'Where's Ute?' He hadn't seen the other sister yet.

Dieter's mother looked away. 'She's out . . . seeing a friend.' He knew what she meant; Ute had found herself a Russian protector. The soldiers had reached the garage showroom upstairs now, he could hear them knocking over rows of tyres. 'Too late to be worried now.' She was trying to sound casual but her eyes told him something. She'd already been raped. He hoped his face didn't betray him.

'Get in.' He held up the sacks. 'Quick.'

She hesitated. He pushed her down. A table crashed to the floor, followed by the clatter of falling bicycle chains and the liquid sound of hundreds of small nuts and screws sprinkling onto the floor.

'There are overalls hanging up at the top of the stairs,' Frau Braun hissed from under the sacks. 'Put them on and rub some oil into your face. There's a can up there too.'

He'd look more proletarian dressed as a mechanic. He ran up the steps and pulled on the rank-smelling overalls. The oil can was empty so he wet his fingers and ran them over the dusty floor, rubbing the resulting mixture into his cheeks. He walked through the door and found himself standing in Dieter's father's office. He let himself look anxious but not so anxious they'd guess about the hidden women. '*Was ist's?*' he asked.

'*Gretchen?*' asked the first soldier, raising his gun. 'Where?'

'*Aus.*' He nodded towards the street. 'Sick – she go for doctor. Bad sick.' He dabbed at his cheek, trying to indicate spots. Perhaps the threat of typhus would scare them off.

The second soldier approached. '*Gretchen?*' He lifted his revolver and pointed it between Gregor's temples.

Clearly they were unafraid of infection. Gregor thought quickly. 'Officerski buy *Gretchens*,' he said. 'Give them food.' He patted his stomach. How much easier it would have been to have explained this in his near-fluent Russian. But it seemed improbable that a Berlin garage-hand would speak the language. 'Protection,' he added in Russian. Just that one word to make it clear. And perhaps some others were needed.

'At headquarters. Chief comrade.' It wasn't unknown for German women to offer themselves to an individual soldier to save themselves from multiple rape.

The first soldier pointed a revolver at Gregor. 'You Wehrmacht?'

Gregor rolled up the leg of his overalls, tugged down a sock and showed them the Kolyma scar. 'Invalid. No fight.' He pointed at himself. 'Socialist. Hitler . . .' He spat.

The Russian scowled. 'Hitler.' He spat too. Gregor offered his hand. The Russian stared at it. Gregor's heart missed a beat. Then the first Russian was shaking it up and down as though it were a pump handle and the second was thumping his back.

It took ten minutes of back-patting and grinning to persuade them there was nothing in the garage they needed to take. Gregor padlocked the door behind them, watched them leave and ran through to the back and down to the cellar. Coca and her mother emerged from the sacks, faces black with coal dust.

'Swing Heil!' Coca winked at him but her face wore that glazed expression Gregor'd seen on women everywhere the Soviets went. She pulled out the gramophone player.

'You keep it down here,' he told her. 'I'll never use it.'

Twenty-nine

Gregor pulled open the curtains on another perfect Berlin spring morning. The swan still swam on the temporary lake. The water reflected a blue sky and puffball white clouds, cut by the sharp outlines of bombed apartment blocks. The air reeked of dead bodies and burst drains.

Something was coming back to him. Peter von Matke had owned an apartment here in Berlin. Perhaps Alix was there this very minute. He grabbed his shirt and went to the bathroom. The water was working for once, so he washed and flushed the lavatory. After throwing on his clothes he ran to the study to find a scrap of paper and a pencil so he could leave a message. If only he knew how the hell one got to Woyrchstrasse. He must have known the way once. Outside he found an old man making slow progress up the street, an empty sack hanging on one arm. 'Keep that church tower on your left,' the old man told him.

He crossed another road and another. Quiet here. No Soviet patrols. A woman pushing a pram full of scrap metal frowned at him when he asked for more directions. 'Most of it's gone. Keep heading down there.' She nodded down the road. A group of Russians ambled towards him, shouting at passing women and throwing empty bottles into the gutter. Gregor ducked behind a burned-out tank.

Gregor felt eyes on him. A rat sat on its hind legs, studying him. Sweat bathed his face. He stood. Times like this he could almost hear Reuben and Jacob mocking him, asking him what it felt like to be a member of the master race now.

He caught sight of something else. A sign. Woyrchstrasse. If he hadn't hidden behind the tank he'd have missed it. He racked his memory for the number of the von Matke apartment. An even number, 16 or 18. Residents had chalked little number plates on tiles outside the heaps which had once been their homes. Some had written notes on scraps of paper and weighed them down with broken bricks. Gregor stopped outside number 14 and read one of them.

Astrid, your father was hurt badly and we have taken him to hospital. If you find this, write and tell us where we can find you. Love, Mutti.

The corners of the paper were curled and the pencilled words had almost faded.

Number 18 still boasted a flowering cherry tree, split down the middle, one half blackened, the other waving blossom-clad branches like a stricken but friendly ghost. Gregor didn't remember a cherry tree and moved on to number 16. Two walls, nearly intact, stood at right angles, the space between them already colonized by flowers. He lit another match and found the pencil stub and scrap of paper he'd brought with him. 'A., the pianist is home.'

She'd know what it meant. He weighed down the note with two lumps of scorched brick and trudged home again. *Home*. How quickly and easily that word came to his lips now.

He spent the morning helping Dieter's mother and Coca right the trashed workshop, sorting through jumbled nuts and screws and replacing them in their correct drawers. Ute reappeared at lunchtime, unrecognizable as the quiet girl he remembered, dressed in a tight purple frock, yawning and saying she needed to catch up on some sleep. She produced a net bag, from which she pulled out a loaf of black bread and a small pat of margarine wrapped up in what looked like a piece of notepaper. Gregor noticed her chewed nails and blushed when she caught him staring at them.

The other women cut the bread and spread margarine so finely you could hardly tell it was there. Even as his stomach growled Gregor tried to turn down his slice; it didn't seem right that he should benefit from the fruits of Ute's nocturnal work. Dieter's mother told him to shut up and eat: last night he'd saved her and Coca from the soldiers. First time in years he'd managed to do something he could remember without shame.

Perhaps the rare food in his blood was fuelling his memory, which was good and bad. There were episodes he'd rather not recall.

But back in the apartment, he couldn't stop thinking about it all again: the night with Alix. And about all that had happened before then, the history he hadn't told her. He'd missed out most of what had happened at the logging camp at Kotlas in northern Russia, where they'd sent him after his arrest with Cyrek in Poland in 1940. Or possibly early in 1941. Already dates were blurring. Whenever it was, his hidden story had begun there, when Gregor Fischer had died and Paul Smolinsky had been born.

Thirty

Gregor
Camp near Kotlas, Archangel, 1941

The camp was 500 miles north-east of Moscow. Gregor could barely find the energy to stand by the time they arrived on the wagon, but Polish women were waiting for the new arrivals with sweetened black tea and bread and kind, sad eyes. He'd tried to tell them about his mother, about the Gronowskis and the death of Cyrek in the train, but had found himself incapable of describing these events. Besides, the expressions on their faces told him everyone had experienced similar things.

He'd half hoped to find some of those he'd lost here in the forests, but nobody had heard of Eva Fischer, or Jacob and Reuben Gronowski. A stern voice in his head told him it was time to forget them all for the duration of this next stage. Gregor concentrated on finding his bearings, on regaining strength. The people in his hut seemed kindly – a Dr Skot-nicki, his wife and daughter and their extended family:

assorted teachers and lawyers from towns in eastern Poland. The daughter, Sofia, was about his age but she stared at him with such sharp eyes that he found himself shy in her presence, as though she were accusing him of some kind of weakness.

'How on earth does a German boy come to be deported with a bunch of Poles?' she asked him on their first meeting.

He shrugged. 'My mother was of Polish origin. We were living in Warsaw when the war started.'

'In Warsaw?' She frowned. 'You didn't plan that very well, did you?'

'Leave the lad in peace,' said Sofia's mother. 'He can't help who he is.'

The camp, one of a cluster belonging to a state-owned lumber company, could have been worse. He'd fallen into the company of Poles who'd arrived with some of their possessions, jewellery and money intact. 'We had some warning they'd deport us,' Sofia told him. 'My father managed to withdraw money in dollars.' She looked over her shoulder. 'My mother sewed jewellery into our clothes and we packed up our bedding and cooking pots.'

She was taking a risk, telling him this. Perhaps she liked him more than it appeared. Gregor himself had nothing to offer except his wits and a certain talent for the mouth organ. Russians were supposed to love music.

'You're strong and healthy, given what you've endured.' Dr Skotnicki removed the stethoscope from Gregor's chest. 'Work hard, but don't exhaust yourself. Exhaustion's the killer here. I'll see if I can persuade them to let you help me in my clinic. If you can stay indoors in the harsh weather you'll conserve some strength.'

Skotnicki had been quick to offer his medical services to the camp guards and their families.

'I don't even know exactly where I am,' Gregor confessed. 'I can't remember much of the last few days in the wagons.'

Skotnicki found a pencil stub and a scrap of yellowing paper. 'Here's the Northern Drina river. Here's Kotlas.' He drew the curve of a peninsula. 'Right up here is Archangel.'

None of the places meant anything to Gregor.

The doctor gave a wry smile. 'Moscow is here. Warsaw here.'

Almost off the scrap of paper.

'We're at the end of the world.'

'Not quite. There are places more remote than this.' A shadow passed over the doctor's eyes. 'Places more terrible. We can survive this camp if we keep on terms with the guards.'

On long summer days when the sun barely set Gregor experienced odd hours during which he almost enjoyed camp life, the early starts on the wagon to distant parts of the forest, singing songs and flirting with girls. Working outside all day made his arms and legs ache and the insects seemed to single out his limbs as their preferred restaurant. But at least there were breaks to lie in the sun and eat bread and even, on occasions, curd cheese. He was a German surrounded by Poles, but for the most part they accepted him. 'We hate the Russians more than you.' Sofia Skotnicka swallowed a mouthful of bread and smiled sweetly at him.

'You always know how to make me feel good. And you haven't got a clue what the Germans are doing in western Poland.'

'Don't tell me. Let me stay happy and ignorant, imagining it's all *Lieder* and *Lederhosen*.'

'Sometimes I think that's all you *do* want to imagine.'

She put down her chunk of bread. 'You think you're the only one with a grasp of world affairs, don't you Fischer?'

He was silent. Sometimes he felt like the only person who'd seen what was really happening in western Poland.

She flapped a hand at a mosquito paying close attention to her arm and examined the bump it had left. 'That's the tenth today. Play something on that dreadful instrument of yours to scare them away.'

The mouth organ was about the only possession Gregor hadn't lost. He pulled it out.

'And not that butchering of the Polish national anthem, if you don't mind.'

He chose an adaptation of a Chopin waltz that worked fairly well if he took it slowly. Sofia leaned back against the wheel of the logging cart and closed her eyes, one hand stretched out in her lap in preparation for another mosquito attack.

Gregor had only been back in their quarters for half an hour when Sasha, one of the guards, ran in. 'Doctor?'

Gregor sat up. 'He's at the mill,' he said in his halting Russian. 'A bad splinter.'

'My Vera – she says her ear's on fire.' He walked to Gregor and pulled his shoulder. 'You come and treat her!'

'But I'm not—'

'You come!'

Gregor followed. Vera, a girl of about four, sat up in bed, her small face contorted. Gregor peered into her ear. He had no torch, no way of knowing what was wrong. 'Treat it!' Sasha roared. Gregor thought quickly.

'Do you have a pin?'

Sasha scowled at him.

'Or a needle?'

Sasha bellowed for his wife and a rapid exchange produced a pin. A candle and matches sat ready for lighting at dusk. Gregor motioned at the woman to light the candle. Her eyes widened, probably scared he was going to use the flame on her daughter. He held the pin over the flame and counted to ten. How long did it take to sterilize objects?

Vera watched him from her bed. She'd stopped screaming now. Perhaps this ear infection would heal by itself . . . It might be better to try and explain this to Sasha, remind him that Gregor wasn't yet sixteen years old and—

'You heal her, yes?' Sasha scowled at him. Sasha was a big man and Gregor had seen him knock a Pole to the ground for disobeying some minor regulation.

Gregor removed the pin from the flame and approached the child with what he hoped was a reassuring confidence. He pushed back the child's hair and guided the pin into her ear, the blood in his veins rushing.

He heard a small pop and a stream of yellow fluid ran out of Vera's eardrum.

Sasha pulled him into an embrace which threatened to break his ribs. Sasha's wife brewed tea – the real stuff, not the substitute the Poles drank. Gregor couldn't help feeling like a hero.

Just an ordinary camp day: wood splinters, insect bites and the smell of resin. And Sofia tormenting him. Nothing to warn him about what was about to happen when they returned to the huts. His usual bowl of millet *kasha* sat in his place at the pallet they used for a table, but Sofia's father, Doctor Skotnicki, couldn't meet his eye. Gregor ate, wishing someone'd tell him what was wrong.

The women took the bowls outside to rinse with only a nod to acknowledge his thanks. Dr Skotnicki beckoned him over to sit beside him on his bunk. 'We need to do something about your name, Gregor.' He removed his spectacles and examined the lenses.

'Why?'

Dr Skotnicki stared at him, his naked eyes looking vulnerable. 'You don't know, do you? I suppose the guards in the forest hadn't heard yet.'

'Heard what?'

The doctor sighed. 'Germany invaded Russia a few days ago.'

Gregor sat up, as though an electric charge had passed through him. It only took a second for him to understand. If the guards discovered his real identity . . .

Dr Skotnicki replaced his glasses and pulled something out from under the blanket. 'What I propose is this. Last week in the next camp, Paul Smolinsky, a Polish lad of seventeen, died from diphtheria. His parents are prepared to sell his papers. Otherwise . . .' Dr Skotnicki looked at Gregor.

Otherwise meant the other kind of camps, designed to work you until you died. This was a holiday in comparison with them. Gregor couldn't quell a laugh.

'Sorry,' he said in response to the doctor's frown. 'It's just I keep twisting and turning like a rat trying to escape terriers.'

The doctor put a hand on Gregor's shoulder. 'You'll let me find out more about those new papers?'

'I don't know . . .' Changing his name, losing his old self: it felt wrong, disloyal. He was *Gregor Fischer*. He'd done nothing wrong.

'Gregor, I wouldn't ask you to do this if I didn't think it was imperative,' the doctor said softly.

'What about the guards?' He was playing for time now.

'Don't worry about the guards. Since you sorted out Sasha's daughter's ear he regards you as a god.'

Gregor shifted on the bunk. The doctor had turned white when Gregor had reported his treatment of Vera. 'Dear God, boy, suppose she'd had meningitis?'

'Then she'd have died anyway.'

The doctor had shaken his head. 'Don't ever do anything like that again. You could have all of us shot.'

But yes, the guards would turn a blind eye to Gregor's change of nationality.

'I haven't got any money to pay for the papers,' he mumbled. All he had was the mouth organ and the photograph of his mother.

'You can pay me back through working as my assistant whenever they spare you from the logging. I'm getting on,

271

Gregor. I need help.' And indeed the doctor's hair had turned white very rapidly these last months.

Sitting on the logging wagon early the next morning he pulled out the mouth organ. 'Are we feeling romantic or nostalgic today?' he asked, in his improving Russian. 'Do you want "Olga with the Big Tits" or the one about Babushka's loaves baking in the oven?'

'Shut your mouth and play the one about the red rose,' Ivan with the broken nose told him.

I shall go, I am a young one. Gregor's Russian wasn't good enough to catch all the meaning but he'd translated some of the words. *Flowers scarlet, roses red, I must pluck.*

His mother and Marie had been picking roses in the garden the morning of the dinner party in Pomerania. The world had stopped for a moment and he'd felt that even when it moved on again there'd always be a part of the universe where the women were picking flowers, Marie serene and unhurried in her movements, his own mother moving with more purpose, her fingers darting between thorns, her eyes bright like a bird's. And Alix's father watching the two of them with that unreadable expression on his face.

'What were you thinking while you played that song?' Sofia had been watching him again. Although she frequently told him what a waste of space he was, how stupid and slow and generally *male*, he noticed that her eyes were soft now.

'I was contemplating the relativity of time,' he told her. She sniffed.

*

'Poles and Russians, fellow victims of Fascist aggression.' The commissar folded the letter from Moscow. 'We share glorious Slavic mission to defeat Germans.' He stretched his pitted face into a smile which looked as though it hadn't been used for some years. 'You are free to leave now.'

'Never mind that our Russian friends imprisoned us up here for nearly a year,' Gregor muttered to Sofia. They were standing at the back of the crowd assembled to hear the official announcement of their new freedom.

Sofia glared at him. 'He'll hear you.'

The Skotnickis unrolled a map of the Soviet Union and started planning. They might almost have been organizing a holiday rather than a journey of two thousand kilometres south. Gregor saw Mrs Skotnicka bend down over her bunk and unroll a belt like a bandage she wore the year round under her shirt. He averted his eyes but not before he'd seen the glint of diamonds and sapphires falling onto the blanket.

'As I said before, we had time to prepare for deportation.'

He hadn't noticed Sofia coming in.

'Mama unstrung her necklaces.'

Gregor thought of his own possessions: a tattered photograph of his mother and a mouth organ. The more he considered it the more obvious it seemed that he should distance himself from the family, who could barter and buy their way across the continent. The Skotnickis would feed and clothe him, possibly even pay for his railway tickets, but he couldn't accept their charity. Especially when he felt like he did about Sofia.

He muttered an excuse to her and went outside. Sasha the

guard sometimes gave him bread if he carried out extra work: groomed the horses or helped on the family vegetable patch. He considered trying to persuade Sasha to convert the extra food into roubles.

'And where do you think you're going, young man!'

Gregor froze.

'Get back here and start boiling water. I want all my instruments sterilized before we leave.' But the doctor's eyes were kindly. 'I keep telling you, there's no way I can cope with the thousands of sick people we're going to encounter on this journey if I don't have an assistant, Paul.'

The doctor was careful to use the new name.

'I can't pay you but I can feed you and wherever we travel you'll come with us. You've become,' he coughed, 'well, let's just say I couldn't manage without you.'

When the time came to leave Gregor showed the official his newly acquired Polish papers. The man observed him through his round lenses. An eternity seemed to pass before he nodded him forward to stand with the Skotnickis. Sofia's hand squeezed his. 'Thank God.' She gulped. Sofia was gentler with him these days.

They planned to head south across the Soviet Union to Krasnovodsk, over the Caspian into Persia and the protection of the British. 'New lives for all of us in London.' Doctor Skotnicki rubbed his hands. Gregor knew he was hoping to join the Free Poles as a medic. 'And you will get a place at medical school,' he told Gregor. 'At St Thomas's or Guy's. I'll coach you in the sciences while we travel.'

'What if he doesn't want to become a doctor, Papa?' Sofia folded her arms.

'I wouldn't mind.' Gregor had enjoyed assisting Dr Skotnicki with the patients. Nothing wrong with making medicine his career. His parents would have approved: it was a socially useful calling. But he'd promised himself not to think of his father and mother.

Sofia's hazel eyes had swept Gregor's face with something that looked like approval.

Thirty-one

Berlin, 1945

Gregor pushed aside the daydreams of how his life might have gone had he reached London. Anyway, the British would probably have incarcerated him in a camp for enemy aliens in some damp corner of their cloud-covered island. At least in Berlin he was a misfit in his own home.

He told anyone in uniform who asked that he was Gregor Fischer. A German deserter had stolen his ID and fire had claimed the rest of his papers. 'Foot injury, the Wehrmacht wouldn't take me,' he said. 'Been working as an orderly for most of the war.'

'What about the Volksturm?' asked a sharper Soviet officer. 'Surely they conscripted you at the end? We heard they even dragged men out of hospital wards to fight.'

'They gave us some old guns and sent us east to defend the city, but the officer commanding us sent us back, said it was hopeless.'

'Wise officer.' The officer's pale blue eyes reminded

Gregor of the icy seas during the voyage from Kolyma, waters he didn't intend seeing again.

So Paul Smolinsky and all he represented was gone.

Gregor wrapped his gun in one of his father's silk handkerchiefs and placed it in the piano. Vavilov's creatures would find it in minutes; he'd have to find somewhere better to hide it. He waited for Alix. And for Vavilov. Most of the day he sat in his mother's old chair, windows open so he could smell the lilac. The cordite and burned-metal odour was subsiding but sometimes the scent of death overwhelmed the lilac and he had to close the windows.

He managed to make his way back to Woyrchstrasse the following evening. As he walked past the letter to the girl called Astrid he shone his torch on the paper. 'Astrid, still no word from you?' the writer had added. 'Your father died and the children and I are trying to get out of the city. We need to know where you are, *Liebling*.'

His own note was unanswered.

The next night he tried to return again but the Russians had set up a roadblock and he feared his orderly-with-an-injured-foot story wouldn't get him through it.

Dieter's mother ignored the fever and cough until Coca and Gregor convinced her to take to her bed. 'I'll handle any repairs that come in,' Coca said. 'Gregor can help.'

Ute's Russian protector had vanished and the girls and their mother hadn't eaten for two days. Gregor sold a pair of Eva's shoes, dainty evening pumps with beads around the toes, to an officer. With the proceeds he bought bread. The process took hours. He'd learned how to move through the rubble-strewn streets, dodging Russian patrols, discovering that, even when the piles of bricks seemed impenetrable, there'd be a route through: a miniature mountain pass.

Now the first wave of rapes was dying down, Berlin women were appearing in daylight, heads wrapped in turbans (no point in showing off unwashed hair), to clear the rubble. They worked in groups, stopping for cigarette breaks during which, to Gregor's amazement, they'd often break into howls of laughter. He saw a certain irony in his own situation, but nothing at all comical in theirs. When they saw him looking at them they'd turn away. He understood. Men were redundant in this new world. Having done their worst to the city and the country, males had no role to play in trying to build something new – that was women's work. He thought of Sofia, how she would have nodded her head at these observations. She'd always believed women were tougher, more resilient. And Alix had been tough, too, working the farm while her father was away at war.

It was still Alix who preoccupied him as he negotiated the rubble mountains. Perhaps he'd catch a glimpse of her in a backstreet or at a bread queue. *Alix, Alix, Alix.* Sometimes he realized he'd been saying her name aloud, over and over again. People didn't stare at him; his was a very mild form of the insanity you could see on the streets every day: people rocking and clutching themselves while they muttered, sometimes bursting out with hysterical laughter. The *Kellerkinder* – children sleeping in cellars – were too busy scavenging, and their mothers were occupied with rubble-clearance and cooking whatever could be found to eat.

At the edge of the temporary lake at the end of the street

a man in a peaked cap muttered something about fresh eggs. Gregor stopped. *Eier.* He couldn't remember the last time he'd seen one. Dieter's mother would benefit from a boiled egg. 'Let me see them.'

The man opened his pocket and showed him two creamy-white eggs. Gregor reached into his pocket.

'Not money,' said the man. '*Zigaretten.*'

'How about some brandy? I've got some in my apartment, I can get it in a second—'

He stiffened. Reflected in the stagnant floodwater was a familiar outline. Gregor swore under his breath. He could run but Vavilov would have posted men along the street. The egg vendor slipped away. Gregor checked for the cyanide capsules in his pocket and turned round to Vavilov, keeping his head up, forcing himself to meet the older man's stare.

'Hello, Fischer. Amazing how nature adapts, isn't it?' He nodded at the swan on the water. 'Could we go up to your apartment, Comrade?'

He led the way up, feeling Vavilov's eyes on his bastardized uniform jacket. He should have worn Dieter's suit today; he'd grown careless.

'That's the thing about standard tunics, you can't change the basic shape. Even if you remove the trimmings.'

'Did you come here to discuss tailoring?' Gregor showed him inside. 'I found a bottle of my father's brandy. God knows why nobody drank it during the raids.' He poured them both measures while Vavilov paced the sitting room, picking up books and records, studying paintings.

'Your family lived well.'

'We paid for it.'

'Germans certainly are paying a heavy price.' He took a sip of his brandy and raised his eyebrows in appreciation. 'Tell me about your parents. Your mother went back on the stage for a while after you were born, didn't she?'

He looked amused at Gregor's surprise. 'It doesn't take us long to find Berliners willing to talk.'

'She turned to cabaret, reviews, that kind of thing. She never went on the classical stage here.'

'Why not?' Vavilov's face was inscrutable.

'I think she liked the rawness of some of the new material. But then all those shows started disappearing in 1933. I was only six or seven then but I remember her coming back one evening after a matinee and saying she'd never stand on a Berlin stage again.'

Vavilov gazed at the piano and the photographs. 'She made a comfortable home for you and your father?'

Gregor nodded. 'I can't remember her complaining about missing her work, but she must have done.'

'She wasn't one of nature's hausfraus.'

'No.' Why was he blabbing about his distant childhood to this man? He reminded himself that Vavilov could still send him east. Or blindfold him and order him to kneel on the Persian rug to be shot.

'You had a secure childhood?'

Gregor stared at him.

'I sound like a psychiatrist, don't I?'

'You certainly don't sound like someone who recruited at Kolyma and interrogated Prussian landowners.' Gregor watched the older man carefully and thought he detected a

280

glimpse of some emotion in his countenance. Hard to tell whether it was anger or shame.

'You know, I never thought it would come to this.' Vavilov glanced at the window and the ruined streets outside.

'What do you mean?'

'When Germany invaded Poland I thought the British and French would make a noise but keep out of it. I assumed they'd let Hitler head east to take on Stalin, friendship pact or not, somewhere beyond the Polish border.' Gregor had never heard him volunteer opinions like this. 'The rest of us could have avoided the worst of it and the dictators would have destroyed each other.' Vavilov's hand sliced the air in demonstration. 'Leaving Europe the better off.'

Gregor blinked rapidly. 'But you're a Communist!' he blurted out.

Vavilov seemed to stare straight through him. 'Of course, it would never have worked. I saw that by 1941. By 1942 it had all gone irreparably wrong.'

Marie's interest in this man when they'd been sitting round the kitchen table at Alexanderhof. Suddenly Gregor saw the connection. 'I know who you are.' The words seemed to drop out of his mouth. 'But I don't understand why you turned to the Soviets.'

'The Germans smashed the Polish Home Army Intelligence Service. I had to go somewhere.'

'But why not to the west?'

'Ideologically impossible.'

'It might have spared you the last few months.' Vavilov blinked. 'You've hated it, too, haven't you? All those lists you've made, but you've shot so few people. You've let so many escape.'

'Others will remedy any gaps in my work.' Vavilov spoke very quietly and Gregor had to lean forward to hear him. 'And so, Gregor Fischer, you and I each have information on one another.'

'Yes.'

'And you must have worked out by now that I knew your mother. And the baroness.'

'In Vienna before the war. Where you were called Viktor Vargá. You left Vienna in the mid twenties and moved around between Poland and Hungary and one or two other countries.' It was as though Gregor were reciting it all by heart.

Vavilov raised an approving eyebrow. 'Yes, I found myself compromised and had to leave Austria in a hurry. Then I heard Eva'd gone off to Berlin to marry a young radical German publisher.'

'My father.'

'A bad choice for a half-Jew.' Vavilov shook his head. 'Not that I'd have been much better.'

'You were . . . involved with my mother?' But Gregor hardly needed to ask, he'd sensed it already.

Vavilov nodded. 'She was probably the love of my life. I wasn't good at acknowledging emotional ties in my youth. And politics intervened. Then years later, when I'd washed up in Warsaw, I heard that Eva and her son were also in Poland and needed help getting out of the city.'

'You organized the timber van.'

'That part worked well. But I had no idea the Soviets would jump on the eastern Poles like that.' Vavilov rose and closed the sitting-room door. 'What happened to the Gronowski brothers? I know that Jacob reached Krasnovodsk, where he recognized you.'

Krasnovodsk. Gregor hadn't let himself think about what had happened there.

'They ran into a patrol.' Gregor wondered whether Jacob had recovered and travelled on to Persia. More likely the NKVD had sent him to a camp too.

Vavilov held out his glass for a refill. 'That's what tends to happen to people who associate with me. Deportation. Loss.' Another man might have sounded maudlin; Vavilov sounded matter-of-fact. Gregor recharged their glasses.

'I don't understand you.' Gregor drank his brandy. 'The more you tell me about yourself the more of a cipher you become.'

Vavilov's eyes refocused on Gregor and his words were studiedly neutral again. 'There's probably not much of me to understand. People have often made the mistake of taking me far too seriously. Give me some sunflowers in a field or a swan on a pond and that's all I need.' He looked towards the window. 'I always thought I could keep myself free of some of the misery by distancing myself from the ordinary human ties. But when I see what's happened to this city and Warsaw before it and all the others before that I accept that no man living in the middle of the twentieth century in the middle of Europe can possibly be free.'

'What's so wonderful about personal freedom?' Gregor asked, the spirits emboldening him. 'What's life without other people?'

Vavilov leaned back into his chair. 'I was like you when I

283

was a boy. I was optimistic.' He gave a faint smile. 'It amazes me that you still seem to have some optimism. God knows why.' A cloud must have passed over the sun. The room grew dark. 'I grew up a happy child. My father was a veterinarian and we lived in a country house just outside the town of Cluj, then part of Hungary. After the first war Cluj was given to Romania and we were forced out. We moved to Budapest. We'd lost a lot, but we were still together and my father planned to start a new veterinary practice and I was to study art.' Vavilov's eyes narrowed. 'One day in 1920 my mother went out to buy bread. It was the time of the White Terror. Some drunken militiamen came out of an inn and attacked her. Just for being on the streets. Apparently they thought she was Jewish. She wasn't, in fact.' The lids half lowered over his eyes. 'They kicked in her skull and she died of a brain infection a week later.'

Vavilov was speaking so rapidly Gregor had to strain to catch the words.

'My father seemed to retreat into his own world after that. Stopped eating. Just sat staring out of the window. I tried to help him but I couldn't. Eventually he died too. I decided I would never allow myself to feel pain like that again. I moved to Vienna and devoted myself to . . . myself.' Vavilov raised an eyebrow. 'I'd always spoken several languages well: we spoke German and Magyar at home, my mother taught me Polish because she'd grown up in Cracow and I'd had a Russian governess for a few years. So I could adapt myself to whichever city best suited me. I was entirely free.'

'And yet you have accepted some human obligations,

haven't you?' Gregor could not believe he was daring to say this but something pushed him on. 'You've saved people.'

Vavilov raised an eyebrow. 'The brandy is making you sentimental, my friend.'

'I remember East Prussia,' Gregor said. 'I remember what happened at that big house.'

The rest of the intelligence unit had wanted to question the village pastor, rumoured to be anti-Communist and unrepentant. Gregor had muttered something about clergy not being his area of expertise and found himself walking alone for the first time in months. Ahead of him lay a red-brick manor house. He checked Vavilov's list. The house wasn't listed. This family, whoever they were, had somehow fallen through a crack in the system.

Behind him he heard singing. Another wave of soldiers passing through. They wouldn't be able to resist this manor. The family might have been spared Vavilov's attentions but the alternative was probably worse.

Gregor found his legs pulling him into a run.

The young woman and old man were plucking chickens in the kitchen. Why hadn't they left? Fools if they thought the stories about the Red Army were just rumours. 'Get out!' He waved a gun at them. 'No packing, just go!'

They stared at him, feathers floating round them like snow.

'I must get blankets for the baby.' The woman roused herself and ran for the stairs.

Gregor pushed past them into the orchard. He'd done all he could.

A scream from the first floor told him he'd been too late. They'd got the woman. He crept round the side of the house and in through the back door. The child lay unattended in a baby carriage in the hallway. He was powerless to stop whatever they were doing to the adults but the kid might have a chance. He picked it up and grabbed one of its blankets and ran through the orchard to a farm worker's cottage where an old woman rose from her fireside seat with a wail, holding out her arms for the child. Gregor pulled her coat from the peg on the back of the door and threw it at her. 'Leave now.'

He felt a blade at the back of his neck. 'No, Jean-Luc!' the old woman screeched. 'One of us!'

The blade moved a millimetre. 'In that uniform?'

'He came to warn us. Let him go.' The knife dropped. Gregor put a hand to his neck.

'I thought you were like the others.' The young man spoke good German but the French accent was still marked. He must be a French prisoner-of-war sent out here to work in the fields who'd found kind treatment in this isolated, almost manless, community.

'Just go – they're already in the big house!' Gregor made for the door, anger and pity so muddled together inside him that he thought he might vomit.

Despite everything he was still German, still one of them.

Vavilov was waiting for him outside the farmhouse where they'd set up base. In the gloom the red tip of his cigarette looked like a single baleful eye. Vavilov's own eyes were sleepy as ever. He might have been taking a stroll on his way out to dinner. 'Did you detain all the family members?'

'Not the child.' Gregor looked down at the snow. 'And they got the woman and old man.'

Vavilov threw the cigarette stub into the snow where it hissed briefly. 'That's not your concern, Comrade. You just provide intelligence.'

'There you are,' Vavilov said, when Gregor had finished reminding him. 'I warned you not to let sentiment cloud your judgement.'

'And yet you let some of those people go,' Gregor said. 'You knew they didn't deserve execution or imprisonment and you let them escape.'

'I arrested a fair number, Comrade. And we shot a few of the worst Fascist aristocrats.'

'But you never touched the innocent – not if you could help it. And when we were near Alexanderhof you made sure I saw the list with the von Matkes' names on it. You didn't stop me from going ahead to warn them because that's what you wanted me to do.' He was almost shouting now. 'You used your free will.'

Vavilov's face was so still he might have been turned to stone. But the pupils of his eyes seemed to have expanded as he listened. 'The Catholics must have got to you in Poland or somewhere else, Comrade,' he said finally. 'Your mother would have laughed at all this talk of the innocent and the guilty and free will.' He swallowed the last of his brandy.

'Tell me more about my mother,' Gregor said, when a moment had passed. 'What happened to her when she left Brest?'

'For a while I managed to keep her safe in a labour camp

287

in the Urals.' Vavilov's voice seemed to be coming from far away. 'It was hard but at least she was doing indoor work and the food was regular.'

'Did you see her there?' He could hardly get the words out. His mother – labouring in a camp thousands of miles from civilization, beyond all contact, all help. It was no more than he'd feared for the last five years, but hearing confirmation of her fate was shattering.

'It would have been too dangerous for her to see someone like me. I fell under suspicion, too, within a month of her arriving in the Urals. Then they sent her on somewhere else and I couldn't trace her.'

'So you came to find me . . . there . . . instead.'

'I found you by fluke. I was in Kolyma looking for Eva.'

Gregor found his hands clenching the arms of his chair at the mention of the place. Even its name could conjure up the stink of unwashed bodies and sour breath.

'By then I'd managed to ingratiate myself with the Soviets. The official reason for my visit to the Magadan peninsula was recruitment. They gave me all the files of Poles in that *lager*. I had no idea that Paul Smolinsky was Gregor Fischer until I saw you walking across the yard to the hospital and something about you seemed familiar – I'd seen you before, back in Warsaw, with Eva.'

'You'd seen me with my mother?'

'In a department store one Saturday morning. I was there buying braces or something equally trivial. I saw Eva with a boy.' Vavilov stared at one of the photographs of Gregor's mother. 'I didn't show myself, but I watched you both as you shopped. She was buying you socks. "Don't be so fussy, Gregor," she said. "Just choose a pair."'

Gregor recalled the Saturday morning trips to the Brothers Jablkowski.

'Warsaw was dangerous enough for her before the Germans arrived. There were Polish right-wingers in the city who could have shown – probably *did* show – the Germans a few tricks. But I kept my ear to the ground; found out what I could about her through my network – which included friends of the Gronowski brothers.'

Gregor bowed his head.

'Then, one evening,' Vavilov continued, with an eye on the closed door, 'your mother came to a café I used to visit, a Jewish café. I hadn't seen her since Vienna about ten years earlier. She asked for help to get out of Warsaw. I managed to give her papers allowing her to cross into the Russian zone and found her a place in a truck with a permit to leave Warsaw.'

'Where do you think she is now?'

Vavilov studied the empty glass. 'She may still be alive, thousands and thousands of miles inside the Soviet Union.' His voice grew flat. 'We'll never know.'

Again they let the silence lie between them undisturbed for some minutes. Then Vavilov stood, pulling something out of a tunic pocket, a scrap of paper that looked as though it must have been ripped from a notebook, covered in urgent, hasty writing. 'But there are things we do know.'

Gregor focused on the piano. *Deportation. His mother's death . . .*

'Before we left Alexanderhof a woman's body was discovered. A Baroness von Matke.'

Gregor sat up. 'You didn't tell me.'

'You were under enough suspicion. Just keeping you alive was enough of a job. You were safest knowing as little as possible.' The man sounded harsh now. 'You of all people should know that only the ignorant are safe.'

Why, Gregor thought, why so keen to save me? Just for my mother's sake?

The older man's voice flattened. 'The baroness was in the forest. With Preizler. He still had his Gestapo warrant in a pocket. They had a woman's pistol with them but there were no bullet wounds, no sign of a struggle. They were just sitting together in the snow, dead. Neither of them wore coats.' He removed a piece of paper from his tunic pocket. 'This isn't addressed to you but you might want to read it. It's from Maria von Matke.'

Darling Alix

I'm writing this in haste because it's already dawn. He said he would intercede for Peter. I was never his mistress but I trusted him. Not any longer. I'll ensure he's no longer a threat to you or Gregor and that he pays for what he's done with his life, but I can't leave him for the Russians to torture. Go west to the Rhineland, Alix, my darling. Wait for Papi, but not for too long. Try to find a way to get Gregor west, too. Make yourself a new and happy life and try to remember me with some fondness.

All my love, Mami.

Gregor folded it and placed it in his own pocket, expecting Vavilov to protest, but he didn't. 'I never thought Marie was his creature. She was just trying to help her husband.'

'They went back a long way, Eva, Maria, Preizler and Lena.' Vavilov looked at his watch. 'Which brings us to you, Herr Fischer. You could try and swim over the Elbe to the Americans, I suppose, but I don't rate your chances. I'll do what I can to let you just disappear. But I want your gun.'

Gregor walked to the piano and moved a photograph of Matthias onto the stool so he could open the lid. He handed Vavilov the revolver. 'Why are you letting me go?'

But Vavilov was preoccupied with the photograph Gregor had placed on the stool, scrutinizing the image of the man with the unruly hair and carelessly knotted tie.

'Is it because you've told me incriminating things about yourself and you're worried I'll report you?' Gregor went on.

Vavilov said nothing until he had replaced the photograph. 'I had a theory about you.' He shrugged. 'It wasn't true, I should have known it wasn't. But now I find I can't just throw you to the dogs.'

Gregor felt his puzzlement work its way across his face. 'Don't ask me to explain, Comrade. I won't.' There was an emotion in his tone Gregor couldn't decipher. 'I'll tell them that I believe a desperate SS unit may have taken you prisoner.'

'Thank you.'

Vargá walked to the door and halted. 'Don't.' He sighed. 'I've been putting off telling you something else that was found at Alexanderhof. Another body in the forest. A girl.'

Gregor clutched the side of the piano.

'Her name was written in a book. I'm afraid it was Alexandra von Matke.'

Vavilov said something else but Gregor didn't hear him. He barely noticed the older man opening the door and leaving the apartment. The spring light illuminated motes of dust in the air and outside a blackbird burst out in a flood of notes.

At some stage Gregor must have moved to the window, where he found himself watching Vavilov's progress along the street. He longed to call him back to the apartment, to beg him to unsay what he'd said about Alix. Mechanically he noted Vavilov pause a second or two at the lake to watch the swan, who seemed to have acquired a mate. A woman came towards Vavilov pushing a handcart full of burned timbers. The cart struck a stone and overturned, sending singed chunks of wood tumbling across Vavilov's path. A sixth sense seemed to warn him of the accident before it happened and with a sideways step he glided out of the way, graceful as a dancer.

He turned the corner and was gone.

Part Four

Thirty-two

Alix
Pomerania, July 2002

The train pulls out of the Berlin Ostbahnhof, rather than the elegant old Stettiner Bahnhof I remember from childhood. Mami, Papi and I would sit in a carriage full of excited Berliners on their way to the Baltic coast and look indulgently at the poor city-dwellers, who only had an annual fortnight of salty air to enjoy.

I'm used to the changes in Berlin; I've returned several times since the war, the last time for the service of remembrance for the German Resistance members.

But I've never been back to Pomerania before and I never dreamed I'd return with my son. I still can't keep my eyes off him. I still long to touch him. And yet I probably come across as over formal as I try to control the waves of emotion threatening me. Does he understand that European manners aren't American ones? People here are more circumspect in the way they express themselves. It doesn't mean they don't feel just as much.

My son's eyes are on the view from the window. He's hoping that material from this journey will make an article on post-Communist relations between Germany and Poland. *Time*, perhaps. There may even be enough to produce a book proposal. One of the benefits of freelance journalism is that it allows you the freedom to take off on trips with recently discovered parents. Michael returned to the US after we first met in January and arranged things so that he could make this journey to the past with me. The intervening six months have felt like six years. What Michael doesn't know is that we'll be in Alexanderhof on my seventy-fifth birthday. I recall my eleventh birthday in 1938, the night that Preizler came to dinner.

We're passing through the eastern suburbs with their brutalist tower blocks, exposed pipes and weed-infested bomb sites. At least it's quieter than it was in the *Mitte*, with its drilling and digging and hurry to rebuild. There's some relief from the drabness: dashes of colour from delphiniums, lilies and roses in passing allotments. Little wooden garden houses dot the rows of flowers and vegetables, well kept, cherished. But for the most part it reminds me that I'm journeying between two cultures. And between past and present.

Finally the last of the suburbs are gone and we're looking out at the empty countryside. God knows what Michael makes of what he sees. This was once a prosperous corner of Germany – the very heart of Prussia itself: farms, churches, neat gardens, children's playgrounds, ordered and orderly, even in wartime.

'When it's sunny like this it's so hard to imagine how much snow there was that night,' I say, as much to myself as to him. 'And we were all on the run, babies, old people, all out in the freezing cold.'

'It must have been terrifying, knowing the Red Army was on its way.'

Terrifying hardly begins to describe it. 'We should have left weeks earlier. The authorities wouldn't let us go until it was really too late.'

'They wouldn't let you leave? Even though they knew what was about to happen?'

'The Nazis thought it was defeatism to move civilians out.' I can feel the sneer on my face. 'Stalin must have thought they were mad not to get us out of his way.'

He glances out of the window again, at the empty fields. 'Looks pretty abandoned now. According to this,' he points at the guidebook, 'everyone's left for the west. It must have been like this in parts of the States during the Depression. Mom and Dad used to tell me stories about empty fields and abandoned farms. Of course I only remember America in the postwar boom years when everyone seemed to drive big shiny cars and have enormous refrigerators.'

'I'd love to travel to America.' It's a relief to switch attention to another country.

'Seems strange to me you haven't.'

'I was supposed to go to a conference in New York with Robin years and years ago. But he caught mumps and we didn't go. And we usually holidayed in France or Europe.'

'You'll have to come and stay with us.' He chats some more about the family in America, his journalist wife and teenage sons, how a stomach virus ruined a once-in-a-lifetime trip to Brazil. 'We'd have liked more children,' he says, 'but it wasn't to be. We were lucky with the two we have; they're great kids.'

Lucky indeed. I remember Robin, his crestfallen face the day the specialist made his pronouncement. What bad luck for a grown man to catch mumps.

I didn't deserve my kind husband, who waited so patiently for me to complete teacher training and for the authorities to allow us to marry. And I don't deserve this son, still straight-backed and athletic, who's forgiven me for forsaking him.

'So quiet.' Michael's looking out at the fields again.

'Much has changed.' The crunch of boots through snow, explosions behind us, soldiers shouting as they pushed past, a dog chained to a tree, barking at each fleeing refugee, until it was silenced by a soldier's rifle.

The train stops at a country station. Arrows on an old sign point west to Berlin and east on to Stettin. Soon we'll leave Germany and enter what's formed part of Poland since the war. My heart thumps in anticipation. But when we draw into Stettin the first thing I notice are crumbling brick chimneys and warehouses with weed-covered roofs. As we step down onto the platform beneath the old iron canopy, neglected and decaying, a lump forms in my throat and I can hardly speak to Michael or walk to the taxi rank.

Occasionally we pass a building I knew as a child – one of the soaring red-brick churches, more like forts than places of worship, or a road whose contours feel familiar – and returning memory jolts me.

'Szczecin getting busy now,' says the taxi-driver. 'People come for surgeons.'

'Surgeons?'

'Cosmetic surgery. And dentists. Is cheap here. And German boys come because all their girls go west. German boys like Polish girls.'

German males courting the women their grandfathers believed fit only for slaves.

The taxi-driver ploughs on, showing no fear and obviously possessing an extra sense alerting him to trams. I seem to remember them ringing bells to warn one of their approach. We drive past grass-covered bomb sites. Michael gazes at a church whose windows have been concreted over, presumably to save the expense of glass. Perhaps nobody here feels much emotional connection to this old Prussian city – most of the incomers after 1945 were displaced Poles from the east of the country.

Yet I spot surviving wrought-iron balconies and baroque plasterwork, graceful counterpoints to the modern blocks and few remaining Prussian civic buildings. A right turn takes us through a quarter that looks almost Parisian: boulevards, circuses and squares. Children kick balls on patches of grass and adults sit reading newspapers under trees. 'Grunwaldski Place,' says the driver.

'We used to call it Kaiser Wilhelm Platz,' I recall.

We turn into a wide thoroughfare.

'That's the post office.' I point at the imposing red-brick building.

Michael whistles. 'The Prussians certainly didn't believe

in small-scale public buildings. Strange to think they were such a big presence here for so long.'

'Strange indeed.' For all our pride and military power we were ultimately driven out into the snow.

'Car rental here.' Without warning or signal the driver cuts across two lanes of traffic into a modern hotel complex, causing a bus behind to hoot its horn. We smell burned rubber. 'Drive careful. Drivers here mad.'

This is all so un-Germanic. Papi would have loved it.

The sun bounces off glass-plated high-rise offices and hotels and dazzles me. Gone are the neat little shops behind the castle with their bright awnings into which bustled neat German women with neat baskets to buy bread and meat and fish. Gone are the old gabled merchants' houses. And the barges chugging up and down the river like a staccato accompaniment to the huge seagoing ships with their cargoes of sugar, corn and timber. And yet, on this sunny day, Stettin or Szczecin doesn't feel despondent, there's purpose in the way pedestrians tackle the intimidating junctions and trams tear along the streets. It just doesn't feel like the city I knew as a child.

We cross the Oder, slow and grey in appearance today, and drive through endless out-of-town shopping outlets, attracting dozens of German number plates. It must be worthwhile crossing the border to shop here. In 1945 the Germans left with a few pots and pans and blankets stuffed into handcarts and rucksacks, but their grandchildren are returning to empty the shelves.

Trees and open fields start to smooth the jagged edges of

my memory. On the roadsides, only centimetres away from the traffic, children stand with glass jars of berries and mushrooms. I try to recall whether German peasants once sold produce on the side of the road before the war. I wince as lorries thunder within inches of a boy who looks about ten and want to tell Michael to stop the car so we can buy up all the berries and send the lad safely home. But there'd only be another child around the next bend and another and another.

'You've been very quiet.' Michael is a good travel companion, happy to sink into his own thoughts but ready to respond to any conversational cues I throw his way.

'Just remembering. Papi's car once burst a tyre somewhere here. A storm blew in from the Baltic and he and Mami got drenched while they were changing it.' Mami's long white linen coat never recovered.

The forests add interest to what would otherwise be a pleasant but unremarkable landscape. Birds of prey hover over wheat fields, still green in the early July sunshine.

'It could be anywhere, really, couldn't it?' Michael says.

I open my mouth to dispute the point but realize the truth of what he says. 'That was always the Prussian problem.' I'm remembering Papi's views on the subject. 'No natural barriers apart from the Elbe and the Oder.' Our geography was our destiny.

'The Poles once owned bits of Pomerania before it became German, didn't they?'

'And the Swedes. The Hohenzollerns were almost Johnny-come-latelies in this part of Prussia.'

'Prussia. There's a name you never hear any more. It's been wiped off all the maps. How does that make you feel,

Alix?' Sometimes my son switches into professional mode and I can almost imagine he's interviewing me for his article.

'Churchill blamed us for everything: Hitler, the war. Perhaps he was right. Many Junker families joined the Party. Even some of our cousins.'

'Really?' He raises an eyebrow. 'I suppose I liked to think the family kept itself aloof from the Nazis.'

'Few families managed that completely. And it was just the people who should have known better – the doctors, lawyers and educated classes – who joined.' I can hear the acid in my tone.

'At least the Prussians made up for their earlier failures when it came to July 1944, didn't they?'

'The Bomb Plot?' I cross my arms. 'My father joined an old Prussian regiment with traditions going back hundreds of years. But some of those noble officers had been in the east. They knew what was happening. They did nothing for years. That's why Papi left, to join the Abwehr, military intelligence, and see if he could make contact with the Allies.' All those trips to Switzerland and Sweden Papi made, all those raised hopes . . . 'And then when he and his friends finally decided to show Churchill and Roosevelt they were serious, they couldn't even organize it properly.' I must have re-examined all these details in my head a hundred times.

'If they'd acted earlier it would have been easier. But they waited. I suppose I find that hard to understand. But Papi was brave and he and his friends reclaimed a little of our lost honour. For that I am grateful.' The heaviness suddenly shrouding me must be tiredness. I long to be back in my drawing room in London with a cup of tea and the *Times* crossword.

'And you'll tell me about my father when we reach the house?' He asks the question very softly.

'Yes,' I say. 'Yes I will.' And I blink hard. 'I'm sorry you had to wait all these months to come out here.'

'It wouldn't have been a comfortable journey in the winter and I had to wait for Steph to finish for summer.' Steph's a university lecturer, very clever. I've enjoyed a few telephone conversations with her. But the mention of Gregor has made me nervous again. Gregor, so long unheard of.

I look out of the window for something else to talk about. 'Somewhere around here there used to be an enormous baroque house with its own art gallery – hundreds of Old Masters, Vermeers, Rembrandts, you name it. The family sent some of them west in time but the Russians took most of the pictures.' We both stare at the empty space. 'They probably razed it and turned it into a pig farm.' Suddenly I feel every year of my age. 'I could only make this journey after Robin died. And when you turned up it seemed particularly appropriate to do it together.'

When Michael frowns two little dimples form, one on each temple. So like his father. 'Are you saying Robin didn't know the truth?'

'Oh, I told him eventually. But not the whole story.'

'He didn't . . .?' He flushes. 'I'm sorry, it just seems strange that he didn't want to know about it all.'

'Not Robin. But people were different back then, Michael. Openness wasn't considered such a virtue. Reticence was admired.' I sound so dry.

'I'm so sorry.' His voice has that American warmth to it. I'm lucky, having him turn up in my life and be so wonderful. He might have hated me. He'd have justification. 'Tell me more about my grandfather.'

No interrogation. He reminds me of Papi himself: so discreet, so gentle with people.

'You already said he was a clock fanatic.'

'To the point of insanity.' I recite the litany of attempted repairs, the regrets when clocks that had been taken to pieces couldn't be reassembled, the triumphs when spare parts were obtained from shops in distant parts of Europe and ageing timepieces could be persuaded to move their hands. 'Poor Papi, we took his two best specimens in the wagon with us but they were lost when the Russians attacked. The carriage clock found its way to Munich of all places. Robin put word out that we were looking for certain timepieces and eventually a dealer made contact. It's the only thing I have from the house apart from the boots I wore when we left.'

'You kept your boots?'

'They were good boots. Papi always told me to look after my footwear. I couldn't bring myself to throw them away when I came to London so I kept them.'

We turn a bend in the road that feels familiar. Trzebiatow, the sign says. Treptow in my time. Michael drives over a stone bridge. Below the river curves a lazy bend around the steep banks. Boys skim stones and men fish. I point to a soaring church tower. 'Luther preached his sermons there and persuaded German Pomeranians to turn Protestant. Now it's a Polish Catholic church.'

Michael smiles at the irony.

'You're supposed to be able to see the house from the tower but we never could.' We pull up outside the town's only hotel, a plain but neat establishment on the square. Some of the gabled houses have been repaired but most are crumbling.

'Must have been a smart little marketplace once.' Michael gets out and walks round the car to hold the door open for me.

'It was.' I can see it all: Papi smiling as some heifers reached more than he'd expected; grain merchants jostling with farmers; Lena gossiping with a friend; Mami sitting in the café drinking coffee and smoking. 'When *they* came to power some of the chatter died down.' The market lost its bustle. 'People looked over their shoulders before they spoke. And the Jewish merchants slowly disappeared.'

'We could check in now if you want.'

'Let's see if we can find the caretaker and get the key. Then I can relax.'

The trip involves several U-turns and consultations with a street map. At last we find the apartment block where the caretaker lives and Michael rings the bell. A boy in a Manchester United shirt runs down to tell us in a mixture of German and American-English – of which he's very proud – that his mother is out. He goes upstairs to find the house key and returns empty-handed. 'Perhaps old man has it?'

'Which man?' Michael asks.

'Man who phone.' The boy shrugs.

We agree to come back after dinner when the mother will have returned and walk back through peaceful streets to the hotel. 'Look.' Michael points up to the roof of an old house. 'A stork's nest.'

'I wonder if they still build nests on the stable roof at Alexanderhof.'

'You never told me who actually owns Alexanderhof now,' Michael says.

'The Polish state. They used it as a children's home until about five years ago.'

'You're not tempted to buy it back?'

'What would I do with a decaying old house? For me it will be enough to see it again.'

'Sounds like the kind of place that might make a hotel.'

The idea appeals. 'Perhaps it would be the best thing for the old house, people coming and going, fresh faces. It would . . .'

'What?'

'Help drive out the ghosts, I suppose.' Erase the image of the four of us sitting in the kitchen with the snow falling outside.

We unload the car and check into the hotel. 'Nice little place. Did you come here as a child?'

'Frequently, before the war. And even after it had started. Right up until the time . . .' Right up until the day Papi was arrested.

Michael's expression tells me I don't have to explain which event I mean. 'We came into town to try and buy sugar for the jam we were making. It was impossible – all the sugar had gone and Mami said we'd leave it, we'd have to make do with what we had at home. Mami wanted to be outdoors. She said she felt calmer in the fresh air.'

Thirty-three

Pomerania, 1944

A short shower had cleared the muggy July air and flowers and shrubs glowed in the clear evening sun. Alix was thankful they hadn't hoed up all the flowerbeds. She still missed the borders Mami'd had dug up. Carrots and radishes now sprouted where giant poppies, hollyhocks, phloxes and cornflowers had bloomed. Vegetables were essential, naturally, but a few delphiniums and lupins were good for the soul.

Mami hummed as she picked raspberries. 'Times like this I could almost be back in the Tyrol. We grew lots of fruit there. Your grandfather loved cherries.'

Behind them Lena sighed.

'You remember, don't you, Lena? And Anton's father grew fruit too.' Mami grew silent as she always did when she mentioned Preizler's name.

'I remember.' Lena sounded curt. 'All those wasps swarming round.' She held out a hand for Mami's basket. 'Let me take that.' As she passed it over Mami's face seemed to lose its temporary glow. Hope was hard to cling to. It had flourished for twenty-four hours while they'd thought Hitler dead. Then plummeted when they heard his voice on the radio shrieking for revenge. Papi had telephoned Mami and told her he'd stay in Berlin even though his friends had already been arrested.

'Come home for God's sake.' Mami'd sounded desperate. And scared. 'Hide in the forest.'

But he hadn't. Probably scared that if he evaded arrest they'd come for Mami and Alix too. They'd already heard of wives sent to camps, children placed in orphanages or adopted. He'd stay in the open, like a beast drawing the hounds away from the young in the lair.

Lena and Alix carried the baskets through the hall. The telephone rang and Mami came running in, biting her lip. 'Wait in the kitchen with Lena, *Liebling*.' Did she feel a premonition?

Lena closed the kitchen door and rinsed the fruit in huge metal colanders and found precious sugar in the pantry. 'A good haul.' She nodded in approval as she tipped raspberries into saucepans and added the last of the carefully hoarded sugar. 'Watch these for me and I'll pour you a glass of milk. You look parched.'

Alix stirred the saucepans, breathing in the aroma of high summer. Almost impossible to believe in anything bad happening when you could smell blackcurrants, raspberries and sugar. She didn't hear Mami open the door but some sense alerted Alix to her presence. 'When?' she asked her mother.

'This evening. That was one of the Abwehr secretaries.

Poor girl, she's taking a risk just telephoning us.' Mami came in and slumped into a chair.

'I'm fetching you a *Kirsch*.' Lena slammed Alix's milk down on the table and went to the pantry.

'I don't need it.'

'You're having it, Maria.'

Only rarely did Lena call Mami by her Christian name.

'Where did they take him?'

'Plötzensee prison.'

Alix felt herself shake. To control herself she forced herself to focus on the familiar objects in the kitchen: the saucepans and sieves and the pottery sugar jar, the sailing ships on the Dutch tiles behind the stove.

'Drink it.' Lena pushed the glass at Mami. 'Ring Anton Preizler. He might know what's happening.'

'Anton?' Mami sipped her *Kirsch*, the pupils of her eyes large and black. 'I don't know. It might incriminate us in some way.'

'He's your friend, isn't he?' Lena sounded harsh. 'He knows people. He has ideas. Use the connection, Maria.'

Mami pushed aside the glass and rested her head on her hands. 'I don't know, Lena, I just don't know.' She let out a long moan. 'Peter let them take him to save us, God help him.'

Days passed. They heard nothing. Mami went up by train to Berlin in a linen and silk suit and dashing (but not too much so) straw hat. She took a parcel of clothes and a Bible for Papi, spending the night with friends. She returned the following evening, still carrying the parcel. 'They told me he didn't need it.' Despite the heat her face was paper-white. 'I must have talked to twenty people but nobody knew what was happening. He's not on the trial list.'

'That's good.' Lena took the parcel from her. 'That Justice Freisler is demented, a judge from hell.'

Mami removed her little straw hat and white gloves. Her fingernails were buffed and polished as meticulously as if she'd been attending a lunch party.

The telephone rang. Alix answered. 'Tell your mother another six were hanged this morning.' The caller hung up. Alix stared at the telephone.

Thirty-four

Alix
Pomerania, July 2002

I finish my story and brush a non-existent strand of hair off my brow, feeling as though I've exposed myself and wonder whether Michael can see me readjusting, tidying away emotions.

'I can't imagine how you must have felt when you heard the news. It must have been dreadful for you and your mother.'

I manage a nod. He looks around the bar, giving me time to recover. The room's decorated with old sepia photographs of the area, showing men wrapped in layers of fur pulling sleds into the marketplace across thick snow. 'You had harsh winters out here.'

'It's probably milder than it used to be. When I was little we used our sledge most winters. The farm horses would pull us around the estate.' The bells on the Haflingers' harness jingled and the runners swooshed over the snow. I was warm underneath the soft cashmere shawl Lena used to drape over my knees.

'We moved round a lot, but when I was a kid we spent some years in northern Michigan,' he says. 'We had a lake nearby that used to freeze. I loved skating.'

I feel the wistful expression on my own face. I've missed so many years – Michael as a child, skating, tobogganing and building snowmen.

'You had a magical childhood.' Please God, don't let me sound bitter. I have so much to be grateful for.

He puts a hand on mine. 'I was happy with the Whites. That's not to say I wouldn't have been as happy with my real mother. But I think you did the right thing. God, Alix, how could you have managed a child by yourself in Germany, in 1945?'

'Plenty of women managed.' Something's caught up in my throat. 'But I'm glad you were happy, Michael. I always wondered. In those days it was hard to trace adopted children. Nobody would help.'

We've already had this conversation; I've explained how I wanted to find him, how I made inquiries through the Red Cross and various other agencies in the fifties and sixties. But I feel I have to keep repeating my explanation. Perhaps the person I'm really trying to convince is myself.

'Sounds like the only person really hurt in this whole thing was you.' His voice is gentle. His gaze is steady and warm. 'As I grew older I became increasingly curious about my blood parents. The only thing I feared was that you wouldn't want to see me.'

'Never.' How fierce I sound. And yet, I don't know how I would have reacted if Michael had turned up twenty or thirty years ago, I don't know how I would have explained him to Robin.

'Having kids made me desperate to know more about you.'

'I can't wait to meet Stephanie and the boys.'

He pats his pocket. 'I keep trying not to call them all the time. It's darn expensive. But they're all so curious. Steph's been pushing me to find you ever since I saw that damn Bosnian documentary.'

'She understood how dreadful it was for you to believe what you imagined.'

'Yes.' And my son's confident, American voice is almost faltering now. 'She was so pleased when I made that first trip to see you.'

'And tomorrow we see the house.' I put my glass very carefully on the metal table between us. 'And I shall explain about Gregor.' I've tried to talk about him on the train but we've always had other people sitting near us. And Gregor has felt like a phantom, someone I might almost have imagined. I hope that walking round the old house will make him feel more substantial.

'It's all right.' Michael gives my hand a brief squeeze. 'Don't worry about anything.'

And again I might almost be looking into Papi's tender eyes. Papi was always so gentle. It's beyond me how Mami could have done what I suspected she'd done. But I was a young girl when it had happened. Perhaps I misunderstood.

Strange how this trip keeps taking me back to my mother

rather than my Resistance hero father: Mami as a young girl, growing up in the mountains, coming to Vienna to act and then marrying Papi and moving here. What a change it must have been for her.

I blamed my mother for so much, yet now when I think of her I feel a wistfulness that surprises me. I wish she could have seen her grandson.

Thirty-five

Marie
Pomerania, 1926

No matter how she phrased the telegram Marie knew it would cause Anton pain. He was trying so hard to make a success of the job he'd finally found in a Munich timber firm exporting wood from Austria to Hamburg. She hadn't seen him for nearly a year now but Lena had written and told her about his business struggles. Marie had thought of asking Lena to break the news to Anton, but that would be cowardly. She owed him more.

Her guilt felt like a localized dull ache, easily forgettable when wedding preparations swept her up, but apt to throb its way into her consciousness when she rested. She and Anton had never been lovers, never even had a relationship. He had no *right* to make her feel guilty. She'd never felt for him what she'd felt for Viktor Vargá.

Enough of Viktor Vargá. She'd never see him again. Nor

would Eva, probably. It was self-indulgent and shocking even to think of him now.

Peter was a darling and she liked it here in the north. She'd had enough of Viennese life, the gossip, the backbiting. Let her come to live in flat old Pomerania, as Peter described it, and settle down with these sensible north Germans. Peter didn't arouse such contradictory emotions in her as did Viktor and Anton; he wouldn't threaten her peace of mind. He was handsome and clever and straightforward. He'd promised her she could redecorate his eighteenth-century manor house exactly as she wished.

Berlin to Stettin, the nearest sizeable town to Peter's estate, was an easy train ride. Marie was up for the day, sorting out wedding matters with her fiancé. 'We'll have your friend Eva and her husband to stay once we're married,' Peter had said.

'A socialist publisher – in your house?'

'They sound fun. And I want to see Eva perform in one of her Berlin revues.'

'You'd probably be the only Junker in the audience.'

He grinned. 'You'd be surprised.'

And Peter's idea regarding Lena was perfect. They needed a housekeeper, he said. Someone who was more of a friend than a servant. Someone loyal and practical.

Marie sent her telegram from the huge red-brick post office building in Stettin.

Three days before the wedding, when Marie was packing up her things in the Berlin hotel that had been her home for the last three months, a carved wooden box came from the Tyrol with a congratulatory letter from him.

Your news came as a surprise, I'll admit. You must have got to know Peter von Matke very quickly as I don't remember you seeing much of him in Vienna! Clearly, he's a splendid fellow and I offer you both my heart-felt good wishes. What of your career? I hope we'll still see you on the stage?

She folded Anton's letter and put it into the carved box. He'd probably made it for her himself, he had a skill with wood – she remembered that hand-turned bowl he'd given her after her first performance as Rosalind in *As You Like It*. And yes, her career. She'd pushed the thought of next season to the back of her mind when Peter'd asked her to marry him, writing vague letters to the directors she'd worked with in Vienna, saying she'd be away for the summer and promising to get back in touch when she returned. Now perhaps she should admit to herself that she had no intention of returning to the stage.

She felt almost angry with Anton for forcing her to face this fact. She was throwing away all those years at the Academy and the promising start she'd made to her career. Peter had told her he was in no rush to start a family, that she should carry on acting if she wanted, perhaps follow up the interest she'd received from Babelsberg studios. She should devote herself to films, if that was what she wanted. And if she wanted to work in Vienna, he'd rent an apartment for them both and spend as much time down there as he could spare from the estate.

If she never saw Vienna again it wouldn't worry her. Or Viktor. She never wanted to remember the rapture in his face while Eva writhed on top of him. Even now, the memory of that scene filled her with an emotion she could almost label as terror. He hadn't even noticed Marie's reflection in the mirror as she stood watching them. He'd overlooked her and like a small child she'd felt fury. Hurt pride and fascination with something she didn't understand were driving her into marriage.

Just as something mysterious had driven Eva into her sudden wedding to Matthias. Marie had had suspicions, but as months passed she'd decided she'd been wrong. Then she'd seen Eva just last week, for coffee in the Fischers' apartment.

'Thanks for coming here.' Eva moved a pile of newspapers from the sofa so that Marie could sit. 'I've been sick. The doctor says I mustn't travel.' Her clothes seemed to hang less elegantly than before and her face was fuller around the chin.

'What is it, Eva? Why don't you tell me?' Of course Marie had guessed by now. That sudden marriage.

Eva twisted her hands in her lap. 'I'm . . . expecting.'

'I rather thought you might be.'

She gave an apologetic little smile. 'I'm so sorry I'll miss your wedding. You'll love married life. Have I already told you that my Matthias is a darling and I adore him?'

Marie met her dark gaze and saw Eva's eyes were almost overflowing.

'Are you *really* happy, Eva?'

The hands stopped their twisting. 'When I found out . . . when it was clear Viktor wasn't coming back I was desper-

ate. I thought I'd die. Matthias made me laugh. I probably . . .
became close to him rather too quickly.'

'We hardly knew him. At least, that's how I remember it.
He was just someone who came to parties.'

'Perhaps. But sometimes you can tell what a person's like
very quickly. Matthias was the right man for me. He's not like
Viktor – all mystery and things left unsaid.' Eva sat straighter.
'He tells me where he's going and when he'll be back. And
when the baby's born we'll have even more fun.'

Impossible to ask the question about the baby she longed
to put to Eva: *When is it due?*

'When can we come to Pomerania and visit you?' Eva
took Marie's hands in hers. 'You'll find my Red of a husband
a lamb in social situations, so don't worry that he'll alarm the
Junkers.'

'He seems very affable.' Marie remembered Matthias's
quick smile.

'Even Anton Preizler couldn't help liking him.' Eva gave
a dismissive wave. 'But enough of men. Are you going to
follow up that interest from the film directors, darling?'

And Marie's intention of asking Eva directly about Viktor
had come to nothing.

Now here she was in Stettin with her husband-to-be, enjoying their last excursion together before they married. She felt
herself relax. This was the right decision. Perhaps taken for
the wrong reasons, but right nonetheless. How long would a
girl like her have lasted on the stage anyway? Times were turbulent, anything could happen. Peter was a darling, eccentric,

yes, but devoted to her. She could love a man like him. She corrected herself, she already did.

Anton wrote no more letters, and three years had passed when she received a brief note telling her that he too had married, a Clara Becker in Munich. The timber export business was on the point of collapse because of the economic crisis. Somewhere in the letter was an unwritten accusation she couldn't ignore. She couldn't lie and say she hadn't been aware of his unspoken hopes.

But Anton was far away in Munich so she didn't find herself thinking about him often.

The arrival of Alexandra within a year of her marriage, the start of her film career in Berlin, Hitler's rise to power, the unexpected passion that built up between her and Peter; all these things kept her attention from her childhood friend.

Anton's telephone call in July 1938 took her by surprise. He and the family had moved to Stettin so he could take up a new position. Might he and Clara call on Marie and the baron? They'd be driving through that part of Pomerania on the Saturday evening and would very much like to pay their respects.

'Which means we'll have to invite them to dinner,' Peter told her. 'Anton is probably a Party member. Tell Eva to be discreet, he might not realize who her husband is.' For Eva and Gregor were here at Alexanderhof, enjoying a respite from the stifling atmosphere of the capital. Matthias Fischer, that rumpled man with the cheerful grin, gentle manners and left-wing opinions, had been taken off to Sachsenhausen, branded an enemy of the state. Did Anton know this? Marie racked her memory to recall if she'd ever mentioned Eva's sudden marriage to him. She thought he'd been at a job interview in Innsbruck when Eva and Matthias had slipped off to the registry office.

The last thing Eva needed was another encounter with a potentially hostile Anton. But if she was careful there was no reason for Anton to know who her husband was. They'd present Eva to the Preizlers with her maiden name: *Anton, you remember Eva Mauer? We used to share an apartment when we were both at the Academy.*

Marie shook her head. This was *Anton* they were talking about: a decent and kind man, a carver of wooden bowls and boxes.

But the tense expression on Peter's face, so rarely seen until these last few years, made Marie think that perhaps her husband was right and discretion should be the order of the night.

Thirty-six

Alix
Pomerania, 2002

At first glimpse the old house hasn't changed much. The white walls look as impregnable as I remember them, despite the streaks of yellow staining them. The formal parts of the garden have disappeared under grass and weeds, as has the tennis court. Mami's fruit bushes and borders are only a memory, although occasional hollyhocks and foxgloves still sway in the light breeze and the air smells sweet with honeysuckle. Faint white lines on the grass show that a football pitch has been marked out on the upper lawn where Papi once played croquet with Matthias Fischer while they argued about politics and books.

Many of the trees I remember still live on, including the acacias Papi had planted and the oak in the meadow, which was already a giant when my great-grandfather Friedrich was born and Napoleon fought at Austerlitz. Further away the birches and firs sway in the forest, just as they always have done. Early July is a good time of year for the garden – warm but without the alternating droughts and thunderstorms of later summer which played such havoc with Mami's beds of hollyhocks, delphiniums and lupins. The summerhouse has gone, already rotten by the time we left in forty-five. It would never have survived another sixty years of Baltic winters. A small rusty bench now occupies its place.

I think of all the valuables Mami buried in concrete pipes under the vegetables. Perhaps they're still there. Probably not. The Russians must have grown wise to that ruse.

And the house itself. Some roof tiles are missing and weeds grow out of chimneys. One could spend a fortune tending to roofs, Papi used to say as he settled yet another bill for a broken gutter or loose tiles.

Michael parks at the bottom of the steps. Frost has bitten chunks of stone from them, leaving them dangerously crumbly. Distance has deceived. The house is putting on a brave front like a dowager fallen on hard times. Over the decades small maintenance jobs have been left undone.

'Poor house,' I say under my breath. 'Poor house.' It seems smaller, too, which is ridiculous because it's still a three-storey Prussian country house built in the grand style. But now I can hardly see because ghosts are swarming round me: Mami, Lena, Papi and the wagon with its yellow horses, waiting to take us west. And Gregor with his Red Army uniform, Polish insignia and desperate eyes.

'You want to go inside now?' My son's voice, so reassuringly American and relaxed, breaks into my reverie.

'Forgive me. I was miles away.'

We climb the steps of the old house. No wooden troughs of lilies now, no geraniums, just a few cracked flowerpots.

Michael frowns. 'The door's open. *Hello*?' His voice resounds through the emptiness. No answer.

My eyes accustom themselves to the darkness of the hall. The antlers mounted on each side have gone. I never much liked these hunting trophies but I miss them now. I can make out the outlines of doors and rooms farther inside the house. Damp and mustiness has replaced the smells of beeswax and roses. Wallpaper I haven't seen before peels away from walls and wires hang from the ceiling. Someone has covered the black and white marble floor with linoleum, laced with holes and stained orange where the rain's come in. It took Mami ten years before the war to decorate this house. She scoured Paris and London for fine fabrics and wallpapers. I'm glad she never saw this.

Concern furrows Michael's face.

'Do you think it's a burglar?' I ask. Someone shuffles upstairs. Judging from the uneven footsteps the intruder has a slight limp. A cough echoes down the staircase.

'Stealing what?' Michael waves a hand at the empty light fittings and rows of naked curtain hooks hanging from plastic rails.

'It's all right.' Something is telling me that whoever is in the house bears us no malice. I follow my son upstairs, with care, because the treads on the steps groan as I tread on them. Nobody can have replaced or repaired them in the last half-century.

I lingered on this staircase the night of the dinner party in 1938 when Mami accidentally locked Gregor in the cellar, waiting for her and Preizler to wander into the garden so that I could tiptoe down and liberate him. In February 1945 I crept down the staircase again to release him, my heart almost hammering its way out of my chest because Preizler was again in the house, desperate and armed with a revolver.

A noise – familiar yet unexpected – grabs my attention. It's the wall clock still ticking on the landing. I frown. Nobody lives here any more but the clock tells the correct time. Perhaps the caretaker keeps it wound.

A shadow moves towards me from my old bedroom door. A shiver runs the length of my body. My hand flies to my mouth and I feel as cold as death. Perhaps I am dead. Perhaps this is why I see him in front of me.

'Alix!' he whispers.

Thirty-seven

'Gregor Fischer – after all these years,' I whisper, grasping at the banister for support. He *can't* be real. I must have conjured him up. He moves towards me and I shrink back. If he's dead he mustn't touch me. He must know how scared I am because he halts in front of me. When we met here unexpectedly the last time he terrified me so much I couldn't speak. His reappearance now is almost as traumatic.

'Alix?' Same eyes, alert and almost amused. But soft, too. 'It's me.'

I put out a hand and find the courage to touch his arm. The linen jacket feels smooth and warm. 'But how did you know I'd be here?'

'Alix!' Michael strides towards me and puts his arm round me. 'Are you all right?' He shoots Gregor an accusing stare. 'Who is this man?'

'It's all right,' I tell him. 'He's a friend, an old friend.'

'There's an old bench in the garden.' Gregor's eyes haven't left mine. 'Let's go downstairs. I'll explain when we're *im Freien*.' Michael looks confused at the German.

'He says we should go outside,' I mutter, starting to follow Gregor down the staircase. I shake away Michael's protective arm. I don't want Gregor to see me as a frail old woman. I walk straight-backed across the hall, watching Gregor as he moves ahead of me to open the front door. How stiffly he moves that left foot. That aside he seems in good, almost robust, health. The linen jacket, olive in colour, is obviously of good quality and barely creased. His shoes shine. His hair is now completely silver but seems almost as thick as it was sixty-odd years ago.

He can't be here. But he is. In silence we follow him out to the garden. Gregor and I sit on the rusty old seat beside the abandoned football pitch. Michael stands in front, like an anxious parent examining two worrisome children. Gregor stretches the stiff foot out in front of him.

'That Kolyma injury never healed properly,' I say.

'The Kirov wouldn't want me, that's for sure.' He gives that old mocking Gregor smile. His face is lined, but the creases aren't deep. Trust Gregor Fischer to evade the signs of ageing.

We're speaking German. 'Sorry.' I look at Michael. 'Michael, forgive me. This is . . . Gregor Fischer.' I speak the name of Michael's father for the first time in his hearing.

'I can manage a little English,' says Gregor. He was always good at languages. He was always good at *everything*. 'Gregor will go far,' Papi used to say.

'I understood the bit about Kolyma,' Michael says. 'The Gulag?'

'Part of my résumé,' Gregor tells the younger man he doesn't know, doesn't recognize. His eyes turn back to mine, burning with intensity. 'I found you again, Alix. But nearly sixty years too late. But I'm forgetting something: Happy Birthday!' He says the last words in English.

'You remembered my birthday!'

'I didn't know today was your birthday,' Michael says. But for the moment my attention is concentrated on Gregor.

'How did you find me? How did you know I'd be here? How did you even know I'd survived?' Questions burst from my lips. My head is still spinning.

'For years I thought you hadn't survived.'

'It was a close-run thing at times.' I remember the stink of the vodka on the soldier's breath and shudder.

'They invited me to cover the opening of the German Resistance Memorial Centre in Berlin back in eighty-nine – I'd become a journalist by then.'

I glance at Michael.

'I couldn't attend because Coca, my . . . companion, was in the last stages of cancer. But the Centre sent me the press release. Your name was on the guest list with a brief explanation that you were Peter von Matke's daughter, married to an Englishman and living in London.'

'But that was years ago. You never wrote, you never . . .' I think of the dying Coca. 'But of course, your life was complicated. I'm sorry about your companion.'

He nods. 'Coca died and by the time I'd recovered the time for contacting you seemed to have passed. But the Wall came down and all kinds of political changes occurred.' His English is becoming more fluent by the minute. 'Eventually it was possible for Germans to travel back here to Pomerania. I came to Alexanderhof regularly, most summers. And I paid the caretaker a small retainer to telephone me if a Mrs Macdonald ever made contact and expressed an interest in visiting.' He touches my arm, very gently. 'I felt we should meet here, if it were ever to happen. And this year I decided to come to the house on your seventy-fifth birthday.'

'I still have your mouth organ.' I keep it in a box with the few possessions I took from Germany when I married. 'I'd have brought it with me if I'd known . . .' My throat seems to dry up.

'My mouth organ?' His eyes light up. 'I'd reached Berlin before I noticed it was missing. But it didn't seem . . .'

Important.

Michael's eyes move from one of us to the other. I planned to tell him everything but not like this, not with his father present. I need to collect myself. I need Gregor to keep talking so that I can recover from this shock.

'Do you need anything, Alix?' Michael asks. Perhaps he thinks I have pills in my handbag to take for such excitements and stresses as this meeting.

'I'm fine, thank you.' I take a breath. 'It was one birthday surprise I didn't expect.'

'I wish I'd known,' Michael says.

'I didn't want you to know, I don't need cards and presents. All I wanted was to bring you back here with me. That was enough. This—' I nod towards Gregor, 'is something else altogether.' Perhaps I do need some kind of medication. But there's no palliative for the shock caused by such a reappearance.

'I never knew what had become of you after you ran off into the forest that morning.' Gregor is almost whispering. 'I was so scared for you.' His face seems to be that of the young man he was when he sent me into the snowy forest.

'Have I got this right? You two were here together at the end of the war?' Michael asks.

'For one night,' Gregor says. 'Just one night.' He closes his eyes briefly, as though protecting his memories of that night from outside scrutiny.

Michael nods slowly. 'I think I've worked out the answer to the question I asked you in London back in January, Alix. I know exactly who Gregor Fischer is.'

'Yes.' A bee buzzes over a clump of foxgloves, unconcerned with all of us, our secrets, our histories. Something about its unconcern gives me courage.

'Michael is our son,' I tell Gregor. 'Born in the Rhineland in November 1945.'

I feel his astonishment as I would an electric shock and clutch at the edge of the rusty seat to steady myself.

Thirty-eight

Gregor

Whole minutes pass before Gregor can speak. *Son.*

He stares at the man in late middle age sitting next to Alix. His *son.* He opens his mouth to dispute the point: Gregor Fischer has no family; he has lost everyone.

Michael stares back. For whole seconds nobody says anything, nobody moves. Then Michael extends a hand. 'Don't know what the correct form of words is in such circumstances.' He sounds shaken, too.

Gregor ignores the hand and gets up, pulling his son into his arms. This can't be a dream because Michael feels solid, substantial. 'There's no set form of words.' Damn his awkward, rusty English. If this conversation were taking place in Polish or Russian or German how much more eloquent he could be. 'This is a miracle.' He lets Michael go and laughs a shaky laugh. 'I should sit down again.'

'I never dreamed, I never even hoped . . . Meeting my

father was the last thing I thought of. I'm so . . .' The words seem to jam in Michael's throat. 'Relieved.'

'The last thing I thought of, too.' Alix clears her throat. 'I should have guessed when the caretaker said she'd given the key to someone else. But I thought you were dead, Gregor. You didn't come to find me in the Rhineland and you didn't write.'

There's no hint of a complaint and yet her words stab him. 'At the time I thought you were dead too. Vargá—' he turns to Michael, 'he was my superior officer, told me they'd found a dead girl in the forest. She had a book with her, with your name in it.'

'A dead girl?' Alix lifts her head and stares at the birches and firs. 'Who . . .? *Ach*. I remember now. We had a Polish girl working here. What was her name . . .? Jana, that was it. So she never made it home. Poor Jana. She was the only friend of my own age I had during the war.'

He feels her pain, but even while she's mourning the long-dead Jana, Gregor can't keep his eyes off Michael. He can see Matthias in him, the same laughter lines around the eyes. When the Gestapo arrested Matthias he was younger than Michael is now; but Michael shows Gregor how his father's face might have aged, how the small lines around Matthias's eyes would have deepened to wrinkles. His mind brims with possibilities. 'Tell me, my son, do you have children?' he asks greedily. 'Am I even more fortunate?'

'Two boys. I married late so they keep me busy.' Michael pulls out a wallet and shows him a photo. Two dark-haired teenagers with snowboards. Broad smiles, easy grace; they could only be American. His grandsons, great-grandsons of

Eva and Matthias Fischer, late of Berlin. Gregor almost tears the picture from his son. He thinks he can see Eva's cheekbones in the older boy and the younger boy has something of Alix in him.

'*Du lieber Gott*.' Something is shifting inside him, a huge rock that has blocked all emotion for years. Gregor prays he won't disgrace himself.

Michael pulls a mobile out of his pocket. 'I'm going to let you have some time together. I need to digest all this.'

His hands tremble. 'Are you all right, Michael?' his mother asks.

'Yes.' He swallows hard. 'It's just the shock. Can't take it all in.' He waves the mobile. 'I should call Stephanie. She won't believe it.'

Gregor watches him walk down the terrace steps. 'I've scared him off.' He speaks in German. 'It must be bizarre to meet your father after so many years.'

'Our son is a resilient person. He's coped with meeting me again.'

'Meeting you *again*?' Gregor sits up. 'You mean . . . you didn't keep him?'

Very slowly she turns to look directly at him. 'I couldn't, at least I thought I couldn't.'

Gregor remembers what Germany was like in those months after the war. He left this young girl, as she'd been then, to stumble alone across a country undergoing a death spasm, carrying his baby. Of all the things he's done, this has to be the worst. And yet . . .

'I wondered later on whether I might have kept him. My

333

husband was a kind man.' She bites her lip. 'I should have waited longer for you.'

'I had no right to even dream you'd wait.'

She blinks.

'There are things I didn't tell you, Alix.'

'I always knew that.' She gives him one of the knowing looks that remind him of her as a girl. 'Tell me now, Gregor, tell me the part I don't know.'

Thirty-nine

Gregor
Soviet Union, 1942

It was easy to keep close to Sofia in the months that followed
their departure from the logging camp, as they made their
way south – or as approximately south as they could – across
the Soviet Union. By boat. By cattle wagon. By train, each
day falling into the same pattern of rushing for *kipyatok* from
the hot water tap at the railway station so they could make
tea. Praying there'd be a working lavatory so it wouldn't be
necessary to use the tracks beneath the train. Never feeling
completely clean, completely fed, but knowing himself to be
more fortunate than almost everyone else on this trek because
he was with the Skotnickis and their supply of money and
goods for barter. Helping the doctor with chickenpox cases,
infections, dysentery. Occasional quiet times in station entrance halls when the crowds weren't pressing into them
which the doctor filled with lectures on physiology, anatomy
and sometimes even psychology, if Mrs Skotnicka didn't

object to the discussions of theories that contradicted Church teaching. Sofia would sit on the suitcases beside him, listening to her father. But she preferred Latin and French.

The towns and cities that blurred one into the other: dusty and smelling of bad drains and filthy clothes. Go'rky. Kazan. Kuybyshev.

And then long stretches on foot, walking behind a string of camels, the sun growing warmer on his face each morning. He began to feel excited about seeing the Caspian Sea, crossing over to Persia, the land of nightingales and wine, where neither the Gestapo nor the NKVD could follow. Even the bedbugs, the lice, the infections their group always seemed to pick up, couldn't dampen his optimism. 'I'll buy you iced sherbet,' he told Sofia as they sat under the shade of a tree in a railway town in south Kazakhstan. It probably had a name, but Gregor hardly bothered to note place names any more. All that mattered was making for the Caspian. Even if the route seldom took them directly where they wanted to go. 'Or Turkish Delight, if you prefer,' he added.

'What with?'

'I'll play my mouth organ and earn money. Persians love music.'

Something was clouding her hazel eyes.

'Sofia?'

For once she looked uncertain, hesitant. 'Sometimes I think this is the best we can hope for, as long as the war lasts.'

He looked round the dusty town with its boarded-up shops. 'This squalor? Never knowing where we're going to sleep or what we're going to eat?'

'While we're on the move it's hard for them to track us. And we're all together.'

'They let us go, Sofia. We're free now.'

'Perhaps.' She attempted a laugh. 'Perhaps I'm being illogical. But these last few months we've been away from the war, I've felt . . . almost free. Even if I'm always worried I've got lice or I'm about to catch dysentery.'

Had the heat finally unhinged her mind? 'Have some water.'

She pushed the flask away. 'When we lived in Poland, if I was even five minutes late home from school my mother wanted to know what I'd been up to.'

'But this journey . . .' Their fellow logging camp inmates had suffered from almost every infectious illness known to humans. And last week two small children had been left on the train by their mother, who'd disembarked at a station to buy bread and water, believing the stop would be of the usual lengthy duration. The train had moved off while she queued.

'I know. I know it's wicked of me to say that I feel free when so many suffer.' She examined the back of her hand, frowning at the tanned skin. 'But it's how I feel.'

He ought to draw her out further, but there were more urgent needs to meet while it was quiet. He muted the little internal voice that told him he was taking advantage of Sofia's vulnerability and moved closer to her.

She darted away from his detaining hand and he saw her parents walking towards them. Mrs Skotnicka carried a bulging canvas bag. The Skotnicki dollars and jewellery had lasted well and there always seemed to be food of some kind to buy, even if it was just a bowl of curd cheese or milled barley with which to make *kvasha*. Once they'd even found tins of crab from the Archangel peninsula in a roasting hot bazaar. They'd tasted good.

Beside him Sofia sighed. He'd have to wait until later to kiss her and steal a quick touch of her breasts, bunched together like two eggs in a cosy nest under her faded but still reasonably clean cotton frock – Sofia and her mother seemed to find soap in the most remote places. It had taken a full month for Gregor to advance as far as he had, but now Sofia seemed as excited by their explorations as he was.

Nobody knew if the train they were waiting for would arrive today after all. Things either happened or they didn't in the Soviet Republic of Kazakhstan and it was too hot to worry either way. Even Doctor Skotnicki had rolled up his tattered pre-Revolutionary map of the territories round the Caspian, submitting to the forces that decreed that any apparently straightforward journey between two towns in this part of the world would prove to be no such thing. As long as they could eat and remain together nothing else mattered. 'It would be nice to make some contribution to the war,' Dr Skotnicki would say, wistfully. 'I fear we will reach London too late.'

At night Sofia slept in a tent with her parents, but sometimes he could persuade her to squeeze under the canvas and meet him behind the enclosure where they stored luggage and cooking pots. During the day, while they hunted down food and sought news of fellow Poles in dusty street markets, Gregor would carry Mrs Skotnicka's decaying canvas bag and haggle with the vendors for a palmful of dusty tealeaves, a wrinkled orange or some flat loaves. But he'd really be imagining the night to come. While he assisted the doctor in his makeshift surgeries he'd be planning a reconnaissance of one part of Sofia's body: her neck, perhaps, or the back of a knee, or the soft inside of an elbow. 'You'll wear out my skin,' she complained. He knew without asking that there were boundaries he couldn't cross. She was, after all, the niece of a Catholic bishop – probably, by now, a very dead Catholic bishop. As the sun grew hotter the knowledge of these forbidden territories preoccupied him more.

'You could just marry me.' She sat up and fastened her dress. Her parents were out of sight, sitting in the shade of a disused church across the square. 'You're nearly seventeen and so am I. That's old enough in wartime. They'd give you permission.'

Marry Sofia. Live in London with her parents while they both completed their studies. See the war through – it couldn't be many years now. Create a brood of children to replace the family he'd lost. A fresh start.

Gregor sat up too and gazed up at the sky as though there might be messages written across the deep blue. He saw nothing. What was he expecting? He was an exile. If he ever returned to Berlin he'd be a stranger to all the people who'd ever known him. Alexandra would have grown up, too, would be engaged to some baron or count. Probably attending some finishing school in Switzerland. Perhaps she'd grown up to approve of what the Germans had done. She probably barely remembered him. Foolish even to think of her when he had this other girl beside him with her teasing eyes and those nights together when the air felt like warm silk.

'You're very young for an engagement.' Doctor Skotnicki was recovering from his initial shock. 'Neither of you have even finished your education. How would you live?'

'We were hoping . . .' He didn't even know what he *had* been hoping, presuming, more likely. 'I could get a part-time job while I study,' he said.

'I see.' Skotnicki undid his top button and loosened his tie. Even on the road he kept up appearances. 'Naturally we'd support you both. But Sofia? Suppose she's a mother within a year? How's she supposed to combine that with studying for a degree? You know she wants to be a lawyer. I don't think you should marry for two or three years.'

'Papa!' Sofia's eyes flashed. 'It's wartime, we can't wait that long.'

'At least a year, then. Your career matters, child.'

'And you can't possibly want to marry while we're undergoing this terrible journey,' Mrs Skotnicka added.

The doctor got to his feet, extending a hand. 'It's wartime, we should take joy where we can. You and Sofia represent a happier future. You have my permission to engage yourself to my daughter. You can marry her when we reach London. Perhaps Brompton Oratory or Westminster Cathedral.'

'Papa!' said Sofia. 'Two grubby refugees like us! A little Irish-Catholic parish church in North London, more like.' Sofia had done her research into their hoped-for new homeland.

*

By the time the train had pulled into the next town a message had passed along the Polish bush telegraph and a Catholic priest had been tracked down in the third carriage along from the Skotnickis. He would be delighted to instruct Dr Skotnicki's prospective son-in-law.

'I'm not Catholic,' Gregor protested. He'd half-hoped a civil ceremony when they reached England would suffice.

'You can be baptized.' The doctor's eyes twinkled momentarily. 'It will cleanse you of original sin. The priest will give you instruction. By the time we get to London you'll know most of the catechism.'

Gregor didn't like to imagine what his atheist mother and father would have made of this. He could almost hear his father's roar of laughter. But if the Skotnickis wanted Gregor to be a Catholic, he'd be a good Catholic.

So he spent hours with the priest, sitting next to him on a pile of suitcases in the cramped corridor of the carriage and learning about doctrine. Catholicism had a certain logic to it; he could admire the way the Church Fathers had built up their arguments. By the time the lessons ended he could sometimes persuade himself of the existence of God. 'You are a clever young man,' the priest said. 'Too clever, perhaps, for these dangerous times. In more peaceful days you'd have made a good cardinal.' Gregor thought his journey to faith was like this journey: a series of zigzags, the destination seemingly unreachable.

The last part of the journey, a loop south-east through Kazakhstan and Uzbekistan, passed in a blur of long nights and drowsy days catching up on rest, curled up together in a wagon. At least they could sleep in the train, saving precious money on accommodation. Sofia turned up her nose at the sheep's kidneys, which were the only thing her mother could find in the market. 'Eat, child,' her father told her. 'You need protein. We haven't had meat since . . .' He turned to Mrs Skotnicka. 'Where was it we had the lamb?'

He raised his hands in hopeless ignorance. 'The towns have all blurred together. They were all stinking and wretched.'

They reached Krasnovodsk in Turkmenistan, the port for the ship to Iran.

'Four days until we sail,' said the doctor. 'We'll need to set up another temporary clinic, Gregor. This dysentery – I've never known anything like it. The British will block the port if we can't contain it.'

A group of Polish soldiers, recently released, had trailed along with them for the last few days, filthy, lice-ridden and suffering from dysentery. This would have been his own condition by now had it not been for the Skotnickis, Gregor reflected.

Gregor helped construct a canvas surgery beside the docks, sweeping the ground and arranging cushions on it, which he covered with a white tablecloth. Not exactly a sterile examination table but it was as clean as he could make it. From the surgery he could make out the iron hulk of the merchant ship which would take them to Iran. The whiff of oil and coal from its engine room was a friendly foretaste of the voyage to come. He couldn't help whistling as he took the doctor's thermometer and stethoscope out of his leather bag, ready for the first surgery. He wondered how long the British would want to keep them in Iran before they were allowed to travel to England. What route would they take? Perhaps via Mesopotamia and Palestine, and from there through the Mediterranean and round the Strait of Gibraltar. The morning passed in happy contemplation of the coming months.

Passing the huddle of transient Poles waiting to see Dr Skotnicki, Gregor stopped. The tall thin lad shivering under an overcoat. Something about him was familiar. The boy's chin was covered in the beginnings of a beard. His cheeks were sunken.

He didn't know him. He found the box of pills the doctor had requested and walked back past the waiting patients. Again the boy's face jogged a memory. Take away that beard and plump out the cheeks. It could only be Jacob Gronowski – muttering to himself, obviously delirious. Longing filled Gregor. But his old friend could be his death warrant now. Gregor would have to stay away from him until he'd recovered and could be made to understand that Gregor Fischer from Berlin was dead and buried.

Jacob's eyes opened and he stared at Gregor. 'Once knew a German who looked just like you!' A couple of NKVD officers waiting to see the doctor about their sexually transmitted diseases turned their heads. 'Best damn German I ever knew.' Perhaps the NKVD men wouldn't understand Polish. Gregor shook his head and walked away, forcing himself to take his time, pretending to study the notes he was taking to the doctor.

When he reached the entrance he dropped the file and took the opportunity to turn round and look back into the waiting area as he picked it up. One of the officers was kicking Jacob as he lay on the floor. 'What was that you said, Comrade? Where's this German?'

The whippings Gregor received did not make him say anything other than that he was Paul Smolinsky from Pinsk, as verified by his papers. He repeated again and again that he didn't know Jacob, that Jacob had been delirious when he'd shouted all that nonsense about knowing him. They had never met. Dr Skotnicki sat in an interview cell with Gregor and pleaded with the NKVD officers to let Gregor continue to Iran. 'He's of conscriptable age. He wants to fight the Nazis. He'll be off Russian soil tonight if you let him go.'

'He's German.'

'He has Jewish blood. He wants to fight the Germans as much as you do.'

'Shut your mouth or you and your family will go north with him.'

Gregor shook his head at Skotnicki but the doctor continued.

'Here are the testimonials given to this young man by the head of security at the logging camp near Kotlas.' Skotnicki pushed the letters under the officer's nose. 'You'll see he assisted me when I treated many Russians.'

The NKVD brushed the papers aside.

They allowed him half an hour alone with Sofia. She came with the priest. 'He's going to marry us now, even if we're too young—' she held up a hand to halt Gregor's interruption. 'And even if you haven't been received into the Church because he knows I'm going to be your wife now, with or without the Church's blessing.' Her hazel eyes were chips of fury, despair and desire. Sofia nodded at the guard and handed him some banknotes and he shouted something to his colleague in the guard room, who joined the group in the cell. The priest began to mumble words, pausing while Sofia nudged the guards to remind them of their witness duties. '. . . et Spiritus Sancti. Amen.' A final Sign of the Cross, it was done. Priest and guards vanished. It couldn't have taken more than five minutes.

The newlyweds sank to the hut's earthen floor, pulling at buttons and hooks. Her tan seemed to have faded in the last twenty-four hours, Gregor noticed as he plunged into her. It was quick and almost brutal but she seemed to drive him on, whispering at him not to stop, to hurry. When they'd finished he felt shame but she put her hand over his mouth to stop the apology. 'It could be the first and last time. We needed this.'

She rearranged her dress and pushed something into his palm. Precious American dollars. How? He shook his head but she wouldn't take them back. 'I sold some clothes.'

He knew she was down to her last threadbare dresses.

'Please,' she urged. He took the money.

'Don't wait for me,' he said as the guards came back in. 'Get an annulment. Tell the priest we didn't consummate our marriage, say I was too scared to manage it. Don't let your parents talk you out of it.'

'I'll find you again, Gregor.' Her eyes blazed through the tears she wouldn't let fall. She took his hand, pressed it to her lips.

'Don't wait for me,' he called to her.

*

345

In the cattle wagon there was time enough to run the past months through his mind again and again. If only they hadn't married. He'd been weak, agreeing to this just for his brief and selfish enjoyment of her body. He ought to have stopped it even earlier. The Catholics were right, sin was the cause of everything wrong in the world. His sin.

Single, Sofia Skotnicka would have had men queuing up for her in London. She could have continued her studies. Now she'd probably never know for sure whether or not she was a widow. *Please God, if you exist, let her find a way to annul the marriage. Sweet Mother of God, let her be happy.* He cast his mind back to his catechism classes. This must be punishment for accepting a religion for which he felt no belief.

Time enough, too, to run a thorough comparison of this transport with the first one he'd endured from Poland back in the early years of the war. This train offered its passengers proper carriages, which ought to have made it more comfortable. But they were shut in bunks from which they could only emerge once a day to relieve themselves on the tracks. The elderly, sick and young couldn't wait that long. Every time he breathed in he thought he'd vomit. After two days he no longer noticed the stench, and the knowledge that it now attached itself to him as well made him want to hammer at the wooden panels on the side of the carriage in desperation. But there was no point wasting precious energy. Where he was going, he'd need all he had.

'*Za chto?*' he asked himself, in Russian. 'Why? What did

I do to deserve this?' And all round him in the fetid heat he heard others asking themselves the same question.

He shivered despite the furnace-like warmth of the wagon. The friend who'd once joked with him in Warsaw, who'd encouraged him to learn Polish obscenities and teased him about practising the piano, had both denounced him and infected him with his fever without knowing he'd done either.

'You've still got your mouth organ?' In the next bed the man called Piotr's eyes were wide. Gregor looked around the hospital. He'd been here two days. Of much of the rail journey thousands of miles east to the Pacific coast and the subsequent sea voyage north to the Magadan peninsula he had no recollection. Apparently they'd carried him off the train and down into the hull of the SS *Dzhurma* without him regaining consciousness. 'For which you may be truly grateful.' Piotr raised himself on an elbow. 'That hulk was worse than the train. We slept on the floor. The criminals, *Urki*, had the platforms. They emptied their slops over us so we lay there soaked with vomit and piss for days. Then a gang knocked out the lights and went on the rampage. They raped the women and stole everything they could get their hands on.' Gregor looked at the mouldy black lumps on the end of his bed.

Piotr shrugged. 'Bread is sacred. Even to them.'

'Nobody would want to eat this.'

'You'd be surprised. Save it. You can sell it.'

'If you say so.' Gregor looked at Piotr. 'Why did they send you here?'

347

'Someone had my name on a list. And my parents. And my sister.'

'Have you seen them since you arrived?'

Piotr pulled at a thread on his blanket. 'No.'

Gregor looked round at the hospital wing, spartan, stained floors, but paradise in comparison with what had come before.

'Where do we go from here?' Gregor glanced at the barred window.

'Mining. Road building.'

Gregor scratched. The blanket seemed to be alive. 'And if we refuse?'

'Serpantinka. A punishment camp. Even less sunlight than here. And less food.'

A nurse came in and fired off a volley of Russian in an accent he had to strain to understand. 'She's telling you you'll be off to work tomorrow,' Piotr said, closing his eyes. 'Try and think of something you can do that might keep you indoors. Otherwise we'll be in the mines by next week.'

'What do they mine?'

'Gold.' Piotr frowned. 'You don't know much about the Magadan peninsula, do you, Comrade?'

He didn't. The Poles at Kotlas had muttered about these Gulags far, far away to the east, so distant that even the Archangel peninsula seemed metropolitan by comparison. But Gregor had never been able to imagine a place harsher than the camps around Kotlas. And Dr Skotnicki had never wanted to talk about this place, as though superstitious about even mentioning the name of Kolyma.

The nurse returned, clapping her hands, followed by an

orderly pushing a trolley. 'Baths!' She handed each patient a sliver of evil-smelling black soap and ordered them out of bed. Gregor clutched at the iron bedhead, head spinning. 'Go to changing room!' the orderly shouted. 'You'll be given water there.'

'It begins,' Piotr muttered.

And in the chaotic stink of the icy changing rooms where they flung their rags to the floor, knowing they'd never recover their own clothes, Gregor knew he'd reached the point in his own history from which no escape, no reprieve, would be possible.

Forty

Gregor
Pomerania, 2002

Gregor stops and lets out a breath. 'I haven't talked so much about myself for years. And I've never really spoken about that place.'

'Kolyma?'

He nods.

'That name—' Alix swallows. 'It has such terrible associations. Almost as bad as—' She shakes her head. 'It's not for a German to say that any place could be as terrible as our death camps.'

'Perhaps not.' Now is not the time for such a discussion.

'I had no idea just how much you'd endured when I saw you here that night.' Her head is still bowed down, as though she's praying.

'It was one of several things I kept to myself.'

'The other one being your marriage?'

Impossible to read her tone. He shifts his position on the

bench: uncomfortable for lengthy conversations. 'Shall we walk a little, Alix?'

They walk slowly up to the terrace. The shutters on the salon windows have gone and Gregor and Alix can see into the interior – dark and empty.

'I should have told you about my wife.' They'd stood in Alix's bedroom, looking out at the wolf, and his defences had melted away. 'Our marriage – well, afterwards it felt like a dream. Sofia and I were only together for a short time.' Just long enough for them to consummate it – with the guards probably listening in at the door and laughing. 'I let myself be convinced I wouldn't see her again.' A spider drops down a smeared glass pane on a silk thread. 'I should tell the rest of my story, really. Put it all in order.'

They turn away from the window. A pigeon coos in the branches of the big chestnut which once provided shelter for picnics on the lawn. Gregor once owned a photograph of his mother sitting on a plaid rug at one such picnic. It was lost in Kolyma, along with many other things.

Gregor and Alix walk slowly round the house through grass that has already grown long and luscious and past bushes and shrubs that may or may not be the ones planted by Alix's mother in the thirties. Alexanderhof isn't a huge house but is of a size befitting an extended family and its retinue, built to show the neighbourhood – especially the Poles and any other foreign interests who might need reminding – that the Prussians meant business. Gregor knows it will take several circuits of its walls for him to complete his tale.

Forty-one

Gregor
Kolyma, Magadan, Soviet Union, autumn 1943

In the camp's clinic Gregor finished stitching the stab wound and cut the thread. 'Try and keep it clean.'

The patient looked at him as though he were talking in riddles. Perhaps he was. Sometimes he felt as though he'd fallen down the rabbit hole or into the looking glass. But things were better now, he reminded himself. Only three months ago he'd still been working out at the satellite camp, labouring outdoors on the bridge-building programme. The ache in his foot, still barely healed, was a souvenir from the place. Today the foot felt like a slab of marble attached to his leg.

He searched in a drawer and found a sliver of soap. 'Take this.'

'Can't you keep me in here?' An educated voice. She'd probably been a teacher or civil servant. 'I'm sure the wound would heal more quickly and I'd soon be up to full productivity.' *Quota. Productivity. Numbers. Percentages.*

Gregor found it hard to meet the patient's eyes. She looked middle-aged but was probably only in her late twenties. He decided to be candid. 'We've reached our quota because of that logging accident yesterday. If we exceed the quota the guards throw out all the patients.'

Even the six whose hunger-related diseases the doctor and Gregor had almost cured.

The woman rolled back her sleeve. 'I see.' She didn't sound bitter. Everyone understood quotas. 'Do you ever treat the children in the nursery?' She clenched the tiny bar of soap in her hand.

'No. This hospital is purely for adult workers.' And he flushed, aware that his relief must be audible.

'I have a girl in the children's camp.' The words rushed out of her. 'She was a baby when we arrived here, just a month old. You might have treated her because she had frostbite and lost part of her left ear.'

God.

'I worked in the north building bridges until recently.' He turned and pretended to scribble something in a file. If he'd stayed in the construction brigade he wouldn't have had to cope with situations like this. If he'd stayed in the construction brigade he'd have been dead by now. The shattered bone in the foot was nothing. The hospital job was a privilege; they could replace him with fifty, a hundred, a thousand eager substitutes.

'Someone told me they'd misplaced the children's files.' Gregor knew where this was leading. The infants were shipped to orphanages when they were two or three, too young to remember their own names. 'I wondered if someone would pin a label to my child's clothes. So they know her name when she arrives.' She pulled something out of her pocket, a scrap torn from a cigarette carton, with the girl's name scrawled on it. 'You'll know it's her because of her ear. And she has a mole on her chin.'

Gregor's mouth seemed to fill with something bitter. 'I'll try.' He took the carton. 'But your child may already have left.'

He scribbled down a description of the girl. Perhaps he could find a reason to walk over to the nursery, say they were worried about an outbreak and needed to check the children. He avoided the cursed place as much as he could. It wasn't so much the stink, barely covered by the disinfectant, but the silently rocking infants in their iron cots that disturbed him.

As the woman left he wondered whether she'd really been the victim of a knifing. Perhaps she'd inflicted the wound on herself in order to try and find out about the child. She'd expended so much precious energy, needed for finding food and keeping warm every day, on this attempt to find the girl. But perhaps her concern for her child *was* what kept her alive.

The door swung open and Olga Sergeyevna, one of the nurses, bustled in. 'They're asking for you in the commandant's office.' Her face was even paler than normal.

The moment had come. Gregor's mind ran through the mental check-list he'd compiled from the very first day of his arrival in the hospital. 'The patients' files are up to date. Bed number three needs his dressing changing. The doctor should check the wound. We're short on iodine. Oh,' he pulled the label out of his pocket, 'if I don't come back I need you to go to the nursery and pin this to the right kid. Frostbite to left ear. Mole on chin. They're shifting them out.' He caught the expression on her face. Even hardened prisoners tried to avoid seeing the children. 'I wouldn't ask you in any other circumstances. You'll find a loaf of bread in my top desk drawer.'

'You don't have to bribe me.' She took the label.

'Give it to the children then.'

'Hurry up, they're waiting for you.'

'A girl of three months,' he called back to her. 'Don't forget about the damaged ear.'

Those mute rocking infants in their iron cots.

'I won't forget.' And she wouldn't. He'd never seen Olga Sergeyevna smile, hardly extracted a single word from her that didn't relate to the job at hand, but he'd seen her looking at the patients with an expression that made him want to fold her in his arms.

The wind rattled the windows of the interrogation room. November now, and the cold had long regained its cutting menace. Gregor had a coat he'd taken from a corpse, but you weren't allowed to wear outer garments here. Or sit. He shifted his weight to ease the pressure on his left foot and focused on the poster on the wall. *We work for freedom and peace*. We work for a sliver of soap, for a few hundred extra grams of bread. We work because there is no choice.

'What happened?' The tall man behind the desk nodded at his foot. He had a curious accent, not Russian by birth,

Gregor thought, despite the name. His face was expressionless.

'A boulder fell on it when I was working on a bridge.' Gregor didn't bother telling him that a guard had dropped the rock on his foot as a punishment because he'd taken one too many latrine trips when he'd been suffering from dysentery.

'But you're a medical assistant now?' his interrogator went on.

'Yes.' In answer to the man's raised eyebrows Gregor explained, 'I worked with a Polish doctor when we were together in a logging camp. So I had some previous medical experience, although I have no qualifications.'

'No doubt preferable to bridge-building?'

Gregor shrugged. Not that this man with his strange, sleepy gaze would be fooled. What kind of idiot wouldn't prefer working in the hospital to labouring in the open?

'And it was your injury that brought you back to Magadan?'

He nodded. Not a day passed that he didn't thank God or fate or whatever that the brigade leader in charge of the bridge-building had sent him back here with the empty wagons returning for supplies. He might just have locked him up in a cell until he recovered or died from exposure. And the doctor who'd treated the broken foot had just lost an auxiliary to tetanus and needed a replacement . . .

'Why don't you sit, citizen?' They didn't call you 'comrade' in the camp. You lost the right to brotherhood by coming here.

Gregor pulled the second chair out and sat.

'Tell me some more about yourself. It says on this file that you were identified as Gregor Fischer of Berlin while trying to obtain a passage across the Caspian Sea to Persia. But you denied this.'

'My name is Paul Smolinksy.'

'You're sure?'

'Yes, Comrade. The person who misidentified me was running a fever of 105 at the time. It was a mistake.'

'So you are not the son of Eva Fischer, formerly Eva Mauer, the Viennese actress?' Something different in the man's face now, as though the muscles round the mouth and eyes had loosened for a moment. Gregor tried not to react to his mother's name. *Forgive me,* he told her silently. For a moment he could almost smell her scent, feel her softness, hear her laugh – mocking and tender both at the same time.

'My name is Paul Smolinsky,' he said again.

The face tightened again. 'And you explain your German accent how, exactly?'

'I attended German school when my parents moved to Danzig.' Gregor prayed his interrogator – Vavilov, his name was – wouldn't dredge up a native of Danzig to ask searching questions about the port city. 'And then we spent some time in Berlin before it became too dangerous for us.' Give him some of the truth. 'My father moved in radical circles. We were in Pinsk when the war started and the NKVD removed us from the border area for our own protection.' Gregor hoped he'd managed to keep the irony out of his voice.

'And what are your impressions of Kolyma?'

What if he just said nothing? Or laughed? Perhaps Vavilov

would think he'd lost his mind. A psychiatric case. That would mean the end of the job in the warm hospital. Almost certainly they planned to send him back to the boulder-building brigade. In the hospital he received occasional meat, once even a pickled herring, as well as black bread and soup. At the satellite camp, *Urki,* criminals from Moscow, ran the food-distribution system.

'The system of correction allows no questioning of the strength of the State's response to counter-revolutionary activity.' Not bad, but probably not good enough. Vavilov raised an eyebrow.

'The strength of the State's response, eh?' He sat back in his chair and examined Gregor. 'Would your commitment to your patients preclude any interest in defeating Germans as part of the counter-revolutionary effort, citizen?'

Of course, another trick question, designed to make him confess to his real nationality. Perhaps it was worse than he'd imagined: not boulder-clearing but the gold mine. Perhaps Serpantinka itself. He waited.

'There's a Red Army Polish division, the Kosciuszko division. I work alongside them.'

Alongside the division. What exactly was this man? Some kind of commissar perhaps. Gregor didn't think this Vavilov was a Pole either. Something about the careful way he spoke the language made him sound as though he'd learned it as an adult.

Vavilov rose. 'I'm not a Pole myself.'

And he could read minds too.

'But then, many who claim Polish nationality aren't either.'

Through the barred window Gregor could see the mountains above the city of Magadan, still white and glistening in the afternoon sun. When the sunset caught them later on they'd shimmer red and orange. The *zeks*, inmates, said that the souls of those who died from cold, dysentery, starvation or beatings fled to those mountaintops for eternal rest. Probably the only kind you could hope for in Kolyma. And yet it was a beautiful view. Even when Gregor's stomach ached with hunger and his skin burned with a hundred insect bites, he'd find himself stopping and marvelling, detesting the view for forcing him to admire it.

Until ten minutes ago he'd imagined he might be looking at the mountains for the rest of his life. This was the offer of release; he ought to be delirious with joy. But nothing was ever as it ought to be in Kolyma. The prospect of leaving was almost chilling. He was almost scared of the world beyond the Magadan peninsula. There were certainties here: the certainty of hunger, of filth, of fear. Hope upset these certainties. Hope was dangerous.

'What are you thinking about, Comrade Smolinsky?'

Comrade now. He must have fallen back through the looking glass.

'About mirrors.' None of his previous interrogators had ever asked Gregor for his thoughts.

'What about them?'

'I was wondering how I must appear to you, Comrade Vavilov,' Gregor lied.

Vavilov lowered his head to the papers on the desk. 'Pack up your things and say goodbye to the patients, Smolinsky.' His voice sounded suddenly strained.

Outside on a patch of scrubby ground some arctic flowers were opening. The *zeks* claimed that Kolyma flowers were scentless because it was too cold. Gregor picked one and let its sweetness fill his senses. He thought suddenly of Alix, how her lips had felt like petals when he'd kissed her. But that was years ago, she'd only been a little girl.

On board the *Felix Dzerzhinsky* Gregor and his fellow Polish conscripts were given a bucket they could empty twice a day. They'd even allowed Gregor a warm shower before he'd left Kolyma, with real soap, not the foul-smelling black tablets usually provided. The doctor Gregor had worked for had examined his foot. 'You might even make it, Smolinsky. You might just. You'll suffer from arthritis in that foot when you're an old man, I'm afraid.' Gregor almost laughed at the thought of himself surviving to old age.

Olga, the nurse who'd gone to the nursery for Gregor, had clasped his hand when he'd come to say goodbye. 'When you get home what will you tell them about this place?' she'd asked.

He'd shrugged, doubting he had the vocabulary for adequate description. He didn't even know where 'home' was. Possibly with Sofia, assuming she'd reached England. He supposed he ought to try to get another letter through to her. She'd never written to him. Or if she had, the letters had never arrived. Rumour had it there was a warehouse full of intercepted letters and parcels. He was unlikely to reach London now he'd joined Vavilov. Already his memories of Sofia were growing fainter. It was the earlier parts of his life that preoccupied him now: that other girl and her family.

Vavilov hadn't told him where they were going. It was only when he talked to other prisoners that Gregor built up a picture of what was in store. Rail journey west across the Soviet Union. Training camp near Moscow. Then west through Poland and into the Reich itself. 'The Allies are due to land in France sometime soon,' one of the Poles told Gregor. 'And we'll be part of the push from the east.'

Gregor blinked. The Allies in Europe. Americans and British pouring through France into Germany itself. His veins warmed with excitement. But it was foolish even to dream of seeing Alix again.

Vavilov's summons to join him on deck came as a surprise. A guard hauled Gregor up the iron steps towards the daylight. He blinked and gulped in sea air, remembering the occasional ferry crossings to Sweden or Denmark he'd made with his parents before the war. God, the air was sweet after the stench down below. Unlike the situation on the voyage out to Magadan the bucket was changed twice a day in concession to the prisoners' new-found status as soldiers. But the odour never left the hold where the men lay on wooden platforms.

Vavilov was leaning against the rusty railings, watching the waves. Perhaps he was worried the ship would fail to avoid the rocks in this dangerous stretch of water with its narrow straits and the Japanese enemy territories so close. Gregor noticed Vavilov's shining boots and wondered where he obtained the polish, now rumoured to be as rare as real coffee. Vavilov was tall, broad-chested, athletic; even in this environment he conveyed a certain distinction. 'Let's talk about what you'll be doing when we reach Prussia.' He didn't turn towards Gregor and his words were casual.

'I imagined I'd be fighting. Or carrying out medical duties.'

Vavilov tossed a cigarette end overboard and turned. 'What I want from you is what's up here.' He touched Gregor's forehead briefly, his hand as light as a woman's, its fingers long with short but well-maintained nails. 'You speak fluent German. You're obviously from a professional family. None of those qualities would benefit you in battle. But there may be other uses for you.'

Gregor'd known. Of course he'd known. No other reason for them to want him. He had no military experience and a shattered foot.

'You want me to carry out intelligence work, Comrade.'

Vavilov was watching him. 'Does the prospect alarm you?'

The sun was falling over the receding mountains. The blood-red land looked like a cruel beauty, taunting him, asking him if he'd miss her, if he thought it was worth selling himself.

'Tell me more.' Gregor turned his back on the scene.

Forty-two

Alix
Pomerania, 2002

We must have walked round the house six times. Gregor is limping. He needs to rest his foot.

'Shall we find somewhere to sit?'

'There are chairs in the kitchen.'

I take his arm and glance over my shoulder for our son. He's stayed at a distance while we talked, like a friendly satellite, just out of earshot. Probably giving us privacy. Americans are so polite.

'Be with you in a moment,' Michael calls. 'Still some shots I want to take.' He waves his camera.

We walk through the entrance hall with its bare walls and smell of damp. Someone has put up a plywood door at the top of the cellar steps but the kitchen itself opens off the passage just as it did in my day. Inside it an old Formica-topped table and metal-framed chairs stand where once we had an oak table and chairs. Gregor sits down but I examine the old

rusting stove on the wall. 'This doesn't look like our range.'
I remember the gingerbread men Lena used to bake for me.
Officially she was our housekeeper, not the cook, but we lost
servants to the war effort and little by little Lena assumed
most of the domestic roles. 'Lena would do anything for us,'
Mami used to say. 'She has given her whole life to this family.'

'They probably ripped your range out to ship back to
Russia. I used to see whole wagonloads of stoves and other
domestic appliances heading east.'

'Lena would have had something to say about that.' I
remove a handkerchief from my bag and rub at the tiles above
the stove. 'These are our tiles, though. See, the ships and the
monkeys.' The old blue tiles from Holland depict voyages to
the Spice Islands and the exotic treasures the merchant sailors
found. 'They'd be valuable now. Someone missed an opportunity here.' I shake out the handkerchief and start to wipe
down one of the chairs.

'Let's not stay in here.' Gregor's words make me blink. 'It
feels . . .'

'Sad.'

Perhaps, like me, he's haunted by the ghosts of that night
when the four of us sat here and waited for the Red Army to
arrive. I suspected my mother of adultery and would barely
speak to her. I can still feel the tension, the unspoken words,
the fear.

'We'll go back to the bench in the garden.' Gregor rises.
'My foot will be fine.'

'If you're sure.' I take his arm again and we walk back
into the hall. It's a relief to see the sunlight stream in through
the front door. 'You've told me so much but I still need to
know how you came to West Germany.'

Forty-three

Gregor
Berlin, 1948

Like many others Gregor would cross to the western sector with little trouble a couple of times a week to see friends or watch a film, the guards checking his papers and nodding him through. Usually he spent the time with Dieter, back from POW camp in the Soviet Union and living in an apartment in a western suburb. Dieter's mother, Coca and Ute had abandoned the garage, somehow wangling their way to Bavaria, where they had cousins who could find them jobs.

'Shame to leave the old place.' Dieter's mother had hugged Dieter and Gregor. 'But I've had enough of those *verdammte Kommis*. Look after each other. Try and get him to move into the western sector, Dieter. He shouldn't stay here. Nor should you, not with your health.' Dieter had never fully recovered from the TB he'd suffered in the camp. His mother looked back at the old garage with Gregor's apartment block overshadowing it.

'You know what he's like, Mutti. Stubborn as a mule.'

Coca, shutting a suitcase, made a tssking noise in the back of her throat. 'Don't worry about Gregor. He'll get by.' She lifted her head from the case and he caught the irritation blended with softness in her expression. Gregor and Coca'd had an on and off *thing* for a couple of years after the war; not serious, but enjoyable. Now, like all the other women in his life, she was moving on. Coca had been different; she'd asked for nothing except sex and access to his gramophone player. He knew she'd seen other men. He'd miss Coca. But not badly enough to move away from Berlin.

Dieter certainly knew how to look after Gregor. His care took the form of seeking out every bar in the western side of the city. And every available woman. 'All those years in Russia to make up for.' He sipped a *Weissbier*. 'Mutti's right. You'd have more fun if you moved in with me.'

'The apartment's all I've got left of the past.'

'It's on the wrong side of the city. And why do you want to cling to the past, anyway?' Dieter leaned back in his chair. 'I'm doing all I can to forget it.'

'I've noticed.'

Gregor left the city at weekends whenever possible. He'd travel as far east as he could, walking or cycling the last miles to the coast at Heringsdorf or Bansin so he could gaze eastwards across the Baltic towards Pomerania, now all but abandoned by those Germans who'd remained after the war. He'd walk along the sand remembering childhood summers on Pomeranian beaches, how he'd buried Alix up to her neck in sand, how he'd caught crabs and tormented her with them, how the mosquitoes had driven them mad. He thought of her more often than he did of his wife.

When the sun shone on the Baltic it became a deeper blue, almost the colour of Alix's eyes. But her eyes had probably been closed for years now. He'd made inquiries with the Red Cross but they'd failed to find any information about her other than that she'd left a displaced persons camp near Erfurt in the summer of 1945. The Russians had taken over control of that part of the country soon afterwards. Perhaps they'd discovered her Junker parentage and killed her.

He'd return to his apartment after these excursions and sit alone, without reading or listening to music, willing the years to pass. Return to work on Mondays came almost as a relief – he'd found a job as an agricultural writer for the government. He could probably have pursued his earlier ambition of training as a doctor in this new socialist state, but he couldn't regain his enthusiasm for medicine.

He churned out copy on whatever subject they chose. Usually it was collectivization. Franz the farmer needed educating about the benefits of giving up his family farm to the state. Georg, his neighbour, was delighted with the price guarantees he'd received for his grain and keen to explain the benefits to his doubting friend. Gregor wrote what he was told to write, ignoring the little voice inside himself that occasionally wanted to make Franz point out that the state was in fact stealing land on which he'd successfully grown wheat for the country all through the war years and long before.

While others complained of threadbare clothes and growling stomachs, he barely noticed them. Sometimes he found himself a girl. Two bodies were warmer than one in a cold bed. These relationships lasted a month or two until the girls became possessive. Plenty of choice in a city where war had claimed so many men.

In August 1961 after a typical night out with Dieter in the western zone, Gregor headed back to his apartment just before dusk. Piles of scorched bricks still peppered the city. Where the rubble had been removed, patches of grass showed the rectangles of old foundations and walls, shadowy in the half-light. A ghost city. Gregor sometimes still imagined he heard guns firing and grenades exploding.

As he turned a corner he saw soldiers rolling out barbed wire across the road. A small crowd had gathered. Gregor caught the eye of an old man in a cap. 'Bastards are sealing off the Soviet sector. Too many people going west, they say.'

'Can't imagine why.' A youth next to him rolled his eyes.

A woman with a baby in her arms and a toddler clinging to her skirts ran past the soldiers towards Gregor. When she reached him she dropped to the ground, still holding the baby, laughing. 'Didn't even have time to pack any clothes. But we'll be on the right side. That's what matters.'

'What are you going to do?' the old man asked Gregor.

'I don't know. I've got an apartment over there.' *And an old gramophone, books, photos, a piano I never play any more . . .*

The old man cackled. 'And the Russians.'

Gregor's feet bound him to the pavement while people rushed towards him. Guards fired shots into the air and the crowd hissed and spat at them.

It wasn't until he found himself standing outside Dieter's door that he realized his legs had turned of their own accord and walked him back into the western sector.

He found a job on a West Berlin business magazine. The editor rolled his eyes when Gregor described the kind of writing he'd done on the other side. 'You wrote about the joys of the collective system and the benefits of socialism for farmers?'

'Yes.'

The editor leaned back and studied him. 'It won't be like that here.' He pulled a packet of chewing gum out of the desk drawer, unwrapped a stick and threw the wrapper into an overflowing wastepaper bin. So many Germans had adopted the American habit of gum-chewing. Gregor could imagine the disdain on his mother's face. The editor would confirm her views that *die Amerikaner* were bovine, uncultured capitalists.

'I shouldn't have thought so, no.'

'Tell me, when you were a boy, what did you think you'd grow up to be?' The editor was leaning back now, hands folded behind his head.

'A pianist. Or perhaps a doctor.' Gregor remembered Dr Skotnicki showing him how to use the blood-pressure sleeve and the stethoscope, how to read a patient's health from his skin colour, the brightness of his eyes, the pinkness of his tongue, the strength of his fingernails. But then he'd graduated from the University of Kolyma.

'What's amusing you?' The editor carried on chewing.

Perhaps he was a former smoker attempting to replace nicotine with gum.

'I'm sorry. I grew up during the war years. It warped my mind, I sometimes think.' Part of him had perhaps rotted in the hold of the NKVD prison ships or in the hospital in Magadan.

The editor gave a wave with one hand that was both dismissive and understanding. 'Probably neither of us ended up where we thought we would.' The hand bore a long scar across its back. Shrapnel, or possibly a fragment of glass from a window shattered in an air raid. They both looked around the office, purpose-built, new. The scene outside was of other new buildings, hazy sunlight reflecting off glass panes. This was still Berlin, Gregor told himself. Still his city. Even if it felt foreign.

'No,' Gregor said. 'We ended up somewhere different.'

Forty-four

Alix
Pomerania, 2002

A thrush bangs a snail shell on a stone and I am back sitting on a bench in the garden at Alexanderhof with Gregor. Michael has finished his photography now and sits on the grass in front of us.

'And you never married again?' I ask Gregor.

He shakes his head. 'I was never completely sure whether Sofia was still alive somewhere, even though I could never trace her or her parents. Perhaps they travelled on to South Africa instead of London.' He pauses. 'Whatever she did, I hope she found great happiness. As for me, in the end Coca and I managed to settle down together quite happily, though we never actually married.'

'Where did you live?'

'Hamburg.' A wrecked city, but no ghosts of family or loved ones to haunt them. 'We never had children.'

'I didn't have any children with Robin,' I tell him. 'It just didn't happen. I thought I'd mind, but I didn't. Children have always been part of my life.' I rise. 'Shall we go back indoors? I'd like to look at the salon.' The other two follow me.

'You continued to teach?' Gregor asks as we climb the front steps.

'When we came back to England I went from teaching German children English to teaching English children German.'

He's grinning that old Gregor grin.

'What is it?'

'I remember the school you made in your bedroom with all those stuffed toys.'

'I made a school for my toys?' What a memory he has.

'I always imagined your parents would marry you off to some young blade from the *Almanach de Gotha* and you'd spend your life mixing with the elite.'

'At least I escaped that fate.' By the end of the war my life had changed so utterly I'd never have made a society wife. 'I enjoyed my career. It was an exciting time to be working with young people. Terrible as it was, war and exile gave me a peculiar kind of freedom.' But at some cost. I find it hard to keep my voice from trembling now. 'I never forgot about the two of you. Not for a single day, not a single day. Michael, I always regretted that I'd given you away. That's why I wanted to bring you to Alexanderhof, so I could express that regret to you here, where it all started.'

I won't tell them of the days of my early marriage, how I moved to the rhythms of life without hearing the notes that would make me feel truly alive. And yet Robin was so kind. Eventually, after years, I started to feel pleasure in the ordinary things: the first frost whitening the trees in the square outside our house; the first smell of honeysuckle on summer nights. I started to tolerate my guilt, as though it were contained in a bag I had to carry everywhere but wasn't required to unpack. We're in the salon now. Some of the plaster work has survived but has been repainted in brown gloss.

'Neither of you owe me any apologies,' Michael says. 'My God, I've read accounts of what the Red Army did to those who got in its way. You could have terminated the pregnancy. Or left me on church steps or in a box beside the road. But you didn't. You gave me to good people, people who'd give me the best start in life. And now you've put my mind at rest.'

He turns away to examine the carvings on the salon fireplace.

His father and I stand together on the spot where Gregor once played Chopin to me. 'I was a coward,' he says, 'afraid you'd reproach me for never coming to find you.'

'There's so much we didn't know back then.' I don't blame him for anything that happened after we spent the night together here. 'You'd have found it impossible to track me down just after the war. I'd married. I'd changed my name.'

The three of us walk round the dilapidated room looking for signs of the past. There are none. The only noise comes from a sparrow pecking at the few bits of gravel remaining on the drive. Where did all the furniture go? The Soviets must have sent it all west. Perhaps the Poles chopped it up for firewood. If I hoped to find many traces of my family here I was mistaken.

'When you came to the house that evening, what were you looking for?' I ask Gregor eventually. 'I always wondered.'

'You.' Our eyes lock. 'Officially Vavilov sent me here to check whether your father was in the house.'

'To arrest him?'

'He'd heard of his part in the July Plot and wanted to ensure he was kept safe. He might have viewed your father as one of the few Germans worth saving.'

'He was taking a hell of a risk for a man he'd never even met.' Michael moves to one of the shutterless windows and gazes out over the terrace. 'I've read a little about Soviet views on Junkers. They treated them with savagery, and if they thought Vavilov had sympathies they'd have pushed him onto a train back to Siberia with no restaurant car.'

'Vavilov had met both Peter von Matke and his wife,' Gregor says.

Michael turns to us. 'When?'

'Where?' I add. Then I remember Mami's curiosity about Gregor's superior officer – something about a missing fingertip.

Gregor's face shows wry satisfaction at the reaction he's elicited. 'In Vienna between the wars, when he was my mother's lover. He was called Vargá then.'

I can't remember Mami mentioning that name. But so much has been forgotten.

'That's why he got her out of Warsaw, he thought she'd be safe farther east. And that's why he found some reason to come to Kolyma four or five years later – he thought she might have ended up in that hell.'

'But he didn't find her,' Michael says softly.

'He knew she had a son – he'd seen us together in War-saw. Because he was recruiting for an intelligence unit he was allowed to read some of the files on Polish prisoners at Kolyma. My name and area of origin were wrong but the NKVD file on me stated I'd been arrested on false identity charges, which had never been proved. I might, in fact, be German.' Gregor's sigh was soft. 'I might be Eva's son. I might, in fact, be *his* son, because I'd been born nine or ten months after he'd left Vienna back in 1926. When he came to the apartment in Berlin he couldn't take his eyes off my father's photograph. I suppose he saw the truth there – that I was Matthias's son, not his.'

Photographs can sometimes show the less obvious, deeper physical likenesses between people. When he was laughing or arguing or furious or expressing love Gregor looked like his mother. But in repose his face resembled his father's.

'When Vavilov realized the truth he could have handed me over to the NKVD for desertion. But he didn't.'

'Because he loved your mother.' And what a love that was.

'He never stopped loving her. I don't believe he ever stopped looking for her, either.' As though following some secret signal, Gregor and I go to stand beside Michael at the window. How long have we been here now? The chestnut's shadows have lengthened on the grass. I am thinking of Eva's beauty, not, perhaps, as classically perfect as my mother's, but so vivid, so vibrant. Our housekeeper Lena distrusted Eva; she didn't approve of her stunning evening dress the night of the dinner party.

I put a hand on the French window catch and pull it. The window opens and I walk out onto the terrace. Years ago I stood here, watching Papi as he himself watched Eva picking flowers with Mami. I felt all that bitterness towards Mami because I thought she'd been having an affair and all the time perhaps it was Papi who'd strayed. This thought I will keep to myself.

'My father adored my mother, too.' Gregor follows me onto the terrace. 'And she loved him, I never doubted that. But our comrade Vavilov, he was something different. He was "the love of her life", as the English say.' He shakes his head. 'He gave the impression of only looking out for himself, of being beyond loyalties or affections. But I think he was a true romantic.'

'What became of him?' asks Michael, standing behind us in the salon.

Gregor smooths out a crease in the smart linen jacket. He hasn't lost his love of clothes in old age. 'I am an old man now, I probably indulge my own little fantasies. But years ago, just after the Berlin Wall went up, I received a letter from my mother. Just the one.'

The hairs rise on the back of my neck. 'From a camp?'

'Somewhere east of Moscow. She said she was in good health, that the work wasn't too arduous.' He gives a wistful smile. 'That bit was probably to spare me. But her hand-writing was firm and clear. She said she'd never given up hope of coming home to Berlin. But then she said something else.' He pauses. 'She wrote, "He is . . ."'

'What? He is what?'

'That's all I could read. The censor had struck out the rest of the sentence. *He is dead. He is in another camp. He is in the west.*' Gregor's hands open to express the ambiguity.

'He is *here*?' says Michael. 'Could it be she was saying that she and Vavilov were together?'

It might be possible. Other reunions – like our own – have occurred.

'There was nothing else,' Gregor continues. 'The censor had done a ruthless job, except for her name at the bottom.' He purses his lips. 'Vavilov was probably swallowed up by Stalin's postwar neurosis and thrown into a Gulag, just like me. He'd crossed too many borders, played too many roles. But sometimes . . .' Gregor hesitates, looking very young now, very unsure, 'sometimes I indulge myself and imagine that he got himself sent to where my mother was, that they ended their days together.' He comes to a halt and stares out towards the chestnut. I know he's seeing his mother and Vavilov in some distant settlement, seeing out their days with their shared memories of Vienna, talking about the friends of their youth.

Our son is still standing behind us, waiting patiently. 'Did you manage to speak to Stephanie?' I ask.

'She was asleep. But she agreed all this news was worth waking her up in the early hours. She sends her greetings to her new father-in-law.'

'Perhaps I can meet her and the children soon,' says Gregor. I can almost see him struggle to throw aside the past so he can embrace the possibilities of the future.

'Don't worry. She's already making plans to redecorate the guest rooms so you can both come over.' He rolls his eyes. 'But she's giving me grief because she says I haven't explained it all properly.'

'Steph's right.' Gregor gives a rueful grin. 'It's like rolls of film all tangled up together. Your mother and I were, naturally, the centres of our own universes when we were young. We could probably barely even imagine our parents as young people at all. What would *they* know about falling in love?'

'But they knew right enough,' I say.

'I'm building up a picture.' Gregor speaks the words very slowly. 'I think it all goes back to Vienna, Vienna in the Twenties. Marie and my mother are young actresses. Preizler's a disappointed young Tyrolean looking for a mission, and Vavilov, or Vargá as he was then, is a dispossessed Hungarian who's lost everything. An insider with an outsider's objectivity, if you like.'

Gregor's voice takes on a more intense note. 'None of the others can quite make him out, but they're fascinated by him. At least the girls, our mothers, are.' He raises his eyebrows. 'These are just my theories, mind you, I've no proof. He dabbles in radical politics but doesn't really seem to care that much. It's like a kind of hobby for him, ducking the Heimwehr – they were a right-wing militia,' he adds for Michael's benefit. 'Women are a hobby, too. But then he falls in love. With my mother Eva. And Marie, Alexandra's mother, perhaps falls in love with him too. But meanwhile Anton Preizler has fallen for Marie. Perhaps he'd been in love with her since they were children.'

'A series of love triangles?'

'Exactly.'

'What do you think happened between Mami and Preizler on that last morning in 1945?' I ask.

'I can only guess. She was furious that he hadn't managed

to get your father safely released and that he'd threatened you the previous night. She was terrified that they were now captives and the Reds were in the grounds of the house. She hated him for that and yet . . .' He breaks off. 'I can only put together bits and pieces about them – and Lena too.'

'Lena?' Again I think of our housekeeper's dislike of Eva.

'It's just supposition,' Gregor says. 'But this is what I think happened.'

Forty-five

Marie
Pomerania, 1945

Marie ran to the boot room. As she passed the cellar steps she heard Gregor open the front door. A male voice, cultured and deep, spoke to him. She knew she should hurry but she couldn't help pausing to listen. It sounded like . . . It *was* Viktor. It was really him. After all these years. She shivered in her furs. Gregor was showing him into the salon. 'You made yourself at home, then?' he said to Gregor before they closed the door. Marie sank down on the steps.

She could go into the salon now and stand underneath all those photographs of herself in various tragic and heroic roles. He couldn't harm her. He'd always liked her, not loved her, but liking and respect would be enough. He'd know that Maria Weissmüller wasn't one of *them*. And Gregor would speak up for her. She groped for the stair rail and pulled herself up the steps and towards the salon. Gregor had shut the door. She was reaching for the handle when she remembered

Anton. Upstairs. Bound. Helpless as a baby. Her eyes switched from the closed salon door to the staircase. Anton hadn't shouted out to her, hadn't begged her to help him, but it was as though he were calling her name over and over again: Marie, Marie, Marie.

She was eleven again and Anton was begging her to tell him the answers to the arithmetic test. She couldn't let him sway her. She'd walk into that room and reintroduce herself to Viktor. Place herself in his custody with dignity and the certainty that he'd do what he could for her. Let Anton take the consequences of his actions.

Damn, damn, damn, she couldn't do this. She let go of the door handle, found herself moving towards the staircase. Fool, fool, for not running into the forest after Alix. She was placing herself in alliance with a Gestapo officer now. Viktor would not be able to protect her if she continued up these stairs. Prison. Torture. Rape. The cattle wagons heading east: Gregor had said almost nothing about Kolyma but Marie knew what the name meant. Peter had told her about Soviet camps. Or perhaps they'd just take her onto the terrace and . . .

Still time to go back downstairs and plead with Viktor. *Please Marie! Don't leave me.* She had to untie him so that he could at least defend himself.

Once she unlocked his door she was irrevocably commit-ted. She found herself continuing to climb the stairs and walk down the passage to her room. The key turned in her hand and the decision had already been made. Anton tried to sit up, wincing as the silk scarves dug into him. 'You came at last,

Marie. I knew you would. Can we get to Peter's shotgun, do you think? If we had a weapon we could put up a fight.'

'We're not going to fight.' She found nail scissors in a drawer and sliced through the silk scarves. 'Come on! The Russians are already in the salon. We have to get past the door quickly.' Anton's legs shook after his night of confinement; he grabbed at her for support and her coat slipped from her shoulders. She put a finger to her lips. She led him down the stairs; he was still moving stiffly after his night tied up, and every time he stood on a loose board she winced, expecting the salon door to burst open. At the bottom she hesitated until she'd heard the murmur of voices in the salon. 'To the boot room,' she whispered. 'Very quickly.' He managed to keep that boot from squeaking as they crept over the marble floor. As they passed the salon door Marie shuddered. Just two centimetres of wooden door between the two groups. Centimetres and whole ideologies, whole lives. She hurried Anton past the door.

In the boot room he started to talk, to protest. She pulled out the little pistol she'd kept in her coat pocket. 'There are soldiers out there.' She put her head out of the door and listened. No sound of the guttural voices. They must have moved back to the front of the house.

'Maria . . .' Anton put up a hand in protest. The effort seemed to cost him; his eyes rolled and he staggered.

'Shh.'

'There's still a chance, you know. Our troops are only kilometres away, we could still—'

'Viktor Vargá is already in the house. He's working with Soviet intelligence.'

He looked disbelieving. 'How—?'

'Vargá and Vavilov are the same man.'

Now Anton understood her questioning of Gregor about his superior last night. 'Marie, you should go back, he won't harm you. Leave me here.'

'No.' She kept the gun pointed at him and he walked out into the snow. 'It's too late now. I'm implicated.'

If she let Viktor catch Anton he'd have to pass him on to the NKVD. The NKVD would extract from him the information that the Baroness von Matke had released him. They'd hunt her down like a beast. And yet she'd done all this for a man who last night had pointed a gun at Alix's head and threatened her. He'd failed to help her release Peter. The Gestapo officers in Berlin had all but laughed at Anton when he'd taken her to that meeting, saying that they didn't have any idea where Peter von Matke was now. Their supercilious gazes had fallen on her too. 'Go back and defend your family,' they'd told Anton. 'Take your fancy woman with you.' And she'd insisted on him doing just that, hoping against all common sense that Peter would have found his way back home. Even then Anton had insisted on packing that ridiculous hamper, as though this were a romantic winter outing.

All his promises had been like those biscuit tins in grocers' shops: full of nothing. She should shoot him herself really. Return to Viktor and tell him where to find the body. But by now he'd have found the unlocked bedroom, the cut silk scarves. She was no longer an innocent civilian. She'd have to plead and beg. And she couldn't, not to Viktor.

And she was tired, tired. Peter was lost to her. If he wasn't here and he wasn't in Berlin, he'd be in a camp. She knew what happened in those camps as Allied soldiers approached, they took out prisoners and executed them.

And then there was Alix. Her body almost shook with longing for her child. Alix might yet survive, but she had mis-understood everything last night. There'd been no chance to explain. Her daughter, her adored daughter, still hated her. Life, past and present, seemed to have tied itself round her and weighed her down in its chains. She couldn't act her way out of this scene.

She noticed that Anton's foot still gave him trouble; he dragged it through the snow. Perhaps that was why he hadn't joined the Wehrmacht . . . How differently things might have played out if he had.

They'd reached the forest now. He was shivering.

And this play had run to its conclusion. It was almost time for the curtain. She knew now how it should go from here. Peter's image flashed through her mind, disturbing her calm-ness, causing her to hold her breath in pain. But he'd only gone ahead. She would join him.

Anton tripped in the snow and for a moment she felt remorse. But there really was no other way.

She thought she heard voices, guttural men's voices speak-ing a foreign language. Time was running out. She pointed at a hollow beside a beech tree.

'Maria!'

'Sit here with me, Anton.' She lowered herself into the hollow. The snow was hardly cold at all now. She sighed as her body relaxed. Anton flopped next to her. She tightened her grip on the gun, considering how she could remove the pillbox from her pocket with her left hand.

'It's all right, you don't need that now.' His voice was calm. 'I understand. But if the Russians come . . .'

She nodded, praying it wouldn't come to that. Let it be like one of those summer excursions back in Meran when they'd walk out with a picnic to the Botanical Gardens and sit talking among the scented flowers.

She put down the gun and took out the pillbox. In another minute her fingers would be too cold to operate the clasp. Four sleeping tablets each – that should be enough in this cold. Gregor had watched her last night in the kitchen as she'd taken out the tablets to use on Anton. She'd been hoarding them for so long, but the doctor had never asked any questions when she asked for more. She'd hoped the young ones would use the night to escape but they hadn't. The snowstorm had detained them . . .

Anton stared at the pills. 'I've got a flask,' he said at last. 'Best French brandy.'

Better than the melted snow she'd thought they'd have to use. She and Anton might have been having a picnic. The thought almost made her smile as she washed down the tablets, the brandy setting her body aglow.

'It could have been different.' Anton took back the flask. 'There was a moment, years back . . . I could have chosen something different. I see that now.'

She hardly had the energy to ask him what he meant, but something was still on her mind, something she'd wondered about for years now. Last night Gregor had accused Anton of being responsible for having him and Eva driven out of the country. Anton had denied it. And yet it didn't seem likely to have happened without his involvement.

'Tell me something.'

'What?'

'Gregor Fischer and his mother. I didn't believe you when you said it wasn't you that had them deported. You told your friends in Berlin all about Eva's Jewish father. As if having a politically unsound husband wasn't enough. God knows what happened to her.' She remembered Eva acting Celia to her own Rosalind in that other forest, the one where there was no clock.

'It wasn't me.' He spoke quietly.

'You met her here again when you came to dinner all those years ago. You remembered who she was and you made sure the authorities knew.'

'No.' He held out a hand for his tablets. So he'd accepted this ending as inevitable. 'Not me.'

'Gregor said it was the Gestapo.'

'Berlin . . . not me. Wouldn't interfere with them. And I was never interested in Jews . . . High society was my area.'

'They sent you to spy on us.' It didn't seem to matter now.

'I tell you I didn't, Marie.' He turned to look her in the eye. 'This is the end, no time for lies.'

'So why did Berlin suddenly pick on Eva? They left most half-Jews alone until later in the war.' How complicated it all seemed. Perhaps her mind was already slowing down.

'Someone simply didn't like Eva. Someone wanted her gone. I'm certain it was personal. It used to happen all the time. Children would ring up and denounce their mothers for listening to the BBC.' He placed his tablets in his mouth and took a mouthful of brandy. 'It's a mortal sin, suicide.' But he was going to do it, anyway. How he'd loved her, all these years. Enough to do this for her.

'You must throw yourself on God's mercy,' she told him. But what he'd just said preoccupied her fading consciousness. 'Who on earth could have anything against Eva?' He'd taken the tablets now, there might not be time for him to tell her everything.

'I came to the house, the day after the dinner party in thirty-eight. Only you and Lena were here. Peter had taken Eva and the children sailing.'

Six years ago her darling husband had removed them from the heaviness oppressing the house following the dinner party. She'd stayed behind with a headache.

'You were very jolly,' Anton said.

Well, she was an actress after all. Quite capable of putting on a good show.

'But Lena wasn't jolly. She dropped a glass, do you remember? So unlike Lena.'

He remembered. Marie had looked up at the sound of breaking glass. 'Are you all right?' he had asked.

'I do apologize.' Lena sounded calm but her hands trembled.

'It doesn't matter.' Marie frowned. 'How hot you look, Lena. Sit down and rest.'

'I'll get a cloth.' Lena tugged at a piece of hair that had escaped her usually neat bun.

'I must be going too.' Anton had picked up his cap.

'What is it?' he asked, closing the salon door and following

387

her into the hall. Something was going on; Lena didn't just start dropping glasses without good reason.

'Nothing, Anton.' She smiled at him, a tired smile that barely reached her eyes. 'How's the foot?'

'Hardly troubles me at all.' Her shrewd stare told him she knew he was lying. So now they both knew the other was trying to cover up something.

'Tell me, Lena.'

'I'm just worried about someone, that's all. A friend. Nobody you know.' She clenched the broken shards of glass so hard her palm began to bleed.

'Your friend's lucky to have you to worry about her. But you always were loyal.'

'Her husband's smitten with someone else. Supposing he leaves her?' Her words were coming out in a gabble. 'I don't know what to do about it.'

His heart ached for her, so worried for her friend. He remembered Lena herself as a small girl going to school without warm clothes or brushed hair because her mother'd run off with some wastrel. It was always the likes of Lena and her friend who suffered, those who couldn't take care of themselves. Just like his father. That's what had attracted Anton to the Party, their recognition that the little people counted, that families mattered. They were all Germans together and needed to take care of one another. This case of Lena's friend was one where the state should step in. 'Can the other woman be sent away?'

She looked at him. 'What do you mean?'

'Just one call to the rival's local Gestapo HQ. Or a letter.

That's all it takes. Tell your friend to say the other woman tells jokes about the Führer.'

Poor misguided Lena. And yet Marie didn't have the strength to feel anything more than sadness for her. Snatches of prayers the nuns had taught her flitted through Marie's mind, forgotten all the years she'd been married to a Protestant. Anton's words were coming more slowly now. She no longer felt the cold.

'There's so much that needs forgiving.'

He nodded like a small boy doing what the nuns told him. *Salve regina, mater misericordiae*, she heard him slurring the words. Minutes passed. *O dulcis virgo Maria*, he murmured, each word seeming to cost him more strength than he had. Then he must have fallen asleep. She felt relief, wanting only to think of Peter now. She really didn't feel frightened any more. The pillbox fell out of her hands. Shadows gathered round her and she could smell the blossoms in the Botanical Gardens back at home in Meran.

Forty-six

Alix
Pomerania, 2002

Minutes pass before anyone speaks. I shake my head. 'So he told my mother then that it was Lena who informed on your mother?'

Gregor sighs. 'Lena loved your mother more than anything else. It makes a kind of sense. I *did* believe Preizler back in 1945 when he insisted he hadn't told the authorities about Mami.'

I consider the main players in our story. Eight dancers facing each other in a quadrille: Gregor and I, Mami and Papi, Eva and Matthias, Lena and Preizler. But then there was that ninth interloper: the man sometimes known as Vargá, sometimes as Vavilov. And now there's Michael, too, only he isn't an interloper at all but the key that makes sense of it all. While I've been contemplating the reasons for Mami's actions my son's been coming to terms with the circumstances of his conception.

'You told me back in London that I wasn't the offspring of a . . . crime,' he says. 'But to meet my father, to see him with my own eyes and understand all that happened, not just to you two but to your parents before you . . .' His voice thickens. 'It's magic.'

Gregor's sigh seems to fill the garden. 'I'm glad you think that. I've been worried that some of the unhappiness of that winter night all those years ago might have harmed you, might have made you hate me. I took advantage of your mother, after all.'

'You didn't take advantage of me,' I say. 'I was in love with you. Probably always had been since you kissed me in the cellar on my eleventh birthday. And I have my own reasons for guilt.'

'There is no guilt. I absolve you both,' our son tells us. 'I wipe out guilt and blame.' He gives a throaty chuckle.

I'm about to say that it can't be that simple, but find myself understanding that it can.

A breeze picks up, moving through the beeches and firs in the forest so that they dance and bow as though possessed by friendly spirits.

The sparrow finishes its work in the gravel and flies up into an acacia. Somewhere in the distance a dog howls. The world is ordinary and wonderful again.

Acknowledgements

My special thanks go to my editor Will Atkins for his wonderful work on this book. Thanks also to Christina Skarbek for her help with Polish expressions and family names.

As far as I know there is no von Matke family who ever lived in an eighteenth-century house called Alexanderhof near the town of Treptow (which does exist, now under the Polish name of Trzebiatow). I have used accounts by Prussian families forced out of the area east of the Oder in the period 1945–7 to create the von Matkes.

The following books were particularly helpful when I was researching *Restitution*:

Berlin, Antony Beevor. The definitive account of the Soviet push for Berlin: harrowing and almost unbearably sad to read. I couldn't have written much of the book without it.

The Ice Road, Stefan W. Waydenfeld. An autobiographical account of a Polish professional family's deportation to Siberia and subsequent journey across the Soviet Union to the Caspian Sea and the freedom of British-administered Persia (Iran).

Gulag, Anne Applebaum. A comprehensive examination of the savage Gulag system in the Soviet Union, which provided most of the details for Gregor's time on the Magadan peninsula.

The Hidden Damage, James Stern. An Anglo-American's account of civilian life in Germany immediately after surrender.

The Past Is Myself; The Road Ahead, Christabel Bielenberg. An Englishwoman's life in Germany under Hitler and in the year just after the war ended.

The Berlin Diaries, Marie 'Missie' Vassiltchikov. A White Russian's life in Berlin, working for some of the conspirators behind the Bomb Plot.